THE CHILD HAD BEEN
MISSING FOR HOURS

"It looks like we might have a new fagin operating in town," said Police Chief Alvarez.

The hairs on the back of Tirrell's neck stirred. Gem smugglers were businessmen, opponents to match wits with; fagins were more on a level with vermin. "What's happened?"

"Four-year-old boy kidnapped in broad daylight at Vaduz Park—kidnapped so casually that his sitter didn't even realize what had happened until an hour afterward."

*   *   *

For a long moment Jarvis gazed into the sleeping child's face as an odd mix of emotions swirled inside him. The decision on whether to proceed was still not irrevocable . . .

But the moment passed. Reaching over to the end table, he prepared the hypo he would need, marveling again at how innocent the clear brown fluid seemed. Certainly there was nothing in its appearance to suggest that it might very well turn Tigrin society upside down as drastically as the sudden appearance of the telekinetic talent had nearly two hundred years earlier. Brown dynamite—a kiloton of it in every hypo.

TIMOTHY ZAHN
A COMING OF AGE

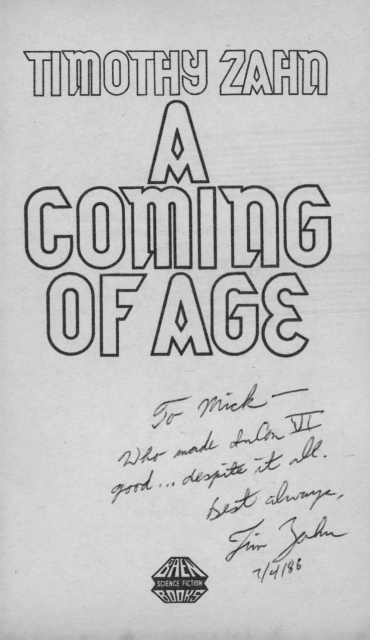

To Mick —
Who made AnCon VI
good ... despite it all.
best always,
Tim Zahn
7/4/86

BAEN
SCIENCE FICTION
BOOKS

A COMING OF AGE

Copyright © 1984 by Timothy Zahn

A Baen Book

Baen Publishing Enterprises
260 Fifth Avenue
New York, N.Y. 10001

First Baen printing, July 1986

ISBN: 0-671-65578-7

Cover art by Jael. Map by Eleanor Kostyk.

Printed in the United States of America

Distributed by
SIMON & SCHUSTER
TRADE PUBLISHING GROUP
1230 Avenue of the Americas
New York, N.Y. 10020

A COMING OF AGE

To Anna—
who was there
for all the
beginnings.

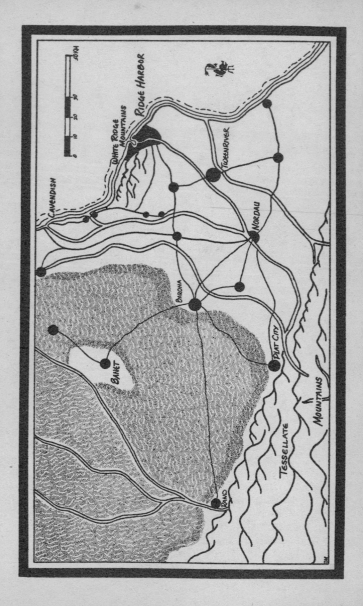

Chapter 1

The dome of the sky arched majestically above her as she flew high above the woodlands, soaring effortlessly amid a flock of batlings. Their chirps filled the air around her and she answered in kind, not understanding any of it but pleased to be joining their conversation. Suddenly they shot up . . . and a second later she was falling toward the tightly rolled spiral shapes below—falling—falling—

Lisa Duncan awoke with a start, heart pounding loudly in her ears, and instinctively burrowed deeper under her blankets. For a moment her brain held on to the image of the woodlands rushing up to meet her; but then it cleared, and around her she saw the comforting familiarity of her room at the Dayspring Hive.

Swallowing hard, she looked across to the other bed, wondering if she'd made enough noise in her nightmare to wake her roommate. But Sheelah's breathing was still slow and even, and in the faint light sneaking in around the curtains Lisa could see her lying wrapped in her blankets with the kind of rag-doll limpness only a sleeping person can achieve. Lisa's watch was just visible on top of her dresser; teeking it over, she saw that it was five-fifty. Ten more minutes and the gently insistent wake-up buzzer would sound, officially beginning the hive's day.

Teeking the watch under the blankets, Lisa fas-

1

tened it onto her wrist, debating whether or not to
just go ahead and get up. The bed was awfully comfortable; but on the other hand, hitting the floor
bathroom ten minutes ahead of the other girls was
definitely worth the sacrifice. Sliding out of bed, she
floated through the air to the door, teeking it open as
she got there, and flew out into the hall.

The large, chrome-and-ripplestone room was, as
she'd expected, deserted. Entering the nearest booth,
she took care of the first order of business. Then she
moved to one of the washbasins, shucked off her
nightgown and gave her face, hands, and arms a
quick wash. Tossing the damp washcloth and towel
into the corner hamper, she picked up her nightgown
. . . and hesitated. "No," she muttered out loud, resolutely turning her eyes away from the full-length
mirror fastened to the side wall. "Just morbid curiosity, that's all." But as she slid the nightgown back
over her head, her hands quietly stole across her
chest, confirming what she suspected but had forbidden her eyes to learn.

Fourteen years old, and still flat as a board.

Sighing with a mixture of relief and guilt, she
straightened her gown and returned to her room,
forcing herself to walk this time. Flat-chested or not,
the end of her preteen life was far too close to ignore.
Most of her friends already had their breast buds.
Several of them had the first bits of pubic hair, as
well . . . and in those preteens the loss of their teekay
was already beginning. She'd better get used to staying
on the ground.

Unbidden, tears filled Lisa's eyes; angrily, she
rubbed them away. *Stop it!* she told herself harshly.
*You're acting like a little girl. You think you're the only
preteen in the world who doesn't want to grow up? Act
your age!*

The pep talk didn't help. Closing the door behind
her, she crossed the cold floor and climbed back into
bed. Dejectedly, she stared at the ceiling, watching
the shifting pattern of light as the conetree outside
the window swayed in the breeze, her mind churning

with resentment and bitterness. The wake-up buzzer, when it sounded, was almost a relief.

"Sgnorf!" Sheelah said suddenly, a sort of enunciated grunt that punctuated her return to consciousness. "Grack, it's cold in here. Did you sneak the window open last night, Lisa?"

"Just a crack." Lisa slid out from under the blankets and stood up. "Come on, get up—it's not *that* cold."

"Tell that to my blood," Sheelah's muffled response came as she pulled the blankets up over her nose. Her single visible eye rotated, and the curtains drew back, letting in a dazzling blast of sunlight. Squinting in the sudden glare, Lisa watched as she teeked the window closed.

"Looks like a nice day," Sheelah commented, climbing out of bed and stretching like a cat. Her own emerging breasts were little lumps under her nightgown, and Lisa felt a flash of jealousy. Sheelah's teekay would begin to fade any time now—would be gone by the end of the year—and yet she remained invariably cheerful. Maturing gracefully . . . Feeling worse than ever, Lisa turned her back on her roommate and began to dress.

By the time the two preteens emerged together from their room, the hallway outside was alive with chattering ten and eleven-year-old girls. Some, still in night dress, were heading for the bathroom; but most were going the other direction, toward the stairway and breakfast. Halfway down the hall, there was a sudden outbreak of giggles, and a head rose above the general level of the crowd. Another followed immediately, and the aerial game of tag was on.

"Back on the floor!" Lisa snapped, with more heat than was really called for. "You know the rules!"

Guilty faces glanced around and disappeared as the two girls hastily dropped back to their feet. Lisa lengthened her stride, intending to catch up with them, but had only taken two steps when Sheelah caught her arm. "Hey, take it easy," she said in a low tone.

"No one's allowed to fly in a hall where three or more other people are present," Lisa quoted stiffly, even as her anger cooled.

"You're telling *me?*—who still holds the Dayspring point-loss record for that particular offense?"

Lisa sighed and gave up. "Rena and Ajie are supposed to know better, though."

"So they're extra lively today." Sheelah shrugged. "It's not worth ruining their day over." She peered closely at Lisa. "What's eating you this morning, anyway?"

"Nothing—just a little grouchy, I guess," Lisa said, reluctant to talk about her feelings even to Sheelah. "Come on, let's get downstairs."

Within a few minutes they had walked down the five flights of stairs to the spacious dining room that sat between the two living-area wings. Going through the serving line, they arrived at their table to find most of the others already present and attacking their trays with the exuberance and noise eight-year-olds always seemed to be able to generate. Lisa wrinkled her nose slightly. Overseeing the table was enough of a chore even at the best of times—the Eights had nearly half the teekay strength they would ever possess but were a long way from the maturity and self-discipline that would keep it under control, and Lisa was forever having to ground floating salt shakers and block the completion of spur-of-the-moment pranks. Today, feeling as she did, even having to look down the table at their youthful faces was going to be painful.

For a few moments, though, the ordeal was going to be postponed. Sitting on the table at her place was a yellow triangle, signifying that she was to check in with the Girls' Senior. Leaving her tray, she picked up the yellow paper and headed to the Senior's table.

"Ah, yes—Lisa." Gavra Norward held up a finger and finished her mouthful of food. "We've got a small problem with work assignments this morning," she said when her mouth was clear. "You're going to have to substitute for Kaarin Smale at the power station—she's down with the flu, and no one else I'd trust with a flock of Sevens is available."

In spite of her depression Lisa felt a warm glow at the compliment. Keeping Sevens entertained while they turned a huge flywheel was indeed a difficult job. "What about my team? You're not going to send them to the construction site alone, are you?"

Gavra shook her head. "I've already talked with the foreman there, and he said they could do without you today—if necessary he'll give the riveters a three-day weekend. Anyway, they have no choice—power station's always got priority. Let me see...." She picked up the small notebook lying by her plate and leafed through it. "Okay, you'll pick up your crew—six boys and eight girls—at the front door in forty minutes and take them to the west power station. I guess we'll give your usual group the day off."

Lisa shrugged. "They could come to the power station with me," she suggested. "We could put twice as much energy into the flywheel that way."

"Thanks, but no," Gavra smiled. "Your girls have served their time on boredom duty. We'll just give them a free day."

Lisa nodded and made her way back to her own table. The Eights—most of them at least halfway finished with their food—seemed more subdued than usual, enough so that she wondered if Sheelah had taken advantage of her absence to clue them in on her mood. In a way it made things worse; she remembered vividly a couple of the "evergrouch" preteens she'd been terrified of as a young girl. *I will* not *become like that*, she told herself fiercely, and made a supreme effort to smile at the others before starting to eat. The underlying feeling of tension remained, though. Hurrying through her breakfast, she set her tray on the conveyor and got out.

But harsh moods had never been able to get a solid hold on her, and this time, fortunately, was no exception. Somewhere en route to the west power station her depression vanished into the brilliant June sunshine as she and her chattering Sevens soared high above the rooftops, the younger ones engaging in the sort of free-form tag forbidden inside the hive buildings. Watching them play—feeling the wind in her hair as Barona's buildings rolled beneath them—it was somehow impossible to truly believe she would ever lose her teekay. She chose, at least for the moment, to ignore the quiet voice of logic within her.

Lisa hadn't been to any of Barona's three power stations since she was eight, but the place was no less intimidating now that she was older and bigger. The main room's two massive flywheels, in particular, were still sort of frightening—she could still remember nightmares she'd had where one of them broke loose and she couldn't move to get out of the way. . . .

Giving her head a sharp shake, she put the memory out of her mind. "Let's sit over here, shall we?" she said to her crew, indicating a spot a dozen meters from the flat side of their assigned flywheel. "Everybody bring a chair over and let's get busy."

The task was accomplished with a good deal more noise and banging of chairs than was necessary, but Lisa knew enough to be patient. "All right," she said when they were finally settled. "What would you like to do first?"

"See a movie," one of the boys spoke up promptly.

"Oh, you like movies, do you?" Lisa asked, her eye on the gauge set into the flywheel's housing. The rotational speed, which had been dropping slowly as its energy was turned into electricity, was now holding steady as the kids began teeking. Still lower than the power station people liked to have it, but Lisa knew they'd be able to catch up later. "What sort of movie would you like?"

"Monsters!" the boy exclaimed.

"Can't we sing instead?" a girl spoke up. "Or see a movie about *real* animals?"

"Yeah," another seconded. "Those monster movies are *dumb*."

"Tell you what," Lisa said. "Let's start with something different and save the movies and singing for later. We'll take turns telling stories, okay? They can be as scary as you want," she added as the boy who'd voted for monster movies opened his mouth to object. He closed it again, and a gleam came into his eye.

Leaning back, Lisa stifled a satisfied smile. She'd never yet seen a round of storytelling that couldn't hold a work crew's attention for at least an hour ... and she would still have the movies and singing to fall back on. "Okay, who's ready to start?"

Three hands shot up. Lisa picked one and settled down to listen as the girl launched into a story about three dragonmites and a batling, a story Lisa remembered hearing on the story tapes several years ago. The other kids obviously hadn't heard it, though; they sat in absorbed silence, only the flywheel's rotation gauge showing that they were still doing their job. Across the room, she noted, the flickering light of a projector showed that the group at the second flywheel had already started a movie, though the picture itself—projected against the flywheel's spinning surface—was invisible from where she sat. *He'll learn*, she thought a bit smugly, eyeing the preteen in charge of the other crew. *About an hour after lunch they'll be bouncing off the ceiling with boredom—and he won't have anything in reserve to keep them quiet.*

Glancing once at her watch, Lisa returned her attention to the girl's story and began to plan what they would do next.

Chapter 2

The young man was small and thin and very nervous. Wrapped in a sailor's jersey a size too big for him and with a cap jammed down to eyebrow level, he looked strangely like an eight-year-old dressed in an older kid's clothes. Stanford Tirrell almost smiled at that image; but there really wasn't anything funny about all of this. Keeping his peripheral vision on the piles of crates and equipment lying around the dock, he stepped away from the security gate and walked out to meet the young man.

"Mr. Potter?" the other asked as Tirrell approached. His voice made Tirrell revise his age estimate downward. The sailor couldn't be over twenty-four—barely old enough to be out of school—and the fact that he'd clearly been sailing for a while implied he'd dropped out early. Tirrell felt a surge of pity for him . . . but he had a job to do.

"Yeah," he said gruffly in answer to the other's query. "What'ya got for me?"

The sailor locked eyes with him for an instant before switching his gaze to somewhere in the vicinity of Tirrell's left cheek. "Raellian whiskey—but remember, you gotta pay what you said, 'cause if my usual buyer finds out—"

"Relax," Tirrell cut him off. "I got the money right here." He tapped his coat pocket and nodded over the sailor's shoulder at the weathered freighter rocking gently alongside its moorings a hundred meters away, its logo and number only barely legible. "The stuff still aboard or did you off-load already?"

"Aboard. Gimme the money and I'll tell you where."

Silently, Tirrell pulled out the envelope and handed it over. The sailor produced a long-bladed knife from somewhere and slit the envelope open with a quick flick of his wrist. Reaching in, he leafed through the bills, his lips moving as he counted.

"It's all there," Tirrell growled, wanting to get this over with. "Where's the merchandise?"

The sailor stuffed the envelope into his hip sporran; with a brief hesitation the knife likewise vanished. "Starboard hold, third locker," he muttered. "The back comes off—use a knife on the water sealant and push the bottom; it swings back. The stuff's in the ballast space behind and below, in six mesh bags."

"How do I get aboard?" Tirrell asked. "Is there someone who knows enough to look the other way?"

"No—there's just me." The sailor was backing away, clearly anxious to fade back into Ridge Harbor's dockyard community. "How you get aboard is your problem. I just get the stuff through customs."

"True," Tirrell agreed, reaching into his pocket again. "And I'm afraid that's going to cost you."

Something in Tirrell's voice must have tipped him off, because the sailor was running full-tilt for the security gate before Tirrell even got his ID badge clear of the pocket. Sighing, Tirrell put a finger in his mouth and gave a trilling whistle. If his trusty right-hand was where he was supposed to be . . .

The sailor increased his speed—and suddenly screamed in panic as his feet left the ground. For another second his legs pumped madly, in a cartoon-like pantomime of flight, before abruptly giving up. Hanging motionlessly, thirty centimeters off the ground, he looked like a marionette with invisible strings. Farther ahead, drifting from his concealment near the fence, a grinning preteen appeared, making gift-wrapping motions with his hands as he flew over the gate. Breaking into a jog, Tirrell headed for the dangling prisoner, reaching him the same time the preteen did.

"That basically how you wanted it done?" the boy asked, settling to the ground.

"More or less," Tirrell nodded. "Your sense of humor leaves something to be desired, though." Stepping in front of the sailor, he held up his badge for inspection. "Detective First Stanford Tirrell, Ridge Harbor Police," he identified himself. "You're under arrest for smuggling. Tonio, let him down."

The preteen did so, and under his watchful eye Tirrell relieved the prisoner of knife and payoff money and secured his hands with wrist cuffs. "Let's go," he said, taking the other's arm and pointing him toward the gate. "Tonio, the whiskey's still aboard the ship over there. Make sure no one enters or leaves until the shakedown squad gets here, okay? I'll call them from the car and tell them how to find it."

"Sure," Tonio nodded. "Should be easy. . . ." Gazing over Tirrell's shoulder, he frowned slightly with concentration. Glancing back, Tirrell watched the ship's gangway flip up to balance precariously on its edge. "That should keep the traffic down," the preteen said with obvious satisfaction.

Shaking his head, Tirrell rolled his eyes exaggeratedly heavenward and marched his prisoner away. Only when his back was to his righthand did he allow a smile to reach his face. Tonio still liked to think his sense of humor could annoy his partner.

It was nearly two hours later, and Tirrell was catching up on some of his backlog of paperwork, when the summons came to report upstairs.

"Bad news," Police Chief Alverez said as Tirrell took the seat in front of the cluttered desk and politely declined the pantomimed offer of a drink. "Your smuggler friend's a dead end. A complete amateur, and seems to be a loner, to boot."

Tirrell nodded; the sailor's youth and obvious inexperience had already led him to the same conclusion.

All those hours of digging through the customs office's truly horrible record system—gone, just like that. "How does he account for the diamonds in his last delivery?" he asked.

"He doesn't." Alverez smiled thinly. "He thought we were joking when we asked about that. When we convinced him we were serious, I thought he was going to rupture a blood vessel."

"I'll bet." Tirrell gazed out the window for a long moment. One of the small pleasures—usually the only one, in fact—of being called into the chief's office was the panoramic view the corner windows offered of both Ridge Harbor's sheltered bay and the line of white bluffs that hemmed the city in from the west. "It makes a certain lopsided sense, you know," he mused. "Most of the professional gem smugglers are too well known to move without attracting attention. So you pick a schmuck who's trying to make a few bills and stick the stuff into his whiskey cache. No one's really likely to bother with him. Does he have a record, by the way?"

Alverez shook his head, plucked a piece of paper from a stack in front of him. "Luz Sandur, twenty-three; dropped out of Tweenriver Academy two years ago. Mild sort of troublemaker in his hive, I gather, which meant he never got the necessary points for anything over Basic at school. Saw the handwriting on the wall—"

"Too late, of course," Tirrell interjected.

"They always do. Decided he was in a dead-end position and wangled an apprenticeship in the merchant marine. It apparently wasn't what he expected."

Tirrell shook his head sadly. It was always the same story: preteen on top of the world at his hive, without the brains to look ahead to life after Transition. It wasn't like the event sneaked up on anyone—Transition was as sure as death and paperwork. Still, pretending it wasn't going to happen was an easy trap to fall into, especially given the horror stories that circulated in the hives. Even after twenty years Tirrell's own memories of that time held some sore spots. "What about his buyer here? Have you picked him up yet?"

"Yeah, but I'm not sure it'll lead us anywhere. He claims he doesn't know anything about gem smuggling—says his warehouse was broken into the night after we intercepted that load eight months back." Alverez shrugged. "I'm inclined to believe him—like Sandur, he's too small an operator for professionals to trust."

"Which leaves us whoever in Raella is pulling the Cleopatra act," Tirrell growled. Eight months of hard work, gone like a hole in water.

"I believe Cleopatra was only putting pearls in wine, but you've got the right idea." Alverez scratched his cheek and picked up another piece of paper. "It's Raella's ball now—which is just as well, because something came in half an hour ago that I want you on. It looks like we might have a new fagin operating in town."

The hairs on the back of Tirrell's neck stirred, and suddenly the scenery outside the window didn't seem quite so picturesque any more. Gem smugglers were businessmen, opponents to match wits with; fagins were more on a level with vermin. "What's happened?"

"Four-year-old boy was kidnapped in broad daylight at Vaduz Park—kidnapped so casually that his sitter didn't even realize what had happened until an hour afterward. We've got a shakedown squad out there now looking for clues, but I'm not expecting much."

"The boy's parents been notified?" Tirrell asked, already heading for the door.

"Foster parents, yes. They're on their way to the park now."

Tirrell nodded grimly. "All right. I'll see you later." Opening the door, he left at a fast walk.

The sitter who'd been watching Colin Brimmer was seventeen years old, a student at Ridge Harbor Introductory School picking up a few extra points toward medical training. She was also very near the point of tears, a point which, judging by the puffiness of her eyes, she'd already been by at least once. "I don't know what else I can tell you, Detective Tirrell," she said, sniffing as she fought halfheartedly with her sinuses. "I've told the other policemen everything I know. Please, I just want to go home."

"I understand, Miss Thuma," Tirrell said gently, "but it's important that I hear the story from you, personally, before any of the details begin to fade."

She sniffed once more and briefly closed her eyes. "We got here about two o'clock—Colin, me, and two other children from the neighborhood that I sit for. One of the older men who're sometimes here was sitting over there." She waved toward a nearby bench, the current focus of attention for two of Ridge Harbor's best shakedown men. "I'd seen him three or four times in the past month or two, the last time two days ago. He was about average height and build, I guess, with a gray beard and medium-length gray hair, and he wore glasses."

"Had you talked to him before today?"

"Yes—on Wednesday. That was the first time," she added, sounding a little defensive. "He came up and introduced himself and specifically said hello to Colin. Colin seemed to know him, so I thought he was a friend of the Brimmers."

"How long was this conversation?"

"Just a few minutes. He sounded cultured and well-educated. I—I didn't think he—" She sniffed loudly and got her face back under control. "Anyway, he told me he was a city building inspector who was retiring early for health reasons. He pointed out his apartment building—that white one through the trees." She pointed. "Then he said good-bye and went back to his bench to read. He was still there when we left."

"Okay." Tirrell made a note on his pad. "Now tell me about today."

"He was here when we got here, sitting on his usual bench. He said hello and said he'd brought a small gift for each of the children—they were little model airplanes. They'd been flying them for a half hour when Colin's hit the ground too hard and broke. Mr. Oliver—that's the man—tried to fix it, but he couldn't. He said he would have to go to his apartment, where his glue and vise were, and asked Colin if he wanted to come watch. Colin seemed eager, and—well, he seemed to *know* him—"

"Yes, you told me already," Tirrell said, striving to keep his voice even. He couldn't really blame the teen; she'd probably never had more than a half hour of instruction on the art of child-sitting in her life. Besides, she clearly still had the reflexes of the hive structure she'd so recently left, reflexes geared to obedience toward authoritative adults. "So they left. It then took you a whole hour to become suspicious?"

She nodded, a single forlorn jerk of the head. "I'm sorry," she said miserably.

Glancing around, Tirrell caught the eye of a policeman and beckoned to him. "I'm going to ask you to go down to the station with this officer," he told the teen, "and describe this Mr. Oliver for one of our artists. Okay?"

"Sure." She sniffed once more and left with the policeman, her shoulders curled with dejection. A motion off to his left caught Tirrell's eye, and he turned as Tonio landed a few meters away.

"Couple of messages for you, Stan," the preteen said. "First: the address is a phony. No one there's ever heard of this Oliver guy or anyone with his description."

"Big surprise," Tirrell growled. "You're going to like this guy, Tonio—he's got your warped sense of humor."

"What do you mean?"

"The term 'fagin' originally came from a pre-Expansion Earth book, whose title happens to be *Oliver Twist*. What's the other message?"

"Colin's parents are here."

Tirrell glanced once at the men working on the bench. "Good. Let's go talk to them."

The detective had never met the Brimmers, but their reputation was well-known in official Ridge Harbor circles. Both in their early forties, they had been foster parents to six children over the past eighteen years, providing the close family background that seemed to best minimize the later transitional shocks to hive, school, and adulthood. Their record had been one of the best in the city . . . until now.

They were standing together near the row of police cars, obviously upset but under much better control than the teen sitter had been. The man took a step forward as Tirrell and Tonio walked up to them. "Are you the officer in charge here, sir?" he asked.

Tirrell nodded. "Detective First Tirrell; this is Tonio Genesee, my righthand. You are Thom and Elita Brimmer, of course. First of all, do you know anyone named Oliver, or anyone who has gray hair, a beard, and wears glasses?"

Both shook their heads. "We've had a few minutes to think about it—the policeman who drove us here gave us Lenna's description," Elita said. "We're quite sure we don't know anyone like that. But I wonder whether or not the hair and beard are a disguise. In that case he probably could be almost anyone."

"Good point." Tirrell had come to that obvious conclusion long ago. "Next: is there any reason to suspect Colin may have been kidnapped for purposes of ransom? Or that someone might want him in order to force you to do anything?"

Again, two solid negatives. Tirrell hadn't expected anything else, but the questions had to be asked. "All right. Then I'd like to go to your house with you and look over both Colin's things and any photos you have of him, especially recent ones taken outside. After that I want you to tell me everything you can about Colin, your friends and acquaintances, your daily schedule—everything that could conceivably give us a clue."

"We're at your complete disposal, Detective," Brimmer said. "We want this man caught as badly as you do."

I doubt that very much, Tirrell thought blackly as he led the way to his car. The Brimmers had most likely never seen what could happen to a child who was brought up by a fagin. Tirrell had.

It wasn't something he was anxious to see again.

Chapter 3

Outside the lounge windows the last traces of sunset had finally faded from the sky, and the crescent shape of Tigris's larger moon was occasionally visible through the swaying woodland treetops. Sighing, Lisa straightened up in her chair and looked around her. The lounge was relatively empty; most of the other preteens were probably either outside or else downstairs in the entertainment rooms, enjoying the extra freedom Friday evenings brought. Of the few other girls present, most were sitting alone, either dozing or just enjoying the silence. In one corner five others had teeked their chairs into a circle and were carrying on a muted conversation. Lisa found herself staring at the group, searching their faces for some trace of the depression she herself was feeling.

But if the imminent loss of their teekay was bothering any of them, they hid it well. Laughing and smiling, they seemed as happy and unconcerned as Eights. *Idiots*, she thought peevishly and was instantly sorry. It was *she*, after all, who was behaving like a kid. Closing her eyes, she sighed and willed the world to go away.

A creaking of wood some time later made her open her eyes again. The group in the corner was breaking up. Watching incuriously, she noticed a sort of hand signal pass furtively among the girls as they threaded their way through the circle of chairs and disap-

17

peared out the door. Looking after them, Lisa felt older than ever. Secret clubs were always cropping up in the hive, usually among new preteens. Her own brief stint with such a club had been four years ago, just after her tenth birthday and the move upstairs to her present room. Then, she'd been more than a little scared at the new responsibilities her age was about to bring her ... but on the other hand, the coming Transition had seemed as distant and academic as the end of the universe.

To grow is to change. Gavra Norward's oft-repeated line ran through Lisa's mind, but it wasn't especially comforting. *I don't* want *to change,* she thought angrily. *I like being who I am; I like the power and—*

She blinked as the thought caught her squarely across the face. *The power.* Not just the teekay, she realized with sudden clarity, but also the authority and status that went with it. Preteens were the top of the heap—more important even than many adults, she'd often thought. And as for herself ... well, Gavra had said it just that morning. *There's no one else I'd trust with a flock of Sevens.* Lisa was one of the best, and she knew it ... and she was about to lose it all and become an anonymous student.

Abruptly, she couldn't bear to sit still anymore. Getting to her feet, she looked around the lounge. A few others were still there, but they were all girls she knew only casually. No one she would be comfortable talking to ... and, actually, she didn't really feel like talking, anyway. Stepping to the room's French doors, she opened them and walked out onto the balcony.

For a wonder, the wide ledge was deserted. Leaning on the railing, Lisa gazed down into the hive's landscaped courtyard, picking out figures moving around in the dim light. Above, the night was coming on rapidly, with only a small patch of blue still showing through the trees where the sun had gone down. Here and there she could see the distant specks of other kids flying about, a few off by themselves but most in groups of three or more. A faint giggle reached her along the breeze, adding that much more to her sense of frustration and loneliness. In the west the smaller of Tigris's moons, Sumer, was rising higher, and she had a sudden urge to go and chase it. Glancing around quickly, she stepped back to the building's wall and teeked herself straight up. Technically, flying off of balconies was forbidden, but preteens were generally allowed to get away with it as long as they made sure younger kids didn't see them. A hundred meters above the hive she leveled off and headed west.

The evening air, warm enough when one was stationary, was rather chilly when passed through at forty kilometers an hour, and Lisa wished momentarily she'd stopped by her room first to pick up a sweater. But the sheer exhilaration of flight quickly drove such thoughts from her mind. She passed the other kids without pausing; passed the outskirts of Barona itself; and within a few minutes she was over the woodlands surrounding the city, as isolated from the world as it was possible to get. She'd come out here often lately, as if distance alone would let her escape the pressing reality of Transition. . . .

For a long time she simply played—games of speed and altitude she'd enjoyed as a young girl, and the more daring tricks of free fall and spinning spiral that had once won a brand-new preteen the admiration of both her peers and even some of her elders. Time and again she soared high above the woodlands surrounding Barona and let herself drop, relying more on instinct than on the dimly seen, dark gray-on-black treetops to judge when to pull out of her dive. The hard knot of bitterness underlying her sport she did her best to ignore.

Finally, the tension within her was exhausted, and she leveled out. Flying westward toward Rand and the Tessellate Mountains, she fixed her gaze on the rising moon and tried to sort out the tangled-yarn pattern of her thoughts.

She didn't mind the idea of being an adult; of that much she was pretty sure. People like Gavra Norward and the architects she knew from her building work had shown her that growing up didn't have to mean loss of all power, that being an adult didn't mean being a nobody. The attitude such thoughts implied still bothered her, though—she didn't like to admit that having power over other people was so important to her. *But I* don't *want to push people around, not really,* she decided after a moment of conscience-poking. *I just don't want* them *pushing me around.* And *that,* she realized suddenly, was what she feared most about Transition. She would be beginning school exactly equal with everyone else her age. A new situation, with new rules and relationships—and no teekay to compensate for her small size. Just thinking about it brought a tightness to her jaw.

To her right a flicker of light showed briefly through the trees. Moved by idle curiosity, she veered to investigate.

She could always simply run away, of course. Gavra had once said that over half of Tigris was still uninhabited, so it would be easy to find a secluded spot where she would never be found, using the remaining year or whatever of her teekay to build a house and clear some land. But after Transition . . . without the slightest idea of how to survive in the wilderness, things could turn ugly very fast. Besides, she wasn't really the hermit type. What she really needed was a way to get a jump on her peers at the school itself.

Again, the light flickered. This time Lisa was close enough to recognize it: a car's headlights, moving along the forest road from Barona toward Rand.

For a moment she paralleled the road, wondering what to do. She wasn't especially interested in chasing the car . . . but on the other hand, she'd seldom if ever seen anyone driving west of Barona at night. Perhaps there was some sort of emergency—and if so, her teekay might be the difference between life and death for someone. Dropping to treetop level, she increased her speed and headed toward the lights.

She caught up easily enough; the car seemed to be staying at the posted speed limit, and Lisa didn't have to bother with the road's occasional curves.

How to approach without startling the driver right off the road was a matter for a few moments' thought; she solved it by flying a hundred meters ahead of the car, matching its speed, and dropping to just within headlight range. When she was sure she'd been seen, she reduced both her speed and height a bit more, and soon was pacing the vehicle at window level.

"Are you in some kind of trouble?" she shouted, trying to minimize the nervousness in her voice. Flying at seventy kilometers per hour high above the trees and at a single meter above the ground made for two entirely different sensations, and she was acutely aware that a slight drift in practically any direction would slam her hard into something solid. Keeping her eye on the speed-blurred road beneath her, she opened her mouth to shout again—

The car vanished, and abruptly a bright light exploded in her eyes.

She was three meters up and heading higher before she realized that the driver had simply put on his brakes, dropping him behind her. Thankful that the darkness hid the hot flush spreading across her face, she circled back around, landing next to the car as it coasted to a halt.

"Is something wrong?" the driver asked, rolling down his window.

Lisa ducked her head and peered inside. The driver was a middle-aged man, dark-haired, dressed in a casual but nice-looking outfit. In the backwash of light she could see traces of the tension that some adults seemed to continually carry around with them. "I just wondered if something was wrong with *you*," she explained, suddenly feeling a little silly. "I noticed you driving at night, and . . ." She trailed off.

Surprisingly, the tightness in his face eased and he even smiled. "Oh, no—there's no trouble here. My nephew and I were just going back to Rand from a day in Barona. The time sort of got away from us and I have to work tomorrow."

"Oh," Lisa whispered; she hadn't noticed the sleeping child in the passenger seat. "I'm sorry—I was worried that there might be something wrong—an emergency or something."

"No, we're fine; but thanks for stopping. If it *had* been an emergency, I sure would have been grateful to have your help."

"Oh, that's all right," Lisa said, her face warming again. "I'd better let you get your nephew to bed. How old is he?"

"Almost five," the man said.

"He looks younger," Lisa commented, studying the boy briefly. A pang of sympathy touched the back of her throat; smaller than most of his peers, he was going to run into a lot of the same problems in his hive that she had had in hers.

"His mother was short," the driver said. "Look, we really have to go."

"Oh, sure—sorry." Lisa stepped back from the car. With a wave, the driver rolled up his window and the car again headed down the road.

Lisa watched its taillights disappear around a curve and then, with a sigh, teeked herself into the air and headed back toward Barona. *So much for making a hero of myself*, she thought, rotating once as she flew to get a last look at the glow of headlights. But even as she started to look away the lights made a sharp turn and disappeared behind a particularly thick patch of the woods.

She'd never noticed a turn quite that sharp in the road, and for a moment wondered if perhaps he'd lost control and driven into the ditch. But an instant later she saw the glow again, a little further on. Reassured, she circled back toward the distant slice of pinprick lights that was Barona. With the excitement over, she turned her mind back to the problem that had driven her out here in the first place.

She struggled with it for another half hour, and through all the tangle two thoughts gradually seemed to emerge: one, that to get the edge she desired over her peers she would need to start learning ahead of time the stuff the school would be teaching; and two, that the first thing on that list was reading.

Reading. Even just bouncing around in her head the word was a little scary. Reading was something only adults did, like driving cars or making money— something that took a lot of time and hard work to become any good at. Could she possibly get any- where with it in the few weeks or months she had left? After all, she'd always heard that reading was too hard for kids and preteens to learn—else why wait until after Transition to put people in school?

But I'm almost *a teen,* she reminded herself firmly . . . and now that she thought about it, she couldn't remember anyone ever saying that a preteen couldn't *try* to learn reading. If she could even just learn all the letters it would give her something to build on later. It was certainly worth a try, anyway.

And with unusually good timing the idea had even come to her when she could take advantage of the extra free time the weekend provided. None of the books in the hive's entertainment center had any- thing but pictures, but the Barona Library was open to anyone; and while Lisa had been above the first two floors only once, she knew kids *were* allowed up there. Provided the library opened early enough on Saturdays, she should be able to get busy right after breakfast.

For a moment she frowned, and her thoughts went back to the man in the car. What sort of job did he have, she wondered, where he had to work on Satur- day but not on Friday? The mines in the Tessellate Mountains near Rand worked eight days a week, she'd heard—a few of them a full twenty-one hours a day—but he hadn't looked much like a miner. Perhaps he was a supervisor of some kind. Certainly he'd sounded educated enough to be somebody important.

And that apparently was the secret of adult life. *Education is power . . . and power means not being pushed around.* Smiling to herself, Lisa increased her speed, hoping to get to bed early for a change. To- morrow was going to be a busy day.

*   *   *

Dr. Matthew Jarvis let his car coast to a stop by the cabin wall and breathed a sigh of relief as he flicked off the headlights. For a moment he sat in the darkness, letting his eyes adjust. Then, opening the door, he reached over and scooped up the sleeping boy beside him. Maneuvering carefully to avoid banging either of their heads, he got out of the car and carried the child into the dark building.

Inside, he headed straight for the kitchen table, the only flat surface he was willing to try and get to in complete darkness. He made it without running into anything and laid the boy down. Feeling his way to the nearest door jamb, he flicked on a light and then reached around the door to his study to turn on the lights there. Picking up the boy, he transferred him to the study couch and then went back to the car to retrieve his small travel bag, confirming on the way that the lights didn't show from outside the cabin. Back in the study, he collected the vials and hypodermics he would need and set them out neatly on the end table by the couch. Finally, he pulled a chair alongside the sleeping boy and sat down.

For a long moment he gazed into the child's face as an odd mix of emotions swirled inside him. The decision on whether to proceed was still not irrevocable ... and the fact that he'd made it this far without getting caught meant that choice was now solely in his hands. Even at this late stage that wasn't something he could casually dismiss.

But the moment passed. Reaching over to the end table, he carefully prepared the three hypos he would need: the first with a chemical to neutralize what remained of the sleeping drug in the boy's system, the second with a mild hypnotic. In the third ... Jarvis squinted at the clear brown fluid, marveling again at how innocent the stuff seemed. Certainly there was nothing in its appearance to suggest its creation had cost four years of blood-sweat ... or that it might very well turn Tigrin society upside down as drastically as the sudden appearance of the teekay talent had nearly two hundred years earlier. Brown dynamite—a kiloton of it in every hypo.

Feeling a tension in his jaw, he put the vial down carefully and picked up the first hypo and a disinfectant swab. Cleaning a patch of skin on the boy's upper arm, he injected the neutralizer and swabbed over the needle mark. Moving a couple of centimeters down, he repeated the procedure with the second hypo. Then, his hand on the boy's pulse, he settled back to wait.

He'd preferred to err on the side of caution with the doses, with the result that it took nearly an hour for the child to drift from his original comalike sleep into the half-awake state Jarvis needed. But finally he was ready.

"Colin, can you hear me?" Jarvis asked softly.

The boy stirred, and his eyes opened into slits that still showed mostly white. "Uh-huh," he murmured.

"I'm going to tell you some things, Colin, and I want you to promise me you'll remember. Okay?"

"Uh-huh."

"Okay. Open your eyes and look at me." Colin did so, and Jarvis continued, "My name is Matthew Caleb. I'm a friend of yours and the Brimmers, and you'll be staying with me for a few months—a sort of vacation in the woods. You're very excited and happy to be here, of course, and will want to stay as long as you can. Will you remember all of that?"

"Okay."

There were other things Jarvis wanted to tell him, but they could wait for another day now that the groundwork had been laid. "Good. Now, turn your head and look into the corner over there. Do you see the red disk? I want you to try and lift it straight up along the metal bar."

Colin nodded and Jarvis turned his attention to the corner. The device there was essentially a homemade version of a standard hive teekay tester. Twenty metal disks, each weighing one kilogram, rested on a vertical pole that was tapered from bottom to top; the different sizes of the disks' central holes let them rest a few centimeters apart on the pole. As Jarvis watched, the bottom disk—painted a bright red—wobbled once and began to rise. It picked up the disk above it without slowing; and the next, and the next. When the pile finally came to a halt, it consisted of eight disks and was almost able to lift the ninth.

"That's fine, Colin; very good," Jarvis said, marking the figure down in a small notebook. Average, or perhaps a bit weak for his age, though Jarvis had no doubt a careful brain and metabolism analysis would show the boy to be on the proper teekay curve. Again, that could wait until tomorrow. "You can let the disk down now." The pile returned smoothly to its original configuration, and Jarvis turned back to the boy. "Now, Colin, I'm going to give you a shot. I don't want you to feel it, though, okay?"

Colin nodded. Picking up the third needle, Jarvis prepared the arm and, with only a slight hesitation, injected the brown fluid. His hand was trembling noticeably when he returned the hypo to the table. "Very good, Colin. Now, there's just one more thing, and then I'm going to let you go to sleep. I'm going to have to give you these shots every couple of days for a while, and I don't want it to bother you in any way. So whenever you hear the word 'Miribel,' I want you to go immediately into a deep sleep. You won't wake up again until you hear the word 'Oriana.' Do you understand? Repeat the two words to me."

"Miribel," the child murmured. His eyelids were drifting shut as the hypnotic began to lose its hold on him. "Oriana."

"That's fine, Colin. Now in a minute you'll go to sleep, and when you wake up in the morning you won't remember this conversation. We're going to have a good time here together, and you're going to learn a lot about woodland life. Above all, don't worry about anything, because I care a lot about you. All right? Good. You're a good boy, Colin, and you may go to sleep now."

A moment later the boy was fast asleep, his mouth slightly open, his breathing slow and regular. Check-

ing his pulse one final time, Jarvis carefully covered
him with the blanket he'd had ready. Just as stealth-
ily, he gathered his equipment and drugs and locked
them away in his work table.

With one last look at the sleeping child, he turned
out the study lights and softly closed the door.
Strangely enough, though his hands were still trembling a bit, the earlier tension was gone . . . and the
reason for that was obvious. By illegally injecting
that drug into Colin's body, he had placed himself
neck-deep in the Rubicon.

For all intents and purposes, the decision to proceed *was* now irrevocable.

Chapter 4

There was no wake-up buzzer on Saturdays, but the excitement of the previous night carried over into the morning, nudging Lisa out of bed well before her usual weekend rising time of seven o'clock. Dressing quickly, she headed downstairs to the dining room. Despite the hour, a reasonable number of others were already there, most of them the younger boys and girls who always woke up with the sun no matter what the calendar said. Taking her tray to her table, she was mildly annoyed to find a yellow triangle waiting there for her.

Someone had probably seen that illegal balcony takeoff, she decided, and had complained loudly enough for Gavra to feel she had to take action. From Lisa's point of view the fingering couldn't have come at a worse time—along with a minor loss of points, the usual punishment for such infractions usually included one or more weekends confined to the hive. If Gavra hit her with that one, she would have to postpone her trip to the library until after work on Nultday at the earliest. Hurrying through her breakfast, she went to the Senior's office, bracing herself for the worst.

And was pleasantly surprised. "Ah; Lisa," Gavra smiled as the preteen knocked tentatively at the open door. "Come in—you're up earlier than I'd expected. I wondered if you'd help me welcome a new child

28

this morning. She's coming in with her parents about eight."

Relief washed through Lisa. It was still over half an hour before eight, and it could easily cost the rest of the morning to check a newcomer into the hive, especially if she was as scared as children often were about leaving their parents. But when she compared the task to the fate she'd been contemplating, Lisa couldn't help but feel she'd been let off easily. "Sure, I'd be happy to. Main entrance?"

"Yes," Gavra nodded. "Thanks very much—and sorry about the short notice."

Half an hour wasn't really long enough to do anything worthwhile, but the hive game rooms were always a good place to kill a little time, so Lisa wandered down to see what was going on there. She arrived to find a scene of barely controlled pandemonium, with a group of Sevens having taken over the center of the main gym room for an exuberant game of spinwheel, while some Fives and Sixes cheered from the sidelines and tried to imitate the intricate motions with their own toys. The two preteens in charge—Tens, by their obvious inexperience—seemed to have conceded the center to the Sevens and were instead concentrating on making sure the younger kids didn't get run down or otherwise hurt. They looked so helpless—and so relieved that assistance had arrived—that Lisa changed her original plans and spent the entire half hour helping to calm the boisterous Sevens and restore order. *Overseeing Saturday morning happy hole is* not *one of the things I'm going to miss about the hive*, she thought wryly as she hurried through the halls toward the front entrance. She hoped the new girl's family was late; she'd cut her time a little too closely.

They weren't late, as it happened, but since Gavra was still welcoming them as Lisa arrived, they apparently hadn't been too far ahead of her. "Ah, here she is," Gavra said as Lisa tried to trot up with dignity. "This is Lisa Duncan, one of our preteens. Lisa, this is Jessy Larz and her parents."

"Pleased to meet you," Lisa nodded to the adults as she dropped into a crouch to put herself at the child's eye level. "Hi, Jessy. How are you?"

The little girl didn't answer. Tightening her grip on her mother's hand, she regarded Lisa with wide, unblinking eyes. "My name's Lisa," the preteen went on cheerfully, ignoring the other's silence. "Is Jessy short for Jessica?"

"Can you say yes, Jessy?" her mother murmured.

"Uh-huh," Jessy said reluctantly.

"That's a *nice* name," Lisa said, smiling her best. "And you're a very pretty girl; did you know that?"

"Uh-huh," she said, sounding more confident this time.

The adults chuckled, and Lisa sensed a slight lowering of the child's barriers. Gavra apparently saw it, too, and moved quickly to take advantage of the thaw. "Why don't we all go to the testing room now?" she suggested. "After that we'll show you some of the facilities Dayspring has to offer."

"Oh, that'll be fun!" Lisa exclaimed to Jessy. "We've got a *lot* of neat toys and games here to play with." She stood up and offered her hand to the child. With only a brief hesitation she took it; and although she also kept a firm grip on her mother's hand during the short walk, Lisa decided to consider it a victory.

When they reached the testing room, however, all remaining resistance crumbled. For a moment Jessy stared in amazement at the array of toys set out there; then, with a sort of happy bleat, she ran forward.

"Jessy—" her mother began warningly.

"It's all right," Gavra interrupted her. "The toys are there for her to play with. If you'll both just step over here to the desk, there are some forms we have to fill out."

The adults disappeared into a corner together as Lisa went over to where Jessy was shaking a clear plastic ball full of colorful butterflies, each of which rang like a small bell when it moved. Lisa showed her how she could use her budding teekay ability to move them individually inside their ball and make a

tune. From her delighted reaction it was clear Jessy
had never thought about teeking through solid objects before, and she instantly went on a grand tour
of the testing room trying out her new trick on everything imaginable. It only worked when she could see
through the outer object to the one she wanted to
move, of course, but there were enough toys like that
scattered around to keep her from becoming discouraged. By the time Gavra was ready to begin the tests,
Jessy was chattering away nonstop.

The standard series of teekay tests, designed to
look as much like play as possible, did nothing to
bruise Jessy's new cheerfulness. Afterward, Gavra led
them all on the promised tour of the game and play
rooms, the dining room, and a section of the younger
girls' living quarters. The adults seemed impressed;
Jessy's father, particularly, kept pointing out things
the hives of his own youth hadn't had.

Finally, back in the testing room, Gavra invited
questions. "Would it be possible for us to stay here
for a few days, until Jessy gets accustomed to the
place?" Mrs. Larz asked, almost timidly. "I understand that that's allowed."

"Well, yes," Gavra said, and Lisa prepared herself
for a long lecture. One of the few official rules Gavra
was absolutely dead set against was "the lingering,
painful good-bye," as she often called it. "However,
there are some aspects of that which I'd like to discuss with you," she continued. "Lisa, would you mind
showing Jessy around for a while longer?"

"Sure, Gavra." Fortunately, Lisa had long ago hit
on a way to keep children occupied for long periods
of time. "Jessy, have you ever seen what Barona
looks like from the sky?"

Jessy's eyes lit up. "You mean—flying? But I can't
do that yet."

"You don't need to, 'cause I'll be carrying you. Come
on; you're going to love it."

And love it she did. From her gasp of wonder at
takeoff to their first wet pass through a low-lying
cloud, the little girl was entranced, alternately look-

ing around in awed silence and excitedly pointing
out brand-new discoveries. For her part, Lisa found
herself caught up in the child's fascination, able to
see with some of her same delight things that she
had stopped noticing years ago. It was like being a
child again herself.

They flew around over Barona for a long time,
until the rush of Jessy's excitement began to wane a
bit. Then, dropping to just above the city's tallest
buildings, Lisa unobtrusively began Jessy's first lessons in aerial navigation. "Okay, now the first thing
you'll need to recognize is the hive—it's that building
there, the one with two towers and the fenced-in area
behind it. Over there is the city building—that's where
the mayor works and where the police are; that star
near the top always means police. Right below us is
the shopping area where you'll get to go sometimes—
not by yourself, but with another preteen. See?—if
you fly straight toward the city building from the
hive you'll come right here."

"Uh-huh." Jessy squirmed abruptly in Lisa's arms,
a sure sign that she was getting restless. That posed
no physical danger, of course; Lisa's teekay was holding the child as securely as batling's talons. But like
most Fives, Jessy was bursting with energy, and Lisa
preferred that she expend it at ground level. They
could drop down to the shopping center, perhaps,
and Lisa could show her how to tell what each of the
stores sold by the picture in the window. Or else they
could walk around the city's business area and look
at the tall buildings, or—

Lisa had a flash of pure genius. "Jessy," she said,
turning smoothly and heading toward a spot north of
the city building, "have you ever been to the library?"

Jessy hadn't; and she was delighted. She had, of
course, seen TVs and tape players before—though the
headphones connected to the latter seemed new to
her—but the flashing lights of the video games were
a source of instant fascination. She ran back and
forth among the machines, standing on tiptoe to see
over players' shoulders, occasionally trying to touch

the images or teek them through the screens, and generally making a minor nuisance of herself. The preteens playing the machines, most of whom had probably fled the game rooms at their hives for the express purpose of getting away from younger kids, were not inclined to be patient, and after a few minutes Lisa corralled her young charge and took her upstairs to the second floor. Much of that level was taken up by nature exhibits, and Jessy wandered among them for nearly twenty minutes, stopping by each exhibit and listening to part of its accompanying information tape before moving on to the next. The exhibits ranged from dioramas of Tigris's native plants and animals to cages housing small, furry animals, both earthstock and native; and as she watched Jessy's exploration, Lisa was again reminded of her own girlhood. She could still spend hours here, watching the gerbils and furheads in their cages and imagining what it must be like for them in the wild. Today, though, her mood was more one of impatience than interest as she waited for Jessy's excitement to wane.

Finally, she couldn't wait any longer. Soon they would have to head back to the hive. "Jessy, there's one more place I want to show you," she said, dropping to one knee beside Jessy and the ant farm she was studying.

"Do I have to?" Jessy asked plaintively, her eyes not leaving the scurrying insects.

"Yes," Lisa said. "Don't worry, you'll be able to come here again. But I want to show you what the library is mostly for."

Reluctantly, Jessy pried herself away from the display and followed Lisa up one more flight of stairs.

It was like traveling from the hive to the city building in an instant. Suddenly, everything from the heavy wooden chairs and tables to the quiet colors and quieter footsteps labeled the room as *adult*. Jessy froze just inside the doorway, and even Lisa—who had known what to expect—felt a strange reluctance to go any further. But she was determined, and taking Jessy's hand she forced herself to walk toward the tall shelves she could see off to the right.

It wasn't an easy trip. They first had to pass by a tall desk, from behind which an even taller librarian gazed down at them, then they walked through a lounge area where several adults and a couple of teens sat with books. Lisa could almost feel their eyes on the back of her head as she and Jessy passed, and she sighed with relief when they finally reached the shelves and ducked into the space between two of them, out of sight of the adults.

Jessy looked up at the shelves, packed solidly with books from floor to ceiling. "What are those?" she asked, sounding awed.

"They're *books*," Lisa told her, pulling one out at random and carefully opening it. Neat lines of black letters on white paper stared back at her. "You see, when you get to be a teen and go to school, you'll learn how to read these. You can find out things from them." Gazing at the page, she looked for the handful of letters she knew. They were there, certainly—but in so many combinations!

"Can I hold it?" Jessy asked, and Lisa felt a teekay tug on the book.

Automatically, she countered with her own teekay. "No, Jessy," she said, leafing through the pages in hopes of finding pictures that might give her a clue as to what the words might be.

"I *want* it," Jessy insisted.

"May I help you?"

Startled, Lisa looked up as the tall woman who'd been behind the front counter came down the aisle toward them. Her lips held a pleasant smile, but there was something in her eyes that reminded Lisa of the storm cloud she'd had to pull a Nine out of a year ago. "N-no, not really, thank you," she managed. "I was just showing Jessy what books are."

"I see. Hello, Jessy," the adult said, and Lisa thought her smile a little more genuine this time. Stooping beside the girl, she deftly plucked the book from Lisa's hand and held it open in front of her. "See,

Jessy, this is *writing*. When you grow up you'll learn how to understand what this says."

Jessy reached for the book, but the librarian held it back. "No, no, you mustn't touch," she said firmly. "These are very valuable—some of the last books made from the big spaceship's records before the machines were destroyed in the Lost Generation. They're very durable—much more so than the books printed today—but they *can* be damaged if they're mishandled. That's why we don't allow children or kids to touch them. Do you understand?"

Whether she understood or not, it was clear Jessy wasn't about to buck such heavy adult pressure. "Uh-huh," she muttered.

"That's a good girl. Don't worry; you'll be able to look at the books all you want when you grow up." She shifted her gaze to Lisa. "Was there anything else you wanted?"

"Uh ..." Lisa's tongue locked awkwardly against the automatic *no* that had tried to come out. "I ... is it allowed for preteens to take books out of the library? I'd be very careful with it."

The smile slipped a bit. "I'm sorry, but we can't allow that. But if you really *want* to look at them, you can do so here, out in the reading area." She gestured in the direction of the lounge chairs they'd passed through on their way in.

"Oh. I—thank you." Lisa swallowed hard, feeling a shiver run down her back. To actually *sit* there with all those disapproving adult stares on her ... "I guess we'd better be getting back, Jessy," she said, taking the little girl's hand and mentally bracing herself to pass among the readers again. "Say thank you to the nice lady."

"Thank you," Jessy murmured.

"I think you'll find the library's first two floors more interesting to you," the librarian said as she walked them to the door. "In the future you'd probably do better to stay down there."

It wasn't until they were flying above Barona again that Lisa was finally able to relax. One thing, at least, was clear: she was *not* going to be able to learn reading in the library. In fact, it was likely to be a long time before she even ventured into the building again.

But she wasn't yet prepared to give up. There *had* to be other places she could get books from, places that wouldn't be so hostile toward her. The librarian had said that books were being made, possibly even in Barona . . . but Lisa had never seen any store that sold them. She could, of course, search the whole city in her spare time, but even if she found such a place, she probably wouldn't be allowed to buy a book there. Preteens weren't given actual bills but could buy things only at certain specially marked stores in town by charging the purchase to their hives. It didn't seem likely that any bookseller she found would have the blue hive symbol in its window.

What she needed, really, was a *person* to guide her around the problems she was running into. Someone who would be sympathetic to her ambition, perhaps a teacher from one of Barona's introductory schools or even the university; someone who could break these unspoken rules—

Or someone who could get around them.

"Hey, we're going faster!" Jessy said. "Whee!"

"Yes—we have to get back before your parents start to worry about you," Lisa told her. She didn't add that she was suddenly in a hurry to get back herself, to start asking some careful questions. Maybe —just maybe—she had the answer.

Chapter 5

"Thank you very much for your time, Mrs. Livorno," Tirrell said, making one last note on his pad. "I appreciate your help."

"My pleasure," the older lady said, her thin lips pulling together in a frown that silently proclaimed her distaste for the whole business. "I hope you catch this scum, Detective—I wouldn't want anyone to get the impression this neighborhood is easy pickings."

"Neither would I," Tirrell agreed. "Don't worry, we'll get him."

And if we're lucky, it'll be before Colin Brimmer reaches puberty, the detective added to himself as he walked down the path and headed for his car. At the moment, though, he wouldn't have placed any bets on that.

Tonio had been faster with his part of the afternoon's work, Tirrell saw; the preteen was seated on the curb beside their car, leaning against a red-and-white-checked "stop ahead" post and gazing skyward. At first Tirrell assumed his righthand was simply daydreaming, but a movement in the tree branches above the car caught his eye. It took another dozen steps for him to realize what was happening: Tonio was amusing himself by plucking dead leaves from one of the branches and teeking them over to another limb. "I hope you're not fastening those permanently somehow," he commented as he reached the car.

37

"The city's going to have to cut off that dead branch pretty soon, and I wouldn't want them to take a healthy one, too."

"No problem," Tonio said, his eyes still on his handiwork. "You finished?"

"For the moment, yeah. Let's get back to the office and see if we can dredge anything out of this mess."

"Okay." Tonio stood up, and as he did so there was a sudden rustle overhead and forty or fifty brown leaves drifted down on them. "See?" the preteen said, holding his hands out as if checking for rain. "Instant autumn."

"Just get in the car," Tirrell said, shaking his head.

"Anybody recognize Macvey's drawing?" Tonio asked as Tirrell pulled away from the curb.

"Nope," Tirrell said. "Not that that's a terrific surprise, of course. Macvey didn't have a lot to work with, and drawing a face minus its beard is an iffy proposition at best."

"Especially when your witness isn't very observant."

Tirrell raised an eyebrow. "That comment sounded rather portentious. Is there some juicy bit of evidence you've been saving for my birthday or something?"

"No, I just heard it this afternoon. It seems Mr. Oliver had been hanging around that park longer than Lenna Thuma said."

"How much longer?"

"According to two of the boys Colin played with, they were chatting to the guy as early as the beginning of March. That's over three months ago."

"Yes, I can count." Tirrell gnawed his lower lip. "Did you get any details?"

"Only that he always seemed friendly and they never saw him except on Saturdays. Oh, yes—he also used a bench near the conetrees in the center, not the one Lenna pointed out yesterday. Apart from that—" Tonio shrugged. "Pretty much a blank. None of the children ever saw him anywhere except the park, and they all assumed he knew Colin or his parents from somewhere, which is why they never reported the conversations."

"Only on Saturdays, eh?" Tirrell said, half to himself. "Interesting."

"You think Lenna's on his side?" Tonio asked.

"Whose—Oliver's? I doubt it. She's sat with Colin alone on several occasions recently. If the two were in collusion she could have delivered Colin to him at one of those times and not have had to worry about having witnesses around." Tirrell drummed his fingers on the steering wheel. "No, what I was interested in was the Saturdays-only aspect. That may imply he's an out-of-towner who normally can't get here during the week."

Tonio digested that in silence for a block. "But this week he came on a Wednesday and a Friday."

"He did indeed. What does that suggest to you?"

"Well-l-l. He changed his pattern in case someone was watching for him?"

"Maybe. I'm guessing it's a bit more significant than that, though. Did you happen to note when Colin's fifth birthday was?"

"Uh, no." Out of the corner of his eye Tirrell could see Tonio giving him a puzzled stare. "Is it important?"

"Uh-huh. Colin was going to turn five next Thursday. And since you probably don't know it, I'll mention that Ridge Harbor law requires a child to be brought in to one of the city's hives for teekay testing on the Saturday before his or her fifth birthday, and to be officially admitted the Saturday after that."

"Oh. So if Oliver had come today, he wouldn't have found Colin in the park?"

"That's part of it," Tirrell nodded. "But think it through a bit more. What was your last week at home like—do you remember?"

"Not really. All I remember is that my parents kept me pretty busy visiting relatives and having parties and outings together." The preteen slapped his hands together suddenly. "Aha! If Oliver hadn't grabbed him yesterday he might not have gotten another chance."

"Right," Tirrell nodded again. "And now you're to the crux of my 'interesting' a while back. One more question, and you'll see that maybe our Mr. Oliver's made a mistake—hopefully, a fatal one. Take your time; I'll give you till the station to figure it out."

It was six more blocks to the station. Tirrell drove at a leisurely speed through the moderately heavy Saturday afternoon traffic, Tonio's silence giving him a chance to map out their next move. An examination of the city's records, probably, after a stop by Chief Alverez's office to get the necessary authorization forms.

He pulled the car into the station's level of the attached parking garage and found an empty slot. Sliding smoothly into it, he set the wheels on lock and turned to Tonio. "Well?"

The preteen was frowning. "There's something about this I don't understand," he said, shaking his head. "How could Oliver know when Colin's birthday was?"

Tirrell smiled grimly and patted Tonio's shoulder. "Bull's-eye," he said.

The records keeper was a tall old man, well into his sixties, but still vigorous for all that. He seemed less than happy about letting Tirrell into the vault area. "If you'll just tell me which records you want to see, Detective, I'll bring them to you at one of the tables," he said, halting on the threshold of the massive door.

"If I knew exactly which ones I needed, I'd be happy to do it that way," Tirrell explained patiently. "But all I know is that we're starting with the birth records and probably going on from there."

"What year? I'll get them for you, and you can tell me then what else you want."

"Just let us in," Tirrell sighed, waving his authorization papers gently.

The keeper glanced once at Tonio, as if considering whether or not to forbid the preteen's participation, but apparently decided further resistance would be a waste of time. Muttering something under his breath, he turned and fiddled with the combination lock. A moment later the door swung open, revealing a large, dim room with thick binders stacked in floor-to-ceiling bookshelves. Flipping on the overhead lights, the keeper stalked off without a word—probably, Tirrell thought, to watch them on the vault's interior monitor system. Stepping inside, the detective studied the floor plan taped to the nearest shelf and headed off to the left.

Tonio followed a bit more slowly, looking around in wonderment. "Are *all* the records for Tigris in here?" he asked.

"Oh, no—not by a long shot," Tirrell said over his shoulder, his eyes searching the shelf labels. "Not even for the whole continent—you'd have to go to the university archives in Barona for that. No, these cover only Ridge Harbor, and only since the Lost Generation. Before that everything was kept in a kind of machine called a computer. I've heard that one of those computers could have stored Ridge Harbor's whole history in a single one of these books." He found the proper aisle and ducked into it.

"You're kidding."

"Well, that's what they say." Tirrell pointed to the top shelf. "That's the one—third from the left. Teek it down here, would you?"

The heavy book drifted off its shelf and into Tirrell's waiting hands. Tucking it securely under his arm, the detective led the way to a small table in one of the room's back corners. "Okay, let's see," he muttered as they sat down and opened the binder. "We want June seventeenth . . . June seventeenth . . . here it is. Baby boy, adopted by Thom and Elita Brimmer for the city of Ridge Harbor ... mother's name was Miribel Oriana. . . . Hmm. Says she was twenty-six, unmarried, and originally from Barona. I wonder why she came here to have her baby."

"Didn't want any of her friends to know about it?" Tonio suggested.

"Maybe. I would have thought Barona was more liberal about such things, though." He read further. "Strange. I'd assumed Colin was adopted because his parents died soon after he was born, but I guess not—his mother simply walked out the day afterward and disappeared."

"Sounds like a real winner," Tonio said, a touch of disgust creeping into his voice.

"Yeah. Seems odd, though," Tirrell said, rubbing his chin thoughtfully. "If her partner cut out on her when he found out she was pregnant and she didn't want to raise the baby alone, why didn't she simply arrange beforehand for the baby to be adopted? It would have saved everyone a lot of trouble and given her a little money during the pregnancy, besides."

"Maybe her partner was married and she didn't want to have to name him."

"Maybe." Tirrell sighed and fished out his note pad. "Let's put our supposers on ice for the moment—we may get the chance to simply ask her. Let's see. The obstetrician knew Colin's birth date, of course, and so did the assisting nurses. Any of the staff on that floor would have been able to look at the records for the next month, before they were sealed away. Then there's the Brimmers' neighbors and close friends, and Colin's biological mother if we can find her. Who else?" He stared at the list, pondering.

"Did the Brimmers ever order a birthday cake for him?" Tonio asked suddenly. "Or have professional help throwing a birthday party?"

"Good point. We can check on that." He made another note.

"This isn't going to work, you know," Tonio said, shaking his head. "We're going to wind up interviewing half of Ridge Harbor."

"Oh, it's not *that* bad," Tirrell said soothingly. "Whoever Oliver's informant is, my guess is we'll find he was relatively new to his job when Colin came to his attention. That's because—"

"Wait a second; let me guess." Tonio stared into space for a few seconds, lips moving silently. "Ah.

Because if the informant had been at it longer, we should have had earlier kidnappings like this?"

"Right. Good thinking," Tirrell said, impressed in spite of himself that Tonio had successfully tracked through the logic. "I guess we'll start by calling the Brimmers again, find out about birthday cakes and such. Then we should probably try the hospital." He started to get to his feet.

"Stan?" Tonio had a thoughtful look on his face. "Maybe I'm missing something here ... but what exactly does a fagin do with kids, anyway?"

Tirrell sat back down. "Well, fagins do different things, I guess, depending on how cold-blooded they are and what they think they can get away with. Usually, they have their kids using teekay to steal for them, but I know of at least one case where the fagin was hiring the kids out to an underground mine operation that was so carelessly run the local hives wouldn't let their kids work there. We caught one using the kids to smuggle stuff past customs, too— you may be old enough to remember that one."

"So they just want cheap labor out of them, right?"

"Basically. What they're doing is exploiting the kids, who are either taken young or sucked in by big promises. The real tragedy is when the kids hit Transition and get tossed out by the fagin, and then find out that without a hive record they're not entitled to any education. That doesn't happen very often," he added, seeing the look on Tonio's face, "since we usually catch fagins early enough to give their kids at least *some* hive time. And the last time it happened in Ridge Harbor, the kid got Basic anyway, at city expense. But even beyond that, the whole experience can scar a kid for life."

Tonio was still frowning. "All right," he said slowly. "But if it's just teekay they're interested in, why pick on Colin in the first place? The children I talked to said he was small for his age, and that means he'll be less powerful."

"Not always; and smaller kids usually keep their teekay a little longer as preteens," Tirrell corrected absently, staring at nothing in particular. "But that's still a darn good question—fagins aren't interested in the long-term teekay characteristics of their victims. And this guy Oliver seems to have latched specifically on to Colin a long time ago."

"You suppose it was because Colin was adopted? It might not be as hard on his parents that way."

"Fagins aren't noted for that kind of consideration, either," Tirrell said, a bit tartly. "No, there has to be another reason—something about Colin himself. Something the average person wouldn't know, perhaps?" He got to his feet and started back toward the vault door. "Let's go find out."

The preteen followed him. "We going to call the Brimmers?"

Tirrell shook his head. "I think we'll start at the hospital instead. I'd like to take a good look at the rest of Colin's medical records. And at the people who compiled them."

Chapter 6

"Now look, Kelby, this is ridiculous," Jarvis said as patiently as possible into the radiophone. "I'm supposed to be on vacation out here, remember? Or is one week your idea of a long time away from the lab? I don't want to hear about your troubles."

"Now, now, Matt; let's not overdo the hyperbole, eh?" Even Jarvis's less-than-magnificent equipment couldn't filter out the bluff good humor that was a permanent feature of Kelby Somerset's voice. "In the first place, this is *not* going to become a regular event; and in the second place I doubt very much you're really forgetting about work out there. I'll lay you very heavy odds you've got yourself a cozy little lab in this allegedly rustic cabin of yours. You're probably working your tail off, making twice your usual progress now that you don't have to worry about trivia like staff meetings and faculty lunches—not to mention simple food and sleep—"

"All right, all right," Jarvis interrupted with a sigh. "I give up. Ask your question and let me get back to my book, okay."

"Right. It's about the results of that test you and Cam ran last month—the induced-hibernation one. We've been running through the data and are getting a strange sort of anomaly between the eight- and ten-milligram dosages. The *rate* of decrease of heartbeat, respiration, and brain electrical activity goes

45

way down all of a sudden. As you increase the dosage the decreases plot out smoothly, but that discontinuity's driving everybody crazy. We've looked at the obvious possibilities and they all washed out. I thought you might have a brilliant suggestion or two on something new to try."

Jarvis sighed. "Disturbing my privacy isn't enough—now you want long-distance prophesy, too?"

"Not necessarily. If you want to sneak back to the lab for a day, I promise I won't tell anyone."

"Thanks a lot," Jarvis growled. "All right; read me some relevant numbers, will you?"

"Sure. Here are the blood insulin levels for the eight-milligram subjects. . . ."

Listening with half his attention, Jarvis stretched his neck to peer out the window. Colin was still in sight, playing at the foot of the big conetree next to the grassy path that served as driveway. As he watched, two large seed pods shot past the boy's head; Colin was apparently still playing dogfight. He was good at it, too, for someone his age. Jarvis made a mental note to take a dexterity/control measurement soon.

Somerset finished his recitation, and an expectant silence took its place. With some effort, Jarvis forced his mind back to the topic at hand. "Okay. First off, check to make sure the thyroid isn't suddenly boosting thyroxin production to compensate."

"We've already looked for that—"

"And check carefully, because what the extra thyroxin may be doing is chemically linking to our gamma component, which would not only take both molecules out of play but also keep you from detecting the hormone increase."

There was a brief silence. "I didn't know the two hormones could react together."

"They haven't in lab tests, but if you look closely at the gamma molecule's sulfhydryl end, you'll see there's no particular reason why the reaction can't go. Check for likely-looking enzymes in the neighborhood of the thyroid, and while you're at it check back a step and see if the pituitary increased its own thyrotropin output."

"Already tried that," Somerset said with the distracted air of someone trying to talk while scribbling notes. "Negative result."

"Okay, concentrate on the thyroid region, then." Jarvis considered. "One other thing: try doing a careful study of prostaglandin levels. Our alpha molecule's largely a prostaglandin analogue, and the body mechanisms that degrade those hormones may be attacking it. If so, we'll need to isolate which one the culprit is and put something else in the mixture to suppress it. You think that'll keep you busy for a while?"

"Quite a good while, I think," Somerset said. "Thanks a lot, Matt—appreciate it muchly."

"Glad to help. You find anything interesting, let me know—by writing it up and putting it on my desk."

"Hint received and understood. Talk to you later."

"Much later. Good-bye."

Hanging up, Jarvis glanced out the window once more to make sure Colin was still in sight before heading outside. Walking around the corner of the cabin, he managed to duck as a seed pod came sailing through the air. It rounded the edge and he heard it drop to the ground.

"I can't make it go round the house," Colin complained as Jarvis came up.

"Well, that's because you can't see it after it goes around the corner," Jarvis told him, sitting down beside the boy. "In order to teek something you have to be able to either see it or touch it."

"Why?"

"Well . . ." It was a good question, actually, one nobody had ever figured out a satisfactory answer to. "It's just the way things are, I guess."

"Why?"

"I don't know. Tell you what—why don't we see if you can figure out a way to do it." He glanced around. "Would you teek a seed pod over here, please?"

"Okay." From above them came the *snich* of a green stem being broken, and Jarvis looked up as a pod drifted down. "Why do the branches go around?" Colin asked.

Jarvis reached out to catch the pod as Colin, shifting his attention to the spiral limb arrangement of the conetree, lost control of it. "A lot of plants have leaves that spiral up a stem like that," he explained. "The conetree just takes the process a bit farther and does it with branches, too."

"Why?"

"Probably to let all the leaves get as much sunlight as possible. You see—on that conetree, over there—see how the branches get shorter as you go up? That keeps the upper branches from shading the lower ones and lets all the leaves get sunlight."

"Why do they need sunlight?"

"It's one of the things they eat," Jarvis said briefly. He'd fallen into this trap with Colin already twice in the past two days. The boy wasn't interested in answers nearly as much as he was in keeping the string of questions going as long as possible. "Here, let's do an experiment, okay?" he suggested, holding up the pod.

"What's a 'speriment?"

"A way to keep little boys quiet," Jarvis said, tapping him lightly on the nose with the pod.

Colin giggled and Jarvis moved the pod thirty centimeters away, holding it horizontally by one end at the level of the boy's eyes. "Wiggle the pod a little, would you? Just a *little*," he added hastily as the pod nearly spun out of his hand.

The amplitude decreased until it was a barely detectable quiver. Colin was being a little silly, Jarvis knew, but he could live with that. "All right. Now I want you to look at the pod very carefully so that you know exactly where it is," he instructed the boy. "Then close your eyes and try to teek it without looking. Okay? Okay, close your eyes."

Colin did so, and the pod's vibration abruptly ceased. "Keep trying," he said soothingly as Colin's features twisted up with concentration. Someday, Jarvis told himself, he would get around to studying exactly why direct visual, tactile, or kinesthetic feedback was required for teekay to function. *Someday when Ramsden runs out of projects for me to do*, he thought sardonically.

Thoughts of Ramsden and the university made him frown. Somerset, for all his perpetual cheerfulness, really wasn't as insensitive to others as he often appeared. If he'd felt it necessary to break into Jarvis's officially ordered vacation, it was either because the hibernation experiment was sinking itself into a hole deep enough to strike magma or else because he was getting pressure from either Ramsden or someone higher up. Either way they could very easily be asking him to come back in for a few days long before his vacation was over.

What would he say if that happened? He couldn't very well take Colin back with him; chances were the Ridge Harbor police had papered every police station on the continent with the boy's picture by now. But neither could he leave the child alone in the cabin. He was too young to handle things like meals for himself, and there was always the possibility that he would hurt himself, perhaps badly. The post-hypnotic sleep code word was, of course, there, but Jarvis knew hypnotic commands tended to break down when the subject got hungry or thirsty. He still had a supply of the sleep drug he'd used in the kidnapping, but Colin had already had two doses of the experimental drug and Jarvis had no intention of mixing chemicals like that. Aside from clouding test results, it could be downright dangerous.

The pod twitched, and Jarvis's adrenal flow jumped with it. Jerking his attention back to Colin's face, he was just in time to see the slitted eyelids snap closed. "I saw that," he said sternly, letting his sudden thrill of excitement drain away. "Try it again, and this time don't cheat."

"Do I have to?" the boy asked plaintively, looking up at Jarvis and shifting restlessly on the grass.

"Yes—but only once more," Jarvis told him. "Then you can go play again."

Colin sighed theatrically, "Okay," he said and closed his eyes again.

It was a good thing the Brimmers had instilled such a healthy measure of obedience in the boy, Jarvis reflected as Colin again frowned blindly in the direction of the pod. The boy's teekay strength would be growing rapidly over the next few weeks, which would correspondingly decrease Jarvis's power to physically enforce commands. He could only hope that the boy didn't realize that before he could be returned to civilization. For the first time in his life, Jarvis began to truly understand how the parents of the Lost Generation must have felt.

"I can't do it," Colin said at last, sounding frustrated.

"That's okay," Jarvis told him. "Don't worry about it. Here—why don't you see if you can teek the pod all the way over the chimney, okay? Then you can play for a couple of hours before it'll be time for dinner."

"Okay." Obviously relieved to be back on familiar ground, Colin teeked the pod from Jarvis's hand and sent it skittering between the conetree's lower branches. Craning his neck as he stood up, Jarvis saw the pod sail high over the cabin.

Smiling, he headed back toward the cabin door. Dinner would be trehhost pasta—one of Colin's favorite dishes, he knew from his Vaduz Park conversations. He'd better get started on it; the slow-cooking a trehhost required would take a while.

And later that evening there would be games, conversation, and some unobtrusive testing ... and, perhaps, another shot.

Chapter 7

It had begun to cloud up while Lisa was eating dinner, and as she flew over Barona's lengthening shadows, she decided it would probably start raining by morning. That could be a new headache for the foreman at her construction site; after losing the use of Lisa's group last Friday, he wouldn't be happy if a heavy rain deprived him of their services tomorrow as well. But rain in the eyes could cause kids to lose their grip at crucial times, and no builder was foolish enough to risk that. Gavra wouldn't permit it, anyway.

The Lee Introductory School was in a section of Barona Lisa had only visited once or twice before, and it took some hunting before she finally located the squat three-story building. After the tall, majestic towers of the hive, Lee Intro seemed almost self-consciously earthbound, and it made her feel a little creepy as she landed by its front door. *I'll be just as earthbound soon*, she thought. Steeling herself, she walked inside.

The door opened into a spacious lounge about half-full of teens, many of them frowning intently into colorful books. The room itself was much friendlier and less intimidating than the reading area at the library had been, but still Lisa hesitated at the threshold. Maybe she should just go home and forget all of this—

51

"May I help you?" a courteous voice came from her right.

Startled, Lisa turned and saw for the first time the alcove just inside the outer door. A young adult sat behind a desk there, a telephone and long sheet of paper in front of him.

"I'm looking for Daryl Kellerman," she said, stepping over to him. "He used to be at the Dayspring Hive."

The man ran a finger down his paper, stopped midway and slid it sideways. "Kellerman . . . well, he hasn't checked out and he's not listed on special duty, so he's probably up in his room. You want me to call up there?"

"Yes, please," Lisa said quickly, before she could lose her nerve.

"Who shall I tell him is here?"

"Lisa Duncan."

The man picked up the phone, consulted the paper again, and punched numbers. "There's a Lisa Duncan here to see Kellerman," he said a moment later. ". . . All right. He'll be right down," the man told Lisa, hanging up the instrument.

Lisa nodded and drifted away from the desk, wondering which direction Daryl would come from. Her heart was pounding and she could feel her courage draining away with the moisture in her mouth. *What am I going to* say *to him?* she thought frantically. She hadn't yet come up with a good answer to that when a door on the left side of the lounge opened and Daryl was there. He spotted Lisa and came toward her.

He'd changed a lot in less than a year, she thought as she put on her best smile and walked forward to meet him halfway. His face was longer and thinner and showed the black nubs of a struggling beard on his chin. He was taller, too, and seemed somehow terribly awkward in his movements. *Part of growing up?* she wondered, suppressing a shudder.

They stopped simultaneously, about a meter apart.

"Hi," Daryl said, his voice sounding as tense and awkward as the rest of him looked.

"Hi," Lisa said. "I wasn't sure you'd remember me."

He smiled and some of his tension seemed to disappear. "Not likely. You were either the best worker or worst pest I ever had in a work crew, sometimes both at the same time. Uh . . . you come by just to see me?"

Lisa hesitated—and was suddenly aware of a new silence in the lounge. Conversations had ceased, and she could feel eyes on her from the other teens in the room. Waiting to hear her answer to Daryl's question? A taste of panic splashed her throat. *New rules, new relationships—and I don't know any of them. What do I say?*

"Could we go for a walk?" she suggested, choosing the easiest way out. "It's pretty stuffy in here."

"Sure," Daryl said, a mixture of relief and disappointment in his voice. He looked past her to the man at the desk. "I'll be going outside for a while," he said, sounding very grown-up.

"Be in by eight-thirty," the other shrugged.

As they left, Lisa thought she heard a faint snicker from the teens in the lounge.

"So . . . how is life treating you?" Daryl asked as the door closed behind them.

"Oh, pretty good," she said. "How about you?"

He shrugged. "Fine," he said, his tone not very enthusiastic.

"School kind of rough?"

"A little." He pointed to the left. "Let's go this way; there's that little park a couple of blocks down."

Lisa nodded her agreement, and for a moment they walked along the sidewalk in silence. The neighborhood had a different feeling than the one near the hive, Lisa decided as she looked around. Lee Intro was closer to shops and Barona's busier streets than any of the city's hives were. Because the teens were less mobile than preteens and kids, she wondered?

"How're *you* doing in school?" Daryl asked suddenly.

"I'm still at the hive," Lisa told him.

He stopped. "What?"

She stopped too. "I'm still at the hive," she repeated, frowning at the look on his face. "I haven't reached Transition yet."

"Oh. I thought ..." Abruptly, he started walking again, and she had to hurry to catch up.

"Hey, what's the matter?" she asked, trying to get a clear look at his face through the bounce of their steps. "Did I say something wrong?"

"I just sort of figured you'd come over from Paris Intro down the street," he mumbled, nodding back over his shoulder.

"Well ... you don't have to tell your friends I didn't," she said, taking a stab at the reason for his reaction. Preteens, too, were sometimes kidded for friendships with much younger kids.

He threw her a quick look and slowed down to a more reasonable pace. "No, that's okay. I guess ... it's not easy to lose your teekay and get tossed suddenly into school at the same time, you know."

"I understand. I'm sorry. Do you want me to go away?" She held her breath, afraid he would say yes, yet feeling intuitively she needed to offer him that choice.

"I guess not," he said and managed a smile. "You came all the way out here to see me; I guess the least I can do is be civil."

She smiled back. "So ... tell me about life as a teen."

And for the next half hour he did just that. They arrived at the park and sat together on a bench as he poured out the fears and frustrations of his new life. Lisa listened attentively, striving to keep her own feelings in check as his stories seemed to confirm her worst fears about the coming Transition.

Finally, he ran out of words, and for a few minutes they sat together in silence, watching the rays of the setting sun streaming through cracks in the growing cloud cover. "Thanks for listening," he said at last, reaching over awkwardly to squeeze her hand. "There isn't really anyone I can talk to like that at the school."

"Didn't some of your friends from the hive go with you?" she asked. "I thought Chase and Hari—"

Daryl snorted. "Chase is a furhead. Joined some stupid club and now he's too good to be seen with someone like me. And Hari—" His voice caught. "Hari tried to kill himself a month ago. They took him to a hospital, and I don't know what's happened to him since then."

"I'm sorry," Lisa said softly, feeling a lump in her throat. Hari'd seemed like a nice guy. Something inside her demanded she change the subject, before she could think too much about what that implied about Transition. "Daryl . . . the main reason I came to see you tonight was to ask you for a favor."

His hand, still holding hers, seemed to stiffen a bit. "What kind of favor?" he asked cautiously.

She took a deep breath and braced herself. "I'd like you to teach me reading."

"Me?" He made a sound that was half snort and half laugh. "You gotta be kidding. I'm barely keeping up with that myself."

"But you could teach me the things you already know," she pointed out. "You could lend me books and show me what the words are."

He swiveled on the bench so as to face her, his hand pulling back. "You're not joking, are you?" he said, frowning into her face. "What do you want to waste time with reading for when the whole *sky* is open—" His voice cracked and he fell silent.

"Because I'm afraid of Transition," she said. The words were harder than stubborn Nines to drag out, but he'd been honest with her earlier and she knew down deep a half-truth wouldn't do here. "I don't want to start school cold, without any idea of what's going on."

"The rest of us had to," he said, almost harshly. "Why should you get special privileges?"

"Why should I get stuck behind the other preteens my age just because my stupid body isn't changing?"

she countered, dimly aware of the strangeness of that argument. "I'll be stuck with girls a year or even two younger than me by the time I get to school."

"You're complaining about an extra year of teekay? What kind of stupid furhead *are* you, anyway?"

"I'm not complaining about *that*," she snapped. "I—oh, grack," she sighed, giving up. She'd never been good at keeping her reasoning clear in an argument. "Daryl . . . please help me?"

His face softened a little. "I don't know, Lisa," he said, running his fingers over the hairs on his chin. "I'm awfully busy here—a lot of schoolwork, and I'm trying to earn some extra points on the work crews." He grimaced. "At least that's one thing you won't have to worry about after Transition. You've probably earned enough points to go straight through medical training if you want. I wish I hadn't messed around so much when I was a preteen."

"Any way I could help?"

"Don't I wish." He hesitated. "But maybe there's something you *could* do for me."

"What?"

He licked his lips. "Would you . . . give me a ride?"

"Sure. Where to?"

"Just . . . around."

She got it then. "You miss flying, don't you?"

"Well, wouldn't you?" he flared, as if ashamed to admit such a desire.

"Yes," she said quietly. "I'm sure I will." Standing up, she offered her hand. He hesitated, glanced around, and finally took it; and together they rose into the sky.

It was, at the same time, one of the greatest and one of the saddest flights Lisa had ever made. Even with her teekay wrapped around his entire body— which she knew from girlhood experience damped the instinctive fear of falling—he clung tightly to her hand the whole time. Drawing on her memories of flights they'd taken when he was her preteen overseer, she tried to duplicate the aerial maneuvers he had seemed to enjoy the most . . . but whenever she snatched a glance at his face she saw no pleasure there, just a frozen mask that could have fit a Nine trying not to be afraid or a Six trying not to cry. She tried everything she could think of, but his face never changed, and she finally gave up and returned them to the park.

For a long moment afterward he just stood there, staring off somewhere past her right shoulder. "Daryl, are you all right?" she whispered anxiously.

He stirred, brought his eyes back to focus. "Yeah," he said. He took a deep breath, let it out as if expelling a bad smell with it. "Thanks."

"It wasn't very good, was it?" she said. "I'm sorry; I did the best I could."

"I know. It wasn't your fault." He looked at his watch. "Come on, we'd better start back. I can't afford to lose points by being late."

They started back toward Lee Intro, Daryl once more taking her hand. "If you'll tell me what went wrong, maybe I can do better next time," Lisa said, a bit hesitantly.

"There won't be a next time," he told her, staring straight ahead. "It's ... not the same as flying by yourself. But it's too much like it."

"Oh," she said, not understanding at all.

They didn't speak again until they were in sight of the school. "You really want to learn reading?" he asked.

"Very much," she nodded. "And I can't do it alone. I *need* your help."

"All right," he said decisively. "Come back on Saturday—I'll meet you in the park at nine o'clock. Don't let anyone see you fly, okay?"

"Sure." Her heart was beating faster with the surprise of his answer; she'd expected he would turn her down after that disastrous flight. "I—thank you, Daryl. I don't know how I can ever pay you back."

"Maybe we can figure something out later," he said, his voice sounding too casual.

"Sure," she said, getting the feeling she was missing something significant.

"Good. I'll see you Saturday, then."

They had reached the outside door now. Daryl stopped and turned to face her. "Good night, Lisa," he said; and with the briefest hesitation leaned down and kissed her awkwardly on the lips. Before she could recover from her surprise he was gone.

For a moment she stared at the door, feeling the tingle of his kiss on her lips. *What was* that *all about?* she wondered. She'd heard about things like that from some of the other preteens, but the whole idea had always seemed silly and even a little bit repulsive to her.

Still . . . Turning, she headed down the sidewalk in the direction of the Paris Introductory School Daryl had mentioned. If suffering through a few scratchy kisses was the price she had to pay to learn reading, she was willing to do so. She just hoped that was *all* he wanted; the rumors about what came after kissing were positively grisly.

Two blocks later, well out of sight of Lee Intro, she lifted from the ground and headed for home.

Chapter 8

"I speak the Truth," the Prophet Omega said solemnly, hands raised palm outward to the group of kids sitting cross-legged in the sun-drenched glen.

"The Truth," they repeated in unison.

"Search your souls for that which is impure," Omega said. He stole a glance upward as a small shadow passed over them: four more kids arriving, from the direction of Tweenriver and Ridge Harbor. "Replace the impure with the Truth."

"The Truth."

"To remember my words is to learn; to learn is to grow; to grow is to rise above Transition. The Truth shall set you free."

"The Truth."

"Meditate, all of you, on the Truth."

"The Truth," they repeated one last time and fell silent, their heads bowed.

Omega brought his hands together, checked his watch. He'd timed things well; there would be just enough time to turn the initiates back over to an acolyte and get back to the tabernacle. "Amen," he intoned.

"Amen."

There was a rustling as the kids got to their feet and glanced around, surreptitiously easing the kinks out of their muscles. Omega looked beyond the circle and nodded, and the preteen acolyte standing silently in the shadows came forward. "Heirs of the Truth," she said, her voice causing them to turn. "You have glimpsed the future as it can be, the inner power that can survive even the dark evil of Transition. Now you must show your sincerity, for the deeds of the body mirror the Truth in the soul—"

Omega didn't wait to hear the rest of the spiel but slipped away through the trees to the side of the glen and began working his way back up the small ridge that separated Initiate Grove from the main part of the site. He could trust Camila to do a good job; unlike some of the other senior acolytes, she was genuinely and uncynically sold on the work ethic he preached, and was therefore the best person to sell it to new converts.

He stopped for a moment as he topped the rise, ostensibly adjusting his royal blue robe but actually admiring his handiwork. By anyone's standards it was an impressive sight. Nestled halfway up one of the most majestic peaks in this part of the Tessellate Mountains, the site of the future Temple of Truth was a raw wound in the tree-covered stone. Flitting around it were perhaps two hundred kids, teeking chunks of the stone out of the mountainside and taking it to a dump site two ridges away where it wouldn't mar the natural beauty of the valley below. They were working with a will, digging out the chunks as if their future happiness depended on it. *The work ethic is such a useful tool*, he thought with satisfaction.

The tabernacle—a large tent divided by internal partitions into various smaller rooms—was set up almost directly beneath the temple site. Omega had ordered it put there as a mark of trust in his followers' skill with the loose boulders overhead, a little touch that had encouraged them to be careful to catch even the gravel the digging generated. Omega's quarters were in the tabernacle's rear, accessible through either the main part of the tent or a private entrance. Entering via the latter, he quickly changed from his blue robe to a dazzling white one and donned an elaborately embroidered, gilt-edged stole that had once belonged to a genuine priest. Exactly on time, he stepped out into the main meeting room.

A small crowd of kids waited for him there, grouped near the far end under the watchful eyes of two senior acolytes. Omega raised a hand in the Sign of Truth and intoned a few appropriate words of blessing before walking over to the "confessional," two chairs facing each other surrounded by a gauzy curtain.

Senior Acolyte Axel Schu was waiting there for him. "Good afternoon, O Prophet Omega," he said, the slightest twitch of his lip showing how seriously he took the title. "A full quota of confessors for you today, mostly from Ridge Harbor and Barona."

Omega nodded. Saturdays were always like this, as kids who were too far away to come on weekday evenings flocked in by the dozens. Of course, the extra workers were good to have, but having to spend a full three hours in confession was a pain in the butt and usually a waste of time besides. "Fine," he told Axel. Stepping into the gauze booth, he settled himself in the fancier of the two chairs and composed his brain and face for the task ahead.

It wasn't really anything like work, of course—he'd seen to that when he'd set the whole thing up—and the first four confessions went by as smoothly as puréed oatmeal. Unlike the standard Catholic confession, Omega's concerned itself less with personal shortcomings and more with the way the world around the confessor either demonstrated or denied the "Truth" he taught. That particular emphasis was always harmless and occasionally netted him a nugget or two of useful information.

Today turned out to be one of those times.

The fifth confessor—a police righthand from Ridge Harbor—had hardly begun when he dropped a small bombshell into his monologue: ". . . and they think a fagin has kidnapped him."

Jerking his mind back to full attention, Omega quickly replayed his short-term memory. A child taken from a park in broad daylight? Unbelievable . . . and

dangerous. "It is evil to steal children away, to hide
them from those who may show them the Truth," he
put in solemnly. "Do the police know who is responsible for such a foul act?"

The preteen shook his head. "Detective First Tirrell
is still talking to people who knew him."

Tirrell. Great. Omega felt a gentle shiver work its
way up his back. Putting Tirrell in charge meant
Ridge Harbor was deadly serious about getting this
fagin ... and he knew from experience how often
intense investigations turned up the wrong thing entirely. So far his cult had largely escaped official
notice, and it would be the height of unfairness for
him to get caught in a net meant for someone else.
He would have to find some way to caution his pu-
pils to be extra discreet without having to tell them
why it was necessary.

The rest of the righthand's confession was routine
and uninteresting, and Omega listened with half an
ear until he had finished. "You must strive to main-
tain the Truth within yourself," he said as the preteen bowed his head for the cult's version of absolu-
tion. "And as the Truth requires you to work for your
own growth, it also requires you to seek out those
who are in need of the Truth's power; those who fear
for their future." He paused and then deviated slightly
from the usual script. "And he who must now be
fearing the most is the child, Colin Brimmer. You
must seek to learn all you can of the case and bring
such knowledge to me. Together, the Truth within us
will deliver him."

"Yes, O Prophet," the other said. Bowing deeply,
he left the confessional.

After all, Omega thought as he watched the preteen's indistinct figure heading for the door, *every
potential danger is also a potential opportunity.* If he
could locate this fagin before the police did, the other's kids would likely have been well drilled in obedience and discipline—prime candidates for conversion
to his cult.

And if the fagin turned out to be a newcomer to the

game and Colin his first recruit? Omega smiled grimly. In that case his best bet would probably be to blow the whistle and get the case closed before any of the heat spilled over onto him. Such a thing was normally unthinkable, but Omega had no sympathy for a fagin who was so brazenly obvious in his acquisitions. And such an amateur would probably have no way of retaliating against him, anyway.

The next confessor was outside the booth now. "Enter," Omega said.

"Oh, yes, I remember her very well," Tasha Chen said, peering at the copy of the hospital record sheet Tirrell had handed her. "Miribel Oriana. Had her baby all alone—no husband or friend in for support. Had a boy, didn't she?—oh, yes, there it is. Three point-two kilos—yes, I remember him being small." She gave the paper back to the detective. "What do you want to know about her?"

"Everything you can remember, Mrs. Chen," Tirrell said. "We're especially interested in any visitors she may have had while she was in the hospital, anyone who may have asked about her, or any names she may have mentioned."

"Whumph!" The woman made a face. "That's all, is it? You don't want shoe size or favorite hobbies, too?"

Tirrell smiled politely; the comment might have been humorous if he hadn't heard a hundred variants of it in the past week and a half. "I know; after five years it's pretty hard to remember details about a patient you had for two days. But it's very important that you try."

Mrs. Chen's eyes narrowed, suddenly thoughtful. "Does this have anything to do with the kidnapping down in Ridge Harbor two weeks ago?"

"Miribel Oriana's son was the one taken," Tirrell said, ignoring Tonio's startled look. The police weren't releasing that information to the public, but Tirrell had had enough experience with people of Mrs. Chen's type to know that beating around the bush would be a waste of time.

"I see." The thoughtful look remained. "Well, as it happens, Detective, I *do* remember a visitor Ms. Oriana had the morning after the baby was born. He went in and talked to her for a few minutes and then just walked straight out without stopping to chat with any of us who were on duty."

"Any idea what they talked about?"

"No, but I remember she seemed upset when I went in afterwards. She nearly snapped my head off over something completely trivial."

Tirrell made a note. "You have a good memory," he told her.

She colored slightly. "As I said, she was a rather unusual case."

"True. Do you remember anything of the man's appearance?"

"Not a thing. Sorry."

"Any idea as to his relationship with her—friend, relative, husband?"

"None whatsoever."

"Did you ever see either Ms. Oriana or the man again?"

"Not that I remember. Of course, I was only at the hospital another few months before coming here and setting up my clinic. I haven't been back to Ridge Harbor more than a dozen times since then. Perhaps one of the other nurses could help you, or Dr. Kruse—"

"We've already talked to all of them," Tirrell interrupted, closing his notebook and standing up. "Thank you for your time, Mrs. Chen, and if anything else should occur to you, please call me. The number's on the card I gave you."

"Of course. Good luck, Detective; I hope you catch this man."

"Well, that was as pleasant a way as any to waste an hour or two," Tonio commented when they were once again driving along the coastal road that joined Cavendish and Ridge Harbor. "Is that the whole list, then?"

"Of the hospital people, yes," Tirrell said, inhaling deeply of the salt-laden air coming through the car windows. Having spent the first half of his life in the mining town of Plat City, he hadn't yet acquired the native coastlander's indifference to the smell of sea air. "And don't knock Mrs. Chen's contributions—her story meshes very neatly with everything else we've got on Miribel's mysterious visitor."

Tonio shrugged. "Which is not a whole lot. Average height and build, nothing remarkable in appearance, and stayed just long enough to have an argument."

"Which is an interesting point all in itself," Tirrell said. "If he was interested enough to visit her in the hospital, why didn't he at least take an extra minute to go see the baby in the nursery?"

"Um . . . okay, why?"

"My first-blush guess is that he didn't want to be seen by any more people than necessary, which automatically suggests he had something to hide."

"If he's our fagin, hanging around nurseries would be a dangerous thing for him to do at any time," Tonio suggested. "If the staff suspected he was picking out future prospects, they'd have the police on him in nothing flat."

"True. But with Miribel's collusion he'd have had a perfectly reasonable excuse to do so in this case," Tirrell said, scratching his chin. "That may be a strike against him having anything to do with our fagin." He stared through the windshield, keeping the car on the road by pure reflex, as he tried to get all the facts to jell into something that would hold water. Dimly, he realized Tonio was talking to him. "Sorry—what'd you say?"

"I said we're back to start again," the righthand said with the tone of exaggerated patience preteens often seemed to use when they felt they were being unjustly ignored. "Or have you changed your mind about one of the hospital people being involved?"

"No, not unless one of the background checks turns up something." Tirrell shook his head. "Tonio, this just doesn't make any sense. Look. The kidnapper—

Oliver—almost certainly knew Colin's birthday. If we rule out the hospital staff and various records keepers, we're left with Colin's mother, her hospital visitor, and someone close to the Brimmers as Oliver's possible informant. Most of the Brimmers' friends are above suspicion, and Ms. Oriana might as well have fallen off the planet on her way out of the hospital for all the traces we can find of her. That leaves her visitor, and we both agree the brevity of his walk-on appearance is at least mildly suspicious. But if he *is* Oliver or Oliver's informant, why didn't he at least case the nursery while he had the chance? Even worse, if he was Colin's father, why didn't he petition for custody of the child sometime in the past five years? He probably could have gotten him and dispensed with the kidnapping entirely."

"But then how would the fagin have gotten him?" Tonio asked.

"Dad could have handed Colin over to Oliver and disappeared somewhere," Tirrell shrugged. "Or they could have set up a fake kidnapping that would have been just as plausible and infinitely safer than the real thing. But even if we can somehow hammer all of *that* into a reasonable theory, we're still stuck with your old question: why would a fagin bother with a child as small as Colin in the first place?"

Tirrell ran out of words and shut up, and for a long moment they drove in silence. Ahead, the road branched twice, and Tirrell kept his attention on the red-and-yellow striped markers that indicated Ridge Harbor. A wrong turn would wind them up in a farm cluster somewhere instead; hardly fatal, but certainly embarrassing. "I suppose it doesn't help to assume there's no fagin involved at all, and that Colin's father simply decided he wanted his son back?" Tonio suggested hesitantly.

"If you do, you also have to assume the father is crazy," Tirrell said. "The average adult can't discipline a kid with teekay—why do you think the hive system was set up in the first place?"

"Then I give up," Tonio said, with a touch of exasperation. "Maybe he *is* crazy—then all of it could make sense."

"Maybe. But I doubt it." He glanced sideways at the preteen. "You ever been to Barona, partner?"

Tonio frowned at him. "Yeah, we went to see the university there once. Why?"

"Because that's where we're going next. Colin's mother was from Barona, his father was probably likewise, and the kidnapper was almost certainly not a Ridge Harbor resident—all those Saturday visits, remember?"

"Okay, but why go to Barona ourselves? The police there can handle that part of it better than we can."

"Maybe," Tirrell grunted, "maybe not. Besides, there's not much left for us to do here. We'll check with Alverez as soon as we get back and see if he can wangle us a temporary transfer."

Tonio shrugged. "You're the boss. I just hope it won't be a complete waste of time."

Tirrell smiled grimly. "Somehow, I don't think there's much chance of that."

Across the room Sheelah was sitting in front of the wardrobe mirror, amusing herself by rearranging her hair into a completely outrageous and elaborate mass that wouldn't have lasted half a second without teekay support. Lying on her bed, Lisa watched her roommate with an absorption that owed less to real interest than to simple fatigue. "I like that one," she told Sheelah as the other's hair drifted into a confused-looking bubble surrounding her head. "You can call it the Frolova Light-Socket Special."

Sheelah made a face in the mirror and teeked a pair of dirty socks in Lisa's direction. "If I were you, I wouldn't make any cracks about personal appearance," she said. "That batling nest of yours looks like it hasn't been brushed in a week."

"I just brushed it this morning, when you were in the bathroom," Lisa objected mildly.

"Well, it doesn't look like it." Swiveling around, Sheelah gave Lisa's head a closer scrutiny. "I'm not kidding, Lisa. If you don't get to work on that mess, some of those snarls may have to be cut out." She glanced over at Lisa's dresser, teeked the hairbrush lying there over to land on the bed. "Get busy; I want to see some improvement by the time I get back from my shower."

"Yes, *Senior* Sheelah," Lisa said dryly, levering herself up on one elbow.

"Never mind the sarcasm—just brush." Slipping on her robe, Sheelah teeked a towel to her opened hand and left the room.

Sighing, Lisa sat up and began to run the brush through her hair. It *was* a mess, she realized, wincing as a particularly large tangle tried to take a piece of scalp out with it. Normally, she took at least passing interest in her appearance . . . but these days there were more important things on her mind.

She glanced at the closed door, then reached under her pillow for the flat object hidden there. Sheelah wouldn't be back for at least fifteen minutes, and there was no sense in wasting the privacy. Opening the book Daryl had given her, she turned past the last section they'd worked through together. *The man is walking*, she read, sounding the words out carefully. *The man is ca—cahri—carrying—the man is carrying a*—She studied the picture with a frown. *Box? Box, probably.*

Slowly, she worked her way down the page as, unnoticed, the hand holding her hairbrush came to a quiet halt.

Chapter 9

The secretary in the university's Physiology Department was rather young and quite attractive, with a set to her jaw that Tirrell took as evidence of an uphill battle to prove she was competent as well as decorative. Tirrell himself had no doubts on that score; she'd looked at his badge without batting an eye, informed her boss of his unexpected visitor, and calmly gotten on the phone to do a little appointment juggling. Watching her covertly as he and Tonio took seats near her desk, Tirrell fantasized stealing her away to Ridge Harbor for a few weeks to straighten out the paperwork mess down at customs.

The inner office door opened and a balding man strode briskly out. "Detective Tirrell? I'm Dr. Ramsden—head of the department. Won't you come in?"

"You've got a clear half hour, Dr. Ramsden," the secretary murmured as Tirrell and Tonio stepped past her. "I can get you more if you need it."

"Thank you, Meri," Ramsden said and closed the door. "Won't you sit down?"

Tirrell settled into the single chair in front of Ramsden's desk; Tonio teeked a second over from under the window and joined him. "Dr. Ramsden, this is Tonio, my righthand," Tirrell said when the scientist was back in his own chair. "We're investigating the Colin Brimmer kidnapping in Ridge Harbor last month."

Ramsden nodded. "Yes, I heard about that. A real tragedy. How may I help you?"

Tirrell pulled out his well-worn artist's drawings and pushed them across the desk. "We're looking for a man who may look something like one of these. Do they strike any bells?"

Ramsden's eyes shifted between the drawings. "Not really. Are they all supposed to be the same man?"

"Yes. He was wearing a wig and false beard at the time, unfortunately, which is why the hair and facial shape vary so much. They're our artist's best guesses."

Ramsden shrugged. "If the hair is in doubt, I probably know a dozen men who could conceivably be drawn like that."

Tirrell nodded. "All right, then, how about her?" he asked, handing the other the picture of Miribel Oriana Barona's driver's license files had provided.

Ramsden frowned at the photo for a long minute. "She looks vaguely familiar, but I can't for the life of me say why. Did she ever work in my department?"

"No, she used to work at a coffee shop a couple of blocks away—the Redeye." Which was why, he didn't add, he and Tonio were wading through the various university departments this week. *Someone* must have known the woman, and her restaurant's clientele was as good a place to look as any.

But Ramsden was shaking his head. "No, I haven't been in the Redeye for at least fifteen years—I came down with flu there the day after I got my doctorate, and the decor has made me feel queasy ever since. You sure she never worked here?"

Tirrell felt a small stirring of hope. If Ramsden wasn't just imagining things, this could be the first lead they'd had in five weeks. "Not *absolutely* sure, no, but none of the records we've found mention the university."

Ramsden picked up his phone and punched a button. "Meri, would you check employment records for a—" he looked up, and Tirrell supplied the name— "Miribel Oriana? Better go back at least ten years.

Yes, go ahead; we can fill out the proper authorization forms afterward. Thank you."

He hung up. "We'll know in a few minutes, Detective. Is there anything else I can do for you while we're waiting?"

"Yes," Tirrell said, pulling out his notebook. "You can give me the names of those dozen men you mentioned earlier."

The secretary's report arrived a few minutes later: no one named Miribel Oriana had ever worked in the department. "Meri said she'll check with the university's central records next, see if she might have worked somewhere else on campus," Ramsden added as he hung up the phone.

"Thank you," Tirrell said. Probably a waste of time, but long shots were occasionally worth the effort. "In the meantime, I'd like to talk to the men whose names you gave me."

"Certainly," the other nodded, getting to his feet. "Actually, only five of them work here—the rest are personal friends or colleagues. But you're welcome to talk to the four who are here this afternoon."

"Is the fifth one sick?" Tirrell asked as he and Tonio also stood up.

"On vacation," Ramsden said, gesturing to the door. "Took off June seventh and won't be back for about six months."

Tirrell glanced at Tonio, saw his own sudden interest mirrored there. One week exactly before the kidnapping . . . and gone now for six *months?* "You have a very generous vacation policy here," he said as casually as possible.

"Oh, Matt Jarvis is a special case," Ramsden smiled. "Hasn't had any time off in nearly five years and we finally decided enough was enough. The rules require a certain amount of vacation time per year, you know. Besides, we can't risk him getting a nervous breakdown."

"Not if it's *the* Matthew Jarvis you're referring to," Tirrell agreed.

"It certainly is," the other acknowledged with understandable pride.

"You know this guy, Stan?" Tonio spoke up.

"Only by reputation," Tirrell told him. "He's done a great deal of the quantitative work on the teekay ability—designed the brain and metabolism test they use at your hive to judge a new kid's teekay and to predict Transition time."

"He's also made great strides in understanding the glandular changes at both onset and Transition," Ramsden added, "not to mention his pioneering work with chemical perception-alteration, glandular disease and dysfunction, and hormone-based medical treatment."

"No wonder he hasn't had time for a vacation," Tonio murmured.

"I hope he at least has weekends off," Tirrell put in, picking up on Tonio's lead-in.

"Oh, I understand there *have* been Saturdays when you could find his lab locked up," Ramsden shrugged. "There haven't been many of them, though."

"I'll bet," Tirrell murmured. "Perhaps we could take a look at his lab later, after I've seen the other four men. And I'd appreciate it, by the way, if you'd keep the specific case we're working on to yourself for the time being. There's no need for anyone else to know, and publicity can sometimes be harmful to this kind of investigation."

Ramsden nodded. "I understand."

The four meetings went quickly; as Tirrell had expected, none of the men bore any real resemblance to Oliver's sketched face. All denied knowledge of anyone named Miribel Oriana, and only one thought he recognized her picture. Tirrell made a note for the Barona police to check their alibis for the day of the kidnapping, but that was pure by-the-book reflex, and he didn't expect anything to come of it. Ramsden seemed a bit embarrassed—Tirrell sensed he'd had visions of minor fame as the man who'd provided the case's first solid clue—but the detective assured him that chasing dead-end leads was all part of the job.

Looking only marginally consoled, Ramsden led them upstairs to Matthew Jarvis's lab.

Tirrell had reasonably expected "lab" to be a singular noun, but in this case it turned out to be decidedly plural. Jarvis presided over a fourth-floor complex that included two labs, an office, a preparation room, and a small menagerie of caged animals. "Very impressive," Tirrell said after one of Jarvis's assistants gave them a brief look at the facilities. "I begin to understand how Dr. Jarvis can handle five different projects at once."

The woman, Cam Mbar, smiled. "Actually, he was handling five projects at once long before the department gave him this much room. He just gets all of them finished faster this way."

"What are all these animals for?" Tonio asked, drifting sideways through the air as he scanned the rows of cages with obvious fascination.

"They're used in various experiments," Ramsden told him. "If we're working with a new drug, say, we have to test it on animals to make sure it'll be safe for people to use."

"What happens if it's not?"

"Well, we do more testing and research to try and—"

"I mean what happens to the animal," Tonio interrupted, still gazing into the cages.

Ramsden exchanged a quick glance with Cam. "Well . . . usually the animal dies, I'm afraid."

Slowly, the preteen settled back to the floor and stepped back to Tirrell's side, his face set into an expression that was simultaneously hard and blank. Forcing his eyes back to Cam, Tirrell broke the awkward silence. "I wonder if we could go to the doctor's office now and ask you a few questions, Ms. Mbar."

"Certainly," she nodded with evident relief. Tirrell glanced once at Tonio's face as they all filed out of the animal room, but the other's expression hadn't changed. The righthand's reaction worried Tirrell a bit, and he made a mental note to ask about it later.

The office was considerably smaller than Ramsden's had been, but once Cam had sat down at the cluttered desk and Tonio had drifted up over everyone's head, there was enough room for everyone to breathe simultaneously. "Have you ever seen this woman before?" Tirrell asked Cam, handing her the picture of Miribel Oriana.

Cam gazed at it, shook her head. "No. Sorry."

"Okay. Do you happen to have a picture of Dr. Jarvis available?"

She blinked at the request. "Uh . . . I think there's one on the jacket of his latest book." She scanned the bookshelves. "That's one—end of the shelf, gray cover." She pointed past Ramsden.

"Tonio?" Tirrell said, and the book slid out and flew into the detective's hands. The picture was on the front inside cover, and he studied it for a long moment in silence. It *could* be Oliver's face, he decided; but, then again, the description they had was so limited that nothing conclusive could be drawn from it.

"Cam? Louden? Anyone home?" a voice said from outside in one of the labs.

"In here, Dr. Somerset," Cam called.

A bluff, friendly looking face peered around the door jamb. "Whoops. Didn't realize you were having a party here. I just brought in the latest prostaglandin test results." He stepped in and leaned past Tirrell and Ramsden to hand Cam a piece of paper. As she took it, his head twisted sideways, and he gestured to the photo still lying on the desk in front of her. "Where'd that come from?"

Tirrell had caught the head movement and was already picking up the photo and turning it right side up. "Do you recognize this woman, Doctor?" he asked.

"Sure—Matt was going out with her a few years ago." He focused on Tirrell's face. "Why do you ask, Mr.—?"

"Tirrell, Detective First Tirrell of Ridge Harbor." Tirrell's heart was doing rapid flip-flops in the center of his chest. "Do you remember how long ago this was?"

"Uh . . ." Somerset hesitated, looking questioningly at Ramsden.

"Tell him anything you can, Kelby," the other affirmed. "This concerns a very serious matter, and I've promised the department's full cooperation. Detective, that must be why she looked familiar to me—I must have seen her in the building with Matt."

Somerset still looked uncertain. "Is Matt in some kind of trouble?" he asked.

Tirrell hesitated a split second, decided to give the most favorable interpretation that wasn't an outright lie. "At the moment, we're just trying to locate this woman or find out as much about her as we can."

"Well, I doubt that Matt would be much help with that," Somerset said, still sounding reluctant. "I haven't seen her around for at least . . . oh, at least five years; probably closer to six."

"I see. I understand Dr. Jarvis is on vacation at the moment. Do you know where he is?"

"Sure—he's out at his cabin."

"Where's that?"

Somerset shrugged. "I don't know. Out in the woods somewhere. Cam, do you know?"

The woman shook her head. "I was thinking it was somewhere due north of here, east of Banat perhaps. He's got a radiophone up there, though."

Somerset nodded. "Yes, I've called him a couple of times since he left."

"You *what?*" Ramsden snapped. "Blast it, Kelby, he's supposed to be on *vacation* out there."

"Funny, that's what *he* said," Somerset said blandly. He looked back at Tirrell. "I'm sure he wouldn't mind coming back for a few hours to talk to you, Detective. I can get a radiophone link from the phone here, if you'd like."

"No, that's all right," Tirrell said, his mind racing. "There's no need yet to interrupt his vacation. It's possible we can get all the information we need from other sources, especially if Dr. Jarvis hasn't seen Ms. Oriana in several years. I would, however, like to ask you and Ms. Mbar some questions about Dr. Jarvis's recent work, if I may."

"What sort of questions?" Ramsden asked guardedly. "I don't mean to be rude, Detective, but you'll understand that some of the work here has important commercial applications, and we can't afford premature disclosure of sensitive details."

"I don't expect to need any sensitive details, and any I *do* will stay with me," Tirrell told him. "But it may very well prove vital for me to know of the existence of such details. I'm afraid I'm not at liberty to say more right now."

For a moment the others mulled that over, while Tirrell crossed his fingers and prayed for Tonio to keep his questions to himself. "Well . . ." Somerset said, glancing at Ramsden, "of course we'll be happy to cooperate as much as possible." He paused, but Ramsden didn't interrupt, and he continued, "I have an important appointment in five minutes, but I could probably cancel it if absolutely necessary."

Tirrell shook his head. "No, you can go ahead. Ms. Mbar can give me all the help I'll need for a while. Just come back as soon as you can and don't mention any of this to anyone else." He shifted his gaze. "That applies to you and your secretary, too, Dr. Ramsden. Thank you for your time and help; I'll let you know if I need any further assistance."

Ramsden nodded and, correctly interpreting the comment as a dismissal, squeezed past Somerset and disappeared. "I'll be back in about an hour," Somerset said and followed his colleague.

"If you don't mind, Detective," Cam said, rising from her chair, "I have to get something out of the autoclave before we begin. It'll only take a minute."

"Go ahead." Tirrell nodded, pressing himself back against the wall to let her by. Tonio dropped back to the floor as she left, took a quick look out the door, and turned to face the detective.

"You going to let me in on this game?" he asked in a low voice. "What does Jarvis's recent work have to do with anything?"

"If he's like most scientists I've known, he'll have all his lab book entries dated," Tirrell said. "Ramsden said he was often here on Saturdays; if we can prove he *wasn't* here on the days Colin's sitter and playmates remember seeing Oliver in Ridge Harbor, we may be able to persuade the Barona police to authorize our using direction finders to locate Jarvis's convenient little hideaway."

Tonio frowned. "Why do we need to persuade them? He's a material witness or something, isn't he?"

"Not really—all we know is that someone else says Jarvis once knew Oriana. That justifies our calling him and asking him to come in for questioning, but if he *is* involved in the kidnapping, that would tip him off and might even spook him into deeper hiding. And if Colin is still with him . . ." He left the sentence unfinished.

An odd look flickered across Tonio's face, but before Tirrell could ask about it, he heard the sound of returning footsteps. A moment later Cam appeared with a half-dozen thick binders. "Here are Dr. Jarvis's lab books, Detective," she said, sidling past him back to the desk chair. "What would you like to know?"

Tirrell glanced back at Tonio, but the preteen seemed all right. *I'll ask him about it later*, the detective decided, turning his attention back to Cam. "Let's start with the first of March," he told her, "and look at which Saturdays Dr. Jarvis was working."

The session took nearly an hour and a half, and by the time Tirrell and Tonio left, Barona's four o'clock rush hour was already in progress. Fortunately, the city building wasn't too far from the university campus, and they arrived with Tirrell's temper still in good shape. Passing the front desk and the loungelike duty room, they went up the stairs to the third floor; but instead of going to the cracker-box office the Barona police had assigned them, Tirrell went to another office a few doors down.

Hob Paxton, Detective Second of Barona, was not

amused by the report. "Do you realize who you're talking about, Tirrell? Matthew *Jarvis*. Probably Barona's greatest claim to fame. I can't let you go invading his privacy on the basis of some dates in some lab books."

"Oh, come *on*." Tirrell brought a finger down hard on the notebook resting in front of the other. "Every single day that we know Colin's kidnapper was in Ridge Harbor Jarvis was out of his lab—and they were the *only* Saturdays he was out. What more do you want?"

"Evidence that he was in Ridge Harbor on those days would help a lot."

"All right," Tirrell said. "Get me a records-check authorization and I'll try and find out when he charged up his car around the critical weekends."

Paxton shook his head. "That's almost as bad as the radiophone trace. Forget it. Besides, all that could get you is how many kilometers he drove, not where he went."

"It wouldn't even get you that much if he recharged at the other end of any long trips," Weylin Ellery, Paxton's righthand, put in.

"If he was spying on Colin Brimmer, he wouldn't risk leaving a record of his presence that way," Tirrell said shortly. His dislike of Weylin had begun about five minutes after their first meeting and was still growing like a healthy weed. The preteen combined a subtle self-righteousness with the irritating air of semi-private amusement kids in secret hive clubs often displayed to the rest of the world.

"Well, it's a moot question, anyway," Paxton said. "We simply can't do anything like that without more proof, Tirrell."

Lips pressed tightly together, Tirrell got to his feet.

"Perhaps we should go see Chief Li directly about this."

Paxton's brow darkened just a bit. "If you want to do that there's no way I can stop you; but I can tell you right now the answer'll be the same," he said coolly. "I don't know how you do things out east, though, but in Barona a visiting policeman usually doesn't threaten to go over his liaison's head."

"Out east we're more interested in solving crimes than in carving out political hierarchies," Tirrell countered. "Thanks for your time." Turning, he stalked out of the room, Tonio on his heels.

"What do we do now?" the righthand asked when they were behind the closed door of their own office.

"We're going to find Jarvis ourselves," Tirrell said, still fuming. "Even if he built that cabin with his own hands, he had to buy the materials somewhere, and he may have dropped enough clues along the way to give us a rough idea of where he is. Once we've got that we can scour the area on foot if we have to."

"You're really sure he's got Colin, aren't you," Tonio said, that odd look on his face again.

"I'm eighty percent convinced of it," Tirrell said. "In a couple of days that number may go up." He tapped the book he'd borrowed from Cam. "I want you to take this picture of Jarvis back to Ridge Harbor tonight. You'll ask Macvey to put a beard, glasses, and gray hair on it and then show it to Colin's sitter, and you'll also show it as it is to the hospital people who remember Oriana's visitor. Better make the picture part of a lineup in both cases—Macvey will know how to handle it."

"Okay." Tonio took the book, gazed at and through the picture. "Stan ... what would Jarvis want with Colin? I mean, there's no reason for him to have set up a six-month vacation if he was giving Colin to a fagin, is there?"

Tirrell shook his head. "I can't think of one. I frankly don't know."

"Do you suppose he's doing some sort of experiment on him? Like they do on all those little animals?"

Tirrell studied the other's face. "That really got to you, didn't it?" he asked.

The preteen shrugged uncomfortably. "I used to go to the library and watch animals like those playing around in their cages," he said. "I didn't know people did things like ... that ... to them."

"It has to be done," Tirrell said, trying to remember his own reaction to that revelation when he was in school. But it was buried too deeply. "There are lots of things we have to do to animals to live. All the meat we eat comes from animals; so does leather and furs—"

"I know all that," Tonio interrupted impatiently. "I'm not a child. It's just that ... cows and trehhosts aren't so small and friendly looking. Or so defenseless."

"I understand." Tirrell let the silence hang in the air a few seconds, and then gestured minutely toward the book. "I'd like that picture in Macvey's hands as soon as possible."

Tonio looked up and managed a faint smile. "Okay, I get the hint. You want me to phone the results to you or just fly them back?"

"Better hand-deliver them. Paxton's point about Jarvis being a civic landmark is well taken. I don't want to risk any leaks until we've got a solid case. There's that twenty percent chance he could be innocent, after all."

"Right." Sliding the jacket off the book, Tonio carefully flattened the paper and buttoned it inside his shirt. "See you in a couple of days," he said and disappeared out the door. Swiveling his chair to face the window, Tirrell gazed out, and a minute later saw his righthand rising rapidly into the eastern sky.

But he's not *innocent,* the detective told himself. *One way or another, Jarvis* is *involved.* And that certainty made something very unpleasant crawl around in the pit of his stomach ... because he had no answer for Tonio's question.

What the hell *did* Jarvis want Colin for, anyway?

All the logic Tirrell was trying so hard to build into his case tottered dangerously around that point. For a moment he wondered if Tonio had been right, if Jarvis was Colin's father and simply wanted some time with his son. But Jarvis was surely smart enough to have tried legal channels before resorting to kidnapping if that was his goal. No, it had to be something else entirely . . . and two facts abruptly clicked together in Tirrell's brain.

Jarvis was an endocrinologist, who had done extensive work with the glandular role in teekay.

Colin was at the age where teekay was just starting to become significant.

Tirrell shuddered as the picture of small animals in cages flicked through his mind. Picking up the phone directory, he turned to the business section and began making lists of builders, building supply stores, and renters of building equipment.

Chapter 10

As usual, Lisa dropped to the sidewalk a good four blocks away from the Lee Intro School. It was nearly six o'clock, an hour past sundown, and even with the streetlights shining brightly she had no problem finding a doorway dark enough for her to surreptitiously stuff the two wads of tissues into the training bra she'd borrowed from Sheelah's dresser. Daryl had always seemed nervous about being seen with her until she'd hit upon this way to make herself look older. It had helped, but only for a while, and over the last couple of weeks he'd started acting a little funny again. Distant, sort of. Hopefully, though, the few drops of perfume she'd managed to scrounge would help bring him back around. Sniffing at her wrists, she checked to make sure the flight hadn't blown the scent away.

Daryl was waiting by their usual bench when she arrived, turning the latest book nervously end over end. Playfully, she used her teekay to freeze it suddenly in midair. His eyes bulged for a split second before he looked up at her with obvious irritation. "Knock it off, Lisa," he hissed.

"Hello, Daryl," she said demurely, releasing the book.

"Hi," he grumbled. "You have the other one with you? Good—give it here. All right, now, this one shouldn't have any new words that you can't get from the pictures; if there are any you can't figure out, mark them and we'll talk on Friday. Okay?" He took a step back toward the school.

"Wait a second," Lisa said, puzzled and alarmed. "What's the rush? Anything wrong?"

"Of course not," he said, a little too quickly. "I just can't stay out here all night."

"All night? It's only—"

"Lisa, I've got to go," he interrupted brusquely, and for a second she was a kid again, standing in front of her preteen overseer. "I'll see you on Friday; don't be late."

Numbly, she watched as he strode back toward Lee Intro, his figure alternately clear and indistinct as he passed under the row of streetlights. The abruptness of his manner had scared her down to her toes— something was wrong, and she had no idea what it could be. Had he been caught passing her books? After her library experience she could easily imagine such a thing's getting him in trouble. Perhaps someone had been watching tonight's meeting—maybe that was why he'd left so quickly. Frantically, she looked around, but she couldn't see anyone.

Or else . . .

Daryl was nearly a block away by now. Carefully, trying to match his speed, Lisa set off after him, a new suspicion growing in her mind. He passed Lee Intro without pausing and continued on the three blocks to the Paris Introductory School. He went in the front door while Lisa, not wanting to hang around in plain sight, found a dark tree midway between two streetlights and flew up into it. She didn't have long to wait; a moment later Daryl reemerged, accompanied by a teen woman, and together they headed toward the commercial area near the two schools. Their voices carried distinctly in the still air, and though Lisa couldn't catch many of the words, it was clear they were having a good time. They passed under a light, giving Lisa a glimpse of the teen's long blonde hair, and she noticed for the first time that they were holding hands as they walked. Laughing and chattering, they rounded a corner and disappeared from sight.

A moment later Lisa was high overhead, streaking toward Barona's northern power station and trying to make some sense out of the jumble of emotions chasing each other through her mind. It was a relief, of course, to have her worst fears proved wrong ... and yet, at the same time, the real reason for Daryl's behavior had her so mad she could hardly see straight. How *dare* he treat her like some pestering kid and then sneak off to be with some stupid teen woman? He was acting just like one of those preteens who belonged to secret clubs and wouldn't say anything about them to outsiders. He could simply have *told* her he had a date—she would have understood. It was the *way* he'd dumped her that was so infuriating.

Wasn't it?

Even with the cool wind whipping past, she felt the rush of heat that rose to her face. She had absolutely no interest in Daryl as anything except a teacher—none at all. Was it her pride that had been bruised so badly, the fact that Daryl's interest could switch so easily to someone else? Because she wasn't jealous. Really. *Wasn't.*

Abruptly, she reached up her sweater and angrily ripped the tissues out of her bra, flinging them as far as she could away from her. No more pretending to be something she wasn't for *anyone*.

She'd planned on spending at least half an hour going over parts of the new book with Daryl and was consequently some forty-five minutes early for her shift at the power station. For a moment she considered waiting outside, but there really weren't any places nearby that had both the privacy and light she needed to read. Leaving her book on the power station roof near one of the skylights, she went inside.

The adult supervisor didn't seem surprised to see her so soon. "Lisa Duncan," he nodded, marking something on his clipboard. "You're sure racking up the extra points these days. This is, what, the fourth time in as many weeks you've signed for nighttime power duty? You must be planning to go into science or medicine or something."

"Extra points are nice to have," she said noncommittally. "Should I go ahead and start now or wait until I'm supposed to?"

"Whichever." The man peered through the square of glass set into one of the office's doors. "Charl's doing okay, I think, but he'd probably appreciate a little help. If you start now you get to quit early, too."

"Okay." Nodding to him, Lisa teeked open the door and walked into the big room.

The north power station, the newest of Barona's three, had been built with each of its four flywheels in a separate room, which was the reason Lisa had signed specifically to work here. Charl, a preteen from a different hive, was slouched in a chair near the flywheel's side, gazing at the spinning wheel with an unblinking expression that was both tired and somewhat resentful. Lisa knew his type instantly: he'd probably fooled around most of his life, losing points for disobedience and never volunteering for the extra work that could make them up. Now, with Transition bearing down on him, he was trying desperately to make up for lost time. Teeking over a chair for herself, she sat down a few meters away from him and got to work.

He left an hour later, never having acknowledged Lisa's presence by so much as a glance. That was fine with her; still smarting from the whole thing with Daryl, she wasn't much in the mood for conversation.

One of the technicians on duty came in a few minutes later to check some readings, followed almost immediately by the supervisor, who was checking something else. Lisa waited until they were gone, and then, still watching the flywheel, flew up to the ceiling skylight and opened it. Reaching out, she picked up her book and dropped back to her chair, glancing once at the office door to make sure she hadn't been seen. *The Story of Our Trip to Tigris*, the book's cover said. Settling back into her seat, Lisa opened it and held it out at nearly arm's length, an awkward position for reading but the only one she'd found that also let her see the flywheel well enough to continue teeking it. The need to keep some of her attention on her work cut her reading speed considerably and made it necessary to put off all writing exercises until later, but she didn't mind. There were very few jobs where she had the necessary privacy to do any reading at all, and fewer still where she could earn extra points at the same time. And those points were becoming increasingly important to her as even the very simple books Daryl had given her hinted at facts and ideas which she had never before heard of. There were a lot of unknowns out there, she was beginning to realize, and the more schooling she could get the better would be her chances of learning about them.

And so she sat and read, learning for the first time how the huge flying ships had first brought people to the world. So completely did the book and flywheel hold her attention that she never even noticed the technician who got three steps into the room before seeing her and beating a silent retreat ... nor the supervisor who stood at the window for several minutes afterward with a grim expression on his face.

Through the gauze curtain surrounding the two chairs, the tabernacle's candles were blurry globes of light, flickering like uneasy spirits with every passing breeze. The effect always reminded Omega of a particularly gruesome horror story he'd been frightened by back when he was a kid, one reason he generally didn't take confessions at night. But any rule had its exceptions.

"Speak, young Heir of Truth," he nodded at the shadowy figure across from him.

Weylin Ellery was still a little breathless from his sixty-kilometer flight south—though teeking didn't require any real muscular effort, it wasn't easy to breathe with the air hitting your face at eighty kilometers an hour. "O Prophet, I bring news of Detective First Tirrell and his investigation." He paused for a deep breath. "He's been trying to find people who knew Colin Brimmer's mother, and today he told us he thinks Matthew Jarvis might have kidnapped him."

Omega frowned in the darkness. "*Doctor* Matthew Jarvis? The endocrinologist?"

"I guess so. He's a scientist, anyway, at the university."

"Did Tirrell give any reason for this suspicion?"

"Nothing that Hob—Hob Paxton—thought was any good. Jarvis's lab books show he wasn't working the days Tirrell says the kidnapper was in Ridge Harbor, and he's also out in the woods somewhere on vacation. Tirrell wanted to try and find him—some trick with his radiophone—but Hob told him the department wouldn't let him."

Omega was silent a moment. "Has Detective Paxton questioned you at all about why you asked him if you could be Tirrell's liaison?"

"No, sir. He swallowed the story about me wanting the chance to work with someone from the seaside. He's not too smart, sometimes."

Omega nodded, thinking hard. Could it be that Paxton had swallowed that line but that Tirrell hadn't? In that case this whole thing with Jarvis might be nothing but a decoy designed to lull him, Omega, into a false sense of security. But, no, that was too subtle even for Tirrell. And anyway, why drag a name as big as Jarvis's into it?—besides which, Omega's information indicated that the few police departments who'd even heard of the Heirs of Truth thought it was just another of the secret clubs that grew like weeds among preteens. No, Tirrell couldn't be gunning for him . . . and that made Weylin's story even more intriguing, because whatever else was said about Tirrell, no one had ever accused him of having bad instincts. If Tirrell thought Jarvis was involved, he probably was. Which led immediately to the question, *Why?* "Did Tirrell mention a motive Jarvis might have had?" he asked the righthand.

"Not to us, sir. I think he was mad at Hob for not letting him do the radiophone trick."

"You have done well to tell me this," Omega said. It was time to bring the confession to an end; he'd gotten about all he could out of Weylin for the moment and the preteen had to get back to his hive before lights-out. "Strive to bring peace between Hob and Tirrell, so that you can learn more about what Tirrell is doing. Remember that the man who has Colin, whether scientist or not, is evil; and those of us who serve the Truth must free the boy from his grasp."

A few minutes later he watched from the entrance to the tabernacle as Weylin rose swiftly into the night sky and disappeared among the stars. For a moment he lingered, his eyes picking out the constellations as he thought about this new twist. Was there, then, no fagin involved at all?—or was Jarvis simply acting as agent for someone else? That was a particularly intriguing thought, one that might make it worth re-opening communications with some of his old friends. If someone had found a way to bribe, threaten, or blackmail leading citizens that effectively, the technique might be worth learning.

No. Better to wait a while, at least until Weylin could pump Tirrell for a little more information. After all, he had a good thing going here already, and it would be foolish to risk someone else's muscling in on him.

Smiling in the direction of the temple site, Omega glanced once more at the stars and went back inside.

Chapter 11

"... the fourth ... the fifth ... and the seventh," Cam Mbar said, closing the last of the eight lab books and settling back with a quiet sigh that somehow expressed just how wasteful of time she considered this. "Dr. Jarvis left on the seventh, so there are no more entries," she added.

Tirrell nodded as he finished making little triangles around the dates she'd read off. "That's all the lab books you have?"

"Weren't they enough?" she asked dryly. "I could go get last year's, if you'd like."

"That won't be necessary," Tirrell said, looking over his calendar with growing interest. It had been a long-shot hunch all the way, but it had paid off. "And you confirm he's been here every weekday since the beginning of the year?"

"Every one of them—and most of the days last year, too," she confirmed tiredly. "If you're about to suggest he doesn't deserve such a long vacation—"

"Nothing of the sort," Tirrell assured her. "You might be interested in taking a look at this, though." Turning the calendar around, he slid it across the desk toward her. "The circles are entries he made in his hibernation studies book, the squares are his pituitary studies, the x's his work on that hormone I can't pronounce, the plus signs his Romo's syndrome

cure, and the triangles the work with pre-teekay
children."

Cam glanced at the paper, an annoyed frown spreading across her face. "You must not have been paying
very good attention to me, Detective," she said. "There
are at least half a dozen days in May alone that I
remember that you don't have marked."

Tirrell shook his head. "I marked every date you
read off. But go ahead—check it yourself."

Cam gave him a strange look. Then, clamping her
jaw, she picked up the first lab book and leafed
through it. Tirrell sat back, letting her take her time.
It took several minutes, and when she finally looked
back up her irritation had been replaced by puzzlement. "But I *remember* him working here these days,"
she insisted.

"I'm sure you do," Tirrell nodded, "and I'm not
doubting your word. It would seem, though, that
you're missing at least one of the doctor's lab books."

"But these are always kept in a locked drawer—"
She stopped suddenly. "You think it was stolen?"

"Not really. I think Dr. Jarvis has it with him."

She opened her mouth, closed it again. "But he
never takes his books out of the lab," she objected
weakly.

Tirrell didn't bother trying to argue the point; she
was certainly intelligent enough to see that he was
making sense. "Do you have any idea what else he
was working on, besides these?" he asked instead,
waving at the stack of books.

"No . . . not really." She still looked troubled, as if
she were betraying a confidence. " A lot of time he
worked alone, or gave me routine sorts of tests to
run. We'd all sit down together on Nultday morning
and discuss the work he wanted to get done for the
week, and I never heard him mention any project but
these. Maybe he told one of the other assistants about
it, though."

"I doubt it." Tirrell pondered a moment. Until
Tonio got back from Ridge Harbor, he still wouldn't
have anything Paxton would be willing to move on.

But with a little ingenuity, perhaps he could circumvent the need to see Jarvis's project proposals or any other official records. "I'd like you to dig out all the supply and equipment requisition forms you can find for the past nine or ten months. Who's the best endocrinologist here after Dr. Jarvis?"

"Dr. Somerset," the woman said without hesitation.

"I'd like you to ask him to join us, too, if you would. We're going to try and figure out what exactly this special project is."

Somerset, though not especially enthusiastic about their chances, was nevertheless willing to help. Jarvis, fortunately, was the methodical sort who had kept copies of all his requisitions neatly filed in chronological order; but even so, it took Cam and Somerset the rest of the day to sort through them all. Tirrell, sitting off to one side, listened quietly and cultivated his patience.

Finally, at four-fifteen, Somerset put down his pencil and returned the last piece of paper to the pile. "I don't know, Detective," he said, pushing back his chair and stretching. "It's pretty obvious now that Matt did have something going on the side—there are drugs here that I *know* we haven't used on any of the other projects. But as to what that other thing is, I really can't tell you."

"Make an educated guess," Tirrell said. "Surely you can do that."

"I'm sure I can. But I'm not sure I should." Somerset eyed the detective thoughtfully. "After all, this *is* Matt's private work, and without an official police request, my telling you anything at all puts me on rather thin legal ice. You understand what I'm saying?"

"Perfectly," Tirrell nodded, forcing his voice to remain calm and reasonable. "At the same time, I'm sure you understand that in a police investigation time can be critically important. Of all of us here I'm probably the one most familiar with the laws concerning privacy—that's the main reason I asked Ms. Mbar to read me the dates in the lab books, instead of looking through them myself. If you'd prefer to wait the couple of days it'll take to get proper authorization, that is of course your right. But it would make things a lot easier if you could give me at least *some* idea of what Dr. Jarvis was doing."

He held his breath as Somerset and Cam exchanged glances, but they didn't call his bluff, at least not directly. "Why don't we call Dr. Jarvis and ask him about it?" Cam suggested. "I don't think even Dr. Ramsden could object to interrupting him for this."

"I don't think that would be a good idea," Tirrell shook his head, mind racing. The last thing he could afford was someone tipping off Jarvis that they knew he'd been running a secret project. At best, it would give him time to hide or destroy anything he didn't want seen; at worst, it could spook him into dropping into a hole so deep they might never find him. But it was clear he couldn't voice such thoughts here. "Radiophone conversations are by their nature more vulnerable to eavesdropping than regular phone calls," he said, choosing his words carefully. "If the wrong person heard what you said there could be real trouble."

Vague intimations had worked once before, but this time Somerset wasn't giving in quite so easily. "What sort of trouble?" he asked stubbornly. "You said yesterday you were trying to find this Oriana woman, but today you seem a lot more interested in Matt and his work. If we're going to help you, I think we're entitled to know what's going on."

Tirrell took a deep breath. Somerset unfortunately had a point. "All right. There's a possibility that Miribel Oriana is blackmailing Dr. Jarvis. Knowing what he's been working on may help us identify who's involved." Which was, the detective decided, as misleading a set of true statements as he'd ever heard.

And it had the desired effect. Somerset's expression ran the complete gamut from surprise to anger to determination; Cam's got stuck somewhere in the vicinity of outraged shock. "You'll understand now," Tirrell continued, "why I can't risk broadcasting any hint of my progress over the airwaves. In this game, the less your opponent knows of what you're doing, the better your chances of nailing him."

"Of course," Somerset nodded firmly. "All right. Basically, it looks like Matt was doing something involving the maturation process. Some of these drugs"—he indicated his list—"are known to slow down various aspects of puberty in earthstock lab animals. Others are synthetic androgens—male sex hormones—and some rather hard to isolate pituitary hormones, all of which seem to play a part in growth and puberty. Um ... there are a couple of carriers here, too—those are relatively inert chemicals that can bond loosely to two or more complex molecules at a time. They're used when you want to get a drug to a specific but inaccessible area—the islets of the pancreas, for example—without flooding the whole system. If you choose the carrier's grabber properly, you can get the whole thing to link up with, say, the glucagon molecules in the islets' alpha cells. The drug then drops off and begins its work, while the carrier-grabber combination either disintegrates or also drops off, leaving the glucagon molecule undamaged."

Tirrell had caught about one word in five of all that, but the essence made it through the jargon. "Would this method also be useful if you wanted to get a drug within range of something spread through the whole body?" he asked carefully. "Those growth hormones, say?"

"Yes," Cam spoke up. "Dr. Jarvis has been doing that in some of his induced-hibernation work—using carriers to seek out thyroxin in the blood."

"I didn't know that," Somerset frowned.

She shrugged. "He said it was just an experiment, but it seemed to work pretty well."

Growth and puberty studies, several months for work without interruption ... and Colin Brimmer, a boy whose teekay was just starting its rise. Something in the pit of Tirrell's stomach began a slow tumble. "Tell me," he said without thinking, "is it still accepted theory that the physical changes at puberty are what bring on Transition?"

The other two suddenly looked thoughtful, and Tirrell cursed his carelessness. He should have saved the question for later, when they wouldn't have been so quick to follow his line of thought. "Well," Somerset said slowly, "it's not really that simple. Transition *does* occur sometime during puberty, but it's not a direct result of the sex hormone activity—otherwise childhood castration should eliminate it. There's a theory that even with the testes removed the adrenal cortex puts out enough testosterone to trigger Transition, but that's never been proved." He shrugged. "But why would Matt be so secretive about working on something like that? Every endocrinologist on Tigris has taken a shot at figuring out what starts Transition. Matter of fact, he and I did some work on that four years ago."

"What did you learn?"

"Nothing really useful. We were able to extend the B and M curves—that's brain size and metabolism rate—all the way up to Transition, but that's about all. Matt got interested in artificial hibernation after that and we put it aside."

"I see." Tirrell turned to Cam. "Would you go and see if you can find Dr. Jarvis's lab book for that period, please?"

"If you'd like." She looked at Somerset, eyebrows raised.

"It'll be December and Lucember of three-oh-three and January of three-oh-four," the other told her.

Cam nodded and left. "There's really not much in that notebook worth looking at," Somerset told Tirrell.

"I'm mainly interested in whether the book is here or not," the detective told him. "It seems rather odd that Dr. Jarvis would suddenly give up on something as potentially valuable as teekay research in favor of artificial hibernation."

Somerset smiled. "You underestimate hibernation's value, Detective. For certain operations being able to slow down the patient's metabolism drastically could make the difference between life and death. And if we ever recover the space technology we had before the Lost Generation and want to go looking for other survivors of the Expansion, some form of hibernation will be vital." He waved a hand. "Besides, as I said, Transition research is a pretty crowded field these days. Even more so than teekay work generally. You have to understand that by the time teekay first appeared on Tigris the viral DNA that triggered it had had four generations to ensconce itself in our genetic structure—*and* that all the original physiological baseline records were destroyed in the Lost Generation. What that means is that we're working essentially blind: we know what human biochemistry is like *now*, but we don't know where in the system the critical changes occurred. That makes for a pretty big target for medical science generally, but for endocrinologists the only really practical starting point is Transition."

"And Dr. Jarvis doesn't like following the pack?"

"Not when the pack is nosing uselessly around a locked door, no. But if anyone ever comes up with the key to that door, odds are it'll be Matthew Jarvis."

"Um," Tirrell grunted, and for a few minutes there was silence. Somerset glanced once at his watch, and Tirrell realized with a start that it was approaching five o'clock. He'd have to end this session soon and let the others get home. He was beginning to wonder if Cam had unilaterally made that decision when she finally returned.

"There's nothing for that period in any of the file drawers," she told Somerset. "I looked through the books for at least a year on either side of the months you gave me, and there's nothing at all on Transition B and M."

"Uh-*huh*." Somerset looked at Tirrell. "Well, you called it, Detective, but it doesn't make any sense. Why would a blackmailer want that particular book? The B and M curves we did can be found in every book on teekay published in the past three years."

"It *does* seem odd," Tirrell lied. It was pretty obvious to him that Jarvis had seen something while doing the study and had hurried to quit before his coworker could also pick up on it. "Did the work involve any new techniques or anything?"

"Not really. The basic method was the one Matt came up with ten years ago. We just had to figure out a way to compensate for the wild fluctuations puberty causes in most of the useful test parameters. Matt found a statistical gimmick we could use by following a group of preteens through Transition, backtracking from their adult parameters, and—well, I won't bore you with the details. Suffice it to say that we simply came up with a statistical trick which is of no particular commercial value. It's also been published, by the way."

Tirrell nodded, pursing his lips. "All right. One more quick question and I'll let you both go. I gather you had direct access to the preteens you did this study with. Did you also work directly with the children in the more recent tests? As opposed to letting someone else take the raw data, I mean."

"No, we worked with them right here," Cam said, frowning. "Why?"

"Just curious," Tirrell shrugged. "Well, I very much appreciate your time and help in this, both of you. I hope I won't have to interrupt your work again, and I'll again ask that you keep all of this to yourselves for now."

"You're welcome," Somerset said as they all stood up. "Please don't hesitate to call us again if there's anything else we can do."

"You'll be the first," Tirrell promised. "Good night."

Chapter 12

"No, bring that end *over* the other one," Jarvis said. Sitting cross-legged on the moist ground, he indicated with his fingers the way the knot should be tied.

Carefully, Colin did as instructed, teeking the end of the rope through its last two convolutions and out through the far side of the knot. "Good," Jarvis nodded, glancing surreptitiously at his watch. Thirty-five seconds to form the knot, subtract maybe five for hesitation and uncertainties.... He would have to check that against the B and M tables when they got back to the cabin, but it looked like Colin's teekay dexterity was about where it was supposed to be. That was good; nothing drastic should be happening for a long time yet.

"Now pull this tight?" Colin asked.

Jarvis nodded. "Yes, but not too tight or you'll put too much strain on the smaller branches."

Colin sucked his lip in concentration ... and a moment later a handmade lean-to was standing proudly beneath the lowest branches of the conetree. "Yay!" the boy crowed excitedly, clapping his hands. "It worked! Can I try it?"

"Sure, go ahead." Jarvis watched as Colin crawled carefully under the thick mesh of branches leaning at a forty-five-degree angle to the ground. A new pang slid through his chest like a knife as he once again reminded himself that Colin might someday have to use these outdoor skills for actual survival. If society overreacted—as it easily could—Colin could become an overnight outcast.

"Can I sleep here tonight, Matthew? Can I, huh?"

"I'm afraid not," Jarvis said, smiling despite his gloomy thoughts at the sight of Colin stretched out on the leaf-and-moss rug they'd laid out under the lean-to. "Maybe in a couple of weeks we'll go on a long hike, though, and then we'll sleep out like this every night."

"Why can't we go *now?*" Colin asked.

"Because you haven't learned enough woodlore yet," Jarvis explained. "You need to know how to catch animals for food first, for one thing."

"Okay." The boy scrambled out of the lean-to, coming within an ace of bringing the whole structure down in the process. "How do you catch animals?"

"We'll work on that some other day," Jarvis said firmly. It was already midafternoon, and he had no intention of starting such a topic without a full day ahead of them. Besides, he'd determined two days ago that he needed some information from his office, and he'd put off making that call long enough. "Right now I want you to show me you remember the knots I taught you. Then we'll go home and you can play until it's time for supper. Let's start with a half hitch; and I want you to tie it both by hand and with teekay."

"*Okay,*" Colin said with the theatrical sigh he did so well. Teeking over a piece of rope, he got busy.

It was nearly four o'clock when Jarvis finally sat down at his desk and reached for the radiophone. For a moment he paused, checking his notes, pens, and paper and confirming that Colin was visible through the window, playing happily and showing no signs that he would be bursting into the cabin at the wrong time. Picking up the handset, the scientist punched in the operator code and then his office phone number.

Cam Mbar answered on the fifth ring. "Dr. Jarvis's office."

"This *is* a surprise," Jarvis said lightly. "I used to sneak off work at three when *my* boss was out of town."

"Dr. Jarvis!" Cam said, her voice unexpectedly intense. "Are you all right?"

Jarvis frowned. "Of course. Why shouldn't I be?"

"Uh . . ." Cam audibly struggled for control. "No reason," she said after a few seconds, her tone now exaggeratedly casual. "I just wasn't expecting you to call."

"I see," Jarvis said as something prickly seemed to settle into his neck. "I need some numbers from the second to the last of our hibernation-studies notebooks. Could you get that for me?"

"Sure. You want me to bring it to you? Just tell me where—"

"No, that's okay," he said hastily. "There's only one table I need; you can just read it over the phone."

"Oh." She sounded vaguely disappointed. "All right. I've got it; what do you need?"

The prickly thing on Jarvis's neck dug its barbs in a bit deeper. The cabinet where old lab books were locked wasn't within reach of any of the lab's phones . . . and yet Cam had found it instantly and without having to put down the handset. What would that book have been doing out at four in the afternoon?

"Dr. Jarvis?"

"Uh, yes. Um . . . about page eighty there are some figures on metabolism rate versus brain electrical activity. . . ."

Cam found the place and read off the table, but Jarvis hardly heard the numbers as his hand dutifully took them down. Cam was the stereotypical unflappable scientist type—Jarvis had seen her spill hydrochloric acid down the front of her lab coat without getting as excited as she'd sounded a few minutes ago. Instinctively, his gaze flicked to Colin, who was examining a large dragonmite struggling helplessly in the boy's teekay grip. Had someone seen him putting Colin in his car back in Ridge Harbor and taken down the license plate? But surely the police would have long since found and raided his hiding place if that were the case. Wouldn't they?

His hand was sitting motionless on the desktop, and with a start he realized Cam had finished her recitation. "Thanks," he said, hoping the silence hadn't dragged on too long. "Uh . . . how are things going?"

"Pretty good. We've been getting some good pituitary data the last week or two. Maybe you can come by and see it sometime soon."

"Perhaps. Well, keep busy. I'll probably check in again later. Good-bye." He dropped the handset into its cradle, barely hearing Cam's own good-bye as he did so.

For a long minute afterward he stared at the radiophone, gripping the arms of his chair tightly as beads of sweat gathered on his forehead. Cam's tone of voice, the notebook sitting out for no good reason, her attempt to find out where he was—it was too much to pass off as coincidence. Clearly, someone had been snooping around the lab, trying to find out what he was up to. And that someone couldn't have persuaded Cam to help him without some kind of evidence that Jarvis had indeed kidnapped Colin Brimmer.

So the police were on to him. He'd known they would be, eventually—the trail through Colin's mother Miribel was all too clear. The real question now was whether they'd had the inevitable radio direction finders running as he talked to Cam. If so, his experiment was about to come to an abrupt end. If not . . . well, he might still have enough time.

With an effort, he pushed himself out of the chair. The chances that the police had had everything ready were probably slim. From now on, though, use of the radiophone was out—it might, in fact, be safest to disable the instrument, lest Colin accidentally turn it on while playing inside.

Stepping to the window, Jarvis gazed out at the

small boy, now standing under one of the longer branches of the nearest conetree and trying to jump high enough to catch hold of it. *What will they do to you, Colin?* he wondered. *Human society has always hated those who were different, especially those who were truly superior in some way. How will you respond to that hatred?*

There was no way to answer that question—not yet, anyway. After a minute Jarvis sighed and moved away from the window. Whenever the police came, he would be ready ... but right now, it was time to start cooking supper.

Hob Paxton shook his head as he again leafed through the report Tonio had flown in from Ridge Harbor and peered at the five almost-identical photos. "I wouldn't have believed it," he said. "She really picked Jarvis's photo out of this lineup?"

"Three times straight," Tonio told him with obvious satisfaction. "It was the eyes and cheekbones, she said, and the fake beard didn't hide those features."

"Maybe she was reacting to the retouching on the other pictures," Weylin Ellery suggested from the corner. "Hypnotized people notice details like that."

Tirrell shook his head. "Our artist knows his job. The copy that still looks like Jarvis has touch-up lines over the originals."

"All right." Paxton tossed the stack of paper onto his desk and leaned back in his chair. "But evidence obtained under hypnosis isn't admissible—you know that."

"Of course. But it should be good enough to get those radiophone direction finders I wanted two days ago."

Paxton's expression was that of a man whose shoes were too tight. "Yeah. Yeah, I'll talk to the chief about it." But he made no move toward the phone. "I don't know, though—the whole thing's ridiculous. Why would Matthew Jarvis, of all people, go out and kidnap someone? Or are you going to tell me he's popped his stopper?"

"No, I don't think so," Tirrell said slowly. "I think he's doing some sort of experiment out there, something he doesn't want anyone to know about."

Weylin chuckled. "You make him sound like one of those crazy scientists you see sometimes in hive monster movies," he said. "I quit believing those when I was ten."

Tonio turned irritably toward the other preteen, but Tirrell spoke up before his righthand could say anything. "Of course he's not crazy; I almost wish it were that simple. I think it's probably much worse—that he's stumbled onto something so explosive he doesn't even want hints of it leaking out."

"Like what?" Paxton snorted.

Tirrell hesitated. It wasn't a theory he wanted to toss around too freely, especially if it turned out to be true. But Paxton was still dragging his feet on Tirrell's radiophone detector request. Perhaps a good shaking up would help. "I think Jarvis is fiddling with the Transition point," he said bluntly. "He's stockpiled a supply of growth and puberty hormones; he's apparently taken several critical lab books into hiding with him; and if he's got Colin Brimmer with him, he's got a human test subject to work on. And if we don't get busy and find him, he could knock the props out from under the whole society."

"Holy Mother," Paxton muttered, forehead corrugating into an intense frown. "You think he might find a way to knock out teekay entirely?"

"Or push it past puberty, or make it stronger, or add telepathy or heaven knows what to the ability," Tirrell countered. "How the hell should *I* know what he's up to? But we'd better find out, and fast."

"Yeah." Paxton brought his feet back to the floor with a crash and picked up the papers Tonio had brought. "Let's go see Chief Li. If we hurry we can probably get your direction finders set up by Saturday night. That fast enough for you?"

Tirrell nodded as he and Tonio stood and let Paxton

walk between them to the office door. "Let's hope so," he said as they fell into step behind the other detective. Now, perhaps, they'd make some real progress.

Chapter 13

With a flourish, Gavra Norward signed the last piece of paper and dropped it into the box on her desk. Leaning back, she permitted herself a tired smile as she glanced at her watch. Four o'clock Friday—the end of a long day at the end of a long week; and by some combination of luck and skill all of the hive's paperwork was finished and she had the rest of the evening free. It was hard to believe; in her twenty years as Girls' Senior at Dayspring she'd had perhaps two dozen such Fridays, despite a solemn promise to herself to leave that evening free. *Someone will probably throw up at dinner*, she told herself with whimsical pseudo-cynicism. *Maybe I should leave now and forget to take a beeper.*

She was in the process of stowing her pens and note pads in their desk drawer when someone knocked on her open door. Looking up, she saw Allan Gould, Dayspring's Director, peering around the jamb. "Got a minute, Gavra?"

Gavra sighed inwardly. *Good-bye, Friday night*, she told herself. Aloud, she said, "Of course."

Gould stepped into the office, and only then did Gavra realize the Director wasn't alone. A small, balding man entered on his heels, closing the door behind him. Gould gestured at him as the two men sat down in front of the Senior's desk. "Gavra, this is Raife Jung, assistant Men's Senior at the Lee Introductory School across town. Gavra Norward, our Girls' Senior."

They exchanged nods. "What can I do for you?" Gavra asked.

"I'm afraid we're here on rather serious business," Jung said, his tone and manner more than a shade on the pompous side. Opening a small folder, he extracted three photos and slid them across the desk. "I believe you will recognize both the preteen and what she is doing."

The pictures, obviously taken at one of Barona's power stations, were of only fair quality, but even so Gavra had no trouble identifying Lisa Duncan. And she was holding— "Is that a *book?*"

"It is indeed," Jung said. "Actually, there are two different books shown: lessons seven and eight of Walker's *Elementary Reading*. The photos were taken Nultday and Wednesday of this week."

Gavra impaled Gould with her eyes. "And you waited until now to tell me?"

Gould shrugged uncomfortably. "We wanted to have all the facts before we said anything. One of the technicians at the power station spotted Lisa reading a book with the Lee Intro logo on it a week ago Wednesday. He contacted me, I contacted Mr. Jung, and it turned out the evening door checker remembered a Daryl Kellerman leaving that evening with a book. We followed him this Wednesday and observed the exchange."

Gavra returned her attention to the photos, struggling to adjust her mind to this sudden revelation and to fight down the chill it caused within her. Of all her preteens Lisa was probably the last one she would have suspected of something this insidious ... and yet, in retrospect, it fit Lisa's personality remarkably well. She'd always tended to fight her battles with brains and skill instead of with brute force; and Transition, after all, was a preteen's biggest battle. And for Lisa, unlike some of the others, it would be an intensely private one, as well. The flicker of paranoia within her damped out and she looked back up at Jung. "All right," she said. "So what do you want me to do about it?"

Jung blinked in obvious surprise. "I want Duncan punished, of course. She should be told in no uncertain terms that this sort of activity is not allowed, and then be docked some points or have some privileges taken away. *And* we want the book back."

Gavra glanced at Gould. His expression was as set in concrete as Jung's. The specters of the past were formidable shapers of both opinion and policy; and their influence, as she'd just found out, wasn't totally lost even on those who should know better.

All the more reason, she thought suddenly, *to inject some logic into this. And damn the torpedoes.* "I'm sorry, Mr. Jung," she said quietly, "but I cannot punish someone who hasn't broken any rules."

Jung's eyes saucered in astonishment and he actually sputtered. "Broken any *rules?*" he finally managed. "Just what do you call—"

"Dayspring Hive has no rule that forbids kids and preteens to read," she interrupted him. "For that matter, I defy you to show me *any* law—on city *or* Tigrin books—that makes reading illegal."

"What about the Education Code?" Jung shot back. "Or the Uniform Library Use Acts?"

"Those specify who can teach reading and what books may be lent to whom," she said. "The burden in both cases is on the adult, not the kid. I'm sure you can make a case against Daryl Kellerman—" *probably already have*, she added to herself—"but Lisa is legally blameless."

There was a moment of silence as Jung seemed to fall back and regroup. Gould stepped in to fill the gap. "Don't you think, though, that letting Lisa get away with something like this will at the very least set a bad precedent?"

"For whom?" she countered. "From the evidence you've shown me Lisa seems to be keeping all this well under wraps. In fact, I'd go so far as to say that punishing her would set a more disastrous example. You'd be surprised how many kids will knock them-

selves out to try anything that they've been specifically told not to do."

"All right," Jung said irritably. "What do *you* pro-
pose we do, then?"

"Nothing, aside from the obvious. You'll want to
transfer Daryl Kellerman to another school, of course,
to break things off where they are."

"We've already done that," Jung said. "But never
mind Kellerman. I want to hear your idea of what to
do with Duncan."

"I already told you: nothing," Gavra said. "She's
not likely to be able to find another tutor in the few
months she's got left before Transition. She'll start
school reading above her level, but you're stuck with
that anyway."

"Ms. Norward." Jung's voice dripped bits of ice.
"You don't seem to realize the potential problems
this situation presents. Ever since the Lost Generation the stability of society on Tigris has depended on
the adults retaining exclusive control of knowledge.
Exclusive control. The kids already have most of the
physical power; if they were allowed to learn all the
ways to use that power, the entire system could col-
lapse into anarchy."

"I'm familiar with the facts and arguments," Gavra
said stiffly, annoyed at being lectured. "And I'd like
to remind you—*both* of you—that I'm more familiar
with the actual psychology of these kids than either
of you. Most of them are totally uninterested in starting into the perceived drudgery of school before it's
forced on them. Lisa is an exceptional case. Even if
she wanted to set up the sort of secret reading lessons I imagine you're worried about, she'd get few if
any preteens to join her."

"Oh, of course," Jung said sarcastically. "Naturally, you know better than the men and women who
laid down these guidelines."

"They were living within memory of the Lost Generation's chaos," Gould murmured, unexpectedly coming to Gavra's support. "The two-tiered society's been
stable for nearly two centuries now, with the kids'

position clearly defined for them. That kind of tradition's hard to break."

"Besides which, kids aren't just small adults, no matter what responsibilities and power they have," Gavra added. "They generally lack the discipline to pass up an immediate pleasure in favor of a more distant one—otherwise you'd have a lot more preteens working to earn extra points than actually do so. Most would rather spend as much time as possible flying or otherwise having fun, especially as they get closer to Transition."

"Spare me the psychology review," Jung said acidly . . . but there was a note of resignation in his voice, and Gavra knew she'd won. Temporarily, anyway. "What about the Walker book she still has? Or do you want to argue about *that*, too?"

"We'll do our best to get it back," Gavra told him. "But again, I don't want to make a major fuss over taking it away from her."

"As you choose. But remember that the book is the property of Lee Intro—and if we don't get it back soon, we would be within the law to bring theft charges against Duncan."

"Understood," Gavra said tiredly. The charge wouldn't stick for ten minutes, but she didn't want to put Lisa through that kind of trauma, and Jung obviously knew it. "I'll get you the damn book."

"Good." Jung got to his feet, shifted his glare from Gavra to Gould and back again. "Well. You've both been rather less than cooperative—I hope you're properly satisfied. I think you should know that I intend to go directly to the police from here and give them the whole story."

"Go right ahead," Gavra nodded. She'd anticipated this gambit, and while it sounded impressive, there really wasn't a lot the police could or would do at this stage except circulate Lisa's name and photo among the officers. "It'll be good for them to have the background in case some sort of problem *does* develop," she added, hoping her admission of such a possibility would mollify Jung somewhat.

It had little if any of the desired effect. Nodding stiffly to her, his mouth a tightly compressed line, Jung left the room. Gould threw her a glance too quick to interpret and hurried after him.

Sighing, Gavra got to her feet and followed the same path . . . but only as far as the outer office and the file cabinets therein. Unlocking the proper one, she began sorting through the *D*'s. Jung might be back later, but for the moment he was at least reasonably convinced that Lisa wasn't going to put her newly acquired skill to a dangerous use.

Now all Gavra had to do was convince herself of the same thing.

Withdrawing the thick file labeled *Lisa Duncan*, she glanced at her watch. She could do a quick survey of the preteen's record in the half hour that remained before dinner time. And for the more careful study that would be required . . . well, she had all evening.

Grumbling under her breath, Gavra tucked the file under her arm and trudged back into her office.

The wind rustling the trees had, over the past hour, changed from a pleasant, soothing sound to one filled with foreboding. Twisting her wrist toward the nearest streetlight, Lisa peered at her watch for probably the tenth time in the hour she'd been waiting in the little park. Three minutes after seven. Daryl was over an hour late.

Getting up from the bench, Lisa began to pace restlessly, her eyes probing the inky shadows that writhed like wounded animals as the trees swayed. Her emotions had already passed from annoyance to anger to concern, and were beginning to edge into genuine panic. After six weeks of regular thrice-weekly meetings, he *couldn't* have simply forgotten to show up, and as the minutes ticked slowly by her imagination generated increasingly terrifying reasons for his absence.

She checked her watch. Five after seven.

And suddenly she could stand it no longer. Glancing around her one last time, she flew quickly to the top of the nearest tree and wedged her book securely between two branches. Then, dropping back to the ground, she headed off at a rapid walk.

There were a fair number of pedestrians out—it *was* Friday evening, after all—and Lisa did her best to check the faces she passed. But neither Daryl nor the blonde woman she'd seen him with that once passed by her; and a few minutes later she was standing in front of the squat shape of Lee Intro.

For a moment she hesitated, her mind flashing back to her nervousness the first evening she'd walked up to that door and realizing dimly that what she was about to do could land her in *real* trouble. But concern for Daryl pushed aside all other considerations. Resolutely, she strode forward; but this time, instead of entering, she turned sideways at the door and disappeared behind the decorative bushes lining the walls. Keeping low, she circled around toward the rear of the building.

She had long ago found out from Daryl which of the rear-facing second-floor windows was his. The line of bushes continued around the side of the building and a couple of meters along the rear wall, allowing her to get within eyesight of his room without coming into the open. At that point, though, two problems immediately presented themselves. Like the courtyard back at Dayspring, the area behind Lee Intro was set up as a recreational area, and under the bright floodlights a good twenty teens were running about in what seemed to be a two-dimensional version of raiders. In addition, as nearly as she could tell from the angle she was at, Daryl's window was closed and, presumably, locked.

Lisa's hands were trembling with both tension and an ever-increasing sense of urgency as she looked around her. Obviously, with nearly two dozen teens throwing and kicking a ball nearby, there was no way she was going to get to Daryl's window without being seen. The floodlights—perhaps if she teeked out the power lines at the light posts' bases and plunged the rec area in darkness? But that would leave dangerous cables loose where someone might accidentally touch them ... besides which, the thought of doing that much damage—even for something this important—grated against her hive training.

She was still trying to figure out a plan when inspiration and opportunity dropped simultaneously into her lap. One of the teens, trying to get rid of the ball before he was tackled, gave the twenty-centimeter sphere a tremendous kick in the direction of the school building ... and even as it was still rising, Lisa had it in a firm teekay grip, adding just a shade more lift and range and giving it the slightest bit of sideways guidance until, with a horrendous crash, it disappeared squarely through one of the first-floor windows.

Some things, at least, did not change with Transition. The teens stood rooted in horror for a split second and then took off madly in all directions. Within seconds, the rec area was deserted.

Lisa was at Daryl's window before the sound of running feet had faded into the night breeze. The room was dark, but the curtains were still open, and enough light was scattering in from the rec area for her to see that both beds were empty. She teeked tentatively at the window; it was, as she'd guessed, locked.

It would have been easy enough to break it, but the noise would bring people there much too quickly. But there might be another way, if the adults who would surely be coming to investigate that broken window held off for another minute. With a quick glance behind her, Lisa turned back to the window and teeked the top drawer out of the nearest dresser. Moving it close to the window, she gave its contents a quick scan. She was in luck; setting down the drawer, she teeked out a small hand mirror and brought it up to hover next to the window's lock. Like most locks, this one was shielded from outside view as a routine precaution against teekay opening. But with the mirror Lisa could see enough of the lock's works; and as the outside door beneath her slammed open the window slid up and she slipped inside.

Heart pounding in her ears, she peeked back out the window. Four or five older teens and adults were in the rec area, but none of them was looking up toward her. Quickly, she replaced the dresser drawer and closed both window and curtains. Switching on the light, she made sure the door was locked. Then, feeling excruciatingly vulnerable, she began looking around the room.

Having only the vaguest idea what she was looking for, she stumbled on the vital clue purely by accident. Taped to the wall by each of the two desks was a piece of paper divided up into rectangles, with days of the week printed across the top and hours of the day down the left-hand side. Inside the rectangles were incomprehensible letter-and-number combinations, and it took Lisa a long minute to realize they were the occupants' class schedules. Wondering if Daryl had unexpectedly been given a Friday night assignment, she checked both schedules—and it was only luck that she happened to look at the names on them.

The names were *Mart Kolowitz* and *Ling Spangler*.

Lisa's first, horrible thought was that she'd goofed and got the wrong room. But a heartbeat later she remembered Daryl's mentioning his roommate Mart. So the room was right. Only—?

She never had a chance to try and figure it out. Even as she stared at Ling's schedule, the sound of a key in a lock came from the door.

Lisa reacted instantly, throwing herself in a sort of teekay-assisted jump to a sheltered position by the other desk. Teeking off the light, she ducked down as the door swung open, throwing a wedge of hall light into the darkness. An instant later the room was brightly lit once more, and Lisa peeked around the back of the desk chair to see a tall, dark-haired teen turn back to close the door. The panel clicked shut, and Lisa pounced.

Her teekay leap landed her practically on his back.

One hand touched his left arm, which she promptly froze in a teekay grip; the other arm snaked around his right shoulder and came to rest with her hand over his mouth. Simultaneously, she flicked a glance to the wall and again teeked off the light.

The teen jerked, probably with both shock and fear, but Lisa held him easily. One leg kicked back inexpertly and was promptly captured in its own invisible vise. Teeth clenched hard, Lisa waited silently for his struggles to end, wondering what in blazes she was going to do next. Her attack had been pure reflex—modeled, no doubt, after the action movies she'd loved as a kid—and now that she had the other, she had no idea what to do with him.

"Keep quiet," she muttered, making her voice as deep and masculine as she could. "I'm not going to hurt you."

The other went almost limp. Encouraged, she tried a question. "What's your name?"

She left her fingers on his lips, just in case, but he was either too scared or too smart to try yelling for help. "Mart Kolowitz," he answered in a husky whisper. "What do you want?"

"I'm looking for Daryl Kellerman," she said, only then realizing the sinister interpretation Mart would probably put on the words, given the circumstances. "I'm a friend of his," she hastened to add, "and I think something might have happened to him."

"Well, I don't know where he is," Mart said defensively. "His stuff was gone when I got back from morning classes."

Lisa blinked. That Daryl might have left so abruptly was something that hadn't occurred to her. "When did you last see him?"

"At breakfast this morning."

"Did he say anything about leaving, or was he angry or upset at all?"

Mart shook his head minutely in the teekay hold. "Nope. Said he'd meet me at four for a fast 'pong game, even. Didn't show up, though."

"Look, people don't just disappear," she hissed. "Didn't you ask where he'd gone?"

"The floor supervisor just said not to worry about him."

Lisa exhaled slowly through clenched teeth, apprehension churning her stomach. What could have happened to Daryl that the school would react like this? It was almost as if—

As if they were trying to pretend Daryl had never existed?

Her thoughts flicked to Daryl's story of Hari's attempted suicide, and to the way the school had reacted to his questions about his friend. But—*No. Daryl wouldn't do something like* that.

"Who are *you?*" Mart cut into her thoughts. "What do you want with Daryl, anyway?"

His tone was confident, almost insolent, and Lisa realized with a start that she was running out of time here. Mart's masculine pride was beginning to overcome his caution, and any minute now he might try something foolish. She could probably handle any attack he could come up with, but if he raised the alarm and someone got a good look at her face . . ."All right," she whispered, "I'm leaving now. Don't try to turn around until I'm gone. And don't tell anyone I was here."

Maintaining her grip, Lisa glanced around and teeked the curtains aside. With the extra light from the rec area floodlights she could see Mart clearly enough. Backing carefully to the window, keeping a teekay hold on the teen's arms and head, she fumbled blindly for the catch and slid the pane open. Adult voices were still audible outside, but there was nothing she could do about that except to hope they wouldn't look up. Reaching up, she smoothed her hair back, plastering it against her head and shoulders with teekay to disguise its length. Then, taking a deep breath, she turned and dived out the window.

Concentrating on speed and the necessity of getting her hands up in front of her face, she misjudged the size of the opening and banged her right knee painfully against the sill. She gasped as the shock of it made her falter; but before any of the people grouped around the broken window below could react to the sound she was above the floodlights and out of sight. Still she climbed, fear adding impetus to her flight, until the cool mist of a thin cloud layer on her face jolted her back to reality. With a start, she realized she was a good two or three kilometers above the now hazy lights of the city.

Exhaling a lungful of air, she let herself coast to a stop, her muscles limp with relief. She'd done it—had gotten in and out of the school, probably without being recognized. For the moment, anyway, she was safe.

But how long would that last?

Gazing down at the city far below, she rubbed her sore knee. Daryl had vanished . . . and deep down she was sure she knew why. *They caught him giving me books*, she thought, the panic beginning to bubble up within her once more. *It really is illegal. They arrested Daryl, and they're going to arrest me, too! I have to run away!*

She stared outward, her eyes picking out the moonlit peaks of the Tessellate Mountain range, cutting its solemn way southeast across the continent. Beyond them, much of the territory was still untouched by man. . . .

But a moment later her common sense stubbornly reasserted itself. *Mart said Daryl's things were moved out before lunchtime. If he's in trouble because of the books, why haven't they already picked me up? I was at the hive at noon and for supper, too.*

Relief washed over her like a hot shower in wintertime, dispelling chills she hadn't realized were there. And yet . . . if Daryl hadn't disappeared because of that, what *had* happened to him? Had he been injured or perhaps come down with some kind of sickness, and been moved secretly to a hospital? No, that didn't make any sense. Had he seen some sort of criminal activity, then, and been hidden as a witness? Again the thought of Hari's suicide attempt rose into view—

Lisa shook her head hard. There was no sense letting her imagination run away with her. For now, all she could do would be to retrieve the book she'd left in the park and go back home. Tomorrow . . . well, *someone* had to know where Daryl was. If she could find that someone and ask the right questions . . .

Slowly, and then with increasing speed as she left the damp fog of the clouds, Lisa headed down toward the city. Her chances, she recognized, were poor; but she had to make the effort. She owed him at least that much.

Especially, a dark voice still whispered at the base of her mind, *since the whole thing* could *be your fault*.

Gritting her teeth, she swooped low to orient herself and then headed for the park.

Chapter 14

The young acolyte tapped once on the open door to Omega's private tabernacle quarters. "Senior Acolyte Axel Schu, O Prophet," he fluted, a trace of nervousness apparent in his face and manner.

"Thank you, young Heir," Omega nodded solemnly. "Let him enter."

The Ten stepped back, and the tall preteen strode in, his eyes still puffy with sleep above his hive-issue robe. "You sent for me, O Prophet?" he asked. His voice, at least, was respectful.

"Close the door, Acolyte Schu, and sit down," Omega invited him, waving to the ornate chair opposite his own.

Axel chose to obey the orders in reverse order, settling himself in the chair before turning his head and teeking the panel closed. "Normal daytime hours not long enough for you?" he asked, a little grumpily.

"You didn't give the messenger a hard time, did you?" Omega frowned, recalling the acolyte's nervousness.

"Whatever I gave him he deserved," Axel said shortly. "I thought being a senior acolyte was supposed to keep me from being woken up at—" he squinted at the desk clock—"at two in the gracking morning. I don't stay here on Saturday sleepover very often; I don't appreciate being interrupted when I do."

"Even when the Prophet of Truth has need of you?" Omega asked softly.

Axel emitted a short bark of a laugh. "Oh, come on—you don't have to pull that earwash on *me*. I figured you out months ago."

"Oh, really?" Sitting back comfortably, Omega crossed his legs and eyed the preteen with interest. "And what exactly did you figure me to be?"

"A complete fake, who's leading a whole bunch of gullible jerks by their noses," Axel said promptly, with an air of enjoyment at finally getting to say the words out loud. "I don't know exactly what you're having us build out here, but if it's a temple, I'm a furhead."

"I see," Omega nodded noncommittally, a shiver running up his spine in spite of himself. Axel's hypocrisy was no great revelation, of course, but having his camouflage verbally ripped away was still an uncomfortable experience. "If you feel that way, why are you still hanging around?"

"Oh, for—" Axel waved a hand impatiently. "Whatever you wanted me for, let's get it over with so I can get back to bed, huh?"

Omega remained silent, and after a moment the preteen sighed heavily. "Okay, okay," he shrugged. "I'm sticking around because I want to learn how you do it. I'm going to hit Transition one of these days myself, and when it happens I want to be ready."

"You enjoy having power over people; is that it?"

Axel shrugged again. "Sure. Who doesn't?"

Omega nodded with satisfaction. He'd read the other correctly—and that lust for personal power would serve quite adequately as a substitute for loyalty. "Good," he said. "You'd like to have my verbal power. How would you like to have some *real* power, too?"

"What kind of *real* power do you have in mind?" Axel countered.

"Possibly the ability to delay Transition in anyone you choose," Omega said softly. "Would that be enough power for you?"

Axel's face went rigid. Slowly, the muscles relaxed

and he swallowed carefully. "Yes," he said, almost calmly. "I think it would." He looked around the room once, almost as if seeing it for the first time, and then returned his gaze to Omega. "I don't think there's any chance of me falling asleep on you now—you want to give me the whole story?"

Omega smiled. "Certainly. I had a visitor a few minutes ago—Weylin Ellery, from Barona. You know him?"

"Uh . . . isn't he a police righthand or something?"

"Right. At the moment he's working closely with a Ridge Harbor detective named Tirrell . . . and Tirrell thinks the kidnapper they're chasing is doing some serious experiments with the Transition point." Omega gave the preteen the gist of Weylin's most recent report, carefully emphasizing certain facts and speculations and omitting others.

"Holy grack," Axel murmured when Omega had finished. His eyes fairly glowed. "Holy grack."

"Agreed," Omega nodded, hiding his amusement at the preteen's childlike awe. "The major problem, of course, is that with their direction finders in place now the police will probably find them before we could even begin to search the twenty-thousand-odd square kilometers of forest he could be hiding in."

"Oh." Axel suddenly looked stricken.

"But," Omega continued, "since the police will be mainly concerned with the boy's safety, they should move in slowly. Since we don't have to worry about that, we may be able to get the jump on them, provided we're ready to move."

Through half-closed eyes Omega watched Axel's face carefully. This was the make-or-break point; if the preteen showed any qualms whatsoever over the implication that Colin Brimmer was expendable, Omega would have to dump him and get someone else for this job. But Axel merely nodded thoughtfully. "Yeah," he agreed. "But how will we know when they find them?"

"Weylin has a phone number in Plat City to call when that happens. The man at that number will

radio me here and we'll leave right away." Omega
pointed a finger. "And that's where *you* come in.
We'll need to have at least twenty kids here every
evening from now on. How can we do that?"

Axel frowned. "Well ... we've got sixty kids here
right now, but Saturday sleepover is really the only
time you can get that many to stay overnight."

"Why? I'd think that if you could get your roommate to cover for you one night a week, you shouldn't
have any trouble getting him to do it other nights,
too."

"The problem is timing," Axel said. "Except for
the weekends, most of us have to get up at six and
leave for work by about seven. That would mean
even kids from Plat City would have to leave here by
five or earlier if they didn't want to be caught sneaking back into their rooms. Other kids would have to
leave even earlier."

Omega remembered bed checks and work details
being easier to duck when he was younger. "All right,
then, how about this? We set up a system in each
hive where we can alert one of the kids and he'll pass
the word quickly to all the others. That way we can
make do with only a few here at any one time and
still scare up a sizable force on short notice."

"I guess that'll work," Axel said slowly, doubtfully.
He peered at Omega with narrowed eyes. "You sure
everyone'll go along with you on something like this,
though?"

"I'm sure many of them *won't*," Omega corrected
him. "At the service tomorrow—I mean this morning—
I'll give a talk about the 'evil child-snatcher' that'll
lay the groundwork in case we need to get rough
later. Part of your job will be to assemble a group of
kids—preferably the older ones—who'll obey any order I give without question. They'll be our basic
troops. Anyone else we'll use up to whatever point
they decide not to cooperate."

"Which brings up the other part of my job, huh?"

"You're not squeamish about pushing people around,
are you?" Omega asked mildly.

Axel simply snorted.

"Good," Omega nodded. "Then you might as well go back to bed—you'll want to be alert enough to watch people's faces at the service."

"Okay." Axel got to his feet and tightened his robe sash. "See you later, O Prophet," he added with an elaborate bow. Grinning, he left the room.

Omega sat where he was for another moment, gazing at the closed door. *Ambitious, self-serving cynics,* he thought. *How would we ever accomplish anything without them?* Almost a pity, in a way, that this one would eventually have to be eliminated, but Omega could already see the seeds of betrayal taking root behind the preteen's eyes. By the time Jarvis's technique—whatever it was—was in their hands, Axel would have decided he no longer needed Omega's help and have taken steps to end their relationship. Omega would simply have to make sure *his* steps in that direction were faster.

Sighing, he got up from his chair and went over to his desk. He was dead tired—the Saturday crowd had been unusually wearing—and he'd had barely an hour of sleep before Weylin's arrival, but he needed to at least sketch out what he was going to say to the assembled Heirs of Truth at the morning service. To persuade a group of generally idealistic kids to violate the most basic laws of their society for even their spiritual leader was no mean rhetorical task. Still, the chance to become perhaps the most powerful man on Tigris was certainly worth some effort and a few hours of lost sleep.

If my words really could be backed up by results! If I really could preach and then demonstrate some kind of power over Transition whenever I chose. Spiritual and political leader of Tigris? Why not? Who could possibly oppose me?

For a moment the vision threatened to overwhelm him, rising above his original paltry ambitions for this game like the mountains surrounding the temple site soared over scrubweed. *Master of Tigris.* It was headier stuff than he'd ever before tasted.

But it won't happen unless I get to Jarvis first, he reminded himself firmly. For a moment he gazed down at the papers on his desk, thinking hard. Tirrell wasn't likely to be simply sitting around waiting to get a good trace on Jarvis's phone. He'd be out poking around for leads ... and Omega had had first-hand experience with Tirrell's ability to breathe life into icy-cold trails. If he did it again now, the police could conceivably have the area around Jarvis's cabin completely cordoned off before Omega even heard about it—and a full-fledged battle with the police was the last thing in the world he wanted.

Of course, if *he* could get hold of Tirrell's notes somehow, the odds would be even again. Have Weylin steal them, perhaps? No, that would be about as clever as sending the detective an engraved invitation to the First Annual Matthew Jarvis Race. And besides, Tirrell would be bound to have an extra copy of his data tucked away someplace. What Omega really needed was to get a private peek at the detective's notes.

Send Weylin into Tirrell's office some night with a camera? Risky; cameras small enough to be easily concealed didn't exist, and trying to sneak a larger one in past the desk man would be tricky. Teeking the camera in from outside would be equally hazardous, given the alarms police station windows were invariably equipped with. If only Weylin could get *him* in ... but the old Yerik Martel wanted poster was undoubtedly still posted, and even though he didn't resemble that photo very much anymore, it would still be a stupid chance to take.

With a sigh, Omega put the thought on his mind's back burner. Time enough to worry about beating out the police *after* he had a force to beat them out *with*. Picking up a pen, he began working out his speech.

Chapter 15

"... and sort of light brown eyes," Lisa said, pausing both for breath and thought. "I don't know if he's got any scars or birthmarks or anything."

The burly police sergeant smiled briefly as his scratching pen caught up to where Lisa had finished. "This'll be just fine," he assured her. "You just wait here and I'll go see if we've got any information on your friend." He gave her a reassuring smile as he stood up and left the alcove.

Swiveling in her chair, Lisa watched him cross the duty lounge and disappear through a doorway behind the impassive-faced desk man. Five or six other policemen were working at desks in the lounge area, and two others were talking with people in alcoves similar to hers. It was far more relaxed a scene than the action movies had prepared her for; but despite that, she could almost hear her thudding heart over the quiet conversational background.

Just coming here had taken a tremendous amount of courage. Now, having given Daryl's name and description to the police, she felt uncomfortably like a dragonmite hovering near the edge of a spider web. Despite the fact that Daryl had disappeared nearly a week ago and Lisa had still not been picked up by any group of authorities, she couldn't shake the guilty feeling that she and her books were still somehow responsible. *Maybe they just haven't gotten around to*

me yet, she thought nervously, watching the door and
half expecting the officer to return with two or three
righthands. In her mind's eye she watched herself
undergo the humiliation of being arrested, heard Gavra
announce the shameful news to the rest of the hive
that evening at dinner, saw herself put into a cell—
alone—still not knowing what had happened to
Daryl. . . .

The door opened and the sergeant came out alone.
He said something to the desk man, then walked
back to where Lisa waited. "Well, there's both good
news and bad news," he said as he sat down again.
"The good news is that no one matching your friend's
description has turned up dead in the past week, at
least nowhere this side of the Tessellates. The bad
news is that we don't have any runaways, detainees,
or hospital unknowns like him, either. I guess we still
can't help you."

Lisa sighed. This had been her last hope. "All right.
Thank you anyway."

He gave her a searching look. "Have you talked to
the various schools in town? He must have been
enrolled in one of them."

She nodded. "He *was* at the Lee Introductory School,
at least until last Friday. But he's gone from there
now, and no one there will tell me anything about
it."

"Maybe he was simply transferred. They do that
sometimes."

"Then why won't they *tell* me that? Every time I
call they tell me he's not there, but they won't say
anything more. And why wouldn't *he* have told me
about it before he left?"

Thoughtfully, the sergeant tapped his teeth with
the end of his pen. "Good questions," he admitted. "I
wish I could give you the answers."

"So do I," Lisa sighed, slumping in her seat. The
last bit of emotional strength seemed to have drained
out of her, leaving her more fatigued than long work
days and even fights in the hive had ever made her
feel.

"You all right?" the sergeant's voice came as if from the far end of a Five's play tunnel.

She managed a smile. "Yes, I'm fine. Thank you anyway for your help. I have to get back; it's almost dinner time."

"You're not sick or anything, are you? One of the men could drive you—"

"No. Thank you." Getting to her feet, Lisa nodded and walked past the desk to the exit.

Outside, she stood on the city building steps and took a deep breath, wondering what she was going to do next. The police couldn't help her; Lee Intro wouldn't. She could think of only one more avenue to try, and she would almost rather cut off a hand than take it. The humiliation of admitting her crimes to the one adult whose approval she still valued—

Do it for Daryl. If he's in trouble, it may be your fault . . . and humiliation's easier to live with than guilt.

Blinking away the dampness in her eyes—they were *not* tears—Lisa launched herself into the sky. Tonight, after dinner, she would tell Gavra everything.

"Thirty-eight," Hob Paxton muttered as the radiophone buzzed quietly, indicating a ring on the phone at the other end of the signal. It buzzed again: "Thirty-nine."

"Hang up," Tirrell said to Cam Mbar, feeling a minor wave of frustration wash over him. Once again, it seemed, Jarvis was one step ahead of them.

Cam replaced the radiophone handset and turned to Tirrell. "Do you think something's happened to him?" she asked anxiously.

"No, I think he's probably okay," Tirrell said, automatically soothing. "Maybe he's working outside or something."

But Cam was too intelligent to accept such reassurance blindly, even when it was what she obviously wanted. "Has he been working outside every other day this week, too?" She shook her head. "Something's wrong."

"Well, there's not much we can do about it," Paxton said gruffly. "Not now."

Tirrell threw his liaison an irritated look. Even if Cam *was* partially responsible for Jarvis's silence, there was no point making her feel worse than she already did. "It's also possible he's busy with a project and turned off the phone so he wouldn't be interrupted," he told her. "Or maybe there's a fault in his receiver—that *does* happen, you know."

She nodded heavily. "I hope you're right. If I somehow helped those . . ." She visibly searched for an adequate noun, gave up, and fell silent.

"I'm sure everything'll be okay," Tirrell said with more conviction than he felt. "You might as well go back to the lab—or home, if you'd like," he added, noting it was after four. "We'll have people standing by both here and with the direction finders twenty-one hours a day; if Dr. Jarvis contacts you, just press the button we've put by your phone and then keep him talking as long as you can."

"I understand." Nodding, Cam got to her feet, collected the notes she'd been planning to ask Jarvis about, and left the room.

"You might as well go, too," Tirrell told the two headphone-equipped men standing on opposite sides of the huge table map that dominated the center of the room. "Your relief's due in twenty minutes, and Jarvis wouldn't be able to reach Ms. Mbar before then, anyway."

"Yes, sir."

Paxton waited until the men had left before asking the obvious question. "You think Jarvis smelled the trap and ran?"

"That he smelled *something* seems pretty obvious," Tirrell snorted. "Whatever Cam said last week when she talked to him apparently made him at least suspicious enough to stay clear of his phone."

"Or suspicious enough to pack up and run," Paxton mused. "No, that wouldn't be very smart."

"Especially since we've already postulated his cabin

is as secure a place as he's going to find anywhere near civilization," Tirrell nodded.

"Well, then, we should still have a chance. What about this building contractor search you've been doing? Any leads?"

Tirrell shrugged. "I've checked with every contractor between here and Rand—no luck. Either Jarvis did all the work himself—and supply purchases indicated he at least bought all the materials himself—or else the contractor he hired went out of business sometime in the last four years."

"Four years." Paxton looked thoughtful. "You have the time any more exact?"

"He seems to have started building in April of three-oh-four, just eleven months after Colin was born. At least that's when he was buying and moving his materials."

"Hmm. Three months after he and Somerset quit their Transition studies."

"Right." Tirrell was mildly surprised the other had picked up on that, given how often other equally simple facts had seemed to slide right past him. Perhaps he was finally starting to pay genuine attention to the case. "Possibly significant, but doesn't really tell us anything new."

"Sure," Paxton agreed. "You said he transported all the stuff that same month. How—rented vehicles?"

"Yes, and that's where most of what little we've got has come from. The mileage he put on the trucks he used give us an upper limit on how far from Barona the cabin is."

"Terrific," Paxton said, straightening in his chair. "Why didn't you say so before?"

"Because it's not an especially useful number," Tirrell countered dryly. "All it tells us is that he's somewhere within a hundred kilometers of Barona."

"Oh." Paxton looked deflated. "That's not a lot of help."

"Not much, but a little. It means he can't be in the mountains past Rand with a directional antenna to compensate for the extra distance. Also, the roads around here are not exactly straight, so doing a careful distance check along them shrinks the boundaries a fair amount. And, of course, we should be able to eliminate all the farmland south of the city.''

"Also Plat City and the marshes near Banat," Paxton muttered. "Still leaves a hell of a lot of territory, though—and a fair amount of it in the mountains south of Plat City. That's going to be an absolute pain to search."

"Yeah." Tirrell hesitated. "There is one other thing that might lead somewhere—heavy underline on the 'might.' One of the truck rental owners remembers having to spend six hours scraping rock-mud out of the van's tire tread after Jarvis returned it—says he debated long and hard about sending the usual bill for the work and decided against it because Jarvis was such an important figure."

For a moment Paxton's eyes lit up, but the expression was quickly replaced by a rueful grin. "Damn! For a moment there . . . but we're talking about *April*, aren't we."

Tirrell nodded. "Apparently a lot of the ground around here turns into rock-mud while the snow cover is melting. I've looked up all the available records and have a couple of the university's soil specialists listing the main areas where the stuff is found in the spring. That, plus my map, will at least give me the most likely places to start looking."

"You're going to start a full-scale search?" Paxton said cautiously. "Now?"

"As soon as that rock-mud data is complete, which is supposed to be this evening. Why? You have a better idea?"

"Well . . ." Paxton looked acutely uncomfortable. "Actually, we were wondering if perhaps we ought to go a bit easy at this point. Until we've got a few more facts, I mean."

Tirrell searched the other's face. "The 'we,' I take it, is you and Chief Li—and you're still worried about possible false-arrest charges brought by Barona's leading scientific light. Right?"

Paxton shrugged helplessly. "Face it, Tirrell; the only solid thing you've got is that childsitter's identification of Jarvis—and *that* was under hypnosis. Everything else really just boils down to hunch and intuition."

"Would you like a list of the people my 'intuition' has helped nail?" Tirrell said coldly.

"The rules are different when you're picking on a leading light, as you put it. Always have been, always will be." Paxton shook his head. "I thought the chief was going to have a coronary when he saw the poster you had distributed to the area police stations."

"Why? I only identified him as a material witness in the case, and I said specifically to use extreme discretion in inquiries and contact. Would you rather risk letting Jarvis walk in and out of Banat without anyone even knowing we wanted to talk to him?"

"No. It's just that your methods don't consider the political implications. As an outsider you can maybe get away with that. The rest of us, unfortunately, can't." Paxton shook his head. "Hell with that now. How big a search crew were you hoping to use?"

Tirrell grimaced. "Given the circumstances, I guess I'd better not hold my breath waiting for Li to authorize anything substantial." He paused briefly, but when Paxton didn't contradict him he continued, "So I guess Tonio and I will have to do it ourselves. If I can get the map ready, we can start tomorrow morning. We'll be discreet, of course."

Paxton pursed his lips for a long moment and then sighed. "Well, if you're *that* determined . . . I suppose we might as well make it a foursome. That way it'll only take *half* an eternity to finish the job."

"I appreciate the offer," Tirrell told him, a bit surprised the other had volunteered, given the pressures on him. "But I'd rather you stay here, actually, just in case Jarvis decides to answer his phone after all."

"Maybe there's another way to do this," Weylin spoke up suddenly.

The other three turned to him. "What's that?" Paxton asked.

"Recruit some unofficial searchers," the righthand said. "I know a bunch of other preteens who'd be willing to help us—maybe twenty or thirty of them. Give us each a map and an area to search and we'll have Jarvis found in no time."

"Forget it," Paxton said, shaking his head. "The chief doesn't even want experienced policemen involved in a full-scale search—imagine how he'd feel about a bunch of amateurs running around out there."

"They know how to keep their mouths shut—" Weylin began.

"Actually, the idea has some merit," Tirrell cut in, "and we might be able to try something like it later. But Paxton's right, at least for now."

Weylin made a face. "Well . . . can *I* come help you look, anyway?"

"Sorry, but you should probably stay with your partner—he and the chief would *both* be furious if an emergency came up and you weren't available. Though I daresay that in a few days I'll be willing to risk anything to have some extra help." Tirrell stood up. "Tonio, you and I might as well head over to the university and see if that rock-mud data is finished yet. Good night; we'll probably check in with you next Nultday if not sooner."

Five minutes later Tirrell and Tonio had joined the stream of cars jamming Barona's streets . . . and Tonio finally let loose with the question Tirrell had known he would eventually ask. "You aren't *really* thinking about letting a bunch of Weylin's friends help hunt down Jarvis, are you?"

"Why not?" the detective asked with a straight face. "Don't *you* know a few preteens who'd be simply overjoyed to spend their whole weekend flying between conetrees out in the forest?"

"Maybe two or three at the most—and I wouldn't trust them to do the job right," Tonio snorted. "Maybe you think good righthands hatch in bogs—"

"Oh, no, not at all," Tirrell hastened to assure him.

"I know the screening you had to go through. So why does Weylin think he can dig up thirty qualified candidates just like that?"

"Because he's pompous and arrogant and thinks he can do anything," Tonio snapped back.

Tirrell glanced at his righthand with mild surprise; he hadn't realized Tonio felt that strongly about Weylin. "Arrogant he certainly is," he agreed. "But arrogant *and* very stupid? I don't think so. And I'm not positive, but I *think* this is the first time he's volunteered any kind of help at all on this case. I thought it was worth encouraging him a bit on it, just to keep our options open."

There was a short silence from the other seat. "You're sounding suspicious again," the preteen said. "You think Weylin's got something sinister in mind?"

"Oh, probably not. He's probably just offering the service of his hive's secret society or something, hoping they'll find Jarvis and make him look good. But . . ." He hunted for words, settled instead for a shrug. "Never mind. Let's just concentrate on getting that map put together and turn in early. Tomorrow's going to be a long day."

The facts of the matter did not take long to recite, but with the dryness in her mouth and tension in her throat, Lisa felt like she had talked for hours by the time she finished.

"I see," Gavra nodded from across the wide desk, her tone a flat neutral that was somehow more scary than disapproval or even anger would have been—and much harder to interpret. "You realize, I'm sure, that what you've done is . . . discouraged."

Lisa nodded, a quick bob of her head. "I know that now," she said. "I didn't—I mean, no one actually *said*—" She clamped her lips hard against the excuses that wanted to come out. "I'm willing to accept whatever punishment I have coming to me," she said instead. "But please help me find out what's happened to Daryl."

Gavra pursed her lips, her eyes seemingly avoiding contact with Lisa's. "Where is the book you said you still have?"

"Up in my room. Under the dresser."

"Please go and get it. Bring it back in this," she added, rummaging in a drawer and coming up with a crumpled paper bag. "I don't want anyone to see it."

Silently, Lisa took the bag and left the office. The halls were largely deserted—most of the girls were either still at dinner or already down in the game rooms—and she made the round trip in record time.

Gavra was still seated quietly behind her desk when Lisa again entered the office. Taking the book with a nod, the Senior glanced at the cover and then leafed through it. Lisa waited tensely in her own chair, almost afraid to breathe.

"You've read all of this?" Gavra asked at last, her voice cutting into the uncomfortable silence like blunt scissors. "And understood it?"

"Most of it," Lisa said, not knowing whether to feel pride or guilt. "There are a few words I didn't know, but I could guess at what they meant from how they were used."

"From context. That's called understanding from context. Did you keep up with the writing exercises, too?"

"Some. I was more interested in reading."

Gavra nodded and closed the book, placing it carefully in front of her. For a moment she stared at it, and then raised her eyes to Lisa's face. "First of all, Lisa, let me say that I'm *very* impressed by your achievement. There have been other kids and preteens who've tried to learn reading on their own, but as far as I know, no one else has ever made it to this level before."

"Thank you," Lisa managed, her heart pounding in her throat. Other preteens had done it . . . but she'd never even heard rumors about them. What had happened to them?

What's going to happen to me?

"But I'm afraid you're not going to get to brag to anyone about it," Gavra continued. "From now on you must consider your ability to read a complete and total secret. *Total*. If we find out you've told anyone at all, you'll face total loss of all your hive points and maybe further punishment as well. Do you understand?"

It took several heartbeats for that to sink in; and when it did, it was like flying into the cool of an unexpected cloudburst on a stifling July day. The relief that went rippling through Lisa's body was as intense as the fear it washed away, and it left her weak and even trembling slightly. "Oh, I—Gavra, I—oh, yes, I understand completely. I won't tell anyone—I promise. I—oh, Gavra, I was *so* afraid I would be—you know."

The barest hint of a smile flickered over Gavra's face. "I understand. But I'm serious about what'll happen if you tell anyone. Don't forget that."

"I won't. Thank you for—oh!" Halfway to her feet, Lisa abruptly sat down again. "I almost forgot—Daryl! Can you help me find him now?"

Gavra's face had turned to wood again. "I'm sorry, Lisa, but I think you'd better forget about Daryl, permanently."

The tension flooded back into Lisa's body with a suddenness that threatened to bring up her dinner. "What do you mean? What have they done to him?"

"There aren't specific rules against you getting books from a teen; but there *are* rules against him giving books to you," Gavra said grimly. "Daryl knew the rules and has to accept his proper punishment for breaking them."

"No!" The word burst from Lisa's lips like a small thunderclap as a hundred horrible images crowded into her mind. "No, they can't! It's *my* fault Daryl did it—*I'm* the one who made him give me the books. They should punish *me*, not him!"

Gavra shook her head. "He knew the rules," she repeated. "In this world you have to take the responsibility for your actions—your *own* actions, no one else's. You may have made the original suggestion, Lisa, but the decision he made was his own."

Lisa's breath felt like fire in her lungs. "What have they done to him?" she whispered. "Please tell me. I was his friend."

The Senior frowned. "Are you thinking . . . ? Oh, good heavens, girl—no, no, he's alive and perfectly well. How could you think otherwise?"

The reassuring words made no impression whatsoever on Lisa's panic. "Where is he? If he's all right, I should be able to see him."

"I'm afraid that can't be allowed. I'm sorry."

"Then what have they done to him?"

"*Nothing*, Lisa. Really. I promise."

Slowly, Lisa got to her feet, and for the first time in her life said to Gavra Norward, "I don't believe you."

Gavra said nothing; but the quiet pain in her eyes made Lisa feel even worse than she already did. But she forced herself to continue. "I don't know if you're lying to me or if someone else is lying to you first. But they told Daryl that Hari was all right, too, after he tried to kill himself." She moved toward the door.

"Where are you going?" Gavra asked.

"To find Daryl," Lisa said, her vision suddenly blurring. Angrily, she blinked back the tears, the effort making the soreness in her throat worse. "I have to know what this—this punishment of his was."

"Lisa, he's *all right*. They just don't want you and Daryl to see each other again."

"I'll believe that when I see him." She focused on the doorknob, teeking it around—

"Lisa. Wait."

The preteen hesitated at the command in Gavra's tone, torn between her frightening new spirit of rebellion and her instinctive respect for hive authority. Slowly, she turned back to face the Senior, letting her teekay grip on the knob dissolve. "What?"

"If you go charging off tonight or miss work tomorrow I'll have no choice but to report your actions to the police and . . . certain others. However"—Gavra's eyes caught Lisa's with unexpected intensity—"as long as you behave reasonably, your weekend time is your own, and I have no official control over your activities. You'll have a better chance if you wait until Saturday to do anything about this. Will you do that?"

Lisa stared at her, indecision churning her stomach. Every muscle in her body was screaming at her to start the search *now*—the last thing she wanted was to sit around worrying for an extra day and a half. But even with her emotions riding high, the tiny core of common sense within her knew Gavra's suggestion made sense. *If*... "You're not going to warn them, are you?" she asked flatly.

Gavra shook her head, and Lisa realized it had all come down to a single, very simple, choice: would she or would she not trust the woman standing before her.

It was, strangely enough, a remarkably easy decision to make. For all Gavra's talk of punishment and official duties, Lisa could sense—as she should have known all along—that the Senior was on her side in this mess. "All right," she said at last. "Where would you suggest I start looking?"

"I don't know," Gavra said, her voice tinged with relief. "But you might begin with the intro schools in the nearest towns. All I know is that he's not in Barona anymore."

"All right." Lisa turned and finished teeking open the door. Halfway through the opening, she paused and looked back at Gavra. "Thank you," she said.

"Don't worry about him," the Senior advised her quietly. "Search as long as you like, but don't let panic drive you to do anything foolish. Other people aren't likely to be sympathetic as I am to what you're doing."

Lisa swallowed, thinking about her little invasion of Lee Intro. *Does Gavra know about that?* she wondered. "I'll be careful," she said. Teeking the door closed behind her, she left the office.

She spent the next two hours in one of the preteen

girls' lounges, watching her thoughts spin in their painful circles and feeling her emotions burn down to an exhausted ache. Mercifully, none of her friends came by to talk ... or perhaps something in her manner discouraged approach. When the lights-out warning sounded, she went immediately to her floor's bathroom, completing her bedtime preparations quickly enough to be out before the main crush arrived. Back in her room, she gave one-word answers to Sheelah's cheerful queries about her day until the other took the hint and shut up.

For a long time afterward she lay awake in the darkness, listening to Sheelah's steady breathing and watching the faint pattern of light the curtains allowed into the room. Finally, around one-thirty, she fell asleep.

Her dreams were not pleasant ones.

Chapter 16

The six o'clock wake-up buzzer literally blasted Lisa out of bed, startling her enough to cause an involuntary half-meter teekay bounce into the air. Settling back to her tangled sheets, she rubbed her eyes and took a deep, ragged breath.

"You okay?" came a cautious voice from the other bed.

Lisa ran a tongue over her lips. Her pounding heart was beginning to recover from the shock now, but the headache throbbing in time with it was showing no signs of going away. Her stomach was oddly tender, and her entire body felt like it had been pulled repeatedly through a wringer. "I'm fine," she told Sheelah tiredly.

The other preteen was out of bed now, eyeing Lisa with a mixture of suspicion and concern. "Fine, huh? You look like something a Seven would haul in out of the rain and ask permission to keep. And you were tossing and moaning half the night. I think you're coming down with something. You want me to go call the nurse?"

"No, I'll be okay," Lisa insisted, teeking her clothes over from the chair where she'd laid them out the previous night. "I didn't sleep well; I'm just tired. Um ... I didn't say anything when I was tossing around, did I?"

Sheelah frowned. "Nothing I could understand. But if you want to talk about it now, I'm game."

"Talk about what?" Lisa asked, heart starting to speed up again.

"Whatever's bothering you." Sheelah sat down cross-legged on her bed. "Either you're sick or else you've got one monster of a problem eating away at you. Come on—you want to tell me what it is?"

For a long moment Lisa was sorely tempted. She *wanted* to talk about it, certainly, and from past experience she knew Sheelah could be trusted with even the most personal of secrets. But Gavra's warning still echoed through her mind, and she knew it wouldn't be fair to Sheelah to get her involved in this, too. "Thanks," she told her roommate, "but this is something I have to work out for myself."

Sheelah's expression said she was unconvinced, but she nodded anyway. "Okay, it's up to you. But I'm available anytime you change your mind. And I still think you should go see the nurse."

"Right after breakfast," Lisa promised.

Surprisingly enough—at least to Lisa—she was feeling much better by the time breakfast was over. The food had helped both her headache and tender stomach, and the normal morning activities had eased the worst of the kinks out of her muscles. The hive nurse, as expected, found no evidence of any sickness, and a few minutes later she was flying with her work crew toward their current construction site.

Unfortunately, as her physical condition improved, she found her mind concentrating more and more on Daryl and the awesome task confronting her. Tigris was a horribly big world for them to hide a single teen in, and the more she considered that fact, the more hopeless it all seemed. *I'm going to find him,* she'd declared confidently to Gavra. Was the Senior even now chuckling at such foolishness? Her cheeks burned at the thought.

"Hey! Wait up!" a faint voice came through the roar of wind in her ears.

Startled, Lisa turned around to find her five girls

lagging nearly ten meters behind her. Slowing down, she let them catch up.

"What's the hurry?" Beryl asked with the righteous indignation only a Nine could muster. "You trying for Miss Speed Demon of Three-oh-eight or something?"

"Sorry," Lisa mumbled. "I guess I wasn't paying attention."

"Good way to fly into a building," Beryl said, only partly mollified.

Gritting her teeth, Lisa flew on in silence, furious at herself for getting so wrapped up in her problems. It would be better once they got to work, she promised herself; as soon as she had something else demanding her attention, she would be able to push Daryl back into a corner of her mind for the rest of the day. At least she *hoped* she would be able to.

But it turned out not to be that easy. Standing on one of the bare fourteenth-floor girders of the new building as she directed her girls in lifting and placing new girders in position, she had a great deal of time where all she had to do was watch . . . and try as she might, she was unable to keep her mind on what was happening. Still, that was more annoying than dangerous. Her crew had been doing building work together for nearly five months now, and she could trust them to know what they were doing.

An hour later, that casual assumption was shattered.

It happened without the slightest warning, at least without any that penetrated Lisa's preoccupation. One moment the heavy girder was resting in midair between two uprights, Ncoma and Rena hovering near its center as welders at each end blew clouds of sparks into the light breeze—and the next moment there was a yelp of pain as the heavy steel beam wrenched itself free and plummeted toward the ground.

Her mind busy with other things, it cost Lisa a fraction of a second to switch gears . . . and in that blank moment she did precisely the worst thing she could possibly have done. Instead of staying where she was and trying to teek from a solid footing, she jumped off and angled away from the building in an attempt to get a better view of the falling girder amid the array of steelwork below. It wasn't until she tried to teek the girder to a halt that she awoke to her blunder.

The girder was very near the weight limit of her teekay strength, and with its head start it had built up a great deal of speed. With her entire teekay focused on the girder, she might have been able to stop it; but while she was also holding up her own forty kilograms, there wasn't a chance in the world of her doing so.

She tried anyway, though, her mind working with abnormal speed as she tried frantically to figure out what to do. *Rotation's easier than lifting,* she thought, remembering the power station flywheels, and put part of her effort into turning the beam to the vertical. *Should I let myself fall for a ways and try to at least soften its landing?* But that would be a minor help at best, because no matter how fast it was going when it hit it would crush whatever was underneath it. Catching her lower lip between her teeth, Lisa bit down hard as she threw everything she had into the battle. *Where the grack are the others?* she wondered desperately, afraid to shift even a fraction of her attention away from the girder. Some of them would be busy with their own loads, but surely Neoma and Rena hadn't *both* been incapacitated by whatever had happened up there . . . had they? *Oh, no—please no!*

And then, barely fifteen meters above the ground, the girder's downward rush abruptly slowed. Within ten meters it had halted completely. Hardly daring to breathe, Lisa teeked it carefully to the side, moving it toward the spot where the rest of the girders were stacked. Only when it was safely down on its side did she look over to see Rena and Neoma—the latter clutching her hand—gazing intently down from their perch. Heaving a shuddering sigh of relief, she shifted her eyes to the ground where the girder would have landed. The half-dozen mugs lying by an over-turned bench—and the six men drifting cautiously back to retrieve them—gave silent testimony to the tragedy that had almost happened.

And Lisa began to shake.

The doctor the foreman had summoned laid one final strip of tape in place and cocked her head slightly as she inspected her handiwork. "Okay, Neoma, that should do it," she said, nodding. "You'll need to have the Dayspring nurse change that dressing tonight after she puts more salve on the burn." Pulling a pen and small pad from her bag, she scribbled briefly on it. Lisa, looking surreptitiously over her shoulder, found the marks totally incomprehensible. "I want you to give this to the nurse or your Senior as soon as you get back home," the doctor continued, folding the sheet and handing it to the preteen. "It tells the kind of salve I used, and also the kind of pain pill I gave you."

"Okay." Neoma took the paper with her unbandaged hand and carefully put it in her pocket. Already her face was taking on an almost dreamy expression. "Can I go now?"

"Yes, but not by yourself. That medicine is very strong, and you shouldn't try to fly or do much teeking while you're taking it."

Neoma nodded, accepting that with unusual calmness. Glancing around the silent group of girls standing at Neoma's shoulder, Lisa gestured to Amadis. "Fly her home, will you, Amadis? Make sure she gets to Gavra and then come back here."

"Okay." Amadis stepped forward and took Neoma's arm. The doctor nodded, and together the two preteens headed into the sky.

"Well, if that's all, I'll be going," the doctor said, snapping shut her bag.

"Thanks for coming by," the foreman said, offering her his hand. "Just send the bill to the company; we'll work out any payment problems directly with Dayspring."

The doctor nodded and headed toward the site exit. Sensing perhaps that the excitement was over, the group of onlooking men also drifted away to return to their jobs, leaving the kids and the foreman alone.

"What did you mean by payment problems, Mr. Vassily?" Lisa asked him, a little suspiciously. "Neoma was doing just what she was supposed to when that spark hit her. You're not going to claim she was negligent, are you?"

Vassily waved a hand. "Oh, no, don't worry about that—the company'll pay her medical costs and the standard damage points, all right. I just didn't want the doc sending Dayspring a duplicate bill—they do that sometimes." He nodded to her. "How about you? Feeling any better now?"

"I'm fine," she said, caught a little off guard by the question. "Why shouldn't I be?"

"You were shaking pretty badly when Neoma and Rena came down," he told her, blue eyes gazing steadily into her face. "First big accident you've ever been this close to?"

Lisa felt her face turning hot. Had he noticed the boneheaded mistake she'd made up there? "I guess so," she admitted, hoping desperately he wouldn't say anything in front of the younger girls—the humiliation would be unbearable. "I've never seen people almost get killed before."

"But they *didn't* get hurt—don't forget that," he pointed out. "You girls got it stopped in time, and nothing even got damaged. Right? So take a deep breath and forget it, okay?"

Obediently, Lisa inhaled deeply. It didn't help; her stomach was still full of angry dragonmites. *First the thing with Daryl, and now I almost kill someone*, she thought morosely, her anger and shame beginning to give way to a gnawing fear. *Everything's just falling apart around me. What's happening to me?*

Vassily's voice cut into her thoughts. "Look, kid, you're not in any shape to go back up there right

now. Take your crew home and come back after lunch
if you feel up to it."

"No!" The word came out with a force that startled even Lisa. "I'll be fine. Let's get back to work."

Vassily shook his head. "Not till you've had a chance
to get over this," he said bluntly. "Look, I've seen
this sort of thing too many times. You go back up
there now and you'll be so anxious to keep watching
the load that, first thing you know, you'll make yourself stop blinking. Then, when your eyes dry out,
they'll water so much you'll risk losing it. No, you go
home and come back at one, and we'll see if you've
calmed down enough then. I can have the welders
catch up on the secondary struts."

Lisa dropped her eyes, a painful lump in her throat.
"All right," she muttered. Gesturing to the others,
she headed upward, wishing she were dead.

A bit of the setting sun cut through the tall conetrees
in the distance, sending one final ray of brightness
into the preteen girls' lounge. Closing her eyes against
it, Lisa pretended she was melting into her chair and
wished she could actually do so. *It's the reverse Midas
touch*, she thought bitterly, remembering the story
tapes she used to listen to. *Everything I touch turns to
garbage.* She'd done who knew what to Daryl, was
destroying her body with lack of sleep, and to top it
off had nearly killed someone at work—and then had
had to be sent home like an oversensitive Seven. The
fact that the crew—minus Neoma, of course—had
been able to return to the site and finish out the day's
work was meaningless as far as Lisa was concerned.
She'd been humiliated, and Mr. Vassily, her girls,
and Gavra all knew it. Squeezing her eyelids tightly
together, she wondered if she should seriously consider running away.

"Lisa?"

She opened her eyes, blinking away the tears that
had collected there. The girl standing in front of her
wasn't one whose name leapt to mind. "Yes?"

The girl—a Ten, probably, Lisa thought—gave her

a tentative smile. "Hi. My name's Camila Paynter. You don't know me very well, but I've noticed you've seemed upset for the past week or so. I wondered if I could do anything to help."

Lisa shook her head, unreasonably annoyed that Camila had picked up on something she'd been trying to keep hidden. "Thanks, but I'll be all right."

Camila shrugged slightly. "Sometimes it helps just to talk about your problems, you know. Maybe with someone older and wiser than yourself."

Lisa snorted. "You?"

"Oh, no." Camila's eyes had taken on a serene, faraway look. "I'm talking about someone who has reached the heights Man was meant to reach. A man who has touched the truth and wisdom of the universe—and who loves us enough to share it."

Despite her black mood, Lisa found herself growing mildly interested. There was genuine conviction beneath Camila's words—an unusual trait in a Ten. "Sounds awfully impressive. How come I haven't heard of him before?"

Camila smiled conspiratorially. "Because the other adults would kill him if they knew he was teaching us about the Truth after they rejected him. That's why we meet in secret and only talk about it to each other."

A memory clicked in Lisa's mind: Camila was one of those she'd seen sharing a hand signal in this same lounge the night she'd first decided to try and learn reading. "With hand signals and everything, I suppose, like any other secret club?" she sniffed.

Camila shrugged, not taking offense at the scorn in Lisa's tone. "The signal helps us identify each other when we're away from the temple site. But the Heirs of Truth is nothing like those silly clubs," she added. "Why don't you come with me tomorrow and see? Whatever's bothering you, I know the Prophet Omega can help you."

"I doubt it." Lisa hesitated, but there was something in Camila's voice that seemed to break down the barriers Lisa had built for herself. "Someone I know has disappeared," she said with cautious vagueness, "and I'm worried about what might have happened to him. He—"

"He?" Camila broke in sharply. "Is he a Five from Ridge Harbor?"

Lisa shrank back a little, startled by the intensity in the other's voice. "No—he's a teen who used to be here in Dayspring."

"Oh." Camila seemed disappointed, but before Lisa could ask about it she brightened again. "Well, look—I know for a fact that the Prophet Omega is very concerned about people who disappear. If you'll come with me tomorrow and tell him all about it, I'm sure he'll be able to help you."

Lisa sucked on her sore lip, torn by indecision. If she went with Camila, she would lose valuable time in her search for Daryl. But if this Prophet Omega really *could* help ... "How could he find Daryl for me?" she asked Camila. "And where would we have to go to meet him?"

"Oh, he's got lots of ways to find things out," she said confidently. "And the temple site is only about sixty kilometers from here, up in the mountains." Shyly, she touched Lisa's hand. "Please come, Lisa. I know the Prophet can help you ... and I think you could learn a great deal from him. About how the Truth in life and Transition can give you power."

Transition! Lisa felt a shiver run up her back. It was her fear of Transition, after all, that had pushed her into this whole mess in the first place. The Truth about Transition ... *and* power over it? It was worth a try; the Prophet Omega could hardly foul things up more than Lisa had done already by herself.

"All right," she told Camila. "I'll come with you."

Chapter 17

Saturday dawned bright and clear, with strong southerly winds that promised unusually warm temperatures even for August. Good weather for flying; but despite that, Lisa—her spirits initially revived by the hope Camila had given her—felt herself slipping into gloom again as the two preteens headed south toward the Tessellate Mountains. Second thoughts were beginning to nag at her, and now with this headwind cutting drastically into the speed they could make, this trip was going to take even more time than she'd expected away from her search effort. The universe, she decided glumly, was still out to get her.

Lisa had flown among the lower slopes of the Tessellate Mountains several times in the past, but such trips had almost always been to the west, toward Rand, where the peaks were taller and more majestic. Much of the territory Camila led her over was therefore unfamiliar and, within a very few minutes, began to look disturbingly alike. "How do you find this place?" she shouted to the other preteen.

Camila pointed behind them. "We started into the mountains right where the Nordau River comes out—we passed over an abandoned metal refinery just over the first ridge, if that helps you." She raised her hand and pointed ahead. "See those two funny-shaped peaks there—they look like someone took bites out of them? Stay to the left of those and you fly right into our mountain. We're building the temple on the eastern slope, where we'll be able to watch the sun rise. Wait'll you see the model the senior acolytes have made—it's going to be beautiful."

Lisa made some kind of polite reply and drifted away, settling back to her flying again. Camila had already shown herself more than willing to talk at length about her club, and Lisa was in no mood to hear how the Heirs of Truth was doing wonderful things in someone else's life. Not yet, anyway. *If* this Prophet Omega helped her find Daryl . . . well, maybe then she'd be willing to believe this was more than just another kind of hive club.

The first jolt to her skepticism came as they approached the mountain and began to circle to the eastern side. Four or five figures could be seen at first hovering or darting near the slope; but as Lisa and Camila continued circling, more and more kids came into view until Lisa realized with a shock that there had to be a good hundred of them working on the temple site. The number staggered her—she'd envisioned perhaps twenty or thirty members at the most. *Maybe there is something to all of this*, she thought, daring to hope again. The size of the hole the kids were digging into the mountain gave a second, equally strong jolt. Already it looked deep enough to swallow the fourteen-story building she was helping build in Barona—and according to Camila it had to be made still bigger! For the first time Lisa began to understand the excitement Camila felt for what was happening here.

Coming close, Camila pointed downward. "There's the tabernacle," she said. "You ready to meet him?"

Lisa looked at the tent nestling casually beneath the jagged rocks being teeked out of the mountains. Inside that tent was the man who led all of this. "I guess so," she said. *I hope so*, she thought.

Arrayed in his white robe and gilt-edged stole, his chair flanked by two senior acolytes, Omega listened in silence as Camila explained the newcomer's problem. His first hope—that the "missing friend" she sought was Colin Brimmer—had been quickly dashed, but he was careful not to show his disappointment. *A Prophet of Truth cares about all people*, he reminded himself; and if showing some interest and making some promises could entice a new member into his fold, it was time well spent. It made a good break from all these damn confessions, anyway. His eyes flicked to the silent group of waiting confessors just as another kid slipped through the meeting room door and joined them.

Camila finished and bowed. "Thank you, Acolyte Paynter," Omega said, nodding his head in return. Shifting his gaze to the newcomer, he said, "Please come forward, Seeker Lisa." The preteen took a hesitant step forward and he continued, "The Truth that dwells in us can locate your friend, wherever he may be. Do you believe this?"

Lisa licked her lips. "I'm . . . not sure, sir. I mean . . . it sounds impossible. . . ."

"It sounds impossible because you do not yet recognize that Truth resides within you," he chided her gently. "Like your muscles, the use of your inner power must be trained and exercised. Here, we can train you; but only if you are willing to put forth the effort."

He stopped, watching closely the play of expressions across her face. Camila had jumped the gun, he decided; Lisa wasn't quite ready to join up. Still, she *was* close. With a little effort they might still manage it.

"Sir . . ." Lisa began.

"Do not be troubled," Omega put in kindly. "Your friend is certainly uppermost in your mind right now—that is only natural. When we have found him perhaps you will let us show you the power Truth can give to your life."

A flicker of surprise was followed immediately by relief, and Omega knew he'd played it correctly. The casual reading of her thoughts plus the promise of no pressure had clearly enhanced his credibility in her eyes. "The Truth," he continued, "knows no bounds, no obstacles. If you will tell me everything you know about your friend—everything that you and he have done or spoken of together—the Truth will seek him out."

It was as if a cloud had passed in front of her face. A very dark cloud. "Everything?" she asked, almost whispering.

"The more you tell me, the faster he will be found," Omega told her, his eyes taking in her slim, prepubescent body as he wondered about her sudden mood change. Had they been experimenting with sex? Unlikely . . . but her friend *was* a teen. That might explain both her reticence *and* the teen's disappearance, if they'd been caught at it. But she was never going to admit to something like that out here. "Perhaps you would feel more comfortable if we discussed this in private," he suggested, rising from his seat and extending a hand in invitation. "We can go into my private rooms."

She hesitated, then nodded. "All right." She stepped up to him but didn't take the proffered hand.

Lowering his arm smoothly, Omega nodded to Camila. "Acolyte Paynter, please take the confessors back to the temple site to continue their service. I shall send for them when I am ready."

Camila bowed and headed back toward the group by the door. With a reassuring smile, Omega gestured to Lisa and led the way through the rear curtain of the meeting room and to the door of his office. Opening it, he ushered her through and indicated the chair next to his writing desk. "Please sit down, Lisa; I'll be with you in a moment."

Omega closed the door behind them, then slipped off his stole and hung it carefully across its hooks. Turning around, he took a step toward the desk—and froze with astonishment.

Lisa was leaning toward the desk, her head cocked slightly and her gaze on the copy of the *Bhagavad-Gita* he'd left propped open while working on his

Sunday talk. Even from the door he could see her eyes tracing a rhythmic left-right pattern.

She was reading *the book!*

The first word that came to mind was one he hadn't used since escaping from Ridge Harbor. Lisa jerked her eyes away from the book with guilty speed, but fortunately she didn't seem to know what the word meant. Forcing a smile, Omega continued forward, swiveling his desk chair to face Lisa and then sitting down. "You are interested in the ancient Scriptures?" he asked her, indicating the *Bhagavad-Gita*.

"I . . . was . . . just looking at it, sir," the preteen said. Her eyes were wide, with lines of tension around them, and she seemed to be having trouble breathing. "I—it has those shiny edges and—"

"Lisa," he said sternly. "You cannot lie to the Truth within me. Nor should you deny such a great ability," he added in gentler tone. Reaching over, he turned the book to face her. "Please show me how well you can read."

"I can't," she whispered, staring at the book as if it would attack her.

"You must," Omega said, putting all the command he could into his voice. If he could force a surrender on this point, he sensed, all other resistance could be broken with relative ease. "I want to help you, Lisa, but if you deny any of what you are, you will merely hinder the very spirit of Truth which seeks to free your friend. Come; release your fears to the wind and allow your own Truth its freedom."

Lisa swallowed hard and dropped her eyes to the desk. Slowly, haltingly, she began to read aloud.

Omega sat quietly, an eerie feeling of unreality bringing a strange numbness to his limbs. To sit and listen as an unschooled kid read to him was probably the last situation he would ever have imagined himself in . . . and as Lisa's initial qualms faded and her confidence grew the sense of wonder increased. She was good—*damn* good—stumbling over only the most uncommon words and even then sounding them out

correctly half the time. This wasn't a simple case of
selfteaching, he realized; this kid had had help.

Of course.

"That will do," he spoke up, cutting her off in
midsentence. "Your friend taught you well. Is that
why he has disappeared?"

For a second her eyes resisted, but then they dropped
in defeat. "Yes," she murmured. "At least, I think
so." She looked up at him again, her expression plead-
ing. "But I didn't mean for any of this to happen—I
didn't know anyone would *punish* Daryl for lending
me his books."

"Of course not," Omega soothed. "What you are
seeing is one part of the same rejection of Truth I
have suffered among adults, which is why I have in
turn rejected *them*. The Truth within you has given
you the desire and ability to read, which they now
seek to repress. But the Truth can yet overcome and
restore things to their rightful places. And I say now:
it *will* do so."

Lisa seemed to ponder that for a moment. "Does
that mean you're going to help me?" she asked, a bit
timidly.

He gave her his best smile. "Within four days I will
deliver to you his location," he declared confidently.
After all, chances were that Daryl had simply been
reprimanded and transferred to another school somewhere. Once Lisa told him the teen's original school
and last name, it should be a simple matter of having
someone pry the information out of the authorities in
the guise of a relative or interested friend or something.

"You mean that?" Lisa breathed.

"I am a Prophet of Truth," Omega reminded her.
"My word will not come to nothing. *But.*" He raised
a finger. "Before I do this for you, you must agree to
do something in return for me."

"Of course," she nodded eagerly. "Anything I can."

"Good." Omega paused, preparing his words carefully. An incredible opportunity had dropped into his
lap with this girl—an incredible opportunity and an
equally incredible risk. He had to be careful now not

to scare her off. "The Barona police—who serve those who would stifle the Truth within you—have in their possession certain secret papers whose contents I must learn. I would like you to go into their station tonight and read them for me."

Lisa's eyes went wide. "Break into the *city building*? Oh, no. No, I *couldn't*—"

"Peace," he said, cutting her off. "There would be no need to break in; you would be accompanied by one of my acolytes, who serves also as a righthand there."

"Why can't *he* steal these things for you, then?" she demanded hotly.

He had a split-second decision to make on how to react, chose to go with gentle forgiveness. "My young Seeker," he said with a forbearing smile, "I do not steal from anyone. The papers are the police's, and they will keep them. But unless I learn what is in them, a young boy who has been stolen from his parents will remain lost."

"But—" She gestured helplessly. "It would still be *wrong*."

"Is it wrong to try and rescue a terrified child from an evil man?" Omega asked gently. "You fear for your friend Daryl, who is—at the very least—able to understand what is happening to him. Can you imagine how little Colin must feel, alone and frightened?" He shook his head. "No, the wrong is in those who could rescue him but will not do so. What I am asking you to do is the response of the Truth within me. Examine your own heart, Lisa, and you, too, will feel a yearning to see this child freed of his prison."

For a moment he was afraid he'd piled it on too thick; but it was quickly apparent he'd touched a nerve. Lisa obviously liked children, and he could see that his slightly colored version of Colin Brimmer's plight was affecting her strongly. Time, he judged, to give the screw one last quarter-turn. "Will you do this, Lisa? Not for me, but for Colin . . . because you *are* the only one who can do this."

Her surrender came in the form of a long sigh. "I
. . . have to think about it."

"Certainly," Omega said, suppressing a triumphant
smile. "We would be honored if you would spend the
remainder of the day with us, sharing in our work
and fellowship and perhaps learning more of the
freedom Truth gives to us. Later, when the Heir Ellery
arrives, I will give you both more detailed instructions." He reached over and patted her hand in a
warm, Senior-like way. "The Truth will reward those
of us who give unselfishly to others, Lisa. Such is the
first law of the universe." Leaning back, he smiled.
"And so now *I* give to *you*. Tell me all you can about
Daryl, that we may free him from his bondage."

Trudging through the knee-high bristleweeds, Tirrell
rounded the last conetree to find that, as usual, Tonio
had gotten back to the car first. "Well?" he asked the
righthand, sliding gratefully into the driver's seat as
the other teeked the door open for him.

Tonio pointed northwest through the windshield.
"There's a patch about three kilometers away that's
thick enough to hide a cabin from the air—conetrees
mixed with some kind of wide tops. No driveway I
could see, but the main road's only a half kilometer
or so away, and it looks like you could get a car
through."

Tirrell had the map spread across the steering wheel.
"Three kilometers northwest . . . yeah. About five by
road, I'd guess. A little off the edge of the rock-mud
region, actually, but I suppose we ought to check it
out." Refolding the map, he took a quick survey of
their surroundings. "I was right back there, you know;
we aren't going to have room to turn around in here.
You want me to get out before you do your stuff?"

The car rocked gently, rose a couple of centimeters,
and settled back down. "Yeah, I think we'll *both* have
to get out," Tonio admitted.

Sighing theatrically, Tirrell swung open the door
and climbed back out onto the muddy grass. Without
its passengers, fortunately, the car proved easy for

Tonio to handle, and within a couple of minutes the detective was carefully driving along their earlier tire tracks toward the narrow backwoods road they'd been working off of for most of the afternoon.

"I gather you didn't find anything of interest at the last spot?" Tonio asked.

"As a matter of fact, I did," Tirrell told him. "Nice little cabin snuggled up under the edge of one of the conetrees."

"What?" Tonio spun half around in his seat.

" 'Course, half the roof had rotted out and there were scrub bushes growing in the living room," Tirrell went on casually. "I figure it's been deserted ten years or so."

Tonio settled back down. "You rat," he muttered.

Tirrell smiled a bit. "Come on, I deserve the chance to get a good zing in every once in a while—I'm the one who's been walking his legs off in that soggy ground for two days, after all."

"Trade you jobs," the preteen offered. "There's a lot more glare up there than you might think, and staring down at shiny conetree leaves gets awfully hard on the eyes after a while."

"If you've got a headache, there's aspirin in the first-aid kit," Tirrell said. Reaching into the storage area behind the seats, he located one of the canteens. "There's water left to take them with, too," he added, sloshing the canteen experimentally before handing it over.

"Thanks." Tonio was already rummaging through the first-aid kit. "I sure wish this was December— we'd have had Jarvis in nothing flat."

Tirrell nodded. Conetrees exchanged their leaves for pinelike needles in wintertime, cutting down at least a little on the cover Jarvis's cabin would have. More importantly, though, the steam and smoke from the generator and wood-burning stove Jarvis had bought would make a pointer visible for kilometers. "Damn inconsiderate of him not to wait six months to pull this," he commented.

"Maybe that's *why* he grabbed Colin in June," Tonio suggested.

"Maybe. Of course, there *was* the whole thing with Colin's fifth birthday, if you'll remember."

"Oh. Right." The righthand sounded deflated.

Tirrell smiled. Ahead was the road they'd been following, and as he turned the car onto it he glanced first at his watch and then at the swath of sky visible above them. "We've got maybe two hours of daylight left, if your eyes can hold out that long. Show me where this latest patch is, okay?"

Chapter 18

Lisa had always enjoyed evening flights over Barona; but tonight the twinkling city lights had none of their usual cheerfulness. Instead, they seemed more like a sea of unwinking eyes staring accusingly up at her. "I can't do this," she said aloud to the preteen flying beside her.

"Will you relax?" Weylin Ellery snapped impatiently. "The Prophet Omega told us to do this, right? And he wouldn't tell us to do something we'd get in trouble for, right? So just take it easy."

The arguments didn't help much. Prophet or no, Lisa couldn't shake the fear that the Prophet Omega might have forgotten something—surely he couldn't know the inner workings of Barona's police department, for example. And she and Weylin were taking all the risks here. "Why do we have to do this?" she said, more to herself than to Weylin.

"Because some kid named Colin Brimmer was kidnapped last June from Ridge Harbor," the other answered anyway. "Tirrell—he's a detective from there—thinks a scientist has him hidden out in the woods somewhere and is maybe doing some kind of experiment with him. The Prophet needs to know where his hiding place might be so we can go and rescue Colin."

Lisa flew for several minutes in silence, letting Weylin's words bounce around her brain. The Prophet Omega had mentioned Colin's kidnapping, but he

hadn't said anything about any *experiment*. What sort
of thing could this scientist be doing? It brought to
mind the hundred most gruesome monster movies
she'd had to sit through when she was younger. "But
if the police are already trying to find him, why don't
we just let them alone?"

"Because the Prophet wants to find him first."

"Why?"

"I don't know," Weylin said with complete uncon-
cern. "Maybe we can do more to help Colin recover
from whatever Jarvis is doing to him. What difference does it make *why?*—the Prophet *told* us to do
it."

And that, Lisa realized at last, was all the explanation Weylin would ever need for anything the Prophet
Omega said. *It must be nice to have that kind of faith*,
she thought, almost wistfully. Even with Gavra she'd
never had anything like absolute trust—she'd always
been too aware of her own shortcomings to expect
perfection from anyone else. Maybe someday that
would change; but for tonight, at least, Weylin's faith
was going to have to do for both of them.

The windows of the city building were mostly dark
and empty as the two preteens slanted out of the sky
to land across the street. The main entrance, itself
well lit, showed bright lights through its inset windows, but aside from that there were no more than a
half-dozen lights visible anywhere.

"Nine o'clock," Weylin said, looking at his watch.
"Good. The seven-to-eight shift overlap could have
given us trouble."

Startled, Lisa checked her own wrist. With her
mind on so many other things, she'd completely lost
track of the time . . . and for the first time ever she'd
now missed hive lights-out. *Just one more gracking
thing gone wrong*, she thought morosely.

"All right, now just stay calm and remember the
story the Prophet told us to use," Weylin said, taking
her arm. "And let *me* do the talking."

The room beyond the front door seemed larger
than it had on Lisa's visit two days earlier, and the

main reception desk looked somehow taller and more massive. Glancing to both sides as they headed toward the desk, she saw four officers hunched over desks in the duty lounge and—talking quietly together in a far corner—an equal number of preteen righthands. The sight of them made her stomach tighten; if there was any trouble, she and Weylin would be nailed like dragonmites in tar before they got three meters.

"You're out awfully late, Weylin," the desk man commented as they approached. "What's up?"

Weylin gestured to Lisa. "Ran across something that couldn't wait till morning. My friend here is an ex-member of that burglary ring Hob and I were working on before Tirrell tied us up with his kidnapping case."

The officer's eyebrows went up. "I didn't realize there were *kids* involved with that one. Shee-double-it." He looked at Lisa. "Tell me, was there an adult in charge of this group, uh—?"

"Kathi," Lisa supplied through dry lips. "Yes, there's a man telling everyone what to do."

"Damn fagins," the other growled bitterly. His gaze hardened and shifted, giving Lisa the eerie sensation of something hateful standing directly behind her. "Do you know this man's name, Kathi?"

Before Lisa could answer, Weylin cut in. "It isn't one that sounded familiar. I'm taking her upstairs to look through the suspects' album Hob and I worked up—it'll be faster than going through the complete roguery down here."

"Okay." The officer's eyes flicked to the duty lounge. "Palmer?"

"I'd rather do this alone, if that's okay," Weylin said quickly. Lowering his voice, he added, "Uniformed officers make Kathi a little nervous, if you understand."

The other hesitated, then shrugged. "Well . . . all right." Reaching under the desktop, he pulled out a key and handed it over. "Make it fast, though—you're not really supposed to be alone upstairs when you're off shift."

"I know. We won't be long." Taking Lisa's arm again, Weylin led her behind the desk and toward a door flanked on both sides by pieces of paper with people's faces on them. As they got closer, she saw that beneath each photo were several lines of words. "What are those?" she whispered, pointing.

"Pictures of people we're supposed to be watching out for," he whispered back. "We go through here." He teeked open the door and stepped through.

Lisa started to follow . . . and abruptly stopped. "Wait a second," she said, frowning at the photo that had caught her eye.

"Come on," Weylin hissed, looking back at her.

Ignoring him, she stepped closer to the picture. *Yes . . . yes*, she decided; it *was* him. Lowering her eyes to the words below, she read with a growing sense of excitement.

Weylin was beside her again, pulling her arm with a grip that looked gentle but had teekay strength behind it. "Come *on*," he growled in her ear. "You trying to get us caught?"

"This is *Dr. Jarvis*—that scientist!" she told him, standing firm and nodding toward the picture.

"Not so loud! You're not supposed to have anything to do with him, remember?"

"But I *saw* him, Weylin, driving toward Rand back in June," she whispered. "He said he was taking his nephew home—" She inhaled sharply as it suddenly hit her who the sleeping child must have been. "I saw *Colin* too!"

"Later!" he hissed, pulling harder. "Let's get upstairs before someone wonders what we're doing here."

Reluctantly, she let him draw her along, eyes flicking across the other pictures as they again walked toward the doorway. One other face seemed vaguely familiar, but before she had a chance to read more than the man's name, they were through the opening and Weylin had teeked the door firmly shut.

"Okay," he said, taking a deep breath as he glanced around the deserted corridor. "The office is on the third floor; stairway's over there. Come on."

Abandoning the floor, he flew to the stairway and threaded his way up the open space in the middle. Lisa followed, and a moment later they were standing outside a door marked with the name "Stanford Tirrell—Detective First." She teeked the knob experimentally, discovered it was locked. "Now what?" she whispered.

Weylin had produced something that looked like a meter-long strand of limp spaghetti with a combination penlight and eyepiece at one end. "Watch for company," he said tightly and dropped onto his back by the door. Putting the eyepiece to one eye, he teeked the strand's free end under the door.

Or, rather, tried to. "Grack," he muttered as the line refused to go. Wriggling a finger under the door, he felt around for a moment, and Lisa heard the muffled sound of heavy fabric tearing. "Rug was in the way," he grunted. He tried the strand again, and this time it slithered through the gap with ease. He sent perhaps half a meter under and then leaned his head back against the jamb, a look of intense concentration on his face.

"What is that thing?" Lisa asked, afraid of disturbing him but fascinated by what he was doing.

"A spy-scope," he said distractedly. "Sends light along the glass filaments to what I'm looking at and then back to me."

"What are you—?" She broke off, startled, at the click that came from the doorknob.

"Opening the lock, of course," Weylin said with an air of nervous satisfaction as he scrambled to his feet, yanking the spy-scope out from under the door. Sending quick glances both ways down the hall, he teeked the door open and all but pushed Lisa through into the darkened office. A second later he crowded in beside her, teeking the door shut and the lights on.

"Don't touch anything with your fingers," he warned her as she blinked in the sudden brightness. "That stuff they do with fingerprints in detective movies really works."

Her eyes adapted, Lisa looked around the office.

Two chairs, a cluttered desk, a combination bookcase/ file cabinet, and a large piece of paper she finally identified as a map taped to one wall were all the room contained. "What am I supposed to do?" she whispered.

"Whatever the Prophet told you to," he said. "I was just supposed to get you in."

Swallowing, Lisa moved to the desk and began studying the papers lying there. *Everything that talks about Matthew Jarvis's cabin*, the Prophet had said; but everything on the desk seemed to be about that. She'd be here all night if she tried to read all of it. Gritting her teeth, she read a few lines from each of the papers, hoping to find the most useful information quickly. One pile seemed to be from companies that had sold things to Jarvis several years ago; another sheet was covered with some kind of writing she couldn't read. Near the center of the desk was a large booklike folder with the words *Soil Types of the Barona-Banat Region* written on the cover. Teeking quickly through the pages, she found a section that consisted of short entries, each with several words and phrases followed by letters and numbers. Some of the entries were circled in red, and she stared at one for a long minute, sounding out the unfamiliar words and trying to figure out the letters and numbers that followed them. "Do you know what these mean?" she asked Weylin hopefully, teeking the folder up for him to see.

His ear pressed to the door, the righthand shook his head impatiently. "What're you asking *me* for?" he snapped. *"You're* supposed to be the one who knows what to do. And you'd better hurry—someone's bound to check on us eventually."

Lisa's heart was pounding. *Calm down*, she told herself. *Don't panic. The numbers have to mean* something. Her eyes swept the room again . . . and fell on the wall map. The words at the top—*Barona University Geological Survey Map Number One*—were largely meaningless to her; but as she looked closer she saw for the first time that a series of faint lines in both directions divided the whole map into small boxes. A string of numbers ran down the left side, a row of letters and double letters across the top, both in the same light brown as the lines. Lisa stared at them for several seconds, feeling she was on the edge of understanding something . . . and suddenly it clicked. Glancing back to the desk, she teeked the folder over to her and turned to one of the circled entries. The word *location* was near the top, followed by four letter-number combinations. With growing excitement, she found the points on the map where the lettered and numbered lines of each set met, and discovered they formed a sort of squashed square just a little ways from a blob labeled BANAT. *Oh, of course*—Banat, she realized as she sounded out the word. The second entry had five letter-number sets, which formed a shape near the first.

"Lisa—"

"Shh!" she cut Weylin off.

BARONA was easy to find: a good-sized blot in the lower center of the map. *He was on the road to Rand that night*, she remembered, her eyes searching the paper and sounding out the words there. Rand . . . Rand . . . there it was, finally, way off to the left. If the circled folder entries were indeed the places the police thought Jarvis might be, then all she needed to do now was find all those with—she glanced at the top and side—letters *A* through *N* and numbers thirty to fifty. Turning her attention back to the folder, she began to flip through the pages. There was one, and another—

And without warning Weylin flew back from the door. "Someone coming!" he hissed, darting to the ceiling and teeking off the light. Lisa had just enough time to make a grab for the folder in the sudden darkness before the door swung open and a silhouetted figure stepped into the room. He was reaching for the light switch when his head was slammed violently against the door jamb.

Lisa gasped in sympathetic pain as the figure collapsed to the floor. "Weylin! You—?"

"Shut up!" the other snapped. The limp figure of the policeman floated into the room and the door again swung shut; and as the last bit of hallway light was cut off the room's lights came back on.

"Is he dead?" Lisa whispered in horror, her eyes glued to the crumpled body. Her stomach wanted badly to be sick.

"I don't think so," Weylin answered tightly, making no move to find out. "We've got to get out of here—if no one heard that thump, they'll still come looking for him soon. Hurry and finish up, will you?"

Lisa ignored him. Gingerly, she knelt by the policeman, wondering what to do. In the movies someone always felt the person's neck, but she had no idea what that was supposed to prove. The side of his head where he'd been hit was becoming matted with oozing blood; she wondered if she should try and stop the bleeding.

"Forget him, Lisa," Weylin growled. "He's all right. Can't you see he's breathing?"

He was right; she'd been so rattled she hadn't even noticed. "Thank heaven," she breathed.

"Never mind that—we're still in trouble. You'd better get out of here right now."

"But I haven't finished yet—"

"I can't help that. Get out of here and go tell the Prophet what happened." He looked over at the window and frowned in concentration.

"What about you?"

"I'll stay and cover for you. Don't worry; the Prophet told me how to handle something like this." There was a loud click and the window slid halfway open. "Go. And don't get caught."

Swallowing, Lisa nodded and slid out through the narrow gap. The night air was a quiet splash of reality, like the feel of her pillow when she woke up after a bad dream. But this nightmare wasn't going to go away. Dropping to just above streetlight level, she flew swiftly toward the building across the street, heading for its protective shadows. As she rounded the corner a sudden impulse made her glance behind her—

Just in time to see three righthands lift from the city building entrance and head in her direction.

Chapter 19

There was no time for thought, no time for Lisa to consider the possibly lethal consequences of her actions. The guilty fear exploding inside her mind drowned out everything else . . . and a second later she was shooting down the alleyway between buildings at top speed, the nearest wall barely thirty centimeters from her shoulder. Emerging, she flashed over the next street and dodged between two more buildings. A flicker of teekay brushed at her legs as she disappeared into the relative darkness, and with a surge of panic she pushed her speed even higher.

She very nearly piled herself into a streetlight two blocks later, and the shock of that finally jolted her conscious mind into realizing the incredible danger she was in. Gasping for breath, her eyes swimming with tears from the eighty-kilometer-per-hour wind in her face, she was avoiding obstacles by sheer luck. Blinking furiously, she managed to locate the darker shades of another alley ahead and to her right; ducking into it, she came to a stop, pressing herself against the darker of the two buildings. The air felt almost hot in her throat as she gulped it in. Rubbing her aching eyes with the heels of her hands, she looked back the way she had come, wondering if she had lost the righthands.

High overhead, three slowly moving figures caught her eye.

Pressing herself tighter against the wall, Lisa watched the drifting righthands with a crushing sense of defeat. Of course they hadn't been crazy enough to try and match her terrified flight; at three-to-one odds all they needed to do was get someplace where they could see her and then just teek her in. If she hadn't stopped to catch her breath they'd probably have picked up her movement and nailed her by now.

Strangely enough, the panic of a few minutes earlier was gone, leaving Lisa more clearheaded than she'd been since entering the city building. *It's just like hide-and-search*, she told herself, *and you know how to play that game.* Keeping the rest of her body motionless, she looked carefully around her. With streetlights blazing all over the city, there were no shadows really dark enough to hide in for long. All three righthands were still visible in front of her; if she could get to the building at the other side of her alleyway, she would be completely hidden from them, at least for the moment. But the movement might attract their attention . . . and hiding wasn't a real solution, anyway. For all she knew the rest of Barona's righthands might be flying in at any time to do a complete search of the area. No, her only chance was to get out of the city as fast as possible.

Or to get back to the hive.

She frowned suddenly. With Weylin's command echoing through her mind, the thought of going home hadn't occurred to her before. But Dayspring was a lot closer than the temple site and certainly easier to find in the middle of the night. If Sheelah was there to open a window for her—and if she hadn't reported her absence to Gavra—

Without warning, Lisa was yanked away from the wall and pulled upward.

She acted instinctively, not fighting the motion directly but teeking herself sideways to it. The pull wavered a bit as the darkness and her unexpected action apparently interfered with the righthands' view of her. Wavered just enough—and as she all but slammed into the building across the alley their teekay grip was abruptly cut off. An instant later Lisa had dropped nearly to the pavement and was skimming the wall as she shot back in the direction she'd come from.

One of the righthands managed to get overhead before she reached the corner, but it was instantly clear that he'd expected her to continue moving away from the city building and was thus in the wrong place, far to her rear. His tentative grip on her was again cut off as she swung around the edge of her building. Counting two seconds, she came to a sudden stop and reversed direction, flying alongside the building and ducking once more into the alley. The righthand, racing over the rooftops to intercept her, was again taken by surprise, and got even less of a hold on her this time before she was out of his sight. She reached the end of the alley without difficulty and shot across the next street at full speed. A cross street led off a few meters ahead and to her left; shifting direction, she headed down it, again hugging the buildings along one side. Several recessed doorways whipped by, and on sudden impulse she stopped short and ducked into one of them. Pressing back into the shadows, blinking away the latest flood of tears, she breathed deeply and wondered if her move had been seen.

If it had, the fact was not immediately apparent. Faintly, she could hear voices calling to one another overhead, and though she couldn't make out the words the tone sounded more frustrated than triumphant. They'd seen her head down the street, she guessed, but had then lost her. If they now split up, leaving one to search the block while the other two went on—

The conversation ended. Heart pounding, Lisa eased forward and risked a look upward. One of the tiny figures was disappearing over the rooftops in the direction she'd been going; the other two were dropping rapidly toward the ground, apparently heading for opposite ends of the block where she was hiding.

Head pressed against the cold stone of the doorway, Lisa froze, afraid to move the short distance back into the deeper shadows and knowing such an effort would be wasted anyway. A careful search would find her instantly ... and while she might have been able to out-teek a single righthand, there was no way she'd be able to handle two at once. Her eyes shifted back and forth, searching the brightly lit street for inspiration. But there was nothing there; no weapons, nothing to distract them with, nothing that would give her cover for an escape. One of the righthands was drifting along at street level a block away now, and she could see his head turning back and forth as he moved slowly away from her down the street. So they weren't sure which of the two blocks she might have vanished into ... but that was little comfort. The second righthand had disappeared off to her left and was presumably working his way down the block toward her hiding place. She had maybe half a minute before he hauled her out into the light and together the two of them teeked her like a wounded batling back to the city building—

And with the inspiration of having nothing at all to lose, she closed one eye and reached out to one of the streetlights halfway down the next block, teeking the bulb forward as hard as she could.

The faint tinkle of broken glass reached her a half second after the light went dark. Blinking at the purple blob that temporarily blinded her, she switched eyes and shattered the next light in line. With both eyes blocked by purple her third attempt was unsuccessful, but an instant later it proved to be unnecessary, anyway. With a swish of wind the righthand who'd been searching her block shot past, his full attention on the patch of darkness from which their quarry was presumably trying to escape. An instant after that Lisa was heading the other way, keeping close to the wall and hoping desperately she could make it around the corner before they realized they'd been tricked.

No shouts or teekay grips reached her before she

made her turn. Ten blocks and two direction changes later, she paused to cautiously poke her head over the edge of a roof. Off in the distance she could pick out two faint figures circling over the area she'd just left; a third was tracing what seemed to be an ever-expanding spiral around the same place. Slipping back to streetlight level, Lisa continued on, hugging the buildings and flying as swiftly as she dared. *A few more blocks,* she told herself over and over. *Just a few more blocks and you'll be safe.* Safe ... but for how long?

She didn't let herself think about that.

The twin towers of Dayspring were even darker than the city building had been, without a single light showing anywhere. Under other circumstances Lisa might have found the view a little creepy, but at the moment she had far too many other things on her mind to even notice. Keeping to all the shadows she could, with half her attention on the sky and buildings behind her, she flew up to her window, hoping fervently she'd be able to get in.

But that problem, at least, had already been solved. For the first time since they'd become roommates, Sheelah had gone to bed with the curtains wide open ... and looking closer, Lisa realized the window was open a crack, its lock unfastened. Without hesitation she teeked it open the rest of the way and slipped inside, closing it quietly behind her.

"Lisa?" The soft voice coming from Sheelah's bed was alert, without a trace of sleepiness in it.

"Yes," Lisa whispered. She teeked the curtains closed, pulling them the last couple of centimeters by hand as they cut off most of the light from the street. "It's okay; go to sleep."

Her answer was a creak of springs as Sheelah flew out of bed. "Watch your eyes," her voice warned from near the door, and the room suddenly blazed with light.

Lisa squinted momentarily against the glare; and as her eyes adjusted she saw with some surprise that

Sheelah was fully clothed. "Why aren't you ready for bed?"

"I thought I might have to go out looking for you," Sheelah told her. "What happened to you, anyway? Are you all right?"

"Oh, terrific." Lisa walked to her bed and sat down heavily. "Did you report me?"

"Well . . . not really." Sheelah's mouth puckered into a grimace. "But I went to Gavra half an hour before lights-out and told her you'd been gone all day. I was worried about you."

"What did she say?"

"That you were off doing something private that I gather I'm not supposed to ask questions about. She said you'd be okay."

Lisa nodded and closed her eyes. If Gavra told the police she'd been out late . . . but at the moment she was too drained emotionally to even care. "Thanks for waiting up," she told Sheelah. "You'd better get to bed."

The other hesitated for a second, then stepped over and sat down beside Lisa. "You're in some kind of trouble, aren't you?" she asked gently. "How about letting me in on it?"

Lisa shook her head as fresh tears blurred her vision. "I've gotten enough people in trouble already," she mumbled through a tight throat.

"So what's one more?" Sheelah countered, the lightness of the words in sharp contrast to the solemnity in her face. "Come on, Lisa—telling each other our troubles is what best friends are *for.*"

And suddenly all the tension, fear, frustration, and anger turned to water and came pouring out; and leaning into the warmth of Sheelah's shoulder, she began to cry, sobbing with an intensity of anguish and loneliness she hadn't felt since the day after her fifth birthday, the day her parents had brought her to the hive and left her. . . .

And later, after all that remained of the tears were damp shirts and aching eyes, Lisa told her all about it.

*   *   *

"Palmer was just barely conscious when the ambulance took him away, but he was able to tell us what happened," Officer Carylson said tightly as he and Tirrell walked down the hall toward the detective's office. "He was headed for Hob Paxton's office to see if Weylin was having any trouble with his informant when he noticed light coming from under your office door and went over to investigate. By the time he opened the door the room was dark, and the next thing he knew he was waking up with two parameds kneeling over him."

"No idea what hit him, huh?" Tirrell asked, just to get the question out of the way.

"*He* didn't, no, but we know it had to be the kid Weylin brought in. You can see a dent in the doorjamb where she must have teeked his head into it."

Tirrell nodded. They'd reached the office now and the detective paused for a moment outside, taking it all in. "Anything been touched?"

"Nothing but the door—and Palmer, of course. We wanted to let you look things over before we sent in a shakedown squad."

"Thanks. Shakedown'll probably be useless anyway—if she was smart she wouldn't have touched anything."

"True. Nothing to lose by trying, though."

Tirrell nodded again. His eyes lingered on the torn-up section of rug by the door, on the open window, and on the soil-types listing on the floor by the survey map. Stepping carefully into the room, he did a quick mental inventory of his desktop papers. Nothing seemed to be missing, at least nothing of any importance. "How did she get by Weylin?" he asked over his shoulder.

"He said he let her into Paxton's office and she immediately clobbered him with something. We found an ashtray off in the corner with a trace of blood on it."

"Was he unconscious when you found him?"

"Just coming to," Carylson said. "Mad as hell, too—wanted to go right out with the others and look for her, headache and all. I had to order him into the ambulance."

Squatting down, Tirrell lifted one end of the soil-types folder with a pen and peered at the edge where the pages met the binding. If any of them had been torn out, it had been done one at a time and far between; he could see no obvious gaps. "How long did it take you to get someone up here after the open-window alarm went off?"

"Half a minute, tops. And we were onto the kid outside sooner than that."

"So there wasn't any time to bring a camera in through the open window," Tirrell concluded, more to himself than to the other.

"Camera?"

Letting the folder back down, Tirrell stood up. "This was a very slick job, Carlyson. The torn-up rug means a spy-scope or some kind of fancy mirror setup was used to get the lock open; the fact the righthands lost her implies a preplanned escape route—and all this *after* knowing enough about one of Paxton's cases to sucker Weylin into getting her inside. Slick operators usually get what they go after. But if she didn't physically take anything out of here and didn't use a camera, then what did she *get*?"

"Maybe she broke into your office by mistake, thinking it was someone else's," Carylson suggested.

Tirrell shook his head. "According to your numbers, if she clobbered Weylin right away, she had nearly twenty minutes alone up here. Even if it took her five to open the door, figuring out she was in the wrong place shouldn't have taken the other fifteen." He looked around the office again. "I guess you might as well wake up the shakedown squad," he said, moving toward the door. "Maybe they can read things differently than I—"

He froze right at the doorway, his mind spinning furiously as he tried to track down the thought that had suddenly brushed him on the shoulder. Carylson, who had already taken three steps down the hall, hurried back. "What is it?" he asked.

Stepping back to his desk, Tirrell opened the bottom drawer and pulled out a thick stack of paper. All the interdepartmental memos, notices, and low-priority info sheets—the sort of paper that was usually skimmed once and then relegated to wastebaskets or taken home as fireplace kindling. Setting the pile on his desk, Tirrell leafed quickly through it. "Would you describe the girl again?" he asked Carylson, pulling out the sheet he wanted.

"About a meter sixty, slender build—probably somewhere short of forty-five kilograms—dark off-shoulder-length hair, dark eyes, maybe thirteen years old," the other said, frowning at the paper in Tirrell's hand. "You have something?"

"Take a look," Tirrell said, handing the sheet over. "The picture at bottom right."

Carylson glared at the paper as if it had just insulted his mother. "I'll be damned," he growled. "That's her, all right." His eyes shifted to the top of the sheet. "And I *read* this damn thing when it came out, too."

"Uh-huh." Tirrell took the sheet back, feeling cold inside. *Lisa Duncan, 14, of Dayspring Hive*, he read silently. *Has learned to read and write, proficiency unknown. Level 10.* So that was why she hadn't bothered to take anything from the office—for her the soil-types listing would have been just a dangerous nuisance to carry. How very convenient for someone to have had her available . . . and there was just one person who might be interested in his progress who also had the chutzpah and the skill to set something like this up.

"I think we can safely bump her up a few levels now, don't you?" Carylson cut into his thoughts. "Say, to level one?"

Tirrell tuned back in. "Put an all-points pickup out on her? Don't be silly—we can't afford to let anyone know we're on to her." He thought a moment. "All right. Seal my office until the shakedown squad can go through it—you might as well leave that till morning; there's no hurry now. Let me come down to the desk with you and use your phone for a couple of calls." Without waiting for a reply he headed off down the hall.

Carylson hurried to catch up. "Shouldn't we at least move her up to level eight? If someone spots her they should at least call it in."

"Can't risk it—we don't know what sort of surveillance system we're up against." But if Jarvis thought his preteen spy had gotten away with her little escapade, he and Tonio might just be able to pick her up quietly. Then, if he could establish a link between them, he might be able to use the threat of an accessory to kidnapping charge to force cooperation from her. And then—

Tirrell blanked the chain of thought from his mind. *First things first*, he reminded himself sternly. A call to the Skylight Hive to get Tonio awake and over here, another call to Cam Mbar to find out if Lisa Duncan had ever worked as a test subject on one of Jarvis's experiments, and then a quiet midnight visit to Dayspring.

It was likely to be a busy night.

"I still think you should go to Gavra right now with all of this," Sheelah said, looking unnaturally stiff as she sat crosslegged on Lisa's bed. "She might be able to help you."

Sitting next to her roommate, hunched over the pad of drawing paper on her lap, Lisa carefully finished the word she was on before laying down her colored pencil and straightening up. "I wish I could," she said, rubbing the fingers of her writing hand. "But I don't think she could do anything for me without getting into trouble herself. And if she calls the police, I don't know what'll happen to Daryl. My only chance is to hope the Prophet Omega can tell me where he is before anyone knows I was the one who was with Weylin tonight."

"Suppose Weylin tells the police himself?" Sheelah countered. "I don't trust him, Lisa—him *or* this Prophet Omega. If he really cared about you he should've helped you without making you do him a favor first. And what makes you think he can find Daryl, anyway?"

Lisa shrugged helplessly. "Everybody else out there seems to think he can do whatever he says he can. Besides, no one else had been willing to help me. What have I got to lose by letting him try?"

"That's a pretty dumb question from someone who's in as big a downdraft as you are," Sheelah said sourly. She paused, and in a more understanding tone said, "You kind of like Daryl, don't you?"

"Not the way you mean," Lisa told her, shaking her head. "I mean, he's a nice enough guy, but not for—you know. But I've *got* to find him. It's my fault he's in whatever trouble he's in; don't you see? If they've got him in jail or something . . ." She left the sentence unfinished.

"And if they have, *then* what? Break him out like they're always doing in the movies? You'll *really* get in trouble for something crazy like that."

Lisa's laugh was more like a painful cough. "More trouble than I'm already in?"

Sheelah grimaced and fell silent. Picking up her pencil again, Lisa returned her attention to the paper. Writing was much harder work for her than reading had ever been. Somehow, the letters never seemed to come out looking quite like those in the books, and many of the words wound up looking *wrong*, even though she usually couldn't tell why. She wished now she had spent more time on the writing lessons in Daryl's books instead of hurrying to get on to more reading. But it was too late to make up for her laziness now. Doggedly, she kept at it, trying to ignore the vision hovering before her eyes of fifty police righthands hurtling toward Dayspring.

But no one had burst into the room by the time she finally finished. "All right," she said, laying down the pencil with relief and folding the paper twice before handing it to Sheelah. "Give this to Gavra in the morning—not before, understand? If she asks you about it, you don't know anything. You've got to promise me that—I don't want you to lose all your points, too."

Sheelah took the paper gingerly, a dubious look on her face. "I still don't see what good a note will do."

"It'll tell her I'm all right but won't give her a chance to stop me," Lisa said. Teeking off the room lights, she went to the window and opened the curtains enough to peek out. "If I talked to her in person or used the phone, she'd have to call the police or get in trouble herself for *not* calling them."

"She won't have a chance to give you any advice, either," Sheelah pointed out. She sighed loudly. "All right, I'll give her the note. Any righthands out there?"

"I don't see any." Opening the curtains wider, Lisa slid the window up and glanced back into the darkened room. "Don't forget, you don't know anything. Okay?"

"Yeah." The shadow that was Sheelah stepped forward and touched Lisa's arm. "Watch yourself, Lisa, and be careful."

"I will." Taking a deep breath, Lisa slipped out the window and dropped quickly toward the ground. Keeping low, with an eye out for searching righthands, she headed south.

Chapter 20

Dayspring Hive was a towering collection of uniformly dark windows as Tirrell pulled the car silently to the curb and gently opened his door. "Don't slam it," he cautioned Tonio as the righthand slid out his side of the vehicle. "Sounds carry pretty well at night."

The preteen nodded and swung the door to with a barely audible click. "You want me to wait out here and watch?" he whispered.

Tirrell shook his head. "There's no way you could cover the whole building by yourself. Let's try the battering-ram approach first and see if we can get to her before she knows we're here."

Still, the detective kept an eye skyward as they headed up the long walkway to the main entrance.

The outer door was unlocked. Opening it and stepping through, Tirrell found himself in a glassed-in vestibule whose inner door turned out to be locked. In the larger entrance hall beyond, a young adult was sitting at a small desk, a solitaire hand laid out in front of her. Looking up at the visitors, she leaned toward a small microphone. "May I help you?" she said pleasantly, her voice coming through an intercom grille in the vestibule ceiling.

Tirrell held up his badge up to the glass. "Police," he said. "I want to see both your Director and your Girls' Senior right away."

Eyes bulging slightly, the woman nodded and groped at the far side of her desk. With a *snick* the inner door popped open a centimeter or two, and as Tirrell pulled it open, she reached for her phone.

They arrived almost simultaneously from opposite directions a few minutes later—the man in robe and slippers, the woman still dressed. Tirrell wondered why she'd still be up, decided to hold the question for later.

"Detective?" the man asked as he approached, as if there could be any doubt. "I'm Director Allan Gould. What seems to be the problem?"

"I'm Detective First Tirrell," Tirrell identified himself formally. "One of your kids broke into my office at the city building an hour ago and assaulted a police officer. We're here to pick her up."

"What?" Gould's jaw sagged.

"Who?" the woman asked.

Tirrell shifted his attention to her. "You're the Girls' Senior?"

"Yes; Gavra Norward. Whom are you accusing?"

"It's hardly a simple accusation—one of the officers who saw her enter the station has already tentatively identified her from her picture. Her name's Lisa Duncan."

Something flickered over Gavra's face, something that didn't look altogether surprised. "Are you absolutely sure it was Lisa?" she asked, her voice strangely tight.

"That's what we're here to find out," Tirrell said. "Would you take us to her room, please?"

Gavra held his eyes a fraction of a second, then turned to the young woman at the desk. "Has Lisa come in since you've been here?"

The other was already running a finger down a long list in front of her. "Not since the doors were locked at eight-thirty," she said, shaking her head.

"You knew she was out?" Tirrell asked, watching Gavra's face closely.

"I knew she'd missed the eight-thirty sign-in," the Senior replied without hesitation. "She's never missed lights-out before, though, so I had no reason to suspect she'd be late this time."

"Uh-huh." *Or else had suspicions and carefully avoided any direct knowledge.* "I'd like to check her room for myself, if you don't mind."

Gavra glanced past him at Tonio, opened her mouth as if to object to his presence on the girls' side, then abruptly turned and headed back the way she'd come without saying anything. Tirrell fell into step beside her, Tonio following close behind.

The twin towers started three floors above street level, rising above the hive's common areas, and Lisa's room was five more flights up the girls' tower itself. Tirrell pushed the pace, with the result that both he and Gavra were breathing a bit heavily by the time they started down the hallway. Tonio, of course, showed no strain at all from the trip.

Gavra led the way to one of the doors about halfway down the left-hand corridor. "This is it," she said in a soft voice which tried very hard to disguise its tension. "May I knock before you go barging in? Knocking is a hive privacy rule."

Tirrell hesitated, then nodded. "All right, but don't wait for an answer before opening the door."

Gavra grimaced, but turned back to the door without comment and rapped gently on the panel. Twisting the knob, she pushed the door open and stepped inside. "Lisa? Sheelah? It's Gavra," she announced quietly as Tirrell flicked on the light and took a long step past her into the room.

It was, unfortunately, an anticlimax. One of the two beds was clearly empty; in the other a tousle-haired girl, startled awake, was half sitting up with an arm thrown protectively over her eyes. "What—" she gasped.

"It's all right, Sheelah; it's Gavra and a police detective," the Senior said quickly.

"The police?" Still squinting, the girl lowered her arm and peered in Tirrell's direction. "Why is—oh!" She broke off, and her sheet suddenly jumped to chin level.

Beside him, Tirrell heard a sort of embarrassed gulp from Tonio. "Maybe I should wait in the hall," the righthand suggested.

Tirrell's eyes had already completed their sweep of the room without finding any place even an under-sized preteen like Lisa could be hiding. "All right," he told Tonio. "But stay close."

"Right." The other took a breath and got out fast.

Turning his attention to the girl now sitting straight up in bed, the detective gave her his most reassuring smile. It didn't help; above the sheet her expression remained wary. *And she's wide-awake*, he noted suddenly. *A fast waker? Or wasn't she asleep at all?* "Please don't be alarmed, Sheelah," he said. "I'd just like to ask you a few questions, if I may. Have you seen your roommate Lisa this evening?"

The girl's expression didn't change. "No," she said. "She left this morning and I haven't seen her since then."

"Do you know where she might have gone?"

"No."

"Did she leave with anyone else?"

"I don't know."

"I see." Tirrell glanced at the curtained window. "It's been over an hour now since lights-out. Any chance she could have sneaked in and out during that time?"

"The window's locked. You can check if you want."

"I'll take your word for it." Tirrell studied her thoughtfully. "You're certainly taking this calmly, Sheelah. Aren't you even worried about what might have happened to Lisa?"

For the first time Sheelah seemed uncertain. "Lisa can take care of herself," she muttered, looking at the floor.

"Maybe she can, but maybe not," Tirrell said. "The fact is, Lisa is in a great deal of trouble—and running is only going to make it worse. You'd be doing her a favor by telling me where she's gone."

Sheelah's eyes snapped back up to the detective,

guilty surprise plastered across her face. "I don't know what you're talking—"

"Sheelah," Tirrell cut her off quietly, gesturing at Lisa's bed. "You don't have to look very closely at that blanket to see that *two* people have been sitting on it—and I remember enough of hive housekeeping standards to know Lisa wouldn't have left it like that in the morning. You let her in, sometime in the past half-hour or so, you sat on her bed together and talked, and then she took off looking for a place to hide. True?"

Sheelah's gaze was back on the floor, her throat making swallowing motions. In the silence Gavra stepped forward and sat down on the edge of the girl's bed. "Sheelah, is he right?" she asked gently.

The preteen closed her eyes and drew a shuddering breath, but otherwise remained silent. "Look," Tirrell said after a moment, "we know you're trying to protect her, but you're only making things worse for both of you. Aiding a fugitive, especially one who's committed assault, could—"

"Lisa didn't hurt that policeman!" Sheelah flared with a sudden fire that took Tirrell by surprise. "It was that other guy—Weylin something. *He* did it."

"So Lisa *did* come here," Gavra said, her voice tightening. "Why didn't you—?"

"Wait a second," Tirrell interrupted. "What makes you think Weylin was involved? He wasn't even in the same room at the time."

Sheelah's expression was pure puzzlement, without a trace of guile in it. "Yes, he was. He took Lisa there to . . . look at some things."

Tirrell stared at the girl for a long second, his brain adjusting to this unexpected revelation. It could be a lie, of course, Lisa trying to cover up what she had done. But the more he thought about it the more sense it made. Weylin had the necessary skill to use a spy-scope, and faking an attack on himself took nothing but determination and chutzpah. Belatedly, now, Hob Paxton's idle comment several weeks back about how Weylin had nagged him into requesting the liai-

son job took on a new significance. If Weylin had
been spying for Jarvis all this time, then it was no
wonder the scientist had outmaneuvered them at every turn—and in that case Lisa might simply have
been recruited on some pretext for this specific job. If
she had no especial loyalty to Jarvis she would make
a good witness against him . . . *if* she could be found.

Gavra was speaking again. "What was she supposed to look at, Sheelah?"

The preteen shook her head. "I don't know, exactly. This Omega guy who sent her said it had something to do with a child who'd been kidnapped."

Gavra looked up at Tirrell, startled. But the detective nodded. "No, she's right—I *am* working on a
kidnap case. I think Lisa was after our list of the
kidnapper's possible locations. How much she got, I
don't know."

"But why would anyone be interested in something like that?" Gavra asked. "It doesn't make any
sense."

"It does if the man who sent her is also the kidnapper," Tirrell said bluntly.

Sheelah's eyes widened. "You mean . . . but Lisa
said Omega was a *prophet*."

"Prophet, my foot," Tirrell growled. "He's a cold-
blooded kidnapper who thought nothing of snatching
a five-year-old boy for—well, never mind." The detective had no intention of going into the whole story.
"The point is, he's just using Lisa to find out how
close we are to him. Once she's served her purpose,
there's no telling what he'll do to make sure she can't
tell us anything about his hideout."

This time Gavra's eyes went wide, too. "You mean
he might . . . *kill* her?"

"He already faces charges of kidnapping and possibly of suborning a police righthand, depending on
what we find out about Weylin," Tirrell pointed out.
"I'd rather get to Lisa before we find out just how far
he's prepared to go."

But Sheelah's face had gone rigid again. "You don't
believe me, do you? You still think Lisa hit that

policeman, and you're making up this whole thing about Lisa being used just so I'll tell you where she's gone. Well, I won't."

Clamping his teeth together, Tirrell counted to ten, cursing his loose tongue. Of course he wasn't going to pass final judgment on Weylin on Sheelah's unsupported word, but he hadn't intended for the girl to know that. "Sheelah—"

"No! You don't want to help Lisa, so just go away." Flopping down onto her back, Sheelah turned sideways to face the wall.

"All right, this has gone far enough," Gavra said, her voice abruptly hard. "Sheelah, this isn't some kind of game. If there's any chance at all Lisa's in danger, you owe it to her to tell Detective Tirrell everything he wants to know. You'll regret it the rest of your life if something happens to her that you could have helped prevent."

Sheelah said nothing, but Tirrell could see her body shaking with quiet sobbing under the sheet. Studying the back of her head, he decided that threats against her hive points would probably be a waste of time. "All right, Sheelah," he sighed. "We'll find her ourselves—and maybe prove Weylin's guilt or innocence in the process."

"How are you going to do that?" Gavra frowned.

"I'm going to call headquarters and tell them we've picked up Lisa and are bringing her in," Tirrell told her, watching Sheelah. The preteen was still facing the wall, but her shaking had stopped. *If you can convince her you mean this—and can convince* yourself *it'll work*—"I'll tell them that you, Ms. Norward, have told her not to say anything until she's formally charged, and that they should therefore call the hospital and have Weylin come back to the city building to make a positive identification of her."

"But you don't *have* Lisa."

"No, but Weylin won't know that—and if Sheelah's version is the truth, he'll know that the minute Lisa starts to talk his little charade will disintegrate. With any luck, when he runs he'll head straight to his boss's hideout." Tirrell nodded to Sheelah, who had now turned halfway back toward him. "Sheelah, if you can at least tell us which general direction Lisa went, it'll help us pick up Weylin's trail when he takes off."

Sheelah pursed her lips tightly. "South," she said at last.

"Thanks." Tirrell looked back at Gavra. "I noticed a phone at the other end of the hall. Can I get an outside line on it?"

"Yes—just punch one first. Can you find your own way out? I'd like to talk to Sheelah for a moment."

"No problem. Sheelah, whatever you might feel about it now, you did the right thing to tell us what you did. Thank you." Nodding once to Gavra, Tirrell left the room, closing the door behind him.

Tonio was hovering in the middle of the hall, his expression reminiscent of an approaching thunderstorm. "That lousy, rotten, *batling* eater!" he hissed.

"I gather you were listening in," Tirrell nodded. "Good. You think you'll be able to follow Weylin if he runs for it? *Quietly*, I mean, without being noticed."

"No problem." Though his expression said he'd rather teek Weylin into something solid.

"Okay. I want you to get going right away and find a good spot to watch the south side of Mercy Hospital from. Stop by the car first and grab a portacom— the private, not the broad-band; I don't want Weylin listening in if he thought to take a broad-band with him. Weylin or anyone else, for that matter."

"You're not going to tell the other police what we're doing?"

"Not yet. If Jarvis got to Weylin he might have gotten to one of the others, too, or even to some of the officers. For the moment, it's just going to be you and me on this. If and when Weylin leads us to Jarvis we'll think about how to get some help. Get going; I'll give you a few minutes to get in position before I make my call. I'll head out on the Plat City road when I'm done—give me a call when you've got a clear direction."

"Right." Taking off down the hallway, Tonio vanished into the stairwell.

Checking his watch, Tirrell followed more slowly, bypassing the stairs and stopping finally beside the phone fastened chest-high on the wall. *How on Tigris did Jarvis get Weylin in on this?* he wondered, staring at and through the phone. *What could he have promised him in exchange for information? Or was he instead using some kind of blackmail? Or*—and the sudden thought was sobering—*has he come up with a genuinely foolproof method of mind control?* The concept was not as farfetched as most people preferred to think; hypnotic drugs came disturbingly close as it was . . . and Jarvis *had* presumably kept Colin Brimmer under some kind of control these past two months.

There was a footfall behind him, and Tirrell turned to see Gavra Norward approaching, a piece of paper in her hand. "Something?" he asked.

She held out the paper. "Lisa left a note for me," she said steadily, watching his face. "I convinced Sheelah you should see it."

"I know about Lisa," he nodded, taking the paper. The message was short, its painfully blocky letters done in some kind of soft blue pencil. But the words, if not the meaning, were clear enough:

Gavra i am al rite. I hav gone to see the profit omaga. He and the other kids wil find Daril for me if Waylin and i got wat he wanted us to. Plese dont wory il be al rite i did it to help Daril. Lisa.

" 'Daril'?"

"Daryl Kellerman was the teen who taught her to read," Gavra explained. "He's just been transferred from Barona to an intro school in Cavendish, but I've been forbidden to tell her where he is, and she's gotten it into her head that something terrible's been done to him."

"Damn," Tirrell swore gently. He reread the note, a small feeling of uneasiness nagging at the back of his mind. Who in hell were these other kids Lisa was talking about? Colin and Weylin? Or was something else entirely going on out there? *A fagin operation? Ridiculous—world-famous scientists don't become fagins.*

"Is something wrong?" Gavra asked, frowning.

Tirrell refocused on her face. "A *lot* is wrong—and I'm not sure anymore I understand all of it," he growled. "I'd like to keep this, if you don't mind."

Gavra nodded. "If you think it'll help you find Lisa." She hesitated. "You know, I think I've persuaded Sheelah to trust you a little. I'd like to think that trust will be honored."

"Saving one preteen's respect for authority is pretty low on my priorities list right now," Tirrell said shortly. "I'll see what I can do, but if it turns out Lisa deserves getting the book thrown at her, then that's what's going to happen."

Surprisingly, Gavra smiled tightly. " 'The book.' Your choice of words is appropriate, Detective." The smile faded and she nodded. "I understand. Good luck." Turning, she walked back down the hall toward Sheelah's room.

Probably going to prepare her to expect the worst, Tirrell decided morosely. *Jarvis, I think I'm starting to hate you.*

Checking his watch, he turned back and reached for the phone.

Chapter 21

By day, the Tessellate Mountains south of Barona had been as unfamiliar as the buildings of a strange city; but by night, they might just as well have been from another planet. Coasting to a stop for probably the hundredth time since crossing the Nordau River, Lisa gazed out across the shadowy landscape before her, trying to find anything that looked familiar while at the same time fighting down the panic that seemed to have lodged permanently in her throat. The stars blazed brilliantly down from a cloudless sky, and Akkad, the larger of the two moons, was still up, but all of the light seemed to hinder more than it helped. The shadows the moon created were sharp and very dark, confusing the shapes of the mountains and sometimes hiding the smaller peaks completely. The handful of snow-covered mountains were easy enough to identify as such, but except for the slopes nearest her at any given time, Lisa found conetree forests, scrubweed, and bare rock to be virtually indistinguishable.

Just ahead and a little to her right were a pair of mountains that might be the ones Camila had pointed out to her that morning—yesterday morning, now; it was a good half hour past ten. If they were the right peaks, she remembered, she needed to pass them on the left. If they weren't . . . well, in that case, she was probably lost already. Swallowing her fear, she picked up speed again.

So intent was she on the landscape ahead that she failed to see the figure angling down toward her from overhead; failed to notice him, in fact, until his soft voice jolted her into a four-meter swerve to the side. "Weylin? That you?" the voice called.

Heart abruptly pounding, Lisa leveled out, rolling in midair to see who it was. "No, it's Lisa Duncan," she told him, trying to pierce the shadows hiding his face. "Who are you?"

"Senior Acolyte Axel Schu," he said. "The Prophet sent me out here to watch for you. Where's Weylin?"

"The police almost caught us," she told him, a wave of relief at having a guide almost covering up her other worries. "I don't know if Weylin got away or not."

For a moment they flew together in silence. "Well . . ." Axel said at last. "Did you at least get the stuff the Prophet wanted?"

"I don't know," Lisa sighed. "I hope so."

"A little more to the left here," Axel said as they rounded a craggy peak. "I guess you'll find out soon enough," he added, pointing to a glistening cone directly in front of them. "That's our mountain. The Prophet's waiting for you."

"All right," Lisa said, matching his increase in speed. *The Prophet's waiting.* Somehow, that thought wasn't as comforting as she'd expected it to be.

"Still going due south?" Tirrell said into his car's microphone, fighting the wheel with one hand as he bounced over the dusty farmland road.

"Still south," Tonio's voice confirmed.

"Damn," Tirrell muttered to himself. The road he was on was forcing him ever more eastward, toward the central part of the Barona-Nordau farming area, and there hadn't been a right-hand turnoff for a kilometer or two. "How close are you to the mountains?" he asked.

"A few kilometers, maybe—not very far. Weylin's still pretty high; I don't think he's going to land anytime soon."

Tirrell scooped up his map with his mike hand, but it was pure reflex; already he was letting the car coast to a stop. "This isn't going to work, Tonio—there's no fast way for me to get back to you by car. You'd better come and get me before he gets into the mountains and we lose him for sure."

"Okay. I think I can see your lights back there. Blink them once . . . right. I'll be there in a flash."

Pulling off onto the soft dirt at the edge of the road, Tirrell collected his map, flashlight, and jacket and climbed out of the car, leaving the headlights on. Ahead, he could see the barest outline of the Tessellate Mountains as they jutted up to block the stars. *A hell of a place to be playing nighttime hide-and-search*, he thought uneasily, putting on his jacket and stuffing the map into a pocket. A million places Weylin could instantly lose them if he even so much as suspected he was being followed—and a million more places where Jarvis's cabin could be hidden. For a moment he considered sliding back into the car and sending for reinforcements, or at least another few trackers. But he resisted the temptation. Until he knew exactly how Jarvis had suborned Weylin it was better to have one righthand he could trust than fifty he wasn't sure of.

He sensed, rather than saw, the dark object arcing toward him from the southwest, and acted with the sure movements of past experience. Ducking slightly, he reached through the car window and doused the lights; simultaneously, he flicked on his flashlight and pointed it at himself from arm's length. Instantly, the still night air became a hurricane in his face as he was abruptly teeked upward at high speed. Squeezing his eyes shut, he brought up his free arm for extra protection and waited for the wind to ease a bit. A moment later it did just that, and he opened his eyes to slits just in time to reach out and clasp Tonio's outstretched hand. "Good job," he complimented the righthand, flicking off his light and putting it away. "Can you get us back to Weylin before he gets lost in the mountains?"

Already they were heading back the way Tonio had come. "Just watch me," the preteen called over the wind and doubled his speed.

The techniques of breathing in fast flight, once learned, were never forgotten, and Tirrell had the extra advantage of not really needing to watch where they were going. He spent most of those first few minutes with his head turned to the side, windward eye closed tightly and the other open just a crack, breathing through the side of his mouth. Every few breaths he would take a quick look forward, just to keep some idea of their position. Tonio, of course, had to do that a lot more often.

They had been flying for perhaps ten minutes when Tonio abruptly brought them to almost a complete halt. "There he is!" the preteen said, pointing.

Tirrell swiped at his eyes and scanned the area ahead. Sure enough, a dimly lit speck could just be seen tracing a path above the first real mountains of the range. "Looks like he's slowed down some," Tonio commented. "Probably figures he's safe now and doesn't want to miss any turns."

"Neither do we," Tirrell told him with grim satisfaction. "Stay low and back and let's follow him in."

Tonio nodded and they started moving again. Ignoring the conetree tops brushing at his feet, Tirrell kept his eyes solidly fixed on Weylin. This was one game of hide-and-search he was *not* going to lose.

The tabernacle was quiet and dark, but the Prophet Omega was indeed waiting for them. "Lisa; I'm pleased to see you again," he said with a warm smile as Axel ushered her into the office she'd talked to the Prophet in before. The Prophet had changed since then from his white robe to a plainer blue one, but he looked no less impressive for all that. "Come sit by me and tell me all of the evening's events. Acolyte Schu, please wait outside."

Slowly, Lisa walked forward and sat down in the indicated chair by the Prophet's desk. Something was nagging at her, but she couldn't for the life of her figure out what it was. "Don't you already know?" she asked him. "I mean, you told me you had the Truth inside you—"

"Truth and knowledge are not identical," he told her, his tone that of a preteen lecturing a Seven. "Truth is more like wisdom, the ability to distinguish right from wrong. Else why would I have asked you to seek knowledge of the boy Colin for me? Now, begin."

Haltingly—the memory was still painful—Lisa told him everything that had happened from the time she and Weylin entered the city building to the time she escaped from the searching righthands. More from fear of the Prophet's disapproval than anything else, she skipped completely over her trip to the hive and everything that happened there. "So then I came back here to tell you what I could," she concluded. "Are you going to do anything to help Weylin?"

"Acolyte Weylin is in no danger if he followed my instructions," the Prophet said, a slight frown creasing his forehead. "Tell me, did you have trouble finding your way here?"

"Oh, yes," Lisa said, shivering slightly at the memory. "I was afraid I'd get completely lost and have to spend the night out there by myself."

The frown vanished. "That explains the time, then," he said. Before Lisa could ask what he meant, the Prophet picked up a large packet of paper from a corner of his desk and unfolded it into what turned out to be a duplicate of the map on Tirrell's office wall. "Now, Lisa," he said, spreading the paper across the center of the desk, "show me exactly where the circled areas are."

"Well . . ." Lisa swallowed. "I only found a couple in the right part of the map before the—before I had to leave." She found the letters and numbers she remembered and pointed out the spots.

"What do you mean, 'the right part'?" he asked. "Did the papers talk about that?"

"Oh! No—I forgot to tell you. There was a picture of Dr. Jarvis by the door downstairs in the city building—I'm not exactly sure what the pictures were for—"

"They're photos of people wanted by the police," the Prophet told her. "Go on."

"Well, I remembered seeing him. He was driving toward Rand one night last June. And he had a little boy with him who he said was his nephew, but I think it must have really been Colin."

"You *talked* to him? Jarvis, I mean?"

"Yes. I thought he might be having some trouble, driving between cities at night, so I stopped to ask if he was all right."

The Prophet muttered something under his breath and jabbed at the map. "Show me where," he ordered. "The exact spot."

She looked at it in bewilderment. "But . . . how do I—"

"You've flown over that road lots of times, haven't you? Well, each turn and bend shows up here as a curve in the line. Come on; I need to know."

But I wasn't flying along the road that night. Gritting her teeth, she leaned over the map, trying to think. She'd cut off parts of two curves catching up with the car, had stopped it on a smooth stretch, and had watched the car curve a little to the left as it left. "I think it was maybe about here," she said at last, her finger tracing a two-centimeter section of the line.

The Prophet brushed her hand aside and made a circle there with a pen. "Good. Now, let's see how far that is from Barona. . . ." With a small disk-shaped device he carefully traced along the line back into the shape labeled BARONA. Glancing at the device's side, he scribbled a number by the circle. "Lisa," he said, looking up with a smile, "I am even more certain now that it was the Truth that guided you to me."

"You mean I . . . did all right?" she asked cautiously.

"You did wonderfully," he nodded, still smiling. "You see, I already know the boy Colin is being held within a hundred kilometers of Barona. You saw him at a point nearly eighty kilometers away, which means you have narrowed tremendously the area we must search. That plus these—" he touched the two spots she'd first given him—"gives me hope that we will soon have Colin freed from his satanic captor; possibly before this day is over. And for allowing the Truth to work through you, your own desire shall surely be granted."

"You'll find Daryl for me." It wasn't until the words were out that Lisa realized she'd made a statement instead of asking a question. In that moment she suddenly understood why Weylin had been able to trust this man so completely. Looking into his eyes, feeling the warmth of his pleasure at her accomplishment, she felt as if she had finally found something she hadn't even known she'd lost. Somehow, it made everything that she'd gone through worthwhile.

The Prophet nodded solemnly. "I give you my word—"

Abruptly, he broke off, his eyes shifting toward the door. Soft voices could be heard coming from outside the room; but even as Lisa strained her ears, the door swung open—

And Weylin Ellery strode into the room.

"Weylin!" Lisa exclaimed with delight. "I was afraid you'd—"

"How'd you get away from Tirrell?" Weylin interrupted her coldly.

"From who? I went out the window—"

"Tirrell called from your hive—said he'd caught you," Weylin bit out. "Wanted me to go back to the city building to identify you."

"And you ran?" the Prophet asked sharply. Lisa glanced back at him, startled by the sudden change in his manner.

"Of course I did," Weylin said, his belligerent tone cooling some under the Prophet's gaze. "I figured she wouldn't know enough to shut up and let me do the talking."

"In other words, Tirrell set up a trap for you and you flew straight into it," the Prophet snapped. "At the very least he knows you've got something to hide over what happened tonight—and at the worst he had you followed and now knows exactly where we are!"

Weylin actually cringed. "No—no, I'm sure I wasn't followed. I got out too fast and made sure no one was behind me." His eyes swiveled to Lisa, turning angry again. "But why would Tirrell have done something like that in the first place?"

"Why indeed?" The Prophet looked at Lisa, too, his earlier warmth gone without a trace. His eyes were cold and hard, his unsmiling face looking like that of another person altogether. "So you came here straight from the city building, did you? Who did you talk to, Lisa, that you conveniently forgot to mention? Was it Tirrell? Someone at your hive?"

"I . . . didn't—"

"Don't lie to me!" the Prophet thundered abruptly.

"Just my roommate," she blurted, shrinking back into her chair. "Only her—and she promised she wouldn't tell anyone."

"Well, she obviously *did* tell someone," the Prophet shot back. "What did you tell her?"

"I—I—" Lisa fumbled, her tongue tangled with confusion at the Prophet's abrupt change—

And suddenly her mind flashed back to the other picture on the city building wall, the one that had seemed vaguely familiar. "It was *you!*" she said without thinking. "But the name was Yerik Martel, not the Proph—"

"Weylin, hold her," the Prophet said quietly.

For an instant Lisa sat in stunned silence, the order echoing through her mind as she wondered if she had heard him right. An instant after that she launched herself at the door—but she was barely halfway there when Weylin's teekay plucked her out of the air and slammed her down onto the floor. Fighting blindly against the invisible force, Lisa struggled back into the air, jerking sideways in an attempt to break his hold. But the trick that had worked among Barona's shadowy buildings was ineffective in such close quarters, and his grip on her remained firm. Spurred by panic, she abandoned her attempts to fly and instead scooped up all the books and papers she could from Omega's desk, hurling them at Weylin. But the right-hand dodged them without shifting his gaze . . . and a moment later Lisa was spun around and shoved into one of the room's far corners.

"What's going on?" a new voice—Axel's—snapped from behind her.

"Help Weylin hold her," Omega ordered. "I think she's a police spy."

"No—" Lisa managed to croak before her jaw was abruptly teeked shut.

"Grack!" Axel muttered viciously. "What do we do with her?"

"We first of all don't panic," Omega said coldly. "Hold her arms, legs, and head really still; I'm going to check for hidden mikes."

Lisa tried to protest, but her mouth was still being held closed. Footsteps approached; and then Omega's hands were moving firmly over her body, kneading the material of her clothing and feeling the skin beneath it. She squeezed her eyes shut, every muscle painfully tense . . . and finally it was over. "She's clean," Omega told the others, relief evident in his tone. "Maybe she wasn't working with Tirrell, after all."

"We going to let her go, then?" Weylin asked.

"Of course not," Axel put in impatiently. "You think she wouldn't go straight to the police now?"

"But we can't *keep* her here—"

"Peace," Omega interrupted, his voice under control again. "Axel, how many of your people are here tonight?"

"Fifteen or twenty, I think."

"Go and get four of them. No, wait—tell Weylin their names and where they're sleeping and let him bring them."

"All right." Axel rattled off some names and instructions that were incomprehensible to Lisa. "And don't wake up anyone else," he added.

"Right," Weylin said. The teekay grip on Lisa eased some, and there was the sound of a door opening and closing.

"What *are* we going to do with her?" Axel asked.

"Leave her here, of course," Omega said. From the sounds behind her Lisa guessed he was picking up the books and papers she'd thrown at Weylin earlier. "You don't think we're going to take her with us to look for Jarvis, do you? She'll be suitably restrained, of course."

"You know where Jarvis is?"

"Close enough to make it worth trying. Anyway, we have no choice—Weylin's blown his cover and the police'll undoubtedly be making a push now to find him first. We'll leave here at first light—that should only be a couple of hours away now."

"Why not leave as soon as she's taken care of?" Axel suggested. "That area's a good two-hour flight away, and we can fly it just as easily in the dark."

"So you *were* listening at the door," Omega said coolly. "That's not a very polite thing to do, you know." There was a short, brittle silence before Omega continued. "We leave at first light because I want all of the regular kids out of here before we leave, and we never send them back to their hives in the dark. That's a lesson you should learn: breaking familiar patterns draws attention, and that kind of attention is always unwelcome. And we want the regular kids out first to make sure none of them accidentally stumbles across Lisa on their way out. I don't want to find this place swarming with police when we get back."

"Oh," Axel mumbled. "I hadn't thought of that."

"That's lesson number two for the day: leave the thinking to me. You haven't had enough practice at it."

Taking a careful breath, Lisa gingerly tested the teekay grip holding her face to the wall. If Axel's attention wavered even a little, she might be able to turn her head far enough to teek off the light. If she could then get out the door—knocking it flat if necessary—and out of the tabernacle, it should be dark enough outside for her to get away. . . .

She was still probing for an opening when Weylin returned with the other preteens.

They took her outside the tabernacle and up the side of the mountain towering above. At Omega's direction Axel flew into the gaping hole that was the temple site; and a few minutes later he led the group to a small, cavelike hollow the workers had left in one of the sides. Omega pronounced it satisfactory . . . and as Lisa stood motionless within the space, pinned by two of the preteens with a flashlight, the others maneuvered a huge slab of rock into place over the opening. The light momentarily showed a five-centimeter gap between the stone and the roof of her prison. Then it was turned off. The murmur of voices faded into silence, and she was alone.

Drawing a shuddering breath, Lisa clenched her hands into painfully tight fists. "I'm *not* going to cry," she said aloud, mainly to relieve the silence hissing in her ears. Carefully—the rock surrounding her was jagged enough to cut—she felt every centimeter of the cave. She found nothing useful. With the full force of her teekay on it, the slab blocking the entrance would not budge so much as a millimeter, though she tried again and again. Once, she thought she had the answer when she discovered a layer of small stones directly beneath the huge rock. But after a solid half hour of teeking out as many as she could touch, the slab merely settled a few millimeters and, if anything, ended up leaning even more securely over the opening.

Finally, with a weary sigh, she gave up. Sitting down carefully, she closed her eyes, only then realizing how utterly fatigued nineteen hours without sleep had left her. *And I trusted him*, she thought bitterly, wishing she'd listened to Sheelah's doubts. *He used me, got me in trouble with the police, and might even—*

She swallowed. She'd never thought much about death before; certainly never really considered the possibility of dying before she became an adult. Now, it suddenly seemed likely that she would never even see sunlight again. The urge to scream for help bubbled up into her throat, and it was all she could do to choke it back down. *Not yet*, she told herself firmly. *Omega wouldn't have put you anywhere someone could hear you. Save your strength; someone's got to come by sooner or later. One of the kids who's been working here, maybe even the police.* She smiled painfully at the thought of how hard she'd been trying to *escape* from the police a bare four hours earlier.

But one way or another, no one was likely to find her for at least several hours. Stretching out as much as she could in the cramped space, she pillowed her head on her left arm. If anyone came by while she was sleeping, she would just be out of luck. . . . Groaning with the exertion, she sat up again and, maneuvering cautiously in the dark, wriggled out of her pants and underwear. The pants went back on; the panties she dangled outside her prison, anchoring one end securely to the top of the rock slab. It wasn't much of a signal, she knew, but it was better than nothing. And with fatigue dragging at her like a downdraft, it was the best she could do.

Stretching out again, she was asleep within half a minute.

"Sorry, Stan," Tonio said tiredly, drifting onto the bare rock outcrop where the detective was standing. "I can't find any trace of him anywhere."

"Damn," Tirrell muttered, gazing out at the dimly lit mountains, rising like frozen ocean waves around them. To have come so close . . .

"I can try again, if you want," the preteen offered. "Unless Jarvis is growing trees on his roof the cabin's got to be visible from *some* angle."

Tirrell shook his head. "Not worth it, especially now that the moon's gone. But we know he went down somewhere in this valley, and unless he spotted us they're not likely to move before dawn. Which is—" he consulted his watch—"all of two hours or so away now. Let's sit tight and get a little sleep, and we can pick up the search in the morning."

"Well . . . okay." Tonio paused. "Maybe I should go and get some help, though. I could probably get to Plat City and back before it gets light. Unless you're still worried about Jarvis getting tipped off."

"Actually, at this point I'd love to have some help," Tirrell admitted. "Unfortunately—no offense—I'm not at all sure you could find this place again if you left now. Maybe when it's light we can risk that, but not now. Besides which, if you feel like I do, you need sleep more than flying time right now."

"There's that," Tonio sighed. "Okay. Shouldn't one of us watch in case they try to leave or something?"

"Probably," Tirrell conceded. "No rest for the righteous, for a change."

"Come again?"

"Skip it. Move back a ways into that thicket of trees where you won't be spotted and get some sleep. I'll wake you in an hour or so."

Tonio nodded and moved off, and after a moment the sound of rustling leaves was replaced by silence. Moving with the stiffness of overabused muscles, Tirrell carefully seated himself on the ground. Pulling his knees to his chest, he wrapped his arms around them and settled down to watch.

Chapter 22

Tirrell had always been a sound sleeper, especially when overtired; but the hand shaking his shoulders was anything but gentle, and within seconds the colorful dream he'd been having faded and was replaced by Tonio's blurry face. "Wha—?"

"Shh!" the righthand hissed. "You'd better come take a look at this."

Tirrell nodded and rolled onto his stomach, mindful of the dead leaves beneath him. Pushing himself up on his knees, he noted the starlight had been replaced by the stronger glow of early dawn. The highest peaks around them blazed with sunlight, though the deepest parts of the valley were still dark.

From high overhead came the faint sound of laughing voices.

The last remnant of sleep was gone in an instant. Getting to his feet, Tirrell moved to the edge of their concealing thicket and cautiously looked up. At least a dozen kids were visible, fanning out in twos and threes as they flew across the lightening sky in generally northward directions.

"What the *hell?*" Tirrell whispered.

"Agreed," Tonio, at his side, whispered back. "They came from over there." He pointed, and with perfect timing another trickle of figures rose into the sky from the eastern side of a tall mountain several kilometers due south. Tirrell listened closely as they passed overhead, and while the words were unintelligible, the tone was clearly lighthearted and untroubled— not the sort of tone the detective would normally expect from a kidnapper's accomplices.

"This makes no sense at all," Tirrell growled, fatigue putting irritation into his voice. "Have we stumbled onto some hive's weekend outing or something?"

"Hive outings don't break up at five in the morning," Tonio pointed out. "And I haven't seen any of the adults that should have been with them, either."

"Right," Tirrell said, annoyed he hadn't thought of those points himself. "Well . . . have you seen anyone who looks like Lisa Duncan?"

"Uh-uh," the preteen said positively. "I've been watching for both her and Weylin and haven't seen either of them."

More kids were streaming upward now, and Tirrell looked at each carefully as they flew past. No Lisa or Weylin in this bunch, either. "This has *got* to be some kind of coincidence, Stan," Tonio shook his head. "Jarvis can't be mixed up with this many kids and preteens. Weylin must be somewhere else in the valley."

"Maybe," Tirrell said slowly. "On the other hand, he *did* offer us a group of kids to help search for Jarvis. I think it would be worthwhile to ease over there and see just where it is everyone's coming from."

"Okay." Tonio paused. "Wait a second; here comes another group."

More figures were indeed rising into the air . . . but as Tirrell watched them something cold began tracing a path up his spine. This was no loose-knit bunch of kids who had simply happened to leave at the same time. They were staying together, almost flying in formation, without a trace of chatter that Tirrell could hear. Staying just above treetop height, they shot swiftly past, heading northwest.

"Stan!" Tonio whispered. "There's an *adult* with them!"

"I saw him," Tirrell nodded. Buoyed up by two of the kids, his outfit some sort of woodsman's garb, the

man had looked nothing at all like a prophet; but
Tirrell had no doubt he was the Omega in Lisa's
note. And he was most definitely *not* Matthew Jarvis.
"Weylin's there too."

"Yeah. But I didn't see Lisa."

"Me neither." Tirrell looked back toward the mountain, the coldness on his backbone seeping into his
stomach. "Let's get down there right away, Tonio.
And the hell with secrecy—I've got a bad feeling that
everyone who was supposed to leave has already
done so."

Tonio understood. "Grack," he said, very softly, as
he held out his hand.

A second later they were hurtling southward.

The huge tent set up at the mountain's base was
impossible to miss—and probably the last thing Tirrell
would have expected to find. "What *is* this place?"
Tonio whispered as they stood just inside the entrance, looking at the gaudy furnishings.

"The Prophet Omega's headquarters, I'd imagine,"
the detective whispered back, keeping a firm grip on
his feelings. Even recognizing that the place had probably been deliberately designed to manipulate emotions, he couldn't help but feel a touch of awe. To an
inexperienced kid, the effect must have been well-
nigh overwhelming. *No wonder Omega's suckered in
such a large following*, he thought grimly. *What the
hell is he* doing *with them, though?* "Let's do a fast
search," he said aloud to his righthand. "Don't dis-
turb anything too noticeably, but check every place a
preteen could be locked up."

The tent, though large, had only a few rooms, and
it took them only a handful of minutes to go through
it. "Now what?" Tonio asked when they were finished.

"I think," Tirrell said quietly, "we'd better start
looking for a grave."

Tonio sighed. "You don't think he would have left
her tied up somewhere outside?"

Tirrell shrugged. "Maybe, but tying kids up so that
they can't get free isn't easy to do. You can't really

gag them, for starters, and he almost certainly would have needed to keep her quiet. I'd bet my pension the kids who left first this morning weren't involved with Lisa or whatever else Omega's got cooking."

"Maybe that's why Omega's group left last, so that a couple of them could sit on Lisa and make sure she couldn't call for help until the others were gone."

Tirrell thought that over. Probably nothing but wishful thinking. If Lisa wasn't thoroughly on Omega's side, keeping her alive was more dangerous than profitable—but on the other hand there was no special reason to burst Tonio's hopes out of hand. At this point looking for a body, a freshly dug grave, or a prisoner would be essentially equivalent. "You might be right," he told the preteen. "Okay. We'll do a fast search, starting at the tent here and moving outward."

They spent the better part of an hour flying slowly through the trees, and while they located several other places Omega's kids apparently used in their activities, there was no clue anywhere as to Lisa's location or fate. For Tirrell, the hardest part of the search was watching Tonio's almost desperate optimism slowly ground down as their chances of finding her alive diminished. The righthand's reaction to what Jarvis might be doing with Colin had shown up the soft spot in Tonio's character, and his concern now for Lisa merely emphasized it. *Just one more righthand,* Tirrell predicted privately, *who'll leave the force after his year and never come back.*

"I guess you were right," Tonio admitted at last. "We're not going to find her, are we?"

"I don't think so," Tirrell shook his head. "Look, this isn't getting us anywhere. Why don't we figure out how to get back here again, and then get over to Plat City and put out an alarm on Omega. We can send a complete shakedown squad back here to ... finish things. Okay?"

"Sure." Tonio nodded tiredly.

"And we're both in need of food and sleep, anyway." Shading his eyes, Tirrell peered upward. "Before we go, though, I'd like to take a quick look at that gash up there. It doesn't look like any kind of natural formation I've ever heard of, and if it's erosion it's an awfully strange pattern."

"Why bother with it now?" Tonio grumbled.

"Because it would be nice to know if the shakedown squad should keep on the lookout for a sudden rock slide," Tirrell explained, holding on tightly to his temper. Matching grouches with Tonio wouldn't do them any good. "It'll just take a minute, and then we'll be off."

Sighing, Tonio held out his hand.

But the gash turned out to be even more interesting than Tirrell had expected. "Holy hive fruit," Tonio said as they hovered at its entrance, his depression momentarily superseded by astonishment. "It's a *cave.*"

"Sure looks like one," Tirrell agreed. "And manmade at that—that floor is far too level to have been formed naturally. Let's go in, take a look around."

Even with the sun now peeking over the eastern mountains, the angle of the cave was such that the deepest third was still in shadow. Tonio brought them down near the middle of the lighted part, and Tirrell immediately squatted down to examine the floor and the loose stones littering it.

"You suppose Omega's kids dug this?" Tonio asked, drifting to one side and gingerly touching the wall.

"*Somebody's* kids dug it," the detective said. "There aren't any marks a digging machine would have left, and even so it would've taken kids to get one this high up a mountain."

"Shh!" Tonio said abruptly. "I heard something!"

Tirrell froze in place, listening. A faint sound—a voice?—came to his ears. Catching Tonio's eye, he pointed toward the darkened section of the cave. The righthand nodded and flew to a spot on the wall just inside the shadow, where he'd have at least a little cover and yet be ready to help. Flicking on his flashlight, Tirrell started forward, moving carefully on the loose gravel underfoot as he tried to pick out the direction the sound had come from.

He needn't have bothered. The first pass with the light caught the white panties hanging across the pinkish stone, and seconds later he was close enough to see a narrow horizontal gap two meters above the floor. "Hello?" he called. "Who's there?"

"Lisa Duncan," the voice came through the gap. "Who are *you?*"

"Detective First Tirrell. Are you all right?"

"Yes, I'm fine." Seldom before had Tirrell heard such palpable relief in a voice. "But I can't get out!"

"Relax," Tonio said from Tirrell's shoulder. "I'll give you a hand."

"Forget it," Tirrell told him. "That slab must weigh five tons—probably took four or five preteens to put it there."

"But we can't just *leave* her there!"

"We're not going to." Tirrell ran his fingers carefully over the jagged rock. "This thing seems to be mostly quartz, and quartz shatters like glass if you hit it hard enough. I want you to scare up a few good-sized chunks to throw at it. Not too big; you'll want to be able to teek them to a good speed in the distance you'll have."

"Right." Tonio vanished with a whoosh.

"Lisa? Did you hear all that?" the detective called.

"Yes. What can I do to help?"

"Get as far back from the stone as you can and curl up with your back to it. Most of the chunks should bounce back out here, but some might go inward and there's no point in you getting cut."

The operation went flawlessly. Standing well back, where he would both be out of the way and able to illuminate the whole target range with his flashlight, Tirrell watched as Tonio blasted the door of Lisa's prison with a succession of melon-sized pieces of quartz. The righthand's heart was clearly in his work, and it took only a few blows before a dozen hairline cracks could be seen radiating from the impact point. The next three blows gouged out progressively larger showers of the glassy shards; and with the fourth, the top third of the stone abruptly broke off and crashed resoundingly to the floor.

The trapped girl was through the opening in an instant, landing in front of Tirrell with a shuddering sigh. "Thank you," she said, shifting her gaze to include Tonio as the righthand flew over. Taking another deep breath, she looked back at Tirrell. "I'm under arrest, aren't I?" she asked.

"For the moment, let's just say you shouldn't try to leave us," the detective said, running his eyes over her in search of injuries. "Are you all right?"

She nodded. "They didn't hurt me, unless you count scaring me to death in that hole. But I don't know what he had planned for when he got back."

Tirrell's shoulder blades tightened up. There'd been at least fifteen kids flying off with Omega earlier—more than enough to make mincemeat of two preteens and an adult. "Any idea when that'll be? Where were they going?"

"They were going to the Barona-Rand road to look for that kidnapped boy, Colin Brimmer." She dropped her eyes. "I'm sorry; if I'd known what kind of person he was, I wouldn't have helped him."

"But what does this Omega want with Colin?" Tonio asked, sounding puzzled.

"I don't know anymore," Lisa said. "He's lied about so much I don't know what's true anymore. His name's not even Omega; I saw a picture of him with the name Yerik Martel at the—"

"*Yerik Martel?*" Tirrell snapped.

The girl flinched. "Y-yes. I think it was him—"

"Damn, damn, *damn,*" the detective whispered, staring through the back of the cave. Suddenly all the odd pieces of the puzzle that had never quite fit were falling into place . . . and the emerging picture wasn't a pretty one.

Lisa was still watching him apprehensively when he brought his eyes back to focus. "Relax," he told her, managing a smile. "I'm not mad at you. I was just startled to find out Martel was involved here."

He looked at his righthand. "Does that answer your question, Tonio?"

The other was frowning. "Martel's that fagin who got away from you once, isn't he? He must be awfully hard-up if he's going to all this trouble for one kid."

"I doubt if he gives half a bill for Colin," the detective said shortly. "For the time being he's switched specialties. Weylin's told him our theory of what Jarvis is really doing out there, and *that's* what he's after."

"Oh, grack." Tonio's mouth was a tight line. "That's just terrific. Well, at least he doesn't know any better where to start looking than we do. I guess that's something."

"Sir?" Lisa spoke up hesitantly. "I'm sorry, but . . . I think I may have told him something you don't know. I—well, I saw Dr. Jarvis and Colin driving from Barona toward Rand one night last June, and I . . . I told Om—I mean Martel—that."

"What day in June was that?" Tirrell asked.

"The fifteenth."

Tirrell nodded grimly. "That's it, all right. Listen, Lisa, we can't let Martel get to Jarvis before we do—I can't explain, but it's vitally important. Can you take us to the spot where you saw him?"

"I think so. If it'll be faster, I could show you the spot on a map, if we can find one down in the tabernacle."

Tirrell had forgotten she could probably read maps. "As a matter of fact . . ." he said, digging into his pocket and glancing around. "Let's get into the light."

Moving back into the sunlit part of the cave, the detective spread his by-now crumpled map onto the gravelly floor. Squatting down beside him, Lisa touched a spot some sixty-five to seventy kilometers west of Barona. "It was about here, I think," she said. "I also told him about these two spots—I saw them marked in your book." She pointed to two of the rockmud areas straddling the road further on toward Rand.

Tirrell felt his stomach tighten. If Lisa's placement

of the meeting was correct, there were less than a dozen areas left where Jarvis could be . . . and Martel had two of them. "Damn. We've got to get after him right away."

"Wait a second," Lisa said, teeking the map back down as he started to refold it. "I didn't remember when I was talking to Martel—I saw Dr. Jarvis's car turn off the road to the right just after I left him."

"You did?" Frowning, Tirrell peered at the map again. The nearest road marked was at least a kilometer from the place Lisa had indicated. Either her estimate was off or Jarvis had taken something more informal then a real road. Either way—"I guess you're going to have to show us the actual place, after all." He studied her face, noting the fatigue there. "You feel up to it?"

"Sure," she said, straightening her back a bit.

"Good." Tirrell folded up the map and stood up. "There was a well-stocked pantry in the big tent; we'll grab some food and head straight out, if you don't mind eating while we fly."

Both preteens nodded. "We still going to stop by Plat City and report this place to them?" Tonio asked.

"I don't think so," Tirrell said slowly. "I'm beginning to think it's almost certain that Martel's suborned one or more righthands there like he did Weylin, and I'd rather not tip them off that we've found his base."

"Why is it certain? Because Plat City's closer than Barona?"

"No. Because of this." Tirrell waved his hand to encompass the huge cave.

Lisa glanced up. "This? But this is just where he's going to build his Temple of Truth."

"Temple of Truth, eh? I should have figured Martel to come up with something cute. I suppose he has his followers dump the rocks a good distance away; say, by a river somewhere?"

Lisa blinked. "There *is* a river in the valley where the rocks are taken. How did you know?"

"Because the rocks are what he's really after here— the rocks and the free labor to dig them out." Tirrell gestured. "My guess is that he's taken a couple million bills worth of gold out of here already, and the vein's probably got at least that much still in it."

"*Gold?*" Tonio looked stunned. "You said it was *quartz.*"

"Most of it is," Tirrell nodded. "But if you look at the walls closely you can see bits of gold glittering there. How Martel stumbled on a vein this rich I don't know, but the point is that unless he takes the gold down the far side of the Tessellate Mountains, he has to run it through the assay office in either Plat City or Rand, and he's too cautious not to have installed at least one listening ear in each city's police department. That's how he got away from us in Ridge Harbor, and he's not likely to change a winning system." He glanced at his watch. "We'd better get moving—Martel's already a good hour and a half ahead of us, and even if he starts with the wrong areas he's got fifteen or more airborne searchers to our one."

"Our *two,*" Lisa corrected, her voice quiet but determined.

"Forget it," Tirrell told her. "As soon as you've shown us where Jarvis turned off the main road, you're going to go to Barona and turn yourself in to the police as a material witness."

"But I want to help you," she said. "I mean, this whole mess is my fault. Again." Her eyes were glistening with moisture, and Tirrell sensed she was fighting back tears. "I got a friend in trouble who was just doing something I asked him to—and now I've made things bad for you in trying to help him." She turned half away, biting her lip.

Tirrell gazed at her, wondering briefly how things might have been different if the various officials had just told her the plain truth instead of dropping ominous hints about Daryl's fate. "Well . . . first things first. You get us to Jarvis's turnoff and then we'll see."

She took a deep breath and nodded. "Thank you."

"But just for the record," he continued, "your friend

Daryl's not really in all that much trouble. He's actually only been transferred to a school in Cavendish, where he won't be able to continue your lessons."

Lisa's mouth fell open as a flurry of emotions struggled for supremacy across her face. "You're sure?"

"That's what Gavra Norward told me, and I expect she should know. You're not supposed to be told, but I think we've got enough to worry about at the moment, and I'd just as soon get Daryl out of our way."

"I—thank you." She took a deep breath. "I guess it was kind of silly, but I was really *worried* about him."

"I know. Just don't borrow any more books from him, and don't turn me in when this is all over." Tirrell turned to Tonio and held out his hand. "Well, don't just stand there—let's go."

Chapter 23

Flying at a brisk but less than eye-gouging speed, it took them nearly two hours to reach the part of the road Lisa had pointed out; after that they drifted above the trees at much slower speed for several minutes as Lisa searched in silence for the exact spot. Tirrell, having spent much of their flying time imagining what Martel would do with whatever discovery Jarvis had come up with, was almost literally aching with the desire for immediate action. But he managed to keep his mouth shut and let Lisa proceed at her own pace—and within fifteen minutes his patience was rewarded as she suddenly swooped downward.

"This is it," she called decisively, paralleling the road at a height of about three meters. "Here's where I flew next to him; he stopped about *here* and we talked; and then he went around this curve. Then—" she pulled up again, losing Tirrell and Tonio for a half second before the righthand matched her maneuver—"I started to head home, looked . . ." She hovered for a moment, then pointed. "He turned off and I saw his lights go through *there.*"

"Great." Tirrell fixed the view in his memory. "Let's head down and take a look."

There was no real road anywhere near the place Lisa had indicated, but it took only minutes to confirm that the grassy lane cutting between the trees led all the way back to the main road, and that it was both wide enough and firm enough to handle moderately heavy vehicles. "I think," Tirrell said with satisfaction, "that we've got him. Let's go. And watch out for a path leading off a little to the east—we've still got to hit a rockmud patch before we reach his cabin, and the most likely spots on the map are still east of us."

Flying low, they set off between the trees. Lisa fell into formation beside them, and for a long moment Tirrell debated silently the wisdom of letting her come along. Still, it shouldn't really be dangerous if they got there before Martel showed up; and the girl was clearly determined to help; and, actually, an extra preteen really *would* be handy to have along.

His rationalization complete, Tirrell put the question out of his mind and settled down to the task at hand.

Colin was playing in the living room and Jarvis had just finished clearing the dishes from their mid-morning brunch when the knock came on the door. "Dr. Jarvis?" a muffled voice called. "This is the police. Open up, please."

For a long instant Jarvis stood frozen in place. Somehow, he'd expected them to come in a midnight or dawn raid, when the detectors he'd set up around the cabin might have given him some warning. But he always turned them off when Colin was likely to go out . . . and now he had only seconds before they charged in and carted him, Colin, and all of his papers away. Too little time to do anything with the papers—far too little to set off the smoke bombs hidden around the cabin's periphery. But if he could buy a bit more time . . .

Three silent steps took him into the living room where Colin, his cat's-cradle frame sitting ignored in front of him, was looking questioningly toward the door. "Shh!" the scientist whispered, putting a finger across his lips. "Get up onto the couch. Quickly."

Clearly picking up Jarvis's tension, the boy obeyed

at once, and was huddling wide-eyed at one end when Jarvis reached him. "Miribel," the scientist said; and as Colin's eyes rolled up and closed, Jarvis picked up the limp body and shifted it into a prone position. He'd never left the boy in hypnotic sleep for more than half an hour at a time, but past experience with such things suggested it would be several hours before Colin got hungry enough or uncomfortable enough to come out of it on his own. With luck, that might give Jarvis enough time to do what he had to.

He was out of the living room and nearly to the door when it suddenly emitted the crack of breaking wood and swung inward with a crash.

The blurry figure that shot in through the opening actually flew past him before it could react to his presence, and he glanced back just as the boy braked to a midair halt. The adult charging in on foot, of course, had no such problem. "Dr. Jarvis?" he asked with the tone of one who already knows the answer.

"Yes. I *was* coming, you know," he added, eyeing the damaged door.

The other's expression remained cold. "Dr. Jarvis, I'm Detective First Stanford Tirrell, Ridge Harbor Police. We'd like to search your cabin."

"Of course," Jarvis said calmly. "I can save you the trouble, though: Colin's asleep on the living room couch."

A flicker of surprise touched the detective's face— surprise, probably, at such a straightforward admission. "Show us," he ordered.

"Certainly." Turning, Jarvis retraced his steps and, with the righthand hovering watchfully at his shoulder, led the way back to the living room.

"Tonio, watch him," Tirrell said. Stepping to the couch, he gazed at the sleeping boy's face for a moment. "Colin?" he said tentatively. "Wake up, Colin."

"I'm afraid that won't do any good, Detective," Jarvis told him. "He's going to be asleep for the next few hours—a side effect of some medicine I've been giving him. And he mustn't be moved until he awakens, either."

Tirrell favored him with a long, speculative look. "Colin?" he said, louder this time. "Colin!"

There was, predictably, no response. Gingerly, the detective reached down and touched a forefinger to the base of Colin's neck. After a moment he straightened. "And why can't he be moved?" he demanded.

"The drug couples strongly with the inner-ear balance system and several delicate brain structures," Jarvis said, frowning slightly. By now the rest of the police should surely have moved in . . . if there *were* any more police. Could Tirrell possibly have come alone? That was almost too much to hope for. "Shifting his position, even with teekay, could be dangerous."

"How dangerous?"

"I don't know. I didn't think it worth experimenting with," he said dryly.

Tirrell grimaced. "Yeah. All right, we can afford to wait. Maybe." He stepped to the window and gestured. Jarvis waited tensely; but the only person who came through the front door was a slender preteen girl.

"Is he all right?" she asked, ignoring Jarvis completely as she flew into the room.

"I think so," Tirrell told her. "But apparently we're not going to be able to move him for a few hours. I want you to stay with me and help keep an eye on Jarvis here while Tonio watches out for Martel and his gang. Tonio, find some place where you'll be out of sight but have a good view of the area. If you see anyone at all, get down here fast and let me know. Got it?"

"Right," the boy said and disappeared.

Jarvis eyed the girl, who was in turn watching him with a mixture of distaste and curiosity. "Is Ridge Harbor using girls as righthands now?" he asked.

Tirrell shook his head. "Lisa just came along to act as a guide."

The girl's face suddenly clicked. "You're the one who stopped me on my way here last June, aren't you?" Jarvis said, nodding. "What did you do, Detective, send my picture around to all the hives in the area?"

"As it happens, Lisa recognized your picture at the police station." Tirrell glanced around the room. "Where's your radiophone?"

"I'm afraid it's out of order," Jarvis said, almost too quickly.

Tirrell gave him a long look. "How very convenient. Show it to me; maybe I can fix it."

Jarvis glanced once at Colin's limp form, lying there beneath the seascape painting Miribel had given him so long ago. "All right," he said. "But I don't think it'll do any good."

He led the way into the study and pointed out the phone. "Thank you," Tirrell said. "Please sit over there against the wall. Lisa, watch him closely."

Jarvis did as he was told. "Tell me," he said as Tirrell got to work on the phone casing with a pocket screwdriver, "just how widespread is knowledge of my . . . involvement with Colin's kidnapping?"

Tirrell frowned up at him briefly. "Not very. Your poster identified you only as a material witness. Why?"

Jarvis shrugged. "The smaller the number of people who know what I'm doing out here, the better my chances of convincing everyone that it should be kept secret, at least for now."

"So you'd like to keep all this a secret, would you," Tirrell said. "We'd take Colin back to Ridge Harbor and you'd settle back in at the university, career and reputation intact, um?"

"My career and reputation are completely unimportant. Colin—and what may be happening inside him—is just the opposite. We might be on the brink of the most drastic change in Tigrin society since the teekay ability first appeared."

Tirrell snorted. "Impressive words—especially coming from a man who kidnapped his own son to do his experiments on. You'll forgive me if I remain unconvinced."

"His *son?*" Lisa looked startled. *"Colin?"*

"Yes," Jarvis nodded. "Detective Tirrell was just

guessing, of course, but there's no reason now to deny it." He looked back at Tirrell. "Would you care to know just why I chose Colin?"

"Because you knew his birthday, I'd imagine."

"A minor point only. Mainly, it was because I knew he'd have a good chance of handling what I might be doing to him. I knew my own temperament and physical stamina and those of his mother Miribel, so his genetic background is good; and, more importantly, I knew the reputation of the Brimmers, who'd been given custody of him. I knew they would give him solid moral and ethical training. I don't know if that'll be enough. I hope so."

Tirrell looked up from the workings of the phone, where he'd been testing for loose wires. "What *have* you done to him?" he asked quietly.

Jarvis smiled tightly. "I've possibly made him the most important man on Tigris."

"How?"

This was it. The detective was listening; and if Jarvis could convince him of the need for secrecy there might still be a way to work out a deal. If not . . . "I'd be happy to. But perhaps Lisa should wait somewhere out of earshot for the rest of this discussion—outside the window there, for instance, where she could still watch me."

Tirrell held the scientist's eyes a moment longer before turning to look first at the window and then at Lisa. "I don't think that'll be necessary," he said. "She can stay and listen."

Jarvis hadn't expected that. "Detective, as I said before, the fewer that know anything about this, the better. Lisa is only a kid—"

"She's almost a teen," Tirrell interrupted. "And she's demonstrated an ability to keep secrets reasonably well. Besides, I don't especially trust your motives in wanting her outside."

Jarvis looked at Lisa, thoughts tangled with indecision. Even a single hint of this dropped into a hive would start rumors traveling like a firestorm, with effects potentially as devastating. But if he didn't talk now, his next chance would be at an official police interrogation . . . and more than rumors would spread from that. Lisa, he decided at last, was probably the lesser of the two risks. "All right," he sighed. "There is, I think, a reasonably good possibility that Colin will pass the first stages of puberty without undergoing Transition—and if he gets that far he'll have a fifty-fifty chance of keeping his teekay well into adulthood."

Lisa gasped. "You can stop Transition from coming?"

He shook his head. "Possibly . . . but not the way you're hoping. If the method works at all, the treatments will have to be started very young. There's nothing I can do for you; the metabolic changes that would be needed would be far too drastic to be safe. I'm sorry."

"What sort of changes are involved?" Tirrell asked.

Jarvis looked at him, glad for an excuse to turn away from Lisa's disappointment. "For the time being that has to remain my secret," he said.

"So you can make all the money from the process?"

"I'm not going to make a bill on this," Jarvis growled, annoyed at the other's attitude. "If you'd bother to think about it for ten seconds, you'd realize what a potential bombshell a discovery like this is. Handled wrong, it could literally drive Tigris into another Lost Generation situation."

"I realize what a mess this is a damn sight better than you might think," Tirrell retorted icily. "Why the hell do you think I kept your role as quiet as I could, otherwise?" He leveled a finger. "And if you're really worried about the effect on society, why'd you start the project in the first place? You could have thrown away your notes and that would've been the end of it."

Jarvis shook his head. "Because we *need* this, Detective—it's the only way to get back to a stable society. Besides, scientific knowledge can never be buried for very long. If *I* can find the right approach, sooner or later someone else will hit it, too . . . and that someone might not want to let all of Tigris in on it. He might keep it for his own use, or at least play politics with it."

Lisa inhaled sharply. Tirrell looked up at her, his own face rigid. "Yeah," he said to her. "He would, wouldn't he?" Looking back at the disassembled phone, he seemed to come to a decision. "All right, Doctor, you've made your point. You're getting out of here right now, along with all your notes and any of the chemicals you used. Lisa and Tonio will take you to Barona and send more police back to wait with me until Colin can travel."

A cold knot rose into Jarvis's throat. Was the discussion going to be closed, just like that? "Detective—to let more people know about this—certainly before the results are even in—will just cause panic and—"

"Doctor, I'd rather broadcast your story all over Tigris than let a certain person get at you—and that man is right now combing this area. There are police units standing by ready to move in, but if we can't call them the only other thing to do is risk flying you out of here ourselves."

"So why can't you and the kids handle him?" Jarvis frowned, his stomach tightening as the detective's sense of urgency began to seep into him. Tirrell clearly wasn't stupid—and he clearly understood the implications of hauling Jarvis and his notes into a police station, where any chance to keep this quiet would be gone forever. If Tirrell was *that* worried about this guy—

"Because he's a fagin, and his preteen entourage outnumbers us by about seven to one," the detective growled. "Come on, get your stuff together."

Jarvis stood up and made a fast decision. "All right, but you and Colin can come, too. He's just in a hypnotic sleep—I only gave you the other story so you'd stay long enough to hear me out."

"You *what?* Damn it all, Jarvis—All right. Lisa, watch him and make sure he doesn't destroy anything while I go and whistle down Tonio."

He'd taken two steps toward the study door and

Jarvis was reaching for the first of his notebooks when a short, barklike shout drifted in from outside ... and, simultaneously, all the windows abruptly blew outward.

Chapter 24

Jarvis's automatic reaction was to jerk back from the flying glass; but he'd barely turned away from the windows when his body froze in place, as if caught in an invisible, infinitely soft vise. Lisa, in his line of sight, thrashed like a hooked fish for a few seconds more before her body, too, went rigid. Turning his head a few degrees, he could see Tirrell's stiff form balanced precariously halfway to the door.

"Everybody just relax," a youthful voice said from behind Jarvis. "Prophet!" he shouted. "We've got 'em!"

The shout was answered by footsteps; and a moment later a middle-aged man strode into the study, accompanied by two more preteen boys. "Good morning," he said with mock politeness, his eyes flicking across the others and coming to rest on Jarvis. "Doctor, it's a pleasure to meet you."

"I'm sure all the pleasure's yours," Jarvis said coldly. "Who are you, and how dare you break into a private residence?"

The man's smile didn't even flicker. "You may call me the Prophet Omega," he said. "My goal is Truth—and I understand you have a bit of truth I would like to have."

Jarvis felt his blood turn to ice water. "I don't know what you're talking about."

"Of course not," Omega said, still smiling. "I'm

sure you'll figure it out shortly." His eyes swept the room briefly. "Where's the boy?"

"In the living room," Jarvis told him, his brain starting to work again. "But don't touch him—he could die if he's moved."

A slight frown creased the other's forehead. "Why?"

"It's a side effect of the drug I've been giving him," Jarvis explained. "It puts him into a deep sleep and makes his brain extremely susceptible to position changes for several hours."

Omega studied his face for a long moment in silence. Then he stepped back outside the study and looked into the living room. "Watch the boy—make sure he doesn't move," he instructed someone there. "Axel, go see if the righthand confirms that."

One of the boys nodded and flew out the door. "What have you done with Tonio?" Tirrell asked, his tone one of barely controlled fury.

"Oh, we just sneaked up on him from under the trees," Omega said, waving nonchalantly. "He was a bit faster than we expected, actually, but as we were already in position, his warning was a waste of time. He's unhurt, if that's what you're worried about."

"Well, if you want to remain the same, you'd better take your mob and disappear," the detective snapped. "This place is going to be crawling with police inside of half an hour."

Omega looked pointedly at the disassembled phone and shook his head. "Admirable try, Detective, but I doubt seriously we're in any danger at all of being disturbed. Your histrionic anger isn't going to panic us into running until we're good and ready."

"How'd you find this place?" Tirrell asked coldly. The fury was gone from his voice, and Jarvis realized suddenly it *had* been an act, apparently designed to lend credence to the "slip" of telling the other that reinforcements were on the way.

"Oh, it was simplicity itself." Omega stepped over to the desk and began leafing idly through the top notebook. "You see, Tirrell, as usual you made all the

wrong assumptions and wound up one step behind
me. You hear from Lisa that I've taken off and you
immediately jump to the conclusion that the kids I
took with me were the only forces I had. It never
even occurred to you that I might have more in
Rand, Barona, and Plat City, and that I might send
messengers en route to go get them . . . and so naturally you never bothered to look over your shoulder
while Lisa pointed out the turnoff to you. But thank
you—you three saved all of us a lot of work."

Tirrell said nothing . . . but Jarvis felt the first glim-
mering of hope. He knew little about fagins or other
criminals, but he'd long since discovered that people
who couldn't resist explaining how clever they'd been
tended to underestimate everyone else—a weakness
he might just be able to exploit. . . . A moment later
Axel was back. "The righthand says the same thing,"
he reported. "The kid'll die if we move him."

Omega nodded. "I see. Well . . . no matter." He
walked back from the desk to again face Jarvis. "Well,
Doctor, shall we collect all of your notes and be on
our way?"

"You can just go take a flying leap at yourself,"
Jarvis said evenly, a defiant set to his jaw. "I'm not
going with you, and if you think I'm going to just
hand over my work, you're totally crazy."

Omega sighed. "Don't waste my time," he said,
gesturing toward the clutter on Jarvis's desk. "If necessary we can take everything in this place that isn't
nailed down and sort through it at our leisure."

"Only if you've got degrees in biochemistry, endo-
crinology, and cellular physiology—*and* can read the
chicken scratches I use for handwriting," Jarvis retorted. "Besides which, you don't even know what
you're looking for."

"I've got a pretty good idea," Omega said calmly.
But his expression was growing increasingly un-
friendly. "And the simple fact that you're resisting so
strongly indicates your discovery is indeed a valuable one. So let me put it another way." His gaze
switched to Lisa and Tirrell. "If you don't cooperate

in getting your materials together, your two friends here will suffer."

Someone behind Jarvis muttered uneasily, the sound cut off by a sharp look from Omega. Jarvis's own mouth felt dry. "You're bluffing," he said weakly.

Omega's eyes bored into his. "Must I demonstrate?"

Jarvis dropped his eyes, letting the defiance in his face crumble. "You can have my notes, but I won't help you any more than that."

Omega smiled scornfully. "Of course. All right, collect everything together and put them in a file or something for transport." He gestured.

The teekay grip holding Jarvis vanished abruptly, and he almost fell before his leg muscles were able to react. "I want some guarantee first that you won't harm the others," he told Omega.

Omega spread his hands. "I can give you my word, certainly, but I'm afraid you'll just have to trust me on that. But as long as I have your discovery I have no reason to harm anyone."

His voice was quiet, sincere. Jarvis glanced at Lisa and Tirrell—the latter's eyes shifting left and right in an obvious *no!* signal—and then nodded heavily. "All right."

Stepping back to his desk, with a watchful preteen at each shoulder, the scientist began piling together his notebooks and files. When he was finished he reached under the desk and pulled out a portable file box. Setting it on the desk chair, he unfastened the catch and swung the lid back. Carefully, he began to stack the papers at one end, hoping no one would notice that, unlike standard file boxes, this one was completely glass-lined. A moment later he was finished; and setting in a spring-loaded brace rod to hold everything in place, he started to close the lid.

"Now put in all the drugs you've been using," Omega said. "Wrap the bottles carefully, of course."

Jarvis hesitated, making sure none of his grim satisfaction showed on his face. As long as Omega had the notes the drugs themselves were unnecessary, but Jarvis had banked on his being greedy. Letting his shoulders slump a bit more, he stepped to his work table and unlocked its deep drawer. From it he drew four vials of brown fluid, one each containing milky white and pale pink substances, and two large glass-stoppered Erlenmeyer flasks filled to the necks with a clear liquid. Taking everything back to the desk, he wrapped each piece of glassware in strips of material that looked like nothing so much as long, thin sandbags wrapped in tissue paper. Omega, fortunately, didn't wonder why he had such convenient packing material on hand, at least not out loud. Each piece, once wrapped, went into the file box with the notebooks. When they were all in place, he stuffed more of the flexible strips between them, until they were wedged tightly together. Under cover of that activity, he made sure the stoppers of both flasks were loose. Finally, he closed the lid and fastened the catch. "All right," he said, picking up the box and turning to face Omega again. "This is—"

And without warning he flipped the box upside down onto the floor.

Omega's bellow and movement were simultaneous. Crossing the floor in two long strides, he snatched up the box and turned it over. With nimble fingers he pried open the catch and threw back the lid—and barely got out of the way of the waist-high flames that roared up from the opening.

Omega shrieked a blasphemy as pandemonium erupted in the room, but Jarvis paid no attention to the noise and fury. For the moment, at least, every eye was on the fire . . . and he and the others were free.

He got just a glimpse of Lisa as she shot past him and out one of the broken windows; an instant later a hand closed hard on his wrist and Tirrell half led, half hauled him out of the study.

"Wait! What about Colin?" Jarvis whispered as Tirrell skidded to a halt by the cabin door and threw a quick glance outside. Jarvis couldn't see anyone, but from the flurry of shouts it was obvious Lisa had been spotted.

"For now, we leave him," Tirrell whispered back. "It's more important we get *you* out of here while Lisa's got their attention. If I can, I'll come back and get him." He looked outside again. "Okay, *go!*"

Tirrell's shove in the middle of his back ended any chance for argument. With a fast prayer for Colin's safety, Jarvis headed for the densest part of the woods as fast as his legs would take him. It would have been nice to snatch up one of the hidden smoke bombs on the way, but there were none in his immediate path and he didn't dare squander the few seconds he might have by trying to get to one. He'd do better to just concentrate on getting to the dead conetree half a kilometer away where he'd cached the survival gear he'd expected he and Colin would eventually need to use.

The trees were five meters away now, and he could hear Tirrell's pounding footsteps behind him ... three meters away ... two ...

And his rear leg snapped painfully backward as the ground it had been pushing against abruptly vanished from beneath him. Simultaneously, the leg was yanked high above his waist, and with a thud that knocked most of the air out of him he slammed chest-first into the ground.

The stars of his landing had barely cleared when Tirrell landed hard beside him.

The preteen who'd thrown them let them lie gasping for a minute before teeking them up and returning them to the cabin. The study was still in an uproar, though, and they were kept out of the way near the outer door until things quieted down. By the time Omega sent for them, Jarvis's breathing was almost back to normal.

The study was a mess. Water from the frantic fire-fighting efforts lay puddled in various places on the floor, and the air was heavy with a foul stench. Tipped onto its side in the middle of the room, the file box's glass lining was black with soot, the vials and flasks inside barely visible amid the ashes.

"By all rights, Doctor, I should have you killed for that stunt."

Jarvis turned his attention to Omega. "You're probably right," he said coolly, ignoring the tightness in his stomach. His plan had worked, and the expected consequences now had to be faced. "Why don't you go ahead and do it? If your followers are willing to kill for you, that is."

For a long moment Omega said nothing, his singed hair and bright red forehead framing an expression that was nothing short of murderous. Slowly, the fury faded, to be replaced by something merely bitter. "I underestimated you," he acknowledged at last, his voice almost calm. "How did you do that, anyway?"

"Sulfuric acid in the flasks, a mixture of potassium chlorate and sugar wrapped in tissue paper as the packing material," Jarvis told him. "The reaction is extremely exothermic, and when you opened the lid the rush of oxygen caused all the paper to spontaneously ignite. I'd had the stuff ready to use ever since I realized the police were onto me," he added, glancing at Tirrell. "If I'd had a little more warning of Detective Tirrell's visit, I'd have had everything in the box, ready to go."

"I suppose the drugs that were in there were also destroyed?"

Jarvis nodded. "Very much so. Complex organic molecules fall apart easily in that kind of heat."

A movement outside caught Jarvis's attention, and he turned as three kids escorted a rigid-limbed Lisa through the window. "Well!" Omega said, turning as the girl was teeked to the floor. "At least we made a clean sweep. You have any trouble, Case?"

The boy addressed swallowed visibly. "Not too much with her, sir . . . but the righthand got away."

"He *what?*" Omega's satisfaction vanished.

"We couldn't help it, sir—when she flew out the window everyone looked, and he just shook off the hands on him and took off." The words were coming in a rush as the boy tried to vindicate himself. "We tried to catch him, but when we looked back he teeked a bunch of branches right in our faces . . . and by then *she* was loose again, so we had to chase both of them, and . . ." He shrugged helplessly. "Adom and the others are still looking for him, but I don't think they even know where he is anymore."

Tirrell snorted derisively. "Where he is, is halfway to civilization and a police force big enough to mop up your little group in five minutes. If you don't want a genuine battle on your hands, you'd better take your junior goons and get the hell out of here."

"Shut up, Tirrell," Omega said thoughtfully. "Doctor, you've left me no choice. You're going to have to come with us. Now."

"Prophet, if you want I'll take a couple of the others and go look for the righthand," Axel offered. "He can't have gotten *that* far."

"It's not worth it," Omega told him. "Why don't you go get the knapsack from where we left it and bring it here."

"Knapsack?" Jarvis asked carefully as Axel left the room. There had been something new in Omega's voice, something he didn't at all care for.

"I told you I wasn't going to hurt anyone, and I intend to keep my word," Omega said. "I'm going to leave everyone else here, suitably restrained, to wait for the police Tirrell claims will soon be coming."

Jarvis looked at the other's burned face and for a moment dared to hope . . . but with the next heartbeat he knew it couldn't be. Omega couldn't afford to leave Tirrell alive—despite his earlier sneering, it was clear that the detective had been hanging on his tail long enough and successfully enough to be a real danger. And if Tirrell was slated for death, then so was everyone in the cabin . . . including Colin.

It was the darkest, most painful decision Jarvis had ever had to face, and the fact that he'd known from the minute of Omega's arrival that it was coming made it no easier. To confess his lie about Colin's sleep would probably save the boy's life . . . but for what? What would Omega do with him wherever they were going? At the very least, he would surely try to bend Colin's loyalty toward himself, so as to be ready in the event that Jarvis's technique succeeded. Brought up by such a creature, what sort of life could Colin look forward to?

Or to put the question another way, what were the chances Colin could be rescued from the cabin or rescued from Omega's hideaway? Both, he suspected, were vanishingly small.

And then the ghost of an idea brushed across his mind. If Tirrell was truly insightful—and maybe a bit telepathic . . .

Omega's voice cut into his thoughts. "When will it be safe to move the child?"

Jarvis remembered to consult his watch before answering. "Not for two or three hours yet," he lied, knowing that with those words he was now committed. "Unless you want to wait, he'll have to stay here, too."

Omega's eyes bored into his. "Any particular reason he would be necessary to further experiments?"

Jarvis shook his head. "Any kid his age or a year or two older would do just as well. He's had several treatments, but given you'll have to wait until the subject reaches puberty to find out whether it worked anyway, two months isn't really significant."

Omega seemed taken aback. "Puberty? Why can't you tell before that?"

"Because there's no way to know if the small metabolic changes are going to have the desired effect. This is new territory; there aren't any theoretical curves to check experimental results against."

"I see." Omega looked over as Axel came in teeking a heavy-looking knapsack in front of him. "We'll discuss this later. Axel, we'll be tying up Tirrell in this room and putting Lisa in the living room; I want one of the kitchen chairs in each place."

Axel frowned as he let the knapsack drift gently to the floor. "Lisa too? I thought you were going to take her with us."

"That was before she fell in with bad company."

Omega turned to Lisa, still standing rigid in her guards' teekay grip. "I had fine plans for you, Lisa— literate preteens are not exactly common, you know, and you could have been of immense use to me. I'd had hopes of persuading you—with hypnotic drugs, perhaps—to be more compliant. But frankly, right now you're not worth that much trouble to me."

Jarvis looked at Lisa in surprise. *Literate?* No—surely Omega was lying; literacy was still restricted to those past Transition. But Lisa's expression held no surprise at Omega's words, only a sullen anger. And if she could indeed read ... Jarvis's mind shifted into high gear, and for the first time he felt real hope. Maybe—with a properly phrased clue—he could vastly improve the odds he was leaving Tirrell with.

The kitchen chair arrived and Omega set to work.

It was a long-established axiom of Tigrin society— and the basis of the hive system—that a kid could only be controlled or immobilized by an older and stronger kid. But Omega had clearly done some hard thinking on the problem, and when he'd finished tying Tirrell into his chair, he took Lisa into the living room and proceeded to demonstrate his ingenuity.

His first step was to carefully tie her to the chair Axel had placed in the center of the room, positioning the knots behind her back and making sure none of them touched her skin, where they could conceivably be teeked open. His second step was to place a loose black bag over her head, tightening its drawstring snugly around her neck, and again tying it away from direct physical contact. And his final step—

Jarvis gasped. "Is that *dynamite?*"

"It is," Omega confirmed. Lying down on his back by the chair, he put down the stick of explosive and set to work with brackets and a screwdriver. "Lisa, I want you to listen carefully to me," he said as he worked. "I'm fastening a stick of dynamite to the underside of your chair. The detonator—the thing that sets it off—has its trigger fastened by a rope to the floor beneath the chair. If you try to teek the

chair in any direction you'll blow yourself to bits.
Understand?"

"Yes," Lisa's muffled voice answered. Not surprisingly, she sounded scared.

"Good." Omega finished his work in silence and
got to his feet, checking the knots one last time.
"Well, that should keep you here long enough for us
to get safely away," he said with satisfaction. "Don't
bother trying to break the rope, by the way; it's
mountaineer's line and tests at just over two tons.
Doctor, if you're ready . . . ?"

Jarvis hesitated, stepped forward to touch Lisa's
shoulder. "Lisa . . . I know you and Detective Tirrell
don't think much of me, but please believe that I do
care very much for Colin. I don't know if you can
picture me in the role of a loving parent, but—well, I
just wanted you to know." He turned back to Omega
and nodded. "All right, I guess I'm ready."

"Axel, take the doctor and send him on with the
others—they should head southeast," Omega ordered.
"You and I will go collect anyone who's still looking
for that damn righthand and catch up with them
later."

Axel nodded, and suddenly Jarvis felt the floor fall
away beneath him. *This is it*, he told himself bleakly
as he was threaded skillfully through the doorway.
I've done all I could. It's up to Tirrell and Lisa now.

He wondered if he would ever see any of them
again.

Chapter 25

The faint sounds of conversation and movement faded into silence. Trapped for the second time that day in blindness and solitude, Lisa made no effort to stop the tears rolling freely down her cheeks. Omega's promises hadn't fooled her; she'd already had a sample of his version of truth. This time, she felt certain, she was going to die.

"Lisa?" Tirrell's voice, though muffled by the bag, was nevertheless understandable. "I think they're gone. Are you okay?"

"What difference does it make?" she moaned, her silent sobs doubling in intensity.

"Lisa, pull yourself together!" the detective snapped. "We may still have a chance."

He was only trying to console her, she knew, but nevertheless she sniffed hard and managed to bring herself under some kind of control. "I'm okay now," she told him.

"Good girl. The first thing to do is get you out of whatever they've got over your head. Describe it to me and tell me how it's fastened."

She did the best she could. "I can't see anything at all through it," she finished.

"All right. Now, it's tight around your neck, so you should be able to use teekay on it there. Try teeking it outward in all directions and see if you can break the rope."

She tried; but there was just enough give in the rope to move it off her skin before breaking, and the instant that happened she lost the ability to teek it. "I can't do it," she admitted after several frustrating tries. "It keeps moving *away*."

"All right, don't get excited. Try this: throw your head back suddenly so that the bag is resting against your face. Use the contacts with your forehead and chin—or stick out your tongue—and teek the material at those points in opposite directions. If you can open up even a small tear, it'll be right in front of your eyes and the rest should be easy."

Taking a deep breath, she tried it. It took two tries to get the bag touching forehead and chin solidly enough, and several seconds of careful teeking before the first tiny tear appeared like a lighted jewel just past her nose. But with the edges of the tear visible . . . the sound of the bag shredding was perhaps the most satisfying sound she'd ever heard. "I did it!" she called, blinking in the sudden light.

"Great! Now, look carefully under you and see how that booby-trap line is attached to the floor. *Don't* move the chair in the process."

She didn't need the reminder. Leaning gingerly over as far as the restraining ropes would permit, she looked beneath the chair. "The rope goes through a hole cut in the rug," she said. "Should I tear the rug more and see where it goes?"

"Better not," Tirrell said quickly. "You might nudge the rope, or he might even have set things to go off if the tension decreases."

Lisa swallowed. She'd almost torn the rug without bothering to ask about it. . . . *"Now* what do we do?"

"Take a good look around the room. See if there's anything at all sharp enough to slice your ropes. There's a picture on the wall, isn't there?" he asked suddenly.

"Y-yes," Lisa said, frowning at the question. "It's a picture of the ocean."

"Teek it over to you and search it for a hidden

knife or sharp edges. Hurry—I don't know how much time we've got."

"But why should there be anything like that on a picture?" Lisa asked, teeking the painting off its nail and bringing it to her.

"Remember Jarvis's last words to you? It seemed to me he went out of his way to use the word 'picture' —'picture me in the role of a parent,' or something like that. I think he might have been trying to tell us something."

"But there's nothing here," she told him, turning the picture over for the fifth time. "Just a normal picture in a wood frame. There's some writing on the back, but it doesn't say anything that'll help."

"Damn." There was a long pause. "All right, then there's just one thing left to try. Remember—just before Martel's gang broke in—Jarvis said that Colin wasn't drugged but only in a hypnotic sleep? We're going to have to try and bring him out of it. He's not tied up or anything, is he?"

"No . . . but if he's slept through all the noise that everyone's been making in here, how are we going to wake him?"

"Ideally, you'd use the key phrase that he's been told to respond to. In this case . . . the only other way I know of is to make the subject so uncomfortable that he wakes up on his own. You're going to have to hurt him a little, I'm afraid."

Lisa's stomach knotted up. "I can't do that. He's just a little kid!"

"If you don't, he's going to die with the rest of us," Tirrell snapped. "Just use teekay to squeeze his arms or chest a little—see if that'll do it."

Timidly, Lisa tried it. "It's not working," she said a moment later.

"Lisa, you're going to have to grit your teeth and bear down. Martel isn't going to just leave us here—we know too much about both him and Jarvis's work. If he's not coming back to kill us personally, he'll have set something up to do it automatically, probably with more of his dynamite."

"Isn't there some other way?" Lisa pleaded. "Douse him with water or something?"

"If you can get to any supply of water go ahead and try it. Otherwise—" Tirrell broke off suddenly. "Damn! What am I using for brains? Lisa—you said there was writing on the back of that picture? Read it out loud."

Lisa teeked the painting back up. " 'To my darling Matt,' " she read laboriously, fighting her way through the flowing handwriting. " 'From Miribel. Christmas, three-oh-one.' That's all there is."

"Any response from Colin?"

Lisa peered over the picture at the boy's face, looking in vain for some indication of life. "I don't see any," she said, feeling panic rising up her throat. "He's still just lying there."

"Hold on; let me think." For a moment there was silence from the other room. Lisa looked desperately around the room again, searching for *anything* she could use to cut her ropes. The windows, their glass knocked outside and out of reach by the other pre-teens, seemed to mock her with their useless offer of escape; the trees beyond seemed almost part of another world. Turning back to Colin, she clenched her jaw, fear making her decision for her. If hurting an innocent boy was what was necessary to survive, then that was what she would do.

"Ha!" Tirrell said suddenly. " 'The role of a loving *parent'*—of course! *Miribel Oriana!*"

And on the couch Colin stirred and opened his eyes.

"Colin!" Lisa all but shrieked in her relief. "Come here—quickly."

The boy jerked at her voice, and as he focused on her his eyes went wide and he scrambled up into a sitting position. "Who are you?" he asked fearfully.

Lisa swallowed her panic-fueled impatience and resisted the urge to teek him directly over to her. Instead, she forced a reassuring smile onto her face. "My name's Lisa," she said, using the soothing tone that had calmed so many nervous Fives back at the hive. "Don't be afraid—I won't hurt you. But I need your help. Would you go to the kitchen and get me a sharp knife, please? And hurry."

Colin's eyes were still troubled, but he nevertheless nodded and slid off the couch. Just outside the doorway he paused, looking into the study. "Matthew?" he asked, taking a step in that direction.

"No, Colin," Tirrell's voice came. "My name's Stanford. Matthew's been taken away by some bad men—please hurry and get that knife for Lisa so we can go after them."

Colin turned and ran, and a second later there was the clatter of a drawer's being wrenched open. He had barely reappeared in the doorway when Lisa, her patience finally breaking, teeked away the butcher knife he was carrying and brought it flashing across the room to her.

"Don't bother with your hands—just get free of the chair and get us all out of here," Tirrell called, a note of urgency creeping into his voice.

Lisa nodded, too absorbed in her control of the knife to remember he couldn't see the gesture. A few seconds later she was floating gingerly free of the chair, taking care that her tied hands didn't catch anywhere. Turning, she shot toward the doorway where Colin was still standing, an astonished look on his face. "Wow!" he breathed—and yelped as Lisa teeked him into the air in front of her. Barely pausing at the doorway, she snatched Tirrell, chair and all, and made for the cabin door. A second later they were out in the bright midday sunshine, whipping between the trees as Lisa ignored Colin's yelps of alarm and excitement in an attempt to get distance as quickly as possible. Finally, about a kilometer away, Tirrell pronounced them safe and Lisa brought them down with a deep sigh of relief.

She had the detective's ropes untied, and he was working on hers, when the cabin blew up with a roar behind them.

* * *

There was very little left when they returned cautiously to the small clearing. Obeying Tirrell's instructions, Lisa waited with Colin among the trees as the detective walked around the blackened rubble, stamping out small fires and stopping every so often to examine something on the ground.

"Nothing worth salvaging," he said when he returned. He seemed about to say something else but glanced at Colin and apparently changed his mind. "Lisa," he said instead, "go up to the top of this tree and see if you can spot anyone."

She was up and down in less than a minute. "No one," she told Tirrell. "I don't see Tonio and the police you said he was bringing, either."

"I wonder . . ." Putting a finger in his mouth, the detective gave a piercing whistle. "Tonio might have gone to ground instead of heading for help right away. If he did, that should bring him." Dropping down on one knee, he smiled at Colin. "Didn't get a chance to ask you before, Colin, but how are you doing?"

"Fine," the boy said with the grave politeness Lisa had often seen kids adopt in the presence of a hive authority.

"Have you been all right out here these past couple of months?"

"Uh-huh," the boy nodded enthusiastically. "It's the best vacation I ever took. Why did the bad men take Matthew away?"

"Well . . ." Tirrell scooped the boy up and got to his feet. "I'm sure we'll get him back real soon. Until then, how would you like to visit a *real* police station? Hm?"

"Okay, I guess," Colin shrugged. "I like the woods better."

"You'll be able to come back to the woods again sometime," the detective promised. "But for now we have to go."

"We going to take him back to Barona?" Lisa asked.

"No choice," Tirrell told her grimly. "We've got to raise the alarm and get on Martel's trail immediately, before he buries himself and Jarvis in some deep hole on the far side of the Tessellates."

"But won't a lot of righthands in the sky alert him?"

"Maybe, if he sees them. But we have to risk it. All we know for sure is that they left here traveling southeast, and that direction could have changed drastically after he rejoined the main group."

"Stan?"

The voice drifting down from the treetops made Lisa jump; but before she could locate its source Tirrell had whistled again, and with a crackle of conetree branches Tonio landed beside them.

"Boy, am I glad to see you," he exclaimed, giving the detective an unashamed hug. "I heard the explosion and was trying to sneak back to see what happened. I thought maybe you'd been blown to bits."

"Almost, but thanks to Lisa and Colin we got out before the timer ran down," Tirrell told him. "We can now add an attempted murder charge to Martel's list when we nail him. You didn't happen to check out the direction his gang was headed, did you?"

" 'Fraid not—I was afraid to poke my head more than half a meter off the ground." Tonio frowned as he glanced around. "Say, where's Jarvis? Didn't he get out with you?"

"No. The shoe, as they say, is on the other foot." Tirrell waved southeast. "*He's* now been kidnapped by Martel."

Tonio snorted. "Serves him right," he said; but to Lisa his voice lacked real conviction. "I suppose we've got to get him out, though."

"Yeah—and we're going to have to call in some help to find them."

"Maybe they just went back to the temple site," Lisa suggested.

Tirrell shook his head. "No. It's clear that most of his kids aren't in on this with him, and that makes the temple site too public a place to keep Jarvis. Besides, he left under the impression that Tonio was already on his way with reinforcements, so he wouldn't go anywhere that Tonio knew about. However—" He paused, a thoughtful frown beginning to crease his face. "He *doesn't* know we're on to what the temple site really is—and he'll need to have a refinery somewhere where he can separate out his gold."

"You think he might go there?" Tonio asked.

"It's worth checking on. Lisa, we're going to need more of your help, I'm afraid. We're going to fly over to Plat City and drop Colin off at the police station there. Then we'll get some detailed maps of the region and I'll want you to show us exactly where the dump site is. With luck, Tonio and I may be able to find Martel's refinery on our own and determine whether or not he's there."

"What if he is?" Lisa objected. "He'll probably have kids on guard, and if he catches you, you'll be in the same situation we just got out of."

Strangely enough, Tirrell smiled. "Not really," he said. "I think I know how to even the odds a little. Let's get going—we can talk more on the way."

Chapter 26

The dump site was in a grassy valley three or four kilometers from the temple site, an unexceptional place with a handful of trees, a narrow yet surprisingly gentle river, and two or three barren hills poking through the scrubweed. It was only as Lisa guided them to one of the latter that Tirrell could see it was in actuality an immense pile of broken stone.

"They dug all this stuff out of that mountain?" Tonio asked, eyeing the rocks with obvious amazement.

"This isn't half of what they've actually mined," Tirrell told him. "Loose rock always looks bigger than the hole it came out of." Sliding his backpack onto the ground, the detective found a relatively flat slab at the edge of the pile and unfolded the small-scale survey map he'd obtained from the Plat City police. "They've probably been quietly hauling the stuff away, most likely during weekdays when all the kids are at work. Probably leaving this much here on purpose so no one'll realize any of it's missing."

Fiddling with one of the smaller stones, Tonio flew over to land at his side. "You figured out where we are?"

"I think so." Tirrell was actually somewhat more certain than that, having followed their course on the map all the way from Plat City. "We're on the southern edge of the De Sable Plateau, next to the main branch

239

of the Rashoni River. Flows generally south, then goes southwest down the far side of the mountains and off my map."

"Is that why the water's moving so slowly?" Lisa asked. "Because we're on a flat area?"

"Basically. The size and number of tributaries and the channel dimensions are important, too, but you basically can't have anything this slow in mountains except on a plateau."

"Makes it nice and easy to anchor their boat while they load up, doesn't it?" Tonio commented. He teeked his stone hard into the side of the heap, causing a minor rock slide. "Well, what are we waiting for? Let's head on down and find him."

Tirrell was already folding up his map when something in his righthand's voice—overconfidence?—made him pause. *Let's head on down and find him.* It was a perfectly reasonable and obvious statement . . . but this was *Martel* they were dealing with, and Martel had stayed free this long precisely because he worked hard at avoiding the obvious. Still, shipping the ore via water was the simplest and cheapest method available. Why bother teeking the stuff to the riverside if all he wanted was to leave a false clue before carting it away overland again?

Unless . . .

Unfolding the map again, Tirrell studied it closely. Yes . . . yes; it *was* possible. And right or wrong, it wouldn't take long to check out.

"Stan?" Tonio asked impatiently. "We going or not?"

"We're going," the detective answered slowly. "But we're going to start by heading *up*stream. The current's slow enough that even a heavy boat shouldn't have any trouble fighting it, at least for a few kilometers."

"You think he's set up a refinery way up here in the mountains?" Lisa asked, looking puzzled. "Wouldn't that have been the hard way to do it?"

"No, to both questions," Tirrell told her, taking one last look at the map before folding it to show only the region immediately upriver of them. "What I'm thinking might be crazy, or it might be brilliant—and I won't know which until we check it out on the actual terrain."

"Well, let's do it then," Tonio said. "Don't worry, Lisa," he added to the other preteen. "He gets these brilliant hunches all the time. You just have to learn to put up with them."

Tirrell smiled, and a small tight place in his stomach relaxed for the first time in hours. The resurgence of Tonio's sense of humor was a good sign, an indication that the righthand was finally catching up with the emotional shocks and stresses that had been pummeling him all day. To capture Martel at the cost of damage to Tonio's personality was not a trade he would've liked having to make. "So skip the noise and give me a lift," he said, scooping up his backpack with one hand and holding out the other. "You can explain to Lisa on the way that my hunches usually come out right."

They found it a bare kilometer upriver—not the refinery, but the clue that Tirrell, despite his outward confidence, had only half expected to find.

"What are they?" Lisa asked as they hovered over the grooves cut into the narrow band of moist ground separating the riverbank from the harder rock beyond.

"Tread marks," Tirrell told her. "Almost certainly those of a heavy amphibious vehicle."

"This doesn't make any sense," Tonio complained, squinting in the direction the tread marks pointed. "There's nothing but rock over there. No trees, no possibility of a decent cave—how's he going to hide a refinery out in the open?"

"Let's go see, shall we?" Tirrell said.

"But they'll *see* us," Lisa objected, looking around nervously.

"Don't worry; Martel's still kilometers away," Tirrell assured her. "Let's go—you'll understand in about a hundred meters."

The two preteens exchanged glances. Then Tonio

shrugged and they were airborne again, flying low. The ground swelled up into a low rise, and they topped it to find—

Another river.

"Are you going to tell us," Tonio demanded as they landed, "that Martel carts his rocks up one river and across dry land just to ship 'em down *another* river? Why?"

"I am indeed," Tirrell nodded. "And the *why* is twofold: first, because this river—a tributary of the Nordau, according to the map—winds up going down the other side of the mountains, which means that at the cost of relatively little trouble he's managed to point any pursuers in exactly the wrong direction. And secondly—"

"Stan!" Lisa exclaimed suddenly. "There's an old metal refinery where the river leaves the mountains!"

Tirrell nodded. "Right. It hasn't been used in probably twenty years or more—not since the mines southeast of Plat City were played out—but it wouldn't take much to get one of the crushers and a cyanidation tank or two back in operation. I'll lay ten to one odds that's where he's holding Jarvis."

"Yeah—with thirty or forty kids to help him," Tonio muttered.

"No, he doesn't have nearly that many," Tirrell told him. "Remember back to the cabin. Even though he left the temple site with fifteen kids and picked up reinforcements on the way, he hit us with only eight or nine—and recall that Weylin wasn't among them. I suspect that those eight or nine have been trusted with the full story of what Martel's planning with Jarvis and are cooperating less on blind faith than on the more tangible promise of sharing in whatever wealth and power Martel hopes to get. Kids like Weylin who have even a scrap of faith left in them would have done fine at beating the woods for Jarvis, but Martel would have had to cut them out of anything past that. They're probably still hunting through the woods east of Rand right now."

"But Weylin was willing to attack a policeman for

him," Lisa pointed out. "He had to be pretty loyal to do that."

"Breaking laws in the name of religion and seeing your leader break them are two very different things; and that's an even stronger indication that Martel's not taking any chances at all with his group. So he's probably only got those same eight or nine kids with him. The other side of that, of course, is that trying to talk them into mutinying would be essentially useless. We're just going to have to hit them hard and fast, without any call for surrender to alert them."

"That doesn't sound very ... pleasant," Lisa said hesitantly.

"It probably won't be," Tirrell acknowledged. "But with luck you won't have to be there. We're going to head down to the refinery first of all and try to confirm that Martel's there. If we can, Tonio and I will put the place under surveillance while you sneak away and whistle us up some backup forces. Probably from Nordau; it'll be faster than going back to Plat City." He glanced up at the midafternoon sun, already perilously close to the highest mountain peaks. "And we'd better get moving—I want to get things rolling as soon as possible."

Because—he didn't add—if the reinforcements didn't arrive before dark, he and Tonio might just wind up taking on the whole place by themselves.

And that *definitely* didn't sound very pleasant.

"You'll have to excuse the accommodations, Doctor," Martel said with exaggerated politeness as the two adults walked toward the middle of the huge, high-ceilinged room, leaving the small group of preteens to close the door behind them. "But I'm afraid we really weren't set up for visitors here."

Jarvis passed up the scathing reply that came to mind and instead took a good look around. The room was indeed huge, taking up probably an entire third of the building, and was, in addition, stiflingly hot. Thick-paned, wire-reinforced windows covered three of the four walls, presenting a somewhat dust-filtered view of the mountains to the south and east and the river flowing by the building to the west. The floor space was dominated by what appeared to be a furnace and two large tanks, each liberally wrapped up in catwalks, conveyors, control and power lines, and tens of meters of heavy pipe. Other catwalks and stairways crossed to what appeared to be a glass-walled control room stuck above the windows on the south wall. Other smaller pieces of equipment were laid out in a seemingly random pattern, connected to each other and the tanks by more piping. A handful of troughs cut into the concrete floor—emergency drains—were covered with gratings which, flush as they were against the floor, fortunately presented no additional hazard to travel. Jarvis mentally fixed the locations of everything as best he could and looked back at Martel. "What is this place, anyway?" he asked, though he was pretty sure he knew.

"Oh, sort of a business sideline of mine," the other said airily. "Axel—I want four of your boys outside to watch for company," he called, his voice echoing in the huge space. "One on each side of the building."

Axel seemed to stare at Martel an unusually long time before nodding and turning back to the other eight kids hovering near him. Inaudible words were exchanged, and four boys detached themselves from the group and disappeared back out the door. The other four dispersed to the windows, which they proceeded to unlatch and teek open. Watching their curious glances around the room, Jarvis concluded that it was their first visit to the refinery, which meant they weren't any more familiar with the layout than he was. Offhand, he couldn't think of any way that could help him.

Axel flew over and settled down beside Jarvis and Martel. "Now what?" he asked with more than a little truculence. "We can't stay here very long—we're not that far from the temple site, and that's the first place the police will look."

"We'll be safe enough, at least until dark," Martel

said. "At that point we can fly over the mountains to a secluded place I know of."

"And then what? Back at the cabin he said it would take years to figure out if his stuff even worked. You going to sit out there and eat conetree pods that whole time?"

"We won't have any trouble with supplies." Martel was gazing thoughtfully at his preteen aide. "I can keep my business contacts in Rand and elsewhere, and in the next room is the means to finance any purchases we'll need to make through them. We'll be perfectly comfortable out there, I assure you."

"Glad to hear it. And who exactly are you going to find to experiment on?"

"I thought we'd adopt Dr. Jarvis's method, seeing as how it's already worked so well. You and your preteens will simply kidnap some four- or five-year-olds, we'll use whatever trickery the doctor used to keep them from panicking, and that will be that."

"You sure he's going to help us, huh?"

Martel glanced at Jarvis; his frown deepened as he returned it to Axel. "He'll mix up the drugs for us, under the threat of very painful consequences if they don't work."

Jarvis snorted. "You're going to chain me to my bed for ten years, are you? That should be interesting."

"Actually, I have something more sophisticated in mind," Martel said, his eyes still on Axel. "If there are no further questions—"

"There are," the preteen interrupted. "I want to know who these business friends of yours are, where your hideout is, and how you intend to force anything out of him. We're in as deep as you are, Omega, and it's time we got in on more of the planning."

For a long moment Martel simply gazed at the boy . . . and when he finally spoke his words were edged with steel splinters. "You're a slow learner, Axel; did you know that? A slow learner and a glutton for head punches. I told you once today already that you weren't practiced enough at thinking to take over that job from me—and so you've naturally decided you want to take over that and everything else."

"No, I didn't mean—" Axel began, his insistent manner evaporating abruptly.

"Just how far do you think you'd get?" Martel cut him off brusquely. "Even if I was stupid enough to answer all your questions, how many would you forget to ask until you'd disposed of me? How would you go about recruiting new kids when you all hit Transition in a year or so, for instance? Hm? What would you do to persuade the doctor to cooperate if he suddenly decided to be stubborn? How would you even know what chemicals he was using, since you can't even read the damn labels? He could sprinkle poison in your soup and you'd never know it."

Axel threw a glance in Jarvis's direction and swallowed visibly. "I ... All right." He took a deep breath. "All right, then; but if we can't do without you, you can't do without us, either."

"Who ever suggested I intended to?" Martel asked. "You have the strength, I have the knowledge and brains. The arrangement's worked well for Tigris for two hundred years; there's no reason it should fall apart now, is there?"

"But what about Transition?" the boy blurted.

"What about it?" Martel countered smoothly. "I'll need people I can train to act as priests among the kids once we get things going again. The message of Truth isn't dead, you know, just reorganizing. I suspect we're soon going to have more power on this planet than anyone since the Lost Generation."

Axel nodded, his eyes shining, and Jarvis could practically see the boy's embryonic thoughts of rebellion vanish under the weight of Martel's dazzling promises. "He's lying, you know," the scientist spoke up, wishing now he hadn't waited so long to do so. But he still might not be too late. "He doesn't need any priests to share his power. Once you lose your teekay, he'll get rid of you without a second thought."

If the words sank in at all, they did so without

leaving a trace. Axel gave him a cool look and turned
back to Martel. "What should we do next?" he asked.

"Go and check on the lookouts; make sure they're
well concealed," the other said promptly, his busi-
nesslike manner stating the matter was closed. "Then
go through the door over there and check on how
much packaged food we've got. In the room next to
that there should be some small boxes—count the
sealed ones and let me know how many there are."

"Right." He turned toward Jarvis. "What about
him?"

"I'll watch him. Just make sure one of your kids is
always in the room with us."

"Okay." Axel flew across the room and vanished
through the outside door.

"I hope that'll dissuade you from further attempts
to turn my kids against me," Martel said, facing
Jarvis. "They have the loyalty of extreme self-interest:
greed plus the knowledge that I'm the only one who
can protect them from the police."

"Must be an interesting form of greed, given you
don't even know what my project is," Jarvis retorted.
"Or is it your stockpile of gold they're interested in?"

Martel's smile vanished. "How did you know about
the gold?" he demanded, his voice deadly. "Did Tirrell
tell you?"

"Don't be silly." Jarvis waved at a collection of flat
plastic bottles on the floor next to one of the huge
tanks, bottles whose big *NaCN* markings were clearly
visible. "What else would you be doing in an old
refinery with sodium cyanide? Especially when you're
packing the result in small boxes. What'd you do, kill
some mine owner near here and steal his ore?"

"As it happens, I came upon it honestly," the other
said. "Not that it matters. And as to the details of
your project, that can wait until you're ready to tell
me all about it. I already know it involves the Transition point and is something you're rather desperate
to keep secret. There are limited possibilities, and all
of them would be of great value to me." He shook his
head. "I must say, though, that you don't at all fit the

stereotypical image of the brilliant scientist, who is supposed to be both blind and helpless outside his specialty. You're fast, sharp, and not afraid to take risks. It's been a long time since I've had to deal with someone like you."

"I'm delighted to hear it," Jarvis said. "Especially since you're going to be doing it for at least eight years. Unless you want to gamble I'll give you the right formula the first time, of course."

Martel's smile made a tentative reappearance. "No, I don't really expect such cooperation. But I don't intend to have you breathing down my neck that whole time, either."

"What're you going to do—tie me to a tree with a supply of sandwiches?"

"Something like that. I'm going to have you put yourself into hibernation."

Jarvis felt his jaw drop. "You *what*?"

"You heard me." Martel was back on balance now. "Your hibernation work with Kelby Somerset has been well publicized. We'll set you up with a capsule hidden underground, perhaps, with enough oxygen to keep you alive at your reduced metabolic rate."

It took Jarvis a moment to find his voice. "And if I give myself the wrong drugs?"

"Then you've committed suicide," Omega shrugged. "But then, that option will always be open to you. Fortunately—for me—you're not the suicidal type." He glanced around as a breeze drifted through the sluggish air. The kids, Jarvis saw, had finished with the windows and were standing in a loose group studying the furnace. "I'd better go give my kids something to do," Martel said, pointing Jarvis to a spot along the south wall, well away from both the cyanide bottles and any of the room's doors. "Why don't you go sit down over there. I'll get you some paper and you can start making a list of the drugs and equipment you'll be needing. There's no sense in wasting time, now, is there?"

"None at all," Jarvis agreed. It was, after all, just after three in the afternoon, with perhaps four hours until complete darkness. He had just that much time to find a way to escape.

It took Tirrell and his companions less than half an hour to reach the ridge just upriver of the old refinery; the three-hundred-meter trip from there to the detective's chosen observation point took nearly as long. Tirrell himself was used to such slow advances, but both preteens were visibly fidgeting by the time he ordered a halt.

"Now what?" Lisa asked as they settled to the ground between a bush and a stand of tall grass.

"Keep your voice down," Tirrell whispered, slipping off his backpack and squinting down the gentle slope ahead. The south wall of the refinery was about half a kilometer ahead, just visible through a narrow gap in the underbrush. Rummaging briefly through the pack, he pulled out a pair of lightweight binoculars, a headset, and a small microphone attached to a coil of slender wire. "Ready, Tonio?" he asked, plugging the end of the wire into the headset and setting the coil and mike onto his lap.

Tonio nodded and raised the binoculars to his eyes; and with the barest whisper of disturbed grass the mike headed smoothly down the slope. Tirrell watched it go, trying simultaneously to protect the coil of wire from snags and also watch for signs of a sentry. It would have been nice to use a cordless model, but they couldn't take the chance that Martel might have the equipment available to detect its broadcast. Still, as long as the wire didn't break or alert the lookout by suddenly yanking out a swath of grass they should be all right.

The microphone, its motion alone keeping it visible, was almost to the refinery wall. "Looks like the windows are slanted open a bit," Tirrell murmured to Tonio as he slipped on the headset. "Ease the mike through the bottom of the crack and let it sort of edge inside."

"Right."

A moment later it was done. Flipping his on switch,

Tirrell cautiously turned up the volume . . . and within five seconds knew he'd guessed right. "We got 'em," he announced tightly. "Martel's there, and at least a couple of the kids . . . and they just referred to Jarvis." He slid the headset half off and turned to Lisa. "Okay, Lisa, it's up to you now. Get that note I gave you to the Nordau police; with luck, Plat City'll have their squad ready to move by now. Be sure to take it very slow until you're over the ridge, then keep low until you're well away from the area."

"Okay." Taking a deep breath, she set off uphill, flying bare centimeters off the ground. Within a minute she was lost to view among the undergrowth.

"She'll be okay," Tirrell assured his righthand as the latter continued to gaze after her. "Give me a hand unloading the rest of this stuff, will you?"

It took only a minute to empty the backpack and lay its contents in neat rows in front of them. "What are these things?" Tonio asked, fingering one of the three gogglelike devices.

"They're gas masks," Tirrell told him. "They're to protect us against the stuff in these." He tapped one of the half dozen squat black cylinders. "It's called tear gas—acts sort of like concentrated onions in your eyes."

"Never heard of it," the preteen said, looking rather apprehensively at the cylinders. "I suppose it's supposed to keep kids from using teekay?"

"Or at least to limit it drastically. The stuff's hardly ever used anymore, but it was one of the few weapons that worked against the Lost Generation, and it's a law that every police department has to keep at least a little of it on hand."

Tonio nodded thoughtfully. "Stan . . . you guys don't really trust us, do you? Us kids, I mean."

"Well . . ." Tirrell shrugged uncomfortably. "I suppose there's *some* distrust," he conceded, putting as good a face on it as he could. Certainly most adult tension was below the conscious level, where it hardly qualified as true distrust. "After all, with teekay, kids are a lot stronger physically than adults. You probably felt the same way toward the preteens when you were a Six or Seven. Hm?"

"Not really. I mean, if they picked on us too much the Senior would make them get back in line."

"True enough—but I'm sure you realize now that without the preteens' cooperation the Senior has no real power at all. The kids themselves have to enforce his rules; you see?"

"Huh! You know, I never thought about it like that."

"That's because the hive is set up to keep you from doing so. When you're little the preteens enforce the Senior's orders; and by the time you're a preteen yourself you're so used to obeying the Senior you do so automatically."

Tonio sat quietly for a long minute. "Huh," he said again, softly. "So if most of the preteens at a hive decided to disobey some order, that would be it. The Senior wouldn't be able to stop them."

"No. He'd have to call in the police ... and the result could be pretty bad." Tirrell shook his head. "When you get to school and start learning Tigrin history, you'll realize just how much destruction and chaos the Lost Generation caused. For nearly six years they held absolute power on the planet, and if it hadn't been for the unexpected loss of teekay at Transition the generations growing up behind them would have been just as lawless and just as ignorant ... and we might well have lost every scrap of science and learning we ever brought to Tigris. If adults distrust kids, I suppose it's because the knowledge of what almost happened is still pretty fresh."

Tonio actually shuddered. "And Jarvis's drug," he said, "would take away Transition. Wouldn't it?"

Tirrell turned to look at the refinery, his mouth suddenly dry. Somehow, he'd never looked at it quite that way before. "Yes," he agreed quietly. "It would."

Chapter 27

The last of the sunbeams crawling up the east wall faded and disappeared as the sun dipped below the mountain peaks to the west. It was still a good half hour until official sundown, of course, but Martel nonetheless felt heartened in the relative gloom that now filled the refinery. Darkness always made him feel safer.

A breeze tickled the back of his neck, and he turned as Axel landed beside him. "All set," the boy reported. "Those boxes of yours are awfully heavy, but there are only fifteen of them and we should be able to handle two each. They're lined up just inside the door over there."

"Good. What about the food supplies?"

"All packed and ready to go. Everyone's eaten now except you and Jarvis and the kids outside."

Martel glanced at the blue sky outside. "We might as well pull in the lookouts, I guess. Wherever the police are looking they'll have to quit reasonably soon; it's already getting dark in the valley beneath the temple site. Go call the kids in and let them eat. Jarvis and I'll eat after they finish."

Axel nodded and flew off to collect the outside guards. Martel watched him go, wondering exactly what to do with the boy . . . or, more accurately perhaps, when and how he would do it. That fabrication about priesthoods for the kids wouldn't hold

252

him forever, especially with Jarvis right there to breathe on any sparks of doubt that might arise. Eventually, Martel knew, a showdown was inevitable, and he'd better be prepared to win it damn quickly.

Still, all things were possible to those who planned ahead. In a sealed cabinet two rooms over were several more bottles of sodium cyanide, and it would be simplicity itself to add one to the supplies they would be flying out with. When he and Jarvis went to eat, he would find a way to quietly take care of that little chore.

A motion across the room caught his eye. Jarvis, still sitting against the south wall, was shifting position, apparently trying to angle the pad of paper on his knees to catch as much of the waning light as possible. For a moment Martel frowned, wondering what about the doctor seemed different to him ... and then he smiled as understanding came. Jarvis was a good three meters closer to the east door than he'd been when he first sat down. Still smiling, Martel walked over.

Jarvis got in the first word. "Don't you have any lights in this place?" he asked irritably. "I'm going blind trying to write over here."

"Of course we do," Martel told him. "Run by our own private generator and battery bank, since the service from Nordau seems to have been suspended. However, if we wanted to use the lights, we'd first have to close and curtain the windows, and I'm afraid it's still too hot in here for that."

"If I don't get more light, I'll have to quit working," Jarvis threatened.

"Oh, by all means—you've worked so hard for the past hour and a half that you've earned some time off. Besides—" he smiled pleasantly—"it'll give you the chance to devote all your energy to sidling imperceptibly toward the door."

Some of the starch seemed to go out of the scientist. "Damn you," he muttered.

"Come now, Doctor," Martel chided mildly. "Don't

sound so discouraged. Especially since I know it's all an act, anyway."

For a moment Jarvis's eyes blazed with anger. "You're pretty sure of yourself, aren't you?" he said. "You know everything, understand everybody, and never make a mistake."

"Of course I make mistakes—but seldom any of consequence. And the reason is exactly as you said: I understand people. I don't know what if anything Tirrell told you of my background, but I assure you that I've been a master of psychology far longer than you've been studying hormones."

"Then you must know I'll die rather than give you what you want."

Martel shook his head. "I doubt it. You see, Doctor, all your professional life you've been solving problems that at first glance have looked unsolvable. This is just the latest one in a long string, and habit alone will keep you searching for a way around me for a long time yet. Besides, if you die before the project's complete, you'll never know if the damn thing works, will you?"

Jarvis remained silent, and Martel knew at least one of his shots had hit home. A small victory, but a potentially significant one. If he could convince even a fraction of Jarvis's mind that he, Martel, was unbeatable, he would in effect have gained an ally inside the scientist's own brain. "If you'll forgive me now, I have a few more things to attend to before our departure," he said, glancing out the window at the blue sky. "We'll probably be leaving in about—"

He broke off abruptly as something hard and cold wrenched at his heart. Nestling almost invisibly just inside the window's lower left-hand corner was a tiny black cylinder . . . a cylinder hanging from a thin wire.

A microphone.

He took a deep breath, trying to ignore the nausea of fear and anger bubbling in his throat. "Axel!" he bellowed.

*   *   *

"Damn!" Tirrell snarled, ripping off the headphones as Martel's yell echoed off his eardrums. "We're in for it now, partner."

"They've spotted us?" Tonio asked, sounding a lot calmer than Tirrell felt.

"Just the mike, so far. But that'll give them our general direction if they sight along the wire. See if you can pull the mike back out; if not, better break the wire as far away from us as you can."

The righthand was already peering through his binoculars. "Okay . . . got it. Mike's down in the grass now, but I think I was too late. Someone was pulling from the other side. Do we get out of here or stay put?"

"We stay put," Tirrell said grimly, trying to see through the dust coating the refinery windows. "They'll have to fly straight overhead in order to spot us, and once they're out in the open you'll have a strong tactical advantage. Just watch for flanking maneuvers and don't let anyone get too close. At least that crowd they'd left outside got in before the alarm went off; I guess that's something to be thankful for."

"What happens if they all sneak out the far side of the building?"

"Aside from the fact that they don't know we're alone, it wouldn't do them any good." The detective pointed. "Except where the river cuts through, the ground on the north side slopes up, and there's not a scrap of decent cover anywhere this side of that ridge. Ditto for east and west; they'd have nearly a kilometer to cross before they'd even get to any tall grass. No, they'll try to come this way—and they'll try to eliminate us first. So look sharp."

For several tense minutes nothing happened; and the first attack, contrary to Tirrell's expectations, did not come from high-flying preteens. Instead, one of the windows suddenly opened all the way and a large object shot out, heading straight for them.

Tirrell opened his mouth to yell at Tonio—and bit down hard on his tongue as the projectile sailed cleanly overhead and thudded into the ground a good fifty meters upslope. It had barely landed when a second missile followed it, this one hitting less than twenty meters in front of them and nearly as far to the left.

"Trying to flush us out," Tonio murmured.

"Yeah. Waiting to see which shots come close enough for us to deflect." A third object followed its predecessors. "Tonio—if this one's aimed high, deflect it at the last moment to land as close to us as you can."

"Got it."

Tirrell held his breath. The shot was indeed going to be a solid ten meters long . . . and suddenly it jerked in midair and fell, digging itself half into the ground less than a meter from Tirrell's feet. The detective swallowed painfully; but it *had* been what he wanted. "Nice job," he managed.

"Thanks. Now what?"

"They should be throwing everything loose at the place that one was supposed to hit. Deflect as many as you can in any direction you want—*not* so close this time."

The words were hardly out of his mouth when the open window suddenly erupted with a veritable stream of flying objects. Tirrell ducked involuntarily, but Tonio was equal to the challenge. Directly overhead, the stream broke up, its component elements splashing into a roughly circular pattern centered a dozen meters upslope. Gritting his teeth, hating his own inactivity even while recognizing there was nothing he could do, the detective watched and waited . . . and, as abruptly as it had begun, the barrage ceased.

Beside him, Tonio exhaled loudly. "Whew! I'm glad *that's* over. Or are they just collecting more stuff to throw?"

Tirrell risked taking the time for a quick look at the objects littering the ground around them. Several sections of iron grating, what looked like an ingot mold, a wheel off a cart, a small box. "They're certainly throwing everything that isn't nailed down," he said. "But I suspect that last attempt cleaned out their stockpile, at least for the moment. My guess is that they'll try coming after us personally next—we've pretty well proved this approach doesn't work."

Tirrell's prediction was quickly borne out; but with a twist the detective hadn't expected. Without warning, two kids came shooting out the same window the earlier barrage had come from and headed swiftly toward them. Simultaneously, a third boy took off from the building's east side, a small box clutched in his arms. At breakneck speed he headed for the trees a kilometer away.

"Stop him!" Tirrell snapped, pointing at the fugitive. Their only hope was to keep Martel's group bottled up in the refinery until reinforcements arrived, and if they allowed even one of them to get away, the fagin would keep trying until all of them had made it.

Tonio's response was typical of the righthand's sense of humor. Instead of simply trying to halt the other's dash by brute force, he abruptly teeked hard on the box clutched in the kid's arms. Unable to react fast enough as the box suddenly slowed, the boy slammed into it stomach-first, legs shooting by underneath as he wrapped himself around it with a gasping yelp loud enough for Tirrell to hear a kilometer away. An instant later both he and the box were hurtling backward toward the refinery as all resistance to Tonio's teekay vanished into the boy's all-consuming need to get air back into his lungs. Satisfied his righthand had that part under control, Tirrell shifted his attention skyward.

The other two kids were almost directly overhead, drifting slowly now as their eyes swept the ground. Tonio, sitting right next to a large bush, was temporarily out of their line of sight; but Tirrell was perfectly visible from their position, and he knew he had seconds at the most before they spotted him.

There was only one thing he could think of to try. "Get ready to catch me," he muttered to Tonio. Waiting until the searching eyes above them were looking elsewhere, he scrambled to his feet and ran recklessly down the slope toward the refinery, the teargas grenade he'd scooped up concealed in his left hand.

He hadn't covered more than five meters when his feet found themselves treading air. Looking up, he saw one of the kids coming up behind him at a height of a hundred meters or so. The second, close behind, was glaring at the ground, and Tirrell got the impression that a teekay battle was underway between him and Tonio. Mentally crossing his fingers, Tirrell glanced at the ground, perhaps three meters beneath him now, and waved his empty hand at his captor. "Not so high! Not so high!" he yelled, putting an edge of hysteria into his voice.

The kid responded exactly as Tirrell had hoped he would. Instead of lowering the detective, he did just the opposite, yanking him swiftly upward as a fisherman would reel in a catch. Higher and closer he was teeked ... and as the kid reached out toward him, Tirrell pulled the three-second fuse on his grenade, counted two, and threw it.

He had aimed the device to go off directly between the two kids, but whether or not it actually did so he never found out. The flat *crack* of the compressed tear gas bursting free and the cool wave of moisture that followed immediately afterward caught Tirrell with his head turned aside as far as possible, his eyes squeezed tightly shut with hands protecting both them and his nose. That his plan had indeed succeeded, however, was clear from the strangled gasps above him—and from his sudden, uncontrolled tumble toward the ground.

Falling blind was a far more unnerving experience than Tirrell had expected it to be, but fortunately it didn't last long. A new teekay grip was on him in seconds, pulling him to the side and down; and with a moment's hard deceleration, the ground slapped at his feet.

"Tonio?" he whispered loudly, dropping into a kneeling crouch. Brushing his sleeve against the tear gas still clinging to his hair, he risked a quick glance, saw nothing but tall grass.

"Back here," came a muffled whisper from a few meters to his right. "Here—your gas mask."

Something bumped lightly against the side of Tirrell's face. Grabbing it, he slid it on, fumbling a bit before he got the straps properly tightened. Exhaling what was left in his lungs to clear the mask of any traces of gas, he cautiously took a breath. Just as cautiously, he opened his eyes.

Tonio, his own mask firmly in place, slid through the grass to Tirrell's side a moment later, the remaining gas grenades held in a fingertip-and-teekay grip in front of him. "Grack, but you took a chance there," he murmured.

"Had to be done," Tirrell grunted, taking a second to examine the righthand's mask. Tightening one of the straps, he returned his gaze to the now empty sky. "Did you see what happened to them?" he asked.

"I think their friends teeked them back into the refinery. They sure weren't navigating on their own. Are they going to be all right?"

"Oh, they're not in any danger. But I think we can scratch them from any further action for the day." Raising his head cautiously, Tirrell peered over the grasses at the refinery. No activity was visible; the window Martel had been using for his attacks was now sealed against the bluish-looking cloud of tear gas that was slowly drifting toward the east in the light breeze. "In fact, depending on how close everyone else is crowding around them, we may be able to take out the rest of them, too. Grab another grenade, Tonio, and let's try to teek it straight down Martel's throat."

Gasping and rubbing almost viciously at their eyes, Kalle and Barth were teeked back in through the window. "Close that window tight!" Martel snapped to Axel, his stomach threatening to climb up his throat. "All the windows—as tight as they'll go." The kids flew off to obey, leaving him staring out the window. Not at the cloud of gas that had unexpectedly robbed him of a quick victory, but at the place where the man who'd executed the maneuver had disappeared back into cover.

Tirrell. It had been Tirrell.

He swallowed once, hard, and as his brain slowly unfroze, he became aware of a sharp odor in the air. "Get over there—all the way in the corner," he ordered the two disabled kids. "Axel, teek them over there. Everyone else keep away; they've got the stuff on their clothes."

"Something coming!" the boy on lookout two windows away shouted.

Martel jumped to his side. A small black object, heading straight for the window. "Knock it down," he commanded the boy. "No, wait—just stop it and try to pull on anything that seems to be sticking out."

The cylinder hesitated in its flight, wobbled back and forth under the opposing forces, and a small ring near the front abruptly popped free. Seconds later the cylinder seemed to explode into another of the off-white clouds.

"What *is* that stuff?" the boy asked nervously.

"Don't worry, it won't hurt you," Omega growled. "It just makes your eyes water, like sliced onions."

Axel landed next to him. "Can we give Barth and Kalle some water? Maybe if they wash—"

"You!" Omega barked, turning on him. "That was *Tirrell*, damn it! Why the hell didn't you teek him in here when he started falling?"

Axel seemed to draw back from the outburst; but even through his anger Martel could see it wasn't the recoil of puppylike subservience. Axel was regarding him coolly, almost measuringly. "We were busy getting Barth and Kalle back in, we had to pull Doane and that box in over there, and you were screaming at us to hurry up and not let any of the smoke in. If you'd wanted us to grab him, you should have said something."

With an effort, Martel forced himself to calm down.

He couldn't afford to lose control now. "Sorry. But that was *Tirrell*, damn it."

"I saw him. You told me he wouldn't be any more trouble."

"I know." Martel watched the latest cloud move across the landscape. How *had* the detective escaped from the cabin? He didn't know, but he was for damn sure going to find out. "Put one of your kids on each side of the room to watch for attempts to break through the windows," he instructed Axel. "Someone else should make sure Tirrell and whoever he's got out there don't move from where they are. Then I want *you*, Axel, to stack the boxes we're taking with us in front of the door to the rest of the building; I don't want anyone sneaking up on our blind side."

Axel seemed to consider all that, then nodded. "All right. You just going to stay here and supervise?"

Martel made a note of the preteen's sarcastic tone for future reference. "No. I'm going to have a little talk with Dr. Jarvis." Without waiting for a response he stalked away.

He found the scientist seated with his back against the huge furnace, a nervous preteen hovering nearby. "Report to Axel—he has a job for you," Martel told the boy. The other nodded and flitted off, and Martel turned his glare onto Jarvis. "Enjoying the show?" he asked coldly.

"Wouldn't have missed it for the world," the scientist smiled. For some reason, he looked five years younger. "Did I hear you say it was Detective Tirrell out there?"

"Either him or his twin brother. I don't suppose you'd like to suggest how he got out of your cabin, would you?"

"Maybe Tonio didn't go for help after all," Jarvis suggested. "Perhaps he simply waited outside until you were gone and then nipped in and got them out."

Martel had seldom heard such a poor attempt at a lie; but on the other hand at least one part of that explanation fitted with the known facts. "Maybe you're right," he said, watching the other's face. "It's for sure that no one's arrived with any help so far."

A slight frown creased Jarvis's forehead. "What do you mean?"

"I mean the rescue attempt you're looking forward to is far in the future. Tirrell's out there alone, with exactly one kid assisting him."

"What makes you think that?"

"One: a group of police and righthands would have either stormed us by now or have used a loudspeaker to call for our surrender. Two: Barth was struggling with someone on the ground just before Tirrell fired his gas grenade; if there'd been two kids down there, they would have had enough combined teekay to yank Barth out of the sky."

"I see," Jarvis nodded thoughtfully. "So what you're saying is that a single kid out there is successfully pinning down all nine of yours. I think I understand why Tirrell didn't call for reinforcements."

"Then you understand wrong," Martel snapped, unreasonably irritated by the barb. "So far there hasn't been anything but one-on-one confrontations, and both were won only by tricks. They couldn't survive a massed attack, and you know it. If it weren't for that damned gas they wouldn't have a chance against us."

"Well, I suppose you could all sneak out the far side of the building and make a run for it," Jarvis shrugged. "Of course, you'd probably have to leave me and your little stash of bullion if you wanted to be fast enough to outfly any tear-gas grenades that might be thrown at you. But if you'd like to run along, I can assure you we'll be fine here alone."

Martel smiled thinly. "Cute—very cute. But I don't think we're quite that desperate yet. It's just occurred to me that there's another way to keep Tirrell off my back. Or had you forgotten I have a valuable hostage?"

He watched Jarvis's face long enough to get the satisfaction of the other's startled expression and then turned toward the door where Axel was busily stacking boxes of gold. "Axel!" he called. "Come here!"

"Well, so much for that approach," Tonio commented as the second cloud of tear gas floated harmlessly past the refinery. "Martel's got at least one kid in there who's still able to see straight. What now?"

Tirrell shrugged. "We sit tight and enjoy the stalemate, I guess. Those windows are undoubtedly too strong for you to break, especially in this light, so as long as they're alert in there, we're not going to get any reasonable amount of gas inside. Storming the place would be futile—the windows are too filthy to see through when it's as dark inside there as it is, and I don't think we want to get teeked at when you can't teek back. On the other hand, as long as we've got grenades left to throw, they aren't going anywhere, either."

Tonio yawned audibly. "Well, I hope Lisa hurries back with those reinforcements. I'm absolutely dead."

"It has indeed been a long day," Tirrell agreed, his own lack of sleep a permanent layer of sand under his eyelids. "I'd offer you a nap, but we might need fast action."

"I'm okay."

The righthand fell silent. Shifting position a little, Tirrell stared at the dark windows and ran through the calculation one more time. Lisa had left just after four; call it half an hour to get free of the area, another half hour to get to the Nordau Police Station and contact Plat City, at least forty minutes more for the troops to arrive. Five-forty at the earliest—a good half hour away and uncomfortably close to the time when it would be dark enough for Martel's crowd to slip away. Of course, artificial lighting could postpone any break the fagin might be planning, but whether lights could be set up such that the kids inside couldn't teek them off was another problem entirely. He hoped someone in the Plat City team had given the matter some serious thought.

He was just trying to bend his tired brain toward

that question when one of the windows in the refinery cautiously opened a crack and a faint voice drifted across the intervening distance. "Tirrell?"

"Don't answer!" Tonio urged. "They'll figure out where we are!"

"They already know that reasonably well," Tirrell shook his head. Taking a deep breath, he raised the lower part of his gas mask and called, "I'm still here, Martel. You ready to surrender?"

"Hardly," the reply came a few seconds later. "I've got Dr. Matthew Jarvis in here, Tirrell. He's a hostage to your good behavior. I've got him booby-trapped with about a quarter kilogram of sodium cyanide powder. Any attempt to break in or interfere with my kids' teekay and he'll die. You understand?"

It took Tirrell two tries to get his tongue to work. "Understood. What do you want?"

"For now, just stay back and don't try anything cute. We'll talk more later."

"All right. *You* understand that if Dr. Jarvis is hurt, you'll pay with your own life."

Martel didn't answer, and the window was once again closed. "Has he gone crazy?" Tonio demanded.

"No—just desperate." Carefully, Tirrell fastened his mask in place again, a feeling of cold unreality displacing the fatigue in his brain. Could Martel truly be willing to gamble with Jarvis's life? Surely not—surely he was merely bluffing. And yet . . . The detective's earlier conversation with Tonio sprang unbidden into sharp focus. With his drugs and notes destroyed, only Jarvis himself had the clue now to the elimination of Transition. If he didn't survive the night . . .

"Do you think they'll try escaping now?"

With an effort Tirrell brought his mind back into focus. "No, they'll still wait a while. Whatever this booby-trap is, they can't try to leave until it's too dark for you to see the mechanism."

"So it's back to waiting," the righthand said with a tired sigh.

Tirrell nodded, glancing at the darkening sky. "That's right," he said. "Let's hope the support troops hurry." *And hope*, he added silently, *that I know how to advise them when they get here.*

Chapter 28

They arrived just under forty minutes later; dozens of them, appearing suddenly over the surrounding hills with such perfect timing that Tirrell had the instantaneous image of being at the center of a lasso closing silently in across the blue-black sky. The vision vanished quickly, as the figures dropped lower and disappeared into the shadowy landscape. Fumbling out his flashlight, Tirrell turned his back on the refinery and flashed the beam three times against his chest. A moment later two dark figures dropped to the ground beside him. "Detective Tirrell?" the larger of the two murmured.

"Right," Tirrell acknowledged. "My righthand Tonio Genesee's around here somewhere." Tonio snorted at that.

"I'm Detective First Ray Kesner of Plat City," the newcomer told them. "Righthand, Mark. What's the situation?"

"Delicate." Tirrell gave the other a fast summary of the past hour, including Martel's threat against Jarvis's life.

"Damn," Kesner growled. "Any chance he's bluffing?"

"As far as the means are concerned, no. I believe he's been running an illegal gold processing operation in there, and the simplest method for him to be using is cyanidation. Whether he's really willing to carry out such a threat—" He shrugged.

"Any idea why he grabbed Jarvis in the first place?" Kesner asked. "Eggers said you were pretty vague about the whys and wherefores of the situation when you first flew through Plat City four hours ago."

"For the moment all of that's still unclear," Tirrell lied. "Let's worry about it after we get Jarvis out safely, okay?"

"I just thought it would help us figure out how serious Martel is," the other grumbled. Raising a hand to the side of his head, he gave a series of orders into the radio headset he was wearing. He listened for a few seconds and then nodded. "Okay, everyone's in position. Mark, let me have that loudspeaker and we'll see what we can shake loose ... thanks." Raising the cone-shaped device to his lips, he clicked a switch. "Martel?" his amplified voice boomed, echoing off the nearest hills. "This is Detective First Ray Kesner. We have you surrounded and outnumbered. Come out one at a time and surrender or we'll come in and get you."

The echoes faded and for a moment there was total silence as even the nocturnal insects remained quiet in the wake of the loudspeaker's roar. Then, clearly audible, came the faint scrape of an opening window. "You'd better talk to Tirrell before you try anything stupid, Kesner," Martel called. "Move in and Jarvis dies. I mean it."

"All right," Kesner replied, "just take it easy. What exactly do you want?"

"For now, assurance that your people will stay at least half a kilometer away from this building. I'll have the rest of my demands ready for you in a while." Another squeak announced the window's closing and the end of the conversation.

Kesner lowered the loudspeaker. "What the hell is this business about demands? Any idea?"

"I expect it's mainly a smokescreen," Tirrell told him. "All he really wants is to get safely away from there with Jarvis, however many kids he has with him, and a box or two of what I suspect is crude gold bullion. To do that he has to wait until it's pitch black out here, dark enough that we won't be able to neutralize the threat to Jarvis's life. But he's not likely to apprise us of such a move in advance—he obviously doesn't want us working on a way to stop him."

"Seems reasonable," Kesner growled. "Well . . . I suppose we could set some floodlights around the area. As long as it's light out here they can't leave."

"You'd be risking Jarvis's life that way," Tirrell reminded him.

"Not really. He'd have to be completely crazy to kill his only hostage over something like that."

"He wouldn't have to kill him outright," Tirrell said. "If he gave Jarvis a small dose of cyanide he would live for at least a couple of hours before dying. You'd then have the choice of letting Martel go on his terms or waiting around until Jarvis dies."

"Ouch! I hadn't thought of that." Kesner touched his headset again. "Palmyra, have you got an angle where you can see inside? . . . Even with the night glasses? . . . Yeah, I'm not surprised. Anyone else able to see anything?"

Another pause, and Kesner's silhouette shook its head. "Palmyra says that the windows are so filthy that he can't see through them even with the night glasses. I'm not sure that even putting a spotlight on the building from out here would do us any good."

"Do you suppose we could sneak in one of the north doors and get into the south section that way?" Tirrell suggested hesitantly. "There are only nine or ten of them in there—they can't be holding the entire building."

"Probably not. But I had a look at the refinery's blueprints on the flight down, and there seems to be only one door connecting to the south section. Almost certainly they've got it barricaded by now."

"How about air vents or other kinds of openings?" Tonio asked.

"The ventilation system is loaded with filters," Kesner told him, "and all other conduits are either sealed or wind up inside the furnace or somewhere just as useless. Anyway, getting in isn't the point. We could handle them just as well from out here if we had a little bit of light in there."

"I know that," Tonio said impatiently. "But if we could get someone inside, he could take some flares in with him."

There was a moment of silence. "You're right," Kesner said, sounding mildly surprised. "I hadn't thought of that."

"Let's see those blueprints," Tirrell suggested.

With a prolonged rustle of paper Kesner laid them out. Covering the lens of his flashlight with his hand, Tirrell let a faint glow fall on the plans from between his fingers.

"Air vents; crushed ore conveyer; furnace feed, outgas, and slag lines," Kesner said, touching each point as he named it. "I'd say the best bet is to use the furnace feed duct ... except I'm not sure how you'd get out of the furnace once you were inside."

Tirrell nodded. "Tonio?"

"I think it's worth a try," the righthand said promptly. "I'll need a flashlight, some flares, and probably someone to help me get in the other end of this pipe. One of those radios would be handy, too."

"Hold it," Kesner cut in. "Who put *you* in charge of this operation? Tirrell and I will decide if someone's going and who that someone will be."

"I'm afraid we're going to have to skip the parliamentary procedure, Kesner," Tirrell said. "There's no time for a long discussion—Martel could make his move practically any time now. Tonio's volunteered to try it, and he knows the situation and people in there better than any of your righthands do."

"All right," Kesner said heavily. "Technically, I suppose, you can take charge here. But remember that whatever happens will then be your responsibility."

Tirrell nodded. "I know. Now get busy and start collecting the stuff Tonio'll need."

Barely five minutes later Tonio was gone, flying low in a wide circle that would get him invisibly to the north side of the refinery where his three assigned helpers awaited him. Tirrell watched him disappear into the darkness, his feelings badly mixed. One way or another it would soon be over, he knew, and however it turned out Martel would definitely have lost his bid for the power he craved. And yet, down deep, the detective recognized uncomfortably that by sending Tonio in he had effectively forced the most crucial decision of his life squarely onto his righthand's shoulders. Tonio could do his best to rescue Jarvis . . . or could try equally hard to make sure neither the scientist nor his formula survived the night.

And Tirrell had no idea which the preteen planned to do.

For a long, agonizing moment he thought seriously about having Kesner call the boy back. But it was too late for that. Already the brightest stars were visible overhead; any minute now Martel would be opening his window again and announcing his imminent departure. No, Tirrell would have to trust Tonio's judgment . . . and perhaps, he thought suddenly, that was the best decision his tired and irresolute mind had been able to make. Perhaps the best decision it *could* have made.

The thought failed to console him. Staring through the gloom at the almost invisible refinery, he listened with half an ear as Kesner directed his righthand force into position, and tried to ignore the painful thudding of his heart.

Chapter 29

Only the windows themselves were still visible, and they were distinguishable only as rectangles of navy blue set into a pitch-black background. Seated with his back to the huge furnace, his hands tied tightly behind him, Jarvis shifted slightly to ease his muscles.

The figure standing over him stirred in response. "Relax," Axel's voice came quietly. "It won't be much longer."

"I'm sure," Jarvis murmured. "You realize, of course, that the police aren't going to just let all of us fly merrily out of here. And if that cyanide hits me, it'll be *you* who gets charged with murder."

Axel chuckled. "You don't know Omega very well. He'll get us out of here, all right. Don't worry about that."

"Don't underestimate Tirrell," Jarvis warned. Under cover of the conversation, he carefully probed the edge of the furnace's metal plate sheathing with his fingers, searching for another place where the coating of rust was thick enough to abrade rope. Omega was smart, all right, but the pressure was making him careless, and he hadn't bothered to check the metal before sitting Jarvis here. Finding a new spot, the scientist resumed his stealthy rubbing. "And my other comment still stands: *you're* the one holding those bowls over my head, not Omega. He didn't give you this job because he likes you—he did it because he thinks that dragging you in as deep as he is will insure your loyalty to him."

"A lot he knows about loyalty." Axel shifted position again and Jarvis tensed involuntarily. The two small bowls floating rim to rim directly over his head held enough sodium cyanide powder in the space between them to kill him ten times over . . . and the only thing holding it up there was Axel's teekay, transmitted through a single finger touching each bowl. A slight distraction, a flash of light or whiff of tear gas, and it would literally be all over. "Let me tell you a little secret," Axel continued, lowering his voice still further. "As soon as we're all set up in Omega's secret hideaway, I'm going to get rid of him. I don't think he's telling the truth about making us into priests, and I don't want to wait until Transition to find out for sure."

"You aren't going to live even that long." There was a slight jerk in the rope binding his wrists as one more of the fibers broke. Jarvis strained carefully at what was left. Not quite enough. "If you know Omega as well as you say, you must know he won't just wait for you to act against him."

"You let me worry about that, okay? Now shut up," he added as, across the room, Martel began speaking. "I want to hear this."

It was not, as Jarvis had feared, the order to move out, but merely another in Martel's series of speculations as to what the police were doing. The relative silence suited Jarvis just fine, though. Leaning hard into the rusty metal, he put as much power into his efforts as he could without making any noise . . . and with a suddenness that jammed his wrists painfully against the edge, the rope finally broke.

Quickly, hardly daring to believe he'd done it, he worked his hands free from the loops around them. Then, moving carefully lest the sound of rustling cloth alert his guard, he rolled over onto his hands and knees and began to crawl, heading for the back side of the furnace. The first three meters were the hardest, as he waited with nerves on end for the shouts that would mean his discovery. But even to his own hyperalert ears he made no sound, and as he continued on, his fears gradually diminished. By the time he halted, half the circumference of the furnace and an eternity later, his heartbeat was no longer the loudest sound in the room. Leaning back against the furnace, his shirt soaked with sweat, he swiped at his forehead with a trembling hand and took his first deep breath in hours. For the moment, at least, he was free.

But even with darkness to hide him, such freedom would only last a little while past the discovery of his escape unless he could get out of the building. The doors, he knew, were out; any that weren't barricaded against the police would undoubtedly have preteens guarding them. The windows weren't designed for easy egress, and opening them made enough noise to wake the dead, anyway. But there was one more possible escape route . . . one that Martel might not have thought to block.

Jarvis's memory was far from eidetic, but he'd had ample time to study the room's layout through the long afternoon. Slipping his shoes off, he took his bearings from the windows and set off in what he hoped was the proper direction, feeling carefully for obstacles with hands and toes. Ten paces later he found what he was looking for: one of the ladders leading to the network of catwalks high above. With a silent plea to the metal not to squeak, he started up.

His luck held all the way up the ladder and perhaps four steps along the catwalk itself. But his fifth step brought his weight down on what was apparently a rust-weakened section of the grating, and with a loud *snap* that seemed to reverberate forever one of the heavy wires broke under his foot.

He froze, and on the floor below the quiet conversations abruptly ceased. "What was that?" one of the kids whispered nervously—and the words were barely out when Axel's bellow split the air. "*Grack!* Omega—he got away!"

"*Damn* you, Axel—no, hold it, damn it, everyone just stay where you are for a minute. Jarvis, you can't get away—we've got the doors blocked and we'll tear your head off if you try for one of the windows. Give yourself up right now or I guarantee the consequences will be very, very painful."

Under cover of Martel's voice, Jarvis had made it another six steps along the catwalk. Now, as silence again settled onto the room, he paused, hardly daring to breathe. Clearly, no one below had yet realized where the original noise had come from, and he had no intention of giving them unnecessary hints. Pitch darkness or not, once they figured out he was on one of the catwalks they could have him in thirty seconds flat. Squinting into the darkness, he tried unsuccessfully to see how far ahead the next intersecting catwalk was, the one he needed to get on.

"All right, Jarvis, have it your way," Martel snarled suddenly. "Axel, Brody, Royce—go to the east end of the room and start working your way west. Cover every square centimeter of floor and wall and make sure he hasn't climbed onto any of the machinery."

Jarvis had made it to the intersection and onto the proper catwalk by the time Martel finished talking—but he knew his time was nearly up. The mere mention of climbing was bound to bring this aerial walkway to mind, and the minute Martel remembered it he would certainly reach the proper conclusion. Quickly, Jarvis unfastened his belt and took it off, coiling it as tightly as he could. Giving it enough loft to clear the other catwalks, he tossed it as far as he could toward the west wall.

"Aha!" Martel shouted triumphantly. "The *cat*—"

And with a clatter the belt hit the floor.

The flurry of activity at that end of the building was all Jarvis could have hoped for, and he didn't hesitate. Abandoning all efforts at stealth, he ran at full speed along the heavy wire mesh, his hands merely brushing the low guard rails. Distances were impossible to judge in the gloom, but he tried to form an estimate by counting his steps ... and two earlier than he'd expected the door loomed suddenly ahead and he slammed full tilt into it. Beneath him Martel bellowed. Ignoring the stabbing pains in his cheek and right kneecap, the scientist fumbled the door open and staggered into the tiny control room, slamming the door behind him. The pale square of a small outside window gave him direction, and he crossed the room in four quick steps, hands searching the wall for the emergency exit he knew would be there.

It wasn't.

For a long second Jarvis stood perfectly still, his mind doing a slow tumble as all his hopes unraveled like an old sweater. The kids would be on him in seconds; far too short a time for him to try squeezing out through that tiny window, or even to sneak back out onto the catwalk. Not that the latter would help him, anyway. Blind or not, they would have him back in their control soon no matter what he did.

And, almost too late, the answer hit him.

He banged the same kneecap a second time in getting to the long control board spanning the room's right-hand side, and he broke a fingernail against the rim of one of the meters set into it as he desperately threw every switch and spun every dial he could find. Most of the equipment had presumably been disconnected or shut down at the machines themselves ... but Martel had mentioned both a generator and battery bank. If the connections were still intact—

He was halfway down the board and someone outside was fumbling for the doorknob when he found the right section of the board. Without warning, two floodlights blazed on, lighting up the main room with a brilliance that seemed devastating after the blackness. Jarvis squeezed his eyes shut reflexively and got two more switches before he was abruptly yanked off his feet. He got just a glimpse of Axel's face at one of the control room's inside windows, his face distorted almost beyond recognition by fear and hatred, before being slammed hard against the door.

Below, on the floor, Martel was screaming something incomprehensible as he pointed up at the floodlights. There was the sound of breaking glass and one of them abruptly went out—

And with a slap Jarvis heard all the way inside the control room, everyone below suddenly slammed face downward onto the concrete floor. Axel spun around, releasing Jarvis from his teekay hold, and an instant later was flying past the catwalks in a desperate attempt to reach the west windows. But he'd barely covered ten meters before his body seemed to slam into an invisible barrier, and he was plucked from midair to land roughly on the floor beside the furnace. An instant later the outside door was blown in off its hinges and the room began to fill up with police and righthands.

It wasn't until Jarvis walked back onto the catwalk that he saw that Axel was lying facedown in the spilled cyanide powder he'd been holding so recently over Jarvis's head. Lying with unnatural stillness . . .

Chapter 30

"I suppose you're going to gloat now," Martel said, a sardonic smile tightening the corners of his mouth. Leaning back in his chair, he idly scanned the books on the shelf beside him, pulling one out for closer examination.

On the opposite side of the desk, Tirrell took a deep breath, refusing to acknowledge Martel's obvious attempts to irritate him. He would have given practically anything to put this talk off until morning, when he would at least have been able to snatch a few hours' sleep; or, failing that, to have used one of the Plat City Police Department's interrogation rooms instead of Detective Kesner's office. But by morning there would be no chance at all of stuffing the genie back into its bottle . . . and interrogation rooms were always rigged with hidden recording and observation equipment. "Gloating is the last thing on my mind," he told the other. "As a matter of fact, I brought you here to offer you a deal."

Martel turned back to face him, an eyebrow cocked. "Oh, really? I'd never have guessed. Let me see—can I assume my part of it will be to keep quiet about Jarvis's experiment?"

Tirrell grimaced, but he knew he should have expected this. Martel was far too smart to have missed the significance of the detective's choice of meeting room, and he'd obviously put considerable thought into the implications of Jarvis's work. "You're very perceptive," he told the other. "That's precisely what I want you to do."

"It would cause a great deal of chaos, wouldn't it?" Martel mused, as if Tirrell hadn't spoken. "Everyone worried about the changes that might or might not hit the society, wondering whether this was going to start a new Lost Generation type of period—and of course the whole population would be dithering over it for ten years before anyone even knew how successful the project had been. A whole society jumping at its own shadow for a solid decade—that *would* be something to see, wouldn't it?"

Tirrell waited until he was finished. "To see, perhaps, but not to live in. Now—"

"Ah, but *I* wouldn't really be living in it, would I?" Martel interrupted him. "I'm an outcast, remember?— a criminal who's going to be spending the next several years in confinement and supervised service programs. Why should I care what happens to Tigrin society?"

"That's a stupid question, but since you're only asking it to try and raise the value of your silence, I'll ignore it," Tirrell said tartly. "Consider your point made, all right?"

Martel smiled briefly. "All right. So what are you offering in exchange?"

Tirrell took a deep breath. "In exchange for your *absolute* silence regarding everything you know of Jarvis's work, the attempted murder charges against myself, Tonio, Lisa, and Colin will be set aside. In addition, fagin charges stemming from your free gold mine work will be dropped completely, as will various infractions concerning the whole refining and distribution process, though we'll probably hit your confederates with those whenever we catch up with them."

"Interesting," Martel murmured. "What exactly is this 'set aside' business?"

"It means that those charges will still be on the record but that you won't be tried on them."

"That sounds distinctly dangerous. I want them dropped outright instead."

Tirrell shook his head. "No. I need to have something that'll insure your half of the bargain is kept. As long as those charges are merely set aside, I can instigate trial proceedings at any time within the next twelve years. Dropped charges are gone forever."

Martel toyed with the book he still held. "What makes you think you can keep that sort of bargain?" he asked at last. "You don't handle the prosecution directly."

"No ... but I believe I can control the willingness of the involved parties to testify. That brings up one other matter; you'll also have to accept the blame for Colin Brimmer's kidnapping. We can work out some story about you having left him with one of your accomplices out in the woods and Jarvis accidentally finding him, which is how Jarvis wound up in your hands. That charge will also be set aside, needless to say."

Martel smiled thinly. "In order to whitewash Jarvis?"

"And in exchange for his cooperation in setting aside the attempted murder charges," Tirrell shrugged. "Do we have a deal?"

The other hesitated. "Some of my kids know I didn't take Colin."

"As long as the fagin charges are dropped, they won't be called on to testify. Besides, most of them never had any real proof other than your own statement, and we all know what a good liar you are. As to the others—well, I can take statements from them and alter them if necessary, but I gather Axel really didn't tell them all that much. He probably would have made you a fitting successor if he'd lived."

A strange sort of shadow crossed Martel's face. "Perhaps," he said. For a moment he hesitated, lips pressed tightly together, and then carefully returned the book to its place on the shelf. "Very well, Detective, I accept—on the condition that you tell me what exactly it is that Dr. Jarvis has discovered."

"Possibly a method to allow kids to keep teekay after puberty," Tirrell said. There was little to be gained by refusing the request; Martel had probably already guessed, anyway. "We won't know, of course, until Colin grows up. Possibly not even then." Standing up, he stepped to the office door and opened it. "Tonio?"

"Right here."

"Escort Martel back to his cell, if you would, and then see if Dr. Jarvis can come up here for a few minutes."

Martel stood up. "Good-bye, Detective. I'll see you in court."

Tirrell nodded silently and waited until they had left. Then, sinking back into his chair, he propped his elbows up on the desk and rubbed his eyes vigorously. It wouldn't be nearly as easy as he'd made it sound, of course—he would have to talk fast and loud to convince the various court officials that setting aside one set of charges in exchange for a flat-out guilty plea on the other set was a fair compromise for all concerned. But he should be able to pull it off. The crucial question now was how Jarvis would react to the deal he was trying to work out. Tirrell had been battling Martel's kind long enough to know how they thought, but the scientist was still in many ways an enigma to him. Too late, now, he wished he'd gone to get Jarvis personally instead of sending Tonio; tired though he was, the exercise might have awakened his brain a bit.

The office door swung open, and he looked up as Jarvis stepped into the room. "You wanted to see me?"

"Yes." Tirrell waved him to the chair Martel had just vacated. "Tonio, I want you to hear this, too," he added as the preteen started to leave. Without comment Tonio moved into the room and closed the door behind him, hovering with his back to it.

"First of all, Doctor," Tirrell began, "I'd like to know exactly what you've told the other police."

Jarvis eyed him for a moment before answering.

"I've just said that Omega—or Martel, I guess his real name is—suddenly burst into my cabin, took me prisoner, and blew the place up. I've agreed to give more details when I've pulled myself together."

"In other words, you've been stalling. Good. Did you mention Colin to them at all? Or the fact that Lisa, Tonio, and I were there when Martel grabbed you?"

Jarvis shook his head. "No to both questions. I assumed you would want to talk with me before my story got set in concrete, so I tried to be as vague as possible."

"I see." Tirrell leaned back slightly in his chair. "All right. Let's start by finishing the conversation we were having at your cabin when Martel arrived. As I recall, you were about to try and convince me that Tigrin society needed your discovery to become stable."

Jarvis glanced up at Tonio. "I doubt if I have to spell out the more obvious potential problems to you, Detective. Depriving kids of literacy and book knowledge would hamper any attempted power grab they might try, but the physical strength is certainly on their side. They would succeed . . . at least temporarily."

"Only if everyone went along," Tonio said, a bit hotly. "A lot of us wouldn't, you know."

"That's one reason a revolt would ultimately fail," Jarvis acknowledged. "But the threat will always be there, sitting in the backs of people's minds, and the response will always be to keep as tight a rein as possible on the kids. That sort of permanent strain isn't good for anyone."

Tirrell thought of the official overreaction to Lisa's attempts to learn how to read. "Possibly," he said. "But that's not sufficient reason to risk another Lost Generation's worth of chaos."

"Isn't it?" Jarvis shrugged. "Then maybe you'd like to consider the trauma of taking five-year-olds from their parents and sticking them in hives among strangers. Or the way the emotional shock of Transition combines with the physical aspects of puberty itself to make teen suicide rates the highest on the planet. Or maybe—" his face seemed to harden—"you don't mind the way those triple-damned fagins siphon some of the brightest kids away from hives and twist their minds to hell and gone. Every one of those problems would disappear if adults as well as kids had teekay."

Tirrell felt his stomach muscles tighten as, knowingly or otherwise, Jarvis hit the detective's own deepest sore spot. "You don't like fagins, I gather?"

For a moment Jarvis stared at him, his eyes curiously flat. "No, I don't. I take it you don't know why exactly Colin was abandoned in Ridge Harbor in the first place."

Tirrell shook his head. "Why don't you tell us?"

"It was because a fagin in your town got the bright idea of starting with brand-new babies instead of snatching kids from homes or hives," the scientist said bitterly. "Miribel was supposed to deliver Colin to him when she left the hospital."

At Tirrell's right, Tonio growled something. "Just like that?" the detective asked. "Just walk out the front door and hand the baby over?"

"Why not?" Jarvis's eyes were blazing, but Tirrell could tell the anger wasn't directed at him. "No one in Barona knew she was even pregnant. The birth would be recorded in Ridge Harbor, and in thirty-two days it would go into the sealed records and no one would ever find out what happened. The fagin would have someone raise the baby, and when his teekay appeared he'd have a working kid who wouldn't be missed by anyone and wouldn't have any records he could be traced by."

"Why didn't you tell the police?" Tonio burst out.

Jarvis looked at the preteen, shook his head. "It would have gotten Miribel in trouble, too. Even if she'd been using me from the start—and I don't believe she was—I still cared a great deal for her. I couldn't turn her in to face criminal charges."

"So what went wrong?" Tirrell asked, though he now thought he knew.

"I did the next best thing: I phoned in an anonymous tip about the fagin," Jarvis said. "The police caught him redhanded, with two of his kids right there with him."

"Nash Gorman," Tirrell nodded. "I've always wondered who phoned us that tip. So when you told Miribel her prospective market had vanished, she just took off and left Colin to fend for himself?"

"It wasn't quite that heartless," Jarvis sighed. "She was afraid for her own safety, too. Gorman had blackmailed her into doing this for him; the details aren't important. I've often wondered what happened to her after she left the hospital. I hope she's still alive . . . but I don't really think she is."

It was Tirrell who broke the long silence that followed. "So what more would you have to do with Colin?" he asked.

Jarvis frowned. "You mean to complete my experiment? Not much. An injection every two months, dropping off to twice a year when he reaches seven. Keeping records of his B and M profile would be useful, too, though only for future reference. As a matter of fact, I would have returned him to Ridge Harbor within a week or so if all of this hadn't happened."

Tirrell was conscious of Tonio's astonished gaze on him. "All right," he told the scientist. "He's going back to Ridge Harbor a little ahead of schedule, but if you can continue the work without getting caught, you can do so. That's completely unofficial, of course."

"*What?*" Tonio was incredulous.

"There are a few conditions," the detective continued as if the boy hadn't spoken. "First, I'll tell you right now that if any harm comes to Colin because of your drugs, I'll have you arrested and prosecuted, so you'd better make damn sure you know what you're doing at all times. Second, you'll need to coordinate your story with Martel's so that Colin doesn't show up in your cabin at all. Martel's going to take the

blame for Colin's kidnapping, though we're not going
to try him on that charge."

"Awfully charitable of him," Jarvis commented.
"What did you have to promise him in exchange?"

"We're setting aside all attempted murder and illegal gold operation charges. In return he's also promised to keep his mouth shut about you and your
work."

Jarvis made a sound that was half laugh, half snort.
"You don't seriously believe that, do you?"

"Oh, he will. Not for altruistic reasons, of course,
but because he's still hoping to steal your process
and it's in his own best interest to keep anyone else
from knowing about it."

"How's he going to steal anything from a prison-
work program?" Tonio scoffed.

"He can't; but even if he's convicted for both Dr.
Jarvis's kidnapping *and* on the faginism charges still
outstanding in Ridge Harbor, he can probably work
off all the service points in seven years or so. Colin
would only be twelve, with at least a couple of years
to go before the method was proved one way or the
other; plenty of time to try and grab the formula
before its existence became public knowledge."

"So I've got just about seven years to live?" Jarvis
suggested, not entirely humorously.

"Possibly," Tirrell nodded. "You'll be in danger;
but the option is to announce your discovery now."

"Thanks. I'll take my chances with Martel. I'm
sure I'll be able to take some precautions against
him."

"True—and one of those precautions is to make
sure he can't corner the information market with one
blow." Tirrell leaned forward. "Specifically, Doctor,
you're going to tell Tonio and me—right now—exactly
what it is you've stumbled on. That's the condition
for *my* silence on all of this. If something should
happen to you I want to at least be able to point
researchers in the right direction."

Jarvis's eyes flicked back and forth between the
two of them. Finally, he nodded. "I suppose you're

right. Well, in a nutshell, I believe that Transition is the result of an interaction between the slowdown in brain growth and the spurt-and-decrease in the amount of lymphoid tissue, both of which occur approximately at puberty. What I'm trying to do is extend Colin's general growth time—which will change his brain growth-rate curve—while leaving the lymphoid tissue curve untouched."

"What'll that do to Colin?" Tirrell asked.

"The extra growth time will increase his adult height a few percent, but since he's small to begin with that shouldn't be a problem. As far as any other problems are concerned, I've successfully decoupled the two curves in earthstock lab animals without any harm that I can detect. Is that sufficient?"

Tirrell thought for a moment, then nodded. "I think so. Anything else you could say would probably be too technical for us to understand, and I don't want any details lying around in writing." The detective stood up. "Thank you, Doctor. I suggest you continue to decline making any public statement until you've had a good night's rest. In the morning I'll help you coordinate your story with Martel, but I'm just too tired now."

"Understandable." Jarvis frowned and paused halfway to the door. "What about the kids that attacked my cabin? They saw Colin there."

"They've already been sent back to their hives for disciplinary action," Tirrell assured him. "They won't be called on to answer any questions as long as Martel pleads guilty to your kidnapping, and they aren't likely to find out about any discrepancies in the official record. As to the Barona police, I'll just have to be a good sport about suspecting you when you really weren't involved at all with the kidnapping. If you can come up with an explanation of what your 'secret project' was that'll satisfy Ms. Mbar and Dr. Somerset, I think we'll have everyone covered pretty well."

"I suppose that'll work," Jarvis said, sounding a bit doubtful.

"If you've got a better idea I'll be happy to hear it . . . in about nine hours."

The scientist smiled. "Good night, Detective."

Tirrell waited a few seconds after they were gone and then followed, his legs feeling like lead as he clumped down the hall toward the sleeping room Kesner had had set up for them. Only one loose end remained to be tied up, and fortunately that could wait a few days. Tonio would be back up in a couple of minutes, as soon as he'd escorted Jarvis back to the policemen downstairs, and he could perhaps discuss it with the righthand for a few minutes. . . .

When Tonio arrived he found the detective face-down on one of the room's two cots, snoring gently.

Chapter 31

Lisa had been expecting the summons to Gavra's office for two days, ever since her midnight return to the hive with the note the police had given her. Along with her other secret burdens, though, such anticipation was just one more bit of weight; and her dread was thus mixed with a certain amount of relief as she knocked on the Senior's office door and teeked it open.

Gavra was seated, as usual, behind her desk—but the unexpected sight of the room's other two occupants temporarily buried all of Lisa's fears beneath a flood of delight. "Tonio!" she blurted. "Stan! I was afraid that something had—I mean, that you'd been—I mean—"

She stopped, embarrassed by her outburst, but the others merely smiled. "We're all fine, Lisa," Tirrell assured her. "I'm sorry—we should have gotten word to you sooner that we were all right. But we've been very busy."

"I *told* you she'd be worried," Tonio murmured, grinning cheerfully.

"Sit down, Lisa," Gavra said, waving her to a chair next to Tonio's. "I'm afraid we have some unpleasant business to attend to, and Detective Tirrell has asked that we allow him to act as official witness to it."

Lisa nodded and sat down, her happiness at finding Tonio and Tirrell alive abating as she realized what Gavra had in mind. "May I ask Detective Tirrell a question first?" she asked, determined to hold off the hammer as long as possible.

Gavra nodded. "Go ahead."

Lisa turned to Tirrell. "Are Dr. Jarvis and Colin all right? And have you caught Weylin and the others yet?"

"Everyone's fine," the detective assured her. "Colin's a bit confused by all the fuss—apparently Jarvis convinced him he was on a vacation of sorts—but he's back in Ridge Harbor and doing fine. We picked up Weylin and all the others Martel had been using when they got tired of flying around the forest and returned to the temple site. Weylin's going to lose a lot of points for his attack on that policeman, and of course he's lost his righthand position. The others were just sent back to their hives with warnings. They'll probably lose some points for being out after lights-out, but nothing worse is likely to happen to them. When a fagin's involved, kids are usually treated more as victims than as criminals."

Gavra cleared her throat. "Unfortunately, Lisa, your case is considerably more serious," she said, looking unhappy. "Along with several smaller infractions of hive rules, you have deliberately violated my prohibition against telling anyone of your reading ability." She hesitated, and her eyes were moist. "I'm sorry, but I have no choice but to cancel all of your points."

Lisa swallowed painfully, feeling her breakfast churn in her stomach. She'd known this was coming, but it still hit her like a punch in the gut. All her points gone—no possibility of any schooling past Basic—maybe not even that much. Her future effectively ruined ... and all while just trying to help people. *But I did save our lives*, she told herself, thinking back to the cabin. Somehow, at the moment, it didn't feel like a fair trade.

"That seems a bit extreme," Tirrell said. "After all, she *was* a great deal of help to us."

Gavra shook her head tiredly. "I tried, Detective, I

really did. But I have no choice. My own superior, the officials at Lee Intro—I've even talked to the mayor's office to try to win her at least a reduction. No one's interested in sticking his neck out to even help me fight it. The point loss has already been recorded at the city building—I don't know how they found out—and there's absolutely nothing I can do." She looked at him hopefully. "Unlesss *you* can intercede . . . ?"

Tirrell shook his head. "I don't have even temporary authority in Barona anymore," he said. "We're on our way back to Ridge Harbor right now. Tell me, how many points did Lisa have?"

Gavra frowned, and even through her misery Lisa heard something odd in the detective's voice. She looked at him, wondering, but his expression was perfectly calm. It wasn't until she noticed Tonio doing his best to stifle a grin that it began to dawn on her that perhaps their disinterest wasn't what it seemed.

"It was something just over forty-six hundred," Gavra told him, still frowning. "Forty-six forty, I believe."

"That's a lot of points," Tirrell commented, drawing a folded piece of paper and a pen from an inside coat pocket. "Tonio's got more than that, but he's got several months of righthand duty under his belt." Unfolding the paper, he laid it on the edge of Gavra's desk and wrote briefly on it. "As a matter of fact, I was the one who blew the whistle on Lisa. You see, she can only have her points taken away once and I wanted to make sure it was done before I brought this by." He offered Gavra the paper.

The Senior was looking thoroughly confused. "What is it?" she asked, taking it cautiously.

"Didn't you know?" Tirrell's straight face was gone, replaced by a satisfied, almost wicked smile. "Ridge Harbor's had a ten-thousand-bill reward posted for Yerik Martel's capture for nearly four years. With a half-dozen different relationships between bills and hive points in existence, I was able to get official permission to use my own judgment."

Gavra blinked hard, her eyes still moist but all the tension gone from her face. "Lisa . . . Detective Tirrell has authorized the addition of forty-seven hundred points to your hive record."

Lisa's throat felt dry. *Forty-seven hundred points!* Everything she'd lost, and a few extra. "I . . . thank you," she managed. "I . . . I don't know what to say."

"You don't need to say anything," Tirrell told her. "You've done a great deal for us, Lisa, though the world will never know it. A few hundred hive points is no more than you've earned."

A warm glow seemed to fill Lisa's body . . . but she nevertheless caught the extra meaning behind the words. "I understand," she nodded, and meant it. No one would ever learn about what had happened that weekend from her.

"Good." Tirrell stood up. "Well, I'd like to stay longer, but we're supposed to be back in Ridge Harbor by noon, so we'd better be going. Perhaps you can come visit sometime soon, Lisa; just drop in at the police station and someone there'll find us."

"And if you come before it gets too cold, I'll show you what flying over an ocean is like," Tonio added, his manner an odd mixture of shyness and daring.

"I'd like that," she smiled. "I've never flown near the ocean before."

"Good," Tirrell said. "Then we'll see you soon. Good-bye, Ms. Norward, and thanks for everything."

"I was glad to help. Good-bye, Detective; Tonio."

They left. For a moment the room was silent, and then Gavra stirred in her chair. "Well, Lisa," she said, "I guess that about ends it."

Lisa nodded. "Should I go on out to the construction site?" she asked. "I could take over from Kaarin and let her come back here. Unless I'm still on probation, that is."

Gavra smiled and waved the suggestion away. "Tomorrow's soon enough to get back to work. Take the day off and relax—I get the feeling you've more than earned it. And whatever you've promised Detective

Tirrell to keep secret, for heaven's sake make sure you *do* it this time."

Words that could have hurt . . . but spoken with a concern that kept them from doing so. "I will," Lisa smiled back.

Though it might be nice, she thought as she left the office, to know exactly what it was she was keeping quiet about. Perhaps on Saturday she would take the others up on their invitation and fly over to Ridge Harbor for a long talk. And after she got the complete story of what had happened at the refinery, perhaps she would take Tonio up on his offer of a guided tour of the seacoast and ocean.

And after that, there might be time for a quick side trip up to Cavendish . . . where Daryl was.

"So you're going to let Jarvis keep on with his experiment," Tonio said as they pulled away from the curb and headed down the street.

"You disapprove?" Tirrell asked.

Tonio shrugged. "I don't like the idea of him putting stuff into Colin without knowing what it'll do."

"If it hasn't hurt him so far, chances are it's safe enough. And if it's not . . . well, it's probably too late already. But I think it's a risk worth taking, given how things have turned out."

Tonio glanced at the detective. "You're really determined to wipe out all the fagins, aren't you?"

Tirrell grimaced. "It's that obvious, huh?"

"You practically lit up when Jarvis suggested his formula would do that."

Tirrell was silent for a long moment, long enough for Tonio to wonder if he shouldn't have put it quite so strongly. "I've never told you this before," the detective said at last, "but perhaps you ought to know. I nearly became a fagin's kid myself when I was eight."

"You?" Tonio stared at him.

"Me," Tirrell admitted. "Brace and I—Brace was my roommate—we'd already been through all the movies and games Eights were allowed and were

looking for something else to do. And when he ran
into a smooth-talking fagin ...'' He shrugged. "The
promises sounded awfully convincing, even though I
could sense that something was wrong with the whole
setup. It took me two days to decide not to join in.
But Brace did ... and I never tried hard enough to
talk him out of it. He deserted the hive and worked
as a thief and smuggler until Transition, when the
fagin threw him out."

He paused. Tonio waited, afraid to break the silence.

"There was a big official debate as to what to do
with him, and even though he was eventually allowed Basic the whole thing made him pretty bitter.
He quit school twice, got into trouble fighting with
the other teens, and was eventually ordered out. He
drifted through several low-skill jobs, but his record
kept tripping him up, and he slipped into various
petty criminal activities. Eventually ... he became a
fagin himself."

Tonio had sort of guessed where Tirrell's story was
leading, but it still sent a shiver up his back. "It
doesn't make sense," he said, shaking his head. "He,
of all people, should have understood what he was
doing to his kids."

"It doesn't seem to work that way," Tirrell said
with more than a touch of bitterness. "Along with all
the other traumas of Transition, kids like that wind
up feeling rejected by both their fagins and by society, and that's a pretty hard load to carry. Most of
them hang on and eventually manage to fit in reasonably well, but others spend the rest of their lives
trying—at least subconsciously—to get back in their
fagin's good graces."

"By becoming the same kind of people he was?"

"And by proving they're as good at it as he is."
Tirrell sighed. "It's a weird, self-destructive pattern,
Tonio, but no less strong for all of that. Martel was a
fagin's kid, too, and you saw how calmly he was
trying to pass the poison on to someone else."

"Like Lisa," Tonio murmured. "It could have been
her."

"And except for the grace of God and circumstance, it could have been *you*," Tirrell said gently. "You and Lisa both found other interests when the hive's entertainments got dull—her with reading, you by applying to be a righthand. But either of you could just as easily have gone the other way. You see now why I think it's worth the risks to let Jarvis continue his work?"

"Yeah." Tonio stared out the window for a long time. "I guess maybe it's a good thing then that I wasn't able to get out of that furnace," he said at last. He wasn't really sure he wanted to say this, but the memory of what he'd been halfway planning to do in that darkened refinery—what he'd thought Tirrell *wanted* him to do there—was proving to be as uncomfortable a burden as a sore tooth. "If I'd had the chance, I might have tried to make sure—" *Jarvis got killed*, his mind prompted. But the three words remained stuck on his tongue.

"It certainly is a good thing," Tirrell nodded. "You'd have come out smack into that cyanide. I'd say the angel who protects policemen and other idiots was working overtime that night."

Tonio opened his mouth to explain that that wasn't what he meant at all ... and suddenly he realized that Tirrell had understood him perfectly, and that his apparent misinterpretation was his way of saying that everything was all right and that the issue was closed. "Thanks," he murmured.

"No problem." Tirrell glanced at him. "By the way, I know how hard this case has been on you. If you want to resign as my righthand, I'll certainly understand."

"No, I'll finish out my year." He grinned. "Remember, I went into this for excitement in the first place. But ... I'm not sure I'll want to stick with police work after school. There are parts of it I'm not sure I like."

Tirrell shrugged. "You'll find you have to make deals and compromises in practically any profession you go into. But it's your decision, of course. There are certainly other good fields to go into."

"Big of you to notice."

Tirrell chuckled and fell silent, and Tonio settled himself for the long drive ahead, wondering at the uneasiness still nagging at him. Everything seemed to have come out okay ... but he still didn't like what was being done to Colin. Even with Tirrell's assurances it didn't seem either safe *or* right to be experimenting with a real live kid. But until he hit Transition and could start learning things on his own, he was just going to be stuck accepting adults' words on such things.

Unless ...

A strange thought, at least for him—but Lisa *would* be visiting Ridge Harbor soon. Perhaps, if he could get up the nerve, he would ask her to teach him reading.

It was worth thinking about, anyway.

WATCH OUT! THE COBRAS
ARE BACK!

That's right: in the new hit sequel, *Cobra Strike*, the Cobras are back, with all of the excitement and hard-hitting action that made Timothy Zahn's *Cobra* an instant bestseller!

Cobra Strike continues the chronicles of the Cobras, the most powerful fighting force ever created by man. Cobras are, in effect, supermen, thanks to surgical implants that give them fantastic strength, speed, and agility. Their abilities are partially controlled by nanocomputers, and augmented by built-in weaponry including, among other devices, finger lasers.

In *Cobra Strike*, the Cobras must decide whether or not to hire out as mercenaries to their former enemies, the alien Troft. This time, however, it's up to Jonny Moreau's *sons* to carry on the honor of the

Cobra name—which they do admirably, through high adventure and political intrigue with more than a few surprising twists.

Available February 1986 • 352 pp. • $3.50

Announcing one hell of a shared universe!

OF COURSE IT'S A FANTASY . . . ISN'T IT?

Alexander the Great teams up with Julius Caesar and Achilles to refight the Trojan War—with Machiavelli as their intelligence officer and Cleopatra in charge of R&R . . . Yuri Andropov learns to Love the Bomb with the aid of The Blond Bombshell (she is the Devil's *very* private secretary) . . . Che Guevara Ups the Revolution with the help of Isaac Newton, Hemingway, and Confucius . . . And no less a bard than Homer records their adventures for posterity: of *course* it's a fantasy. It has to be, if you don't believe in Hell.

ALL YOU REALLY NEED IS FAITH . . .

But award-winning authors Gregory Benford, C. J. Cherryh, Janet Morris, and David Drake, co-creators of this multi-volume epic, insist that *Heroes in Hell* ® is something more. They say that all you really need is Faith, that if you accept the single postulate that Hell exists, your imagination will soar, taking you to a realm more magical and strangely satisfying than you would have believed possible.

COME TO HELL . . .

. . . where the battle of Good and Evil goes on apace in the most biased possible venue. There's no rougher, tougher place in the Known Universe of Discourse, and you *wouldn't* want to live there, but . . .

IT'S BRIGHT . . . FRESH . . . LIBERATING . . . AS HELL!

Co-created by some of the finest, most imaginative

talents writing today, *Heroes in Hell* ® offers a milieu more exciting than anything in American fiction since *A Connecticut Yankee in King Arthur's Court*. As bright and fresh a vision as any conceived by Borges, it's as accessible—and American—as apple pie.

EVERYONE WHO WAS ANYONE DOES IT

In fact, Janet Morris's Hell is so liberating to the imaginations of the authors involved that nearly a dozen major talents have vowed to join her for at least eight subsequent excursions to the Underworld, where—even as you read this—everyone who was anyone is meeting to hatch new plots, conquer new empires, and test the very limits of creation.

YOU'VE HEARD ABOUT IT—NOW GO THERE!

Join the finest writers, scientists, statesmen, strategists, and villains of history in Morris's Hell. The first volume, co-created by Janet Morris with C. J. Cherryh, Gregory Benford, and David Drake, will be on sale in March as the mass-market lead from Baen Books, and in April Baen will publish in hardcover the first *Heroes in Hell* spin-off novel, *The Gates of Hell*, by C. J. Cherryh and Janet Morris. We can promise you one Hell of a good time.

FOR A DOSE OF THAT OLD-TIME RELIGION (TO A MODERN BEAT), READ—

HEROES IN HELL®	THE GATES OF HELL
March 1986	April 1986 Hardcover
65555-8 • 288 pp. • $3.50	65561-2 • 256 pp. • $14.95

TASTE THE ACTION!

Here is an excerpt from

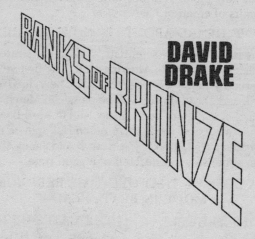

RANKS OF BRONZE

DAVID DRAKE

"How many do you think there are?" Clodius asked. "Sir?"

It was like trying to guess how many roses bloomed in the fields beneath Vesuvius, and an honest guess would have been in horrifying contrast to the five thousand—more or less—legionaries bearing down on those opponents.

Instead of blurting, "Thirty thousand, maybe as many as fifty"—the figures that clicked through his mind—Vibulenas said, "They look like they're all naked, and only the ones in the chariots have shields."

They also looked like they were ten feet tall. Well, maybe eight feet tall.

With no more organization than water bursting a dam, and with the suggestion of equally overwhelming force, hundreds of war cars charged from the enemy line without appreciably diminishing the mass that remained. The rumble of bronze as they approached had an omnipresence that horns or even proper drums could not have equaled. It was as if the legion were approaching a swarm of bees, each of the size of an ox.

The warriors were shouting as their vehicles galloped onward, but their cries were surprisingly high-pitched for all the breadth of their torsos. Plumes of single feathers or perhaps blue-dyed plant fibers trembled stiffly from the sides of each warrior's helmet.

The warriors in the cars each carried a long spear tipped with the black glint of iron. Some of those who clung to their vehicles with their spear hand brandished huge shields, allowing glimpses of breastplates and swords or daggers in belt sheaths.

"The chariots that came first," Vibulenas shouted. He was in effect a rank of his own, a stride behind the leading legionaries and a stride ahead of the second rank, but he was marching in time with the centuries to either side. The strap of his shield was already beginning to chafe the skin of his left forearm, and the unfamiliar effort of holding the piece of equipment advanced was causing his bicep muscle to cramp. "What happened to them?"

Clodius Afer twisted his head enough to look past the cheek pieces of his helmet. He grimaced, a facial shrug because those were the only muscles not bound by armor or clutching equipment. "Not our problem," he shouted back; and he, like Vibulenas, hoped that was true.

"Ready!" called Clodius, facing the men to his left.

Simultaneously, Vabula, the centurion of the fourth century, roared toward the mass of his own unit, "Century—"

The nearest war cars had rolled across the center of the shallow valley and were now climbing toward the legion. The draft animals looked distinctly unlike oxen now that the tribune had a closer view. They had four gnarly horns apiece, one pair in the usual place atop the head and the other on the nose. Vibulenas had not heard of anything like them, even among monstrous births catalogued with omens.

There were so many of the cars that they were jostling for position as they neared the legion. The unyoked draft animals followed their opposite numbers in neighboring teams, and one vehicle upset because its driver did not have room to maneuver around a tree.

"Charge!" shouted Clodius Afer, a fraction of a second before Vabula screamed the same command in a carrying falsetto.

Both non-coms and their fellows from the opposite flanks of each century in the line began to run toward the chariots only two hundred feet away.

For a moment, the centurions and file closers were alone, a ragged scattering ahead of the legion, like froth whipped from the tops of waves. Then the whole legion broke into a run as the right arms of the two leading ranks cocked back, preparing to hurl the lighter of the pair of javelins each legionary carried.

The advancing line stuttered as each man lost a stop when he launched his javelin. Vibulenas, who had finally gripped his flopping sword sheath with his left hand so that he could draw the weapon with his right, found himself once again in front of the remainder of the legion.

The enemy war cars were drawing up, apparently according to plan rather than in reaction to the legion's advance. Drivers swung their teams to one side or the other in a scene of utter confusion, but with fewer real collisions than the dense array had suggested would result. The enemy were, after all, practiced at their method of warfare even if they made no attempt at discipline in the Roman sense. Hostile warriors were springing from the vehicles even as drivers sawed back on their reins as if to lift the teams' forehooves from the ground.

Some fifteen hundred Roman javelins rained down onto them in a space of less than two seconds.

"Rome!" cried Gaius Vibulenus, while the legionaries behind him were shouting that and a thousand other things as they ran toward the foe.

The warrior's shields were big, even by comparison with the bodies they had to cover, and they were solid enough that even hard-flung javelins penetrated only to the barbs of their heads. The teams had been in confusion before the missiles gouged many animals into rearing agony. Now they were in chaos. Several teams raced off in whatever direction they were pointing, spilling their drivers and occasionally dragging an overturned car like a device for field-levelling.

Most of the warriors were unharmed, though a few had been caught as they jumped from their vehicles and now sprawled or staggered. Their chest armor, even when studded with metal, did not turn or stop the missiles the way the heavy shields had done. The weight of the javelins stuck in the shield facings, half a dozen in some cases, was an awkward additional burden. Many of the warriors were trying to tug the javelins clear when the second flight, from the third and fourth ranks of the legion, hit them.

Vibulenus was running downhill, though the slope was no more than an inch in twelve. When a Roman javelin sailed over his shoulder, missing the back of his neck by no more than the blade's width, his bloodthirsty joy and feeling of invulnerability washed away in a douche of fear. The young tribune tried to stop. His hobnails skidded out from under him, and the long spear the warrior thrust at him gouged a fleck of bronze from Vibulenus' helmet instead of plunging in through his mouth and out the base of his skull.

The spearpoint's ragged edge was the result of forging at too low a temperature rather than deliberate serration, but the difference to Vibulenus would have been less than academic had the blade sawn a hand's-breadth slot through his face. As it was, the tribune's shin hurt more where his shield banged it than his head did from what would have been a deadly thrust.

The warrior who was trying to kill him had two feathery plumes that were part of his head rather than clothing as Vibulenas had assumed from a distance. Orange-skinned and with feather-plumes of electric blue, he was half again as high as the tribune, and gave off the smell of something chitinous and dead as he lifted his spear again to finish the job with a second overarm thrust.

COMING IN MAY 1986

65568-X * 320 pp. * $3.50

To order any Baen Book by mail, send the cover price plus 75¢ for first-class postage and handling to Baen Books, Dept. BA, 260 Fifth Avenue, New York, N.Y. 10001.

WE'RE LOOKING FOR
TROUBLE

Well, feedback, anyway. Baen Books endeavors to publish only the best in science fiction and fantasy—but we need you to tell us whether we're doing it right. Why not let us know? We'll award a Baen Books gift certificate worth $100 (plus a copy of our catalog) to the reader who best tells us what he or she likes about Baen Books—and where we could do better. We reserve the right to quote any or all of you. Contest closes December 31, 1987. All letters should be addressed to Baen Books, 260 Fifth Avenue, New York, N.Y. 10001.

At the same time, ask about the Baen Book Club— buy five books, get another five free! For information, send a self-addressed, stamped envelope. For a copy of our catalog, enclose one dollar as well.

SCIENCE FICTION AND FANTASY

ISBN #	Title # Author	Publ. List Price
55979-6	ACT OF GOD, Kotani and Roberts	2.95
55946-1	ACTIVE MEASURES, David Drake & Janet Morris	3.95
55970-2	THE ADOLESCENCE OF P-1, Thomas J. Ryan	2.95
55998-2	AFTER THE FLAMES, Silverberg & Spinrad	2.95
55967-2	AFTER WAR, Janet Morris	2.95
55934-6	ALIEN STARS, C.J. Cherryh, Joe Haldeman & Timothy Zahn, edited by Elizabeth Mitchell	2.95
55978-8	AT ANY PRICE, David Drake	3.50
65565-5	THE BABYLON GATE, Edward A. Byers	2.95
65586-8	THE BEST OF ROBERT SILVERBERG, Robert Silverberg	2.95
55977-X	BETWEEN THE STROKES OF NIGHT, Charles Sheffield	3.50
55984-2	BEYOND THE VEIL, Janet Morris	15.95
65544-2	BEYOND WIZARDWALL, Janet Morris	15.95
55973-7	BORROWED TIME, Alan Hruska	2.95
65563-9	A CHOICE OF DESTINIES, Melissa Scott	2.95
55960-5	COBRA, Timothy Zahn	2.95
65551-5	COBRA STRIKE!, Timothy Zahn	3.50
65578-7	A COMING OF AGE, Timothy Zahn	3.50
55969-9	THE CONTINENT OF LIES, James Morrow	2.95
55917-6	CUGEL'S SAGA, Jack Vance	3.50
65552-3	DEATHWISH WORLD, Reynolds and Ing	3.50
55995-8	THE DEVIL'S GAME, Poul Anderson	2.95
55974-5	DIASPORAH, W. R. Yates	2.95
65581-7	DINOSAUR BEACH, Keith Laumer	2.95
65579-5	THE DOOMSDAY EFFECT, Thomas Wren	2.95
65557-4	THE DREAM PALACE, Brynne Stephens	2.95
65564-7	THE DYING EARTH, Jack Vance	2.95
55988-5	FANGLITH, John Dalmas	2.95
55947-8	THE FALL OF WINTER, Jack C. Haldeman II	2.95
55975-3	FAR FRONTIERS, Volume III	2.95
65548-5	FAR FRONTIERS, Volume IV	2.95
65572-8	FAR FRONTIERS, Volume V	2.95
55900-1	FIRE TIME, Poul Anderson	2.95
65567-1	THE FIRST FAMILY, Patrick Tilley	3.50
55952-4	FIVE-TWELFTHS OF HEAVEN, Melissa Scott	2.95
55937-0	FLIGHT OF THE DRAGONFLY, Robert L. Forward	3.50
55986-9	THE FORTY-MINUTE WAR, Janet Morris	3.50
55971-0	FORWARD, Gordon R. Dickson	2.95
65550-7	THE FRANKENSTEIN PAPERS, Fred Saberhagen	3.50
55899-4	FRONTERA, Lewis Shiner	2.95
55918-4	THE GAME BEYOND, Melissa Scott	2.95
55959-1	THE GAME OF EMPIRE, Poul Anderson	3.50
65561-2	THE GATES OF HELL, Janet Morris	14.95
65566-3	GLADIATOR-AT-LAW, Pohl and Kornbluth	2.95
55904-4	THE GOLDEN PEOPLE, Fred Saberhagen	3.50
65555-8	HEROES IN HELL, Janet Morris	3.50
65571-X	HIGH JUSTICE, Jerry Pournelle	2.95

ISBN #	Title # Author	Publ. List Price
55930-3	HOTHOUSE, Brian Aldiss	2.95
55905-2	HOUR OF THE HORDE, Gordon R. Dickson	2.95
65547-7	THE IDENTITY MATRIX, Jack Chalker	2.95
65569-8	I, MARTHA ADAMS, Pauline Glen Winslow	3.95
55994-X	INVADERS, Gordon R. Dickson	2.95
55993-1	IN THE FACE OF MY ENEMY, Joe Delaney	2.95
65570-1	JOE MAUSER, MERCENARY, Reynolds and Banks	2.95
55931-1	KILLER, David Drake & Karl Edward Wagner	2.95
55996-6	KILLER STATION, Martin Caidin	3.50
65559-0	THE LAST DREAM, Gordon R. Dickson	2.95
55981-8	THE LIFESHIP, Dickson and Harrison	2.95
55980-X	THE LONG FORGETTING, Edward A. Byers	2.95
55992-3	THE LONG MYND, Edward Hughes	2.95
55997-4	MASTER OF SPACE AND TIME, Rudy Rucker	2.95
65573-6	MEDUSA, Janet and Chris Morris	3.50
65562-0	THE MESSIAH STONE, Martin Caidin	3.95
65580-9	MINDSPAN, Gordon R. Dickson	2.95
65553-1	THE ODYSSEUS SOLUTION, Banks and Lambe	2.95
55926-5	THE OTHER TIME, Mack Reynolds with Dean Ing	2.95
55965-6	THE PEACE WAR, Vernor Vinge	3.50
55982-6	PLAGUE OF DEMONS, Keith Laumer	2.75
55966-4	A PRINCESS OF CHAMELN, Cherry Wilder	2.95
65568-X	RANKS OF BRONZE, David Drake	3.50
65577-9	REBELS IN HELL, Janet Morris, et. al.	3.50
55990-7	RETIEF OF THE CDT, Keith Laumer	2.95
65556-6	RETIEF AND THE PANGALACTIC PAGEANT OF PULCHRITUDE, Keith Laumer	2.95
65575-2	RETIEF AND THE WARLORDS, Keith Laumer	2.95
55902-8	THE RETURN OF RETIEF, Keith Laumer	2.95
55991-5	RHIALTO THE MARVELLOUS, Jack Vance	3.50
65545-0	ROGUE BOLO, Keith Laumer	2.95
65554-X	SANDKINGS, George R.R. Martin	2.95
65546-9	SATURNALIA, Grant Callin	2.95
55989-3	SEARCH THE SKY, Pohl and Kornbluth	2.95
55914-1	SEVEN CONQUESTS, Poul Anderson	2.95
65574-4	SHARDS OF HONOR, Lois McMaster Bujold	2.95
55951-6	THE SHATTERED WORLD, Michael Reaves	3.50
	THE SILISTRA SERIES	
55915-X	RETURNING CREATION, Janet Morris	2.95
55919-2	THE GOLDEN SWORD, Janet Morris	2.95
55932-X	WIND FROM THE ABYSS, Janet Morris	2.95
55936-2	THE CARNELIAN THRONE, Janet Morris	2.95
65549-3	THE SINFUL ONES, Fritz Leiber	2.95
65558-2	THE STARCHILD TRILOGY, Pohl and Williamson	3.95
55999-0	STARSWARM, Brian Aldiss	2.95
55927-3	SURVIVAL!, Gordon R. Dickson	2.75
55938-9	THE TORCH OF HONOR, Roger Macbride Allen	2.95

SCIENCE FICTION AND FANTASY (continued)

ISBN #	Title # Author	Publ. List Price
55942-7	TROJAN ORBIT, Mack Reynolds with Dean Ing	2.95
55985-0	TUF VOYAGING, George R.R. Martin	15.95
55916-8	VALENTINA, Joseph H. Delaney & Marc Steigler	3.50
55898-6	WEB OF DARKENSS, Marion Zimmer Bradley	3.50
55925-7	WITH MERCY TOWARD NONE, Glen Cook	2.95
65576-0	WOLFBANE, Pohl and Kornbluth	2.95
55962-1	WOLFLING, Gordon R. Dickson	2.95
55987-7	YORATH THE WOLF, Cherry Wilder	2.95
55906-0	THE ZANZIBAR CAT, Joanna Russ	3.50

COMPUTER BOOKS AND GENERAL INTEREST NONFICTION

ISBN #	Title # Author	Publ. List Price
55968-0	ADVENTURES IN MICROLAND, Jerry Pournelle	9.95
55933-8	AI: HOW MACHINES THINK, F. David Peat	8.95
55922-2	THE ESSENTIAL USER'S GUIDE TO THE IBM PC, XT, AND PCjr., Dian Girard	6.95
55940-0	EUREKA FOR THE IBM PC AND PCjr, Tim Knight	7.95
55941-9	THE FUTURE OF FLIGHT, Leik Myrabo with Dean Ing	7.95
55955-9	THE GUIDEBOOK FOR WINNING ADVENTURERS, David & Sandy Small	8.95
55923-0	MUTUAL ASSURED SURVIVAL, Jerry Pournelle and Dean Ing	6.95
55929-X	PROGRAMMING LANGUAGES: FEATURING THE IBM PC, Marc Stiegler & Bob Hansen	9.95
55963-X	THE SERIOUS ASSEMBLER, Charles Crayne & Dian Girard Crayne	8.95
55907-9	THE SMALL BUSINESS COMPUTER TODAY AND TOMORROW, William E. Grieb, Jr.	6.95
55921-4	THE USER'S GUIDE TO CP/M SYSTEMS, Tony Bove & Cheryl Rhodes	8.95
55948-6	THE USER'S GUIDE TO FREE SOFTWARE, Tony Bove & Cheryl Rhodes	9.95
55908-7	THE USER'S GUIDE TO SMALL COMPUTERS, Jerry Pournelle	9.95